THE PRICE OF LOVE

Also by Anne Baker

Like Father, Like Daughter
Paradise Parade
Legacy of Sins
Nobody's Child
Merseyside Girls
Moonlight on the Mersey
A Mersey Duet
Mersey Maids
A Liverpool Lullaby
With a Little Luck

THE PRICE OF LOVE

Anne Baker

HEADLINE

First published in 1999
by HEADLINE BOOK PUBLISHING

10 9 8 7 6 5 4 3 2 1

British Library Cataloguing in Publication Data

Baker, Anne
The price of love
I. Title
823.9'14[F]

ISBN 0 7472 2308 4

Typeset by Avon Dataset Ltd, Bidford-on-Avon, Warks

Printed and bound in Great Britain by
Mackays of Chatham PLC, Chatham, Kent

HEADLINE BOOK PUBLISHING
A division of Hodder Headline PLC
338 Euston Road
London NW1 3BH

www.headline.co.uk
www.hodderheadline.com

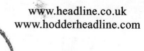

THE PRICE OF LOVE

Chapter One

February 1910

At six o'clock in the morning Kate McGlory slid back the bolts on the shop door and turned the card round to say they were open. Outside it was cold and the street was dark and empty. Her first job was to heave in the great bundles of newspapers that had been dumped on the step.

'Ten Woodbines and a *Chronicle*, miss.' The first customer came in behind her, making her jump. Kate felt very much on edge as she cut open the bundle of *Chronicles* to serve him.

Customers rushed in on their way to work. Those using bicycles left them propped against the kerb outside. She served them quickly, knowing they had to get to work on time.

Some she knew by name; most had familiar faces because they came in every morning. Nearly always they bought the same things. She was reaching for them the moment they came in the shop.

One asked: 'How's your mother, miss?'

That brought the niggle at the back of her mind flaring into life. 'Still waiting, Mr Benbow.'

The waiting seemed endless. The thought made her shiver; if she found it hard, how was poor Mam feeling? A ball of foreboding was building up in her stomach.

Kate set out a selection of the morning's papers for sale, reading the headlines as she did so. Train crash in Bristol. Assassination in Mexico. Big freeze with heavy snow in Scotland. Just what was needed for today's placards.

In between serving customers, she printed those headlines out as clearly as she could on the large sheets of paper kept for the purpose, clipped them to the boards and hauled them outside. It was getting lighter as she lifted them into position under the shop window and wired them in place.

During every lull after that, her thick pencil scrawled house numbers on the top corners of newspapers, as she made up the rounds for the

1

delivery boy. She paused as the date on a copy of *The Times* leapt out at her. It was 24 February already!

Mam's baby should have been here ten days ago. There was an old wives' tale that girl babies came early, and that boys were late. Her mother was always over her dates and they were always boys.

Silently, Kate implored the powers that be: please let it be a girl. She'd once had a sister but she'd lived for only nine months. Mam had been heartbroken about that. Her six boys were all growing up big and strong with hearty appetites. A girl now was what they were all hoping for. They might just be able to welcome a little girl.

Kate pushed the fringe off her forehead and sighed. The rest of her hair was fashioned into a bun as became a respectable shop assistant of nineteen. But whatever she did with her hair, it didn't please her. It was so straight and strong she couldn't make her fringe bend, let alone wave. She didn't like the bright gingery colour either.

She'd tried plaits wound round her head, and though they controlled her hair, the style did nothing for her rather square face. The bun was a little softer and kinder, but she had difficulty anchoring it securely with hairpins.

All her brothers had curly hair in lustrous shades of brown from mid to dark, some with golden highlights. All they had to do when they washed it was to comb it out. Kate could comb their hair into waves and that was how it stayed. It made her very envious.

And it wasn't just her hair that was different. The boys had big brown eyes like Dad's, mostly with long sweeping eyelashes. Her eyes were green and her eyelashes were straight and stubby and almost invisible. The boys were all good-looking, but Kate thought she was not. She was more than slender, too thin really, but so were all the boys. Their trouble was they didn't get enough to eat.

That wasn't her trouble, at least not since she'd come here to work. She'd been lucky with her place. At thirteen, she'd been desperate to escape from home to a live-in job as a maid. She was employed by the Hallidays, a middle-aged couple whose children had left home. Mr Halliday was a newsagent who owned several shops, the largest of which was attached to the house here in Rake Lane in Wallasey. Mrs Halliday didn't work in the business, not any more. She kept house with the help of Kate and a cook, and Mr Halliday bought her flowers every week. Kate felt she was seeing how the middle class lived.

One morning that first winter, when every other customer seemed to be suffering from flu, the early-morning girl didn't turn up at six to open the shop. Mr Halliday was just getting over a virulent bout of flu himself.

Kate was lighting the house fires when he had to ask her for help with the early papers. She'd enjoyed doing it. Mr Halliday was pleased and said she picked up what was needed very quickly. She'd asked if she could continue working in the shop and had been there ever since.

She still lived in; Mr Halliday felt he had more control if she was here on the premises. Kate told him she was more than glad to do so.

'I have a room to myself here, and it's too far for me to come first thing in the morning.' She didn't mention the other reason.

The Hallidays were Quakers and very considerate of their staff. The meals provided were plain and nourishing but generous in amount. They paid the full rate for the job and showed their appreciation of the work done for them. In return, the staff did their best to please them and it made it a happy place to work.

Kate thought Mr Halliday was very good to her. This was the third time he'd allowed her to take her week's annual holiday to coincide with the birth of a new baby so she could look after her mother and the family.

She couldn't stop worrying about how much longer it would be before she heard from home. Mam hadn't been feeling well for months. She'd had so many troubles and so many babies so quickly, it was only to be expected that her health would suffer. Kate glanced up at the clock; it was five minutes to nine.

Almost time! Every morning about this time Jack Courtney came in to buy a copy of *The Times*. She'd already peeped inside to read the headlines that he'd read and smoothed the paper back to look as though it hadn't been touched. Just the thought of seeing him sent little quivers down her spine.

Every time the shop bell rang at this time of the morning, she looked up with such eagerness. It rang less often because the morning rush was dying down.

Two minutes to nine. At this time every morning she was on pins waiting for him to come. Afraid he'd be late, that she'd be having her breakfast and Miss Fisk would serve him instead.

But no, he was here. She could see his top hat through the glass in the door. Very few of their customers wore top hats these days. A little frisson ran through her.

'Good morning, Mr Courtney.'

She was reaching for *The Times* as he swept off his hat. She thought his dark-blond hair curling up from his collar very attractive. He inclined

3

his head in her direction. Surely good manners didn't require him to do all that for a shop assistant?

'Rather a raw morning, I'm afraid. Not very pleasant.'

He was interested in her, she was almost sure, from the way his gentle eyes looked into hers.

'Anything important happening in the world?'

She quoted the headlines. He could have read them on the placards outside.

If it had been anyone else, say young Mr Jones from the hardware shop next door, Kate would have said he wanted to keep company with her. But when Jack Courtney did it, she had to ask herself why. Why he came in to buy a newspaper every day, when copies of four different newspapers were delivered daily to his home. She made up the round herself and sent them out with the paper boy to the Grange. The Courtney name was well known on Merseyside. They were rich shipowners.

She watched him go. Tall and slim and every inch a gentleman. She found it very hard to believe he came to see her.

He held the door open for Miss Fisk. She was elderly and wore pebble glasses. She'd been the manager here for the last twelve years and started work at nine o'clock.

'Morning.' She whipped through the shop to remove her coat. 'Off you go, then.'

Kate was due for a half-hour break and went to the kitchen for breakfast. She and Josie Oaks, the cook, always ate together. Josie was plump and middle-aged and made sure there was always a freshly cooked breakfast.

'Still here?' Every morning this week she'd asked Kate the same thing. 'I thought you'd have gone by now.'

Kate spooned up her porridge. 'So did I.'

'Your poor mother.' Josie was buttering slices of toast to go under the poached eggs. 'She'll be glad when it's over.'

'We all will,' Kate said with feeling.

Mam had been complaining for weeks about being tired, and she had every reason to. Having a baby at the age of forty-two was asking a lot of any woman. Especially when it was her ninth and she had all the work of looking after her older children.

'You're very good to your mother.' Josie's white cap covered half her forehead as well as all her hair. 'Giving up your annual holiday to help her, and it's not as if you don't go home every free minute you have.'

Sunday was Kate's day off. She nearly always spent Saturday night

4

at home too; she wanted to stay as close to her brother Tommy as she could.

In addition, Kate was allowed every afternoon off between one and four thirty, and she often went home to see her mother then. She had to come back to work in the shop; it stayed open until seven, nine on Saturdays.

Kate said: 'Mam's got a lot to . . .' She almost said: *put up with*. She changed it to: 'cope with.'

'It's your mother's life. She shouldn't rely on you. You could be married with a family of your own and not be able to help her,' Josie retorted. 'Not many daughters would do what you do. Everybody expects so much of you. You let them drive you.'

'It's not that . . .'

Mam had a soft, weary smile that drew affection. The whole family strove to do all they could for her; some of the neighbours too. Mam radiated love, she gave it in bounteous amounts to the boys. They were praised if they brought in firewood, lit a fire, or earned a few coppers that could be spent on food for the family.

Kate wanted a share of that love and did her best to earn it. Although she was scared to be at home when her father was there, she still spent every Sunday helping to wash and clean and cook meals. She gave her mother money to buy food and sometimes for boots and jerseys for the boys. She gave up her annual holiday to see her through her confinements.

She often saw Mam's hands going out to caress her boys, though she hardly ever showed affection for her daughter. It was almost as though there was a wall between them. She and Mam couldn't reach each other.

Kate yearned to be loved. She wanted it from Mam but most of all she wanted someone of her own. Someone who put her first always. She felt it as a deep need.

'You're doing too much for your family,' Josie went on. 'You need more time for yourself. You need a bit of life. Get yourself a boyfriend.'

Kate searched the cook's friendly, podgy face and kept silent. She couldn't say Jack Courtney was her boyfriend, but she wanted no other.

'You ought to have a bit of fun. You'll end up an old maid looking after your brothers if you don't watch out. You make yourself a doormat for them.'

Kate sighed as she went back to the shop. She worked hard for Mr Halliday and earned his respect. Dressed all in black with a full set of grey whiskers on his face, he looked more like a preacher than a newsagent. He was checking stock; usually he spent an hour with them early in the morning, and later on went round his other shops.

An old man was waiting to be served. Kate crossed to the far side, where little heaps of tobacco were set out on doilies inside glass dishes.

'Half an ounce of dark shag, miss.'

Kate weighed it out on the special scales. Dark shag was the cheapest tobacco they sold and therefore the most popular.

'And a halfpenny pipe.'

They sold lots of white clay pipes at a halfpenny each to children, who used them for blowing bubbles. Impecunious old men smoked tobacco in them too. They had racks of more expensive pipes, some with carved faces on them, some with metal covers.

Kate went back to weigh out a quarter of humbugs for another customer. She liked to see the bright electric light glinting on the jars of sweets set out on the shelves, and she loved the smell of newsprint that pervaded every corner of the shop.

The doorbell pinged and Kate looked up. The sight of the urchin coming through the door sent a shock wave through her. This was it then, the summons she'd been half expecting and half dreading for the last few weeks. It was an effort to keep her voice steady.

'Hello, Tommy. How's Mam?'

'She wants you to come.'

He hung back by the door, his eyes going round the shop, savouring the sight of so many sweets spread out in their boxes across the counter. Tommy was nine years old, and had a pixie-like face with sparky eyes full of mischief. When people asked about her brothers it was Tommy she spoke of.

He wore no coat though it was a cold, damp morning. A skinny elbow stuck out through a hole in his green pullover and it could be plainly seen that he had no shirt underneath.

Kate could see Mr Halliday taking all this in. The Hallidays set great store by personal neatness and cleanliness. She took great pains to please them, wearing high-necked blouses and trim skirts that swung just clear of her boots. A blue apron was provided to cover most of that.

She asked: 'The new baby, is it here yet?'

'Not yet. Mrs Potter's come. She said it won't be long.' Mrs Potter was the local midwife and nurse.

Tommy looked scruffy; she was almost ashamed to have him come in the shop and say he was her brother. Mam might have darned his elbows for him, but she knew Mam never had time or energy for things like that. At least he had good boots on his feet, though they looked too big for him and he wore them without socks.

'Here, young man.' Mr Halliday was twisting the blue paper they used into a cone and pushing sweets into it: a few each of wine gums, caramels, aniseed balls, pear drops and gobstoppers. He added some liquorice bootlaces.

'Thank you, sir.' Tommy received the bag with eager hands. 'Thank you very much.' He had a cherubic smile.

Mr Halliday beamed at Kate as he went to the till. 'You'll want your holiday money?' He handed over a week's wages. Now that the summons had come, she felt reluctant to leave.

'Today's Thursday – let's see. If you come back here on Thursday night of next week. Just to sleep, so that I know you're here for the early opening.'

'Thank you, thank you.' She felt overwhelmed by his generosity. He was giving her the best part of another day off. He was very kind. The Hallidays were lovely people.

'I'll just get my bag. I'll see you at the tram stop, Tommy. Wait for me there.'

'I'll have to,' he said so they could all hear. 'Mam didn't give me my fare back.'

Kate bounded upstairs to take off her apron and put on her best green coat. Then she skewered her hat on top of her ginger bun.

She'd arrived at the Hallidays' when she was thirteen with all her belongings packed in a brown paper parcel. Josie Oaks had offered her the loan of a handsome brown carpet bag to take on holiday. She'd had it packed ready for more than two weeks. She picked it up now and ran back downstairs.

She couldn't go without telling Mrs Halliday. She wanted them both to think well of her; it was a job she wanted to keep. Shop work was much sought after. Everybody preferred it to housework.

Josie was busy making pastry when Kate looked into the kitchen. 'So you're on your way at last? You'll be glad to go, I dare say.'

When she tapped on the parlour door to say goodbye to Mrs Halliday, the older woman put down the Bible she'd been reading and led the way back to the kitchen.

'I asked Josie to make a big fruit cake for you, and there's a jar of calf's-foot jelly for your mother.' Josie was putting them into a carrier bag.

'Thank you, you're very kind.' Kate felt overwhelmed. She hadn't expected such generosity.

'I know it'll be no rest for you,' Mrs Halliday looked over her half-moon spectacles, 'with the new baby to look after, but you'll enjoy being back in the bosom of your family.'

Kate turned the phrase over in her mind as she walked to the tram stop. In the bosom of her family. Above everything else, it was where she wanted to be. It sounded a comforting place, where she'd be surrounded with love, but she never had been in the bosom of her family and was afraid she never would.

Her place was on the edge of the family circle, not in it. She was different. The only girl, the only one to have bright-red hair. She could go on and on about the differences between her and the rest of her family.

Tom was waiting for her at the tram stop, chewing on liquorice bootlaces. A light drizzle was beginning to fall.

'You'll get wet,' she told him. Already his jersey was covered with beads of moisture. 'Why didn't you put a coat on?'

'Harry took mine to school. Mam's very worried about Dad. Upset because he isn't home.'

Kate had worries she hadn't mentioned at the shop, and this was one of them. Dad often worked away from home; wherever there was maintenance required on the railway lines or a new tunnel to be constructed or bridge to be built. He sometimes spent weeks at home between jobs.

He always used to come home on Saturday nights and stay over Sunday. He'd stay in bed most of the morning, while Kate and Mam cleaned up and cooked the Sunday dinner. He'd get up in time to eat it. Then usually, he'd go out and Kate wouldn't see him again before she had to return to the shop.

Over the last year he'd been coming home less and less. There were some weekends when he didn't come home at all.

The first time he did that, they thought he might have had an accident at work and been put in hospital. That had happened once, but on that occasion his boss had let them know.

The following day Kate had telephoned his boss, who'd told her that Mitch was working with the gang in Neston and confirmed he'd have a day off the following Sunday. But he hadn't come home then either.

She knew Mam had been really worried after that. Neston was near enough for him to come home every night; he could travel free on the trains. He knew how close Mam was to giving birth, he must know she needed him. Must know she was desperately in need of money.

'Did you have a row?' Kate had asked her, afraid they had. He was always carping. 'Is there some reason?'

8

'No.' Mam had looked frightened. 'Well, no more than usual.'

Last Sunday, Mam had been anxious because Dad hadn't been home for three weekends. She didn't know where he was.

'He hasn't been back at all?' Kate asked now.

'No.' Tommy shrugged. 'And he hasn't sent any money. We've got no food, no firing, nothing.'

Kate felt the muscles of her stomach contract. This was the worst yet.

'What's Dad thinking of? Surely he knows Mam can't take in washing in her condition?'

He never gave her mother enough money to feed and clothe the family they had. Mam tried to eke it out as best she could. Yet he provided another mouth to feed almost every year, making matters worse. For Mam, it was a hand-to-mouth struggle.

But she wasn't the only one he treated badly. He was rough and tough, and Kate had made up her mind years ago that she wasn't going to marry a man like him.

From the top of the tram, Kate stared down into the streets. It ought to be a treat to be starting her annual holiday; but how could she enjoy anything when Mam was in trouble?

Tommy got to his feet and clattered down the stairs as they neared their stop, which was outside St Bede's Church School. He was off the tram with her bag before it had drawn to a halt. She knew he should have been there in class and didn't want to be seen. She had to run down Upton Road to catch him up.

Their steps slowed as they went along Boundary Road. It always seemed tranquil here, with the hill on one side and Flaybrick Hill Cemetery on the other. Officially, their address was Flaybrick Cottages, but locally everybody knew them as Cemetery Cottages. The familiar sight of gravestones and marble statues on the other side of the sandstone wall brought Kate a sense of peace.

It had been opened as Birkenhead Municipal Cemetery in 1864. At that time, the local churchyards were becoming overcrowded and a new public cemetery was thought to be a more hygienic place to bury the dead. Many local notables were buried here, including members of the Laird family, who had brought employment in their shipyard to Birkenhead since the middle of the last century.

Kate thought it a beautiful place, with its high trees, ornate gates and two gracious chapels of rest.

The cawing of the rooks followed them as they turned up the unmade cart track towards home. Cemetery Cottages had been built nearly two hundred years earlier; theirs was the third along in a terrace of six.

They were pretty little houses; all were whitewashed, with diamond-paned windows and blue slate roofs. Each had a little garden in the front with a picket fence round it and a small gate.

They followed the cart track round the back. Each cottage had a stone building at the back gate. Part of this was the privy and the other part was meant to house a pig. Their privy had a wooden seat scrubbed clean and white with a bucket below. An old bucket that leaked was considered best because it emptied automatically into the garden and helped grow good vegetables. Nowadays only Kitty Watts at number six kept pigs, and their manure was sadly missed by the gardens. These were long and narrow, and even Mam tried to grow vegetables in hers, but they had neither electricity or running water indoors.

Each cottage had a coal shed and a wash house built against the back wall of the house, but apart from the butts that collected water from the roofs, their only source of water was from standpipes, one at each end of the row.

Tommy burst in through the back door, leaving it open for Kate. She could see that the fire behind the big wire guard had almost gone out. Freddie, last year's baby, was asleep on the hearth rug and the table was a chaotic mess of dirty dishes and the remains of several meals.

Before Kate had taken off her coat and hung it on the peg behind the door, she could hear the thin mewl of the newborn. She straightened up with a rush of relief. The new baby had been born, it was all over.

She could see she had to do something about the fire straight away or she'd lose it. The coal shed was bare except for a little slack. She brought some in on a shovel and with the help of a few morning sticks tried to coax a blaze by blasting away with the bellows.

Then she headed up the stairs that led straight up from the living room to the back bedroom. There she had to step over four-year-old Duncan, who was building with the same wooden bricks she'd played with as a child. Tommy met her at the door to her mother's bedroom.

'It's another boy,' he announced, his face creasing with disappointment. Everybody knew how much Mam wanted a girl.

Chapter Two

Lena McGlory pushed her hair off her forehead. It felt sticky with sweat. Another boy! She couldn't bring herself to look at him. She didn't want him. Couldn't cope with him. Another mouth to feed, and on what? She turned her face over into her pillow and wept.

'There now, Mrs McGlory, it's all over. You can rest now.'

Rest was the last thing Lena felt she could do. She mopped at her eyes with the sheet. Mrs Potter was washing the baby at the marble-topped washstand, using Lena's best china basin and jug. She hoped the midwife would be careful; she didn't want them chipped any more than they were. They'd been a wedding present from her mother, who was now dead. There was a matching soap dish too, and a chamber pot, all decorated with wreaths of poppies. But what did wedding presents matter if Mitch had gone?

Damn him! Waves of anger and resentment washed over her. He'd said he loved her. In the early days she'd seen it burning in his Irish eyes. Now he'd turned his back, walked away. She couldn't think calmly about that. Couldn't believe he'd abandon her and the boys.

'Seven pounds two ounces, he is.' Mrs Potter had attended every birth in Cemetery Cottages for the last eighteen years; every death too.

Lena sniffed hard. She felt put upon. She now had to look forward to another fourteen years of running after this child, providing food and boots and care. She was so tired . . . Too tired.

'Of course, a little girl would have been more welcome, I realise that, with all the boys you have. But we can't help what God sends us.'

Lena swallowed the sob in her throat. Hadn't she been to church every morning after Mitch had had his way. There had been a time when she could accept more children, when she'd actually wanted another girl. For the last five years she'd been very definite that she didn't. Hadn't she gone down on her knees and pleaded with God not to send her any more babies? She'd entreated Him, beseeched Him, implored Him, yet he kept sending her boys. She'd dreaded having yet another.

It wasn't just that she was being selfish; that her body never seemed her own, that her life wasn't her own to spend as she wanted. Child-bearing was making her ill, pulling her down; her varicose veins ached from morning till night. And the clothes she had to wash for them and the food she had to find and cook exhausted her.

Out there in the world there were women who wanted children; who prayed as hard to get them as she did to avoid them. With just a little more care, surely the babies could be sent where they were wanted?

Who could blame her that she couldn't entirely trust in prayer any more? Hadn't she pleaded with Mitch to leave her alone?

'For pity's sake, don't start me with another,' she'd said. He didn't want them either. He'd said he had more than enough sons for any man.

They couldn't afford another. They had no room here for more, but when the drink was in him Mitch didn't care. When he had the need in him, nothing would stop him.

Lena had another little weep. She'd done her best to stay out of Mitch's way. The last thing she wanted was to tempt him. She'd got into the habit of staying up late when he was at home. She'd done her best to prevent him making yet another child. She'd waited until he was asleep before she lay down beside him. She'd stayed downstairs, darning socks and sewing buttons back on the children's clothes, anything to keep her down by the dying fire until it was safe. She'd stayed until she was too tired to see, night after night.

It made her cross and tired in the mornings, more irritable with all of them. She had to get up early to make breakfast for Mitch and cut sandwiches for him to take to work.

She'd kept it up for months, but in the end he'd got her pregnant again. She'd wept on his shoulder.

'Another mouth to feed when we can't feed the children we have now. I can't give them the time they need. I just haven't the energy, not at my age. After Freddie, the doctor told me not to have another, that my heart wasn't strong.'

'Didn't tell you how to avoid it though, did he?' was all Mitch said.

Lena had given up her late nights and gone to bed at a reasonable hour. What did it matter now? Within a month or two she'd begun putting on weight and her tummy had bulged with yet another baby.

To avoid Mitch's attentions had seemed the only thing to do at the time, but he hadn't liked it. He'd said he wouldn't stand for that sort of treatment, no man would. There had been rows; he'd shouted fiercely that she was denying him his marital rights, that she was going right across the teaching of the Church.

12

'Keep your voice down,' she'd pleaded. Kate had been home that night; Lena didn't want her or the older boys to hear that, nor the babies to be wakened.

'You've always talked so much about love. About how much you love me and the kids. About how love is the most important thing to have in this world and that nobody can be truly happy without it. But with you it's all talk.

'I do love you Mitch, truly.'

He'd gone on complaining in a harsh whisper that she didn't.

'You're showing you don't. If you felt one iota of affection for me you'd know you can't do this to me.

'If you won't let me in your bed, there are plenty of women who will,' he'd said over and over.

It had soured things between them. Since then, he'd not been coming home nearly as much as he used to, and when he did, he was off-hand and cold.

He'd called what she did to him rejection. She'd tried to explain why she'd done it so many times. He understood why, it was common sense. Now he was rejecting her, and it was more hurtful than she could have imagined.

She had to blame herself for this. If only she'd gone along with what he wanted, he'd be here with her now. He'd told her he wouldn't put up with what she was doing. That it was her fault didn't make it any easier to bear.

Her nose was running; she had to slip out of bed to get a handker-chief. She caught sight of herself in the mirror on her dressing table. Puffy red eyes, lank, lifeless hair and a flabby, overweight body. It was plain to see why Mitch had gone; here was another reason.

Mitch was wrong, she did love him. How could she be married to a man for fourteen years and bear him eight children and not love him?

Eight? Lena's toes curled in agony. There would have been more if she hadn't done that awful thing . . . but she'd had to. It was what Mitch had wanted. It had seemed the only thing she could do at the time.

She could see her way of life crumbling. Things could never be the same without him.

It frightened her to think of the future. Where was she to get money to feed herself and the boys, if not from him?

From the bedroom door, Kate's gaze went straight to the ornate brass bedstead. Her mother's exhausted eyes stared up from the pillow.

13

'Thank goodness you've come.' Her voice was weak, as though she had no strength left.

'You knew I would, as soon as you sent word.' Kate moved easily in the confined space among the furniture crowding the room. She moved Freddie's cot a few inches closer to the wall, then reached for Mam's hand. Her cheek felt hot and damp as she kissed it.

'Hello, Mrs Potter. Mam's doing well?'

'Yes, all right.'

'And how about my new brother? How's he doing?'

The midwife held up the baby for her to see. Kate's impression was of a crumpled red face above a squirming body wrapped loosely in an old towel. Mrs Potter seemed unusually quiet and lost in thought. Normally, she was full of bonhomie and good will.

The bedroom was warm, made cosy by the fire in the tiny cast-iron grate. It was only ever lit for Mam's confinements.

'I needed you. All this week – haven't felt well. Such awful backache. Couldn't do anything.'

'I'm here now Mam, and it's all over.'

How could she have come sooner? She couldn't expect more than one week off work. Poor Mam! A few years ago, she'd thought her pretty. Now strands of greying hair stretched across her pillow. There was a lot of it still, but once it had been nut brown and curly. Her dentures were out on the bed table, and she looked haggard without them; older than her years, work-worn and weary. It was all too much for her.

Kate sought for words. Mam would be upset because it was another boy; she mustn't make things worse. If only it had been a girl. Girls helped about the house as they grew up, looked after their mothers in their old age. Boys made more work.

Months ago, Mam had wept on her shoulder. 'There's another on the way.'

Kate didn't need to be told. It had happened too often. The signs were there for all to see.

Now, at least it was over. Mam was usually slow to pick up after a birth. She'd be low and depressed over the first weeks. But in time, the baby she'd dreaded having, had fought against having, would become a much-loved member of her family.

Kate thought of her brothers. They were all handsome, healthy boys. She loved them dearly herself, and they captivated the neighbors, but it surprised her that Mam loved them as she did.

Kate marvelled at the power of love. That it could make Mam accept

14

into her family a baby she hadn't wanted. Love made everything possible for Mam's babies. Made everything possible for Mam too. She'd love this new baby within a few weeks. In six months, she'd be nursing him for hours on end and be ready to lay down her life for him.

'What are you going to call him?'

'William after his uncle. Claude as a second name. What do you think?'

'Bill or Billy – yes. A fine name.'

Kate knew it didn't matter what she thought. Mam had a never-ending list of names she wanted to use.

Tommy came back leading Duncan by the hand. From behind his back he drew out a large bunch of hothouse arum lilies. They were fresh, and the raindrops on them sparkled in the firelight.

'I brought some flowers for you, Mam.' He laid them beside her on the bed.

Kate went to the window to hide her smile and her embarrassment that they should be offered in front of Mrs Potter. She must surely know they'd come from the cemetery. No doubt she could even name the grave; it would be the most recent burial.

She drew the heavy chenille curtains further back. They were faded now and dusty but they still kept out the cold. There were lacy net curtains too and the looking glass standing on the dressing table cut out much of the light from the room.

She could hear hens cackling. She looked down. There was a new hen run attached to next door's old pig house.

Her mother said: 'Thank you, Tommy, they're lovely,' and put out her arms to give him a hug.

Kate felt she had to intervene. 'Tommy, love,' she said gently. 'It's not right to take flowers from the cemetery. Really, he should take them back, shouldn't he, Mrs Potter?'

The midwife turned to her. She seemed flustered and upset.

'This baby isn't right.' She'd been dressing him in the clothes Kate had prepared weeks ago. 'I'm sure he isn't right.'

Mam was pulling herself up the bed. 'What d'you mean, not right?'

'He won't grow up right.' She held him up for them to see, then put him down in the bottom drawer of the chest. It was always taken out and used as a cot for newborn members of the family, because the last baby was still using the cot.

'Better get the doctor in to tell you. He'll explain it properly.'

Mam sounded irritable. 'I can't afford one and six just for the doctor to tell me things. Can't you tell me?'

15

'I've seen this sort of baby before . . . He's not right.'

'He seems all right to me,' Mam said, frowning.

'He'll be like Charlie Politt on Powell Street.'

Kate froze. Charlie Politt definitely wasn't right and never would be. She took another peep at the new infant. He seemed to be sleeping peacefully. There were little snorts and gurgles, but all her brothers had made such noises when they were newborn.

'Look at his eyes,' the midwife said. 'They're sort of slanty, and his head's small.'

Mam snorted indignantly. 'I can't see that a small head will be much of a problem.'

Kate quaked inwardly. The nurse was saying the baby wouldn't grow up to earn his own living. That he'd be an extra mouth to feed all his life.

Mrs Potter was putting on her hat and coat.

'Right, I'm going now. There's nothing I need tell you about looking after babies, you've brought up plenty already. Try and get some sleep, Mrs McGlory. I'll be back tomorrow to see how you're both getting on.'

Kate saw her out. Tom had had to cut the lilies down so they'd fit in a two-pound jam jar. She took them back to her mother's room.

'What's this about Dad not coming home? Why doesn't he come?'

Her mother was shaking her head. Kate could see tears glistening in her eyes.

'I don't know. I wish he would.'

Dad had always come home when her brothers were born. He never did much to help except make cups of tea. More often than not he got in the way, but he was always here, showing interest in the new arrival. He set great store by wetting the baby's head down at the pub. He even rewarded Mam by bringing home a bottle of stout and providing money for food.

Kate felt that the thing that really set her apart from Mam and the boys was that she couldn't get on with her father. She'd never been close to him, never felt there'd been any affection on either side. She'd seen him show rough affection for his sons. He called them 'our Joe', 'our Charlie', 'our Freddie', but she was never 'our Kate', as though she truly didn't belong. She hated to be home when he was; he scared her, but she knew Mam needed him and was upset because he wasn't.

Mam croaked: 'It's the money . . .'

It usually came down to money. Two of Kate's brothers were working

16

now. Joe was fifteen and employed by an undertaker. He had ambitions to drive the smart carriages in the cortège, but at the moment he was polishing them and looking after the horses. Charlie was thirteen and had just started working for a builder. They didn't earn a lot, but it was something.

'Don't worry, I've got my holiday pay,' she said. 'I expect Dad'll be back before long.'

Mam smiled wanly. It told Kate she'd given up hope.

'I'm going to the shops now. I'll take Tommy with me to help carry the bags. What about the little ones?'

'Freddie's asleep. I can keep an eye on him anyway.'

'We'll take Duncan with us then.'

Downstairs she helped Duncan into his coat and leggings and unhooked another shabby coat hanging behind the back door.

'Wear this,' she told Tommy.

'It's too small for me.'

'It's better than nothing, it's a raw day. We'll take the push cart, we need more coal.'

They went up the back garden to what had once been the pig pen. Tommy pulled out a wooden box fitted over the wheels of an old pram. Duncan wanted to ride in it.

To Kate, it was like stepping back in time to be buying in the local shops. She'd spent much of her childhood doing it. Everybody knew her and Tommy and asked about her mother. She told them all she had a new brother but not that Mrs Potter was suggesting there was something wrong with him, though she and Tommy had talked of nothing else since they set out.

She bought stewing meat to make scouse for dinner, and stocked up with basic foodstuffs. She knew she had to be very careful with the cash if Dad wasn't going to keep the family any longer. She had a lot of mouths to feed.

They were walking home, Kate weighed down by two heavy bags, Tommy finding it hard work to push the box on wheels. It now held a bag of coal and half a sack of potatoes, and Duncan was perched on top. It squeaked and rattled with every turn of the wheels. Suddenly Tommy stopped. Kate heard his shuddering intake of breath.

'There's Dad.' He was jabbing his finger to show her.

Kate gulped. There was no doubt, it was Mitch McGlory, tall, broad shouldered, big-boned, with a red neckerchief knotted over a collarless flannel shirt. He'd done physical work all his life and prided himself on his strength. He could crack walnuts in his fist to prove it. He was coming out of the Queen's Head public house, and there was a woman with him.

'Who's that he's talking to?' Tommy hissed.

Kate didn't know. The woman looked about thirty. They heard her laugh; she was vivacious, tossing her head as she spoke. Mitch McGlory was bending towards her as though anxious not to miss a word. He kissed her cheek and walked away. The woman looked round, then went back inside the pub.

'Oh no!' Kate was asking herself if Mitch had found another woman.

Tommy pulled at her coat, echoing her thoughts. 'Is she why Dad never comes home?'

'He's going home now,' Kate pointed out. Mitch was stepping out briskly in the direction of the cemetery. 'Where else could he be going? Come on.'

Slowly the wheels of the push cart began to squeak onwards.

'Hurry,' Tommy urged. 'Let's catch him up.'

'No, not with these heavy bags, we won't be able to.' It was an excuse. Kate didn't want to catch him up. She was wary of her father. 'Let's see if he is going home.'

They followed him up the cart track. He went to number three like a homing pigeon. Through the back door without stopping to wipe his feet.

'He's back then,' Tommy whispered.

Kate groaned inwardly. He ought to be at work now; she hoped he still had a job. The last thing she wanted was for him to be off work during this week when she'd be at home.

'I'm going to play out.' Duncan scrambled down from his perch and shot off along the row of cottages.

'He's covered with coal dust,' Tommy said. 'We shouldn't have let him ride on top.'

Kate said: 'Put the coal in the shed and bring a bucketful to the fire before you take your coat off.'

She raked the ash out of the grate and built up the fire. She'd need it to cook the stew for dinner. The whole house would feel more cheerful when it blazed up.

'Get some water in, Tommy, before you do anything else.'

'I want to see Dad. I want to tell him . . .'

'Mam will want him to herself for a little while. She'll want to show him the new baby.'

She could hear voices upstairs, and they sounded angry. 'Go on, get some water.'

Kate started to put her shopping away in the pantry. Having Dad home again was making her quake. His presence seemed to reverberate through the little house. She could never relax when he was here. Not since . . .

When she was just turned fourteen, she'd come home for a day off. She'd been working for the Hallidays but as a housemaid at that time. It had been a Tuesday, because they liked the house staff to work on Sundays when the shop was closed.

Mitch had been between jobs and had had no work for ten days. Mam had said he was getting restless. He did odd jobs for anyone who would give him money for beer and fags, worked his garden and sometimes went poaching.

After a lunch of bread and cheese, Kate went up to the bedroom she shared with Tommy. During the morning, she'd been helping Mam in the house, cleaning and scouring. Now she was going to go shopping for her; that was the job she enjoyed most. The house was empty, the older boys were at school. Mam was drinking tea round at number one with her friend Ada Catchpole. Tommy had followed her, though he said he wanted to come shopping with Kate.

Kate had half an hour to herself. She had a new green blouse to wear. At least, it was new to her. Josie Oaks had given it to her because she'd grown out of it. It was a warm summer day and she wanted to show it off.

She took off her working clothes and washed herself in the bowl of warm water she'd brought up with her. She was thinking of cutting some of her hair off.

She'd just started putting her hair up, winding her two ginger plaits round her head. They were too long and fat to sit well, and too heavy to keep in place with hairpins.

She heard Dad coming upstairs. No one else sounded so heavy. She thought he was going to his own bedroom, though it was something he rarely did in the day. He'd gone to the pub before lunch and they'd left his bread and cheese on the table.

She was drying herself when she heard the latch of her door being lifted. Automatically, she covered herself with the towel as Dad's face came round the door. He didn't shave during the week, and his chin and neck were covered with strong dark stubble. He had clusters of blackheads round his nose.

'What do you want?' she asked.

He came in, closing the door carefully behind him. He'd always had

19

this power of reducing her to a nervous wreck. He had a way of fastening his brown eyes on hers and never dropping his gaze. Almost as though he was stalking her. It made her freeze like a rabbit caught in the light of a lamp.

Suddenly he pounced, lifting a great paw and snatching the towel from her fingers.

'Dad!' She started to scream but a heavy hand clamped over her mouth and forced her back against the bed. It smelled of tobacco. His fingers were jerking at her bodice.

She struggled and fought, tried to push his dirt-ingrained hands away. 'Leave me alone.'

'Shut up!' His fist crashed against her jaw, knocking her head back, making her bite her tongue. She could taste the salt of blood. Her heart was pounding and she could feel the sweat breaking out on her hot face.

He tugged at her skirt of dark-green wool. Kate thought it firmly in place until he found the button at her waist and dragged it off. He ripped off her fine white cambric petticoat with lace edging, and her flannel one followed, though she was fighting him every inch of the way. Screaming when she could get her breath. His face, all bristles, scratched against hers. She tried to bite him.

'You little devil!' He gave the neck of her bodice an almighty heave and it tore. There was still her vest. She fought to keep it down but he was pulling it up to look at her breasts.

'Just buds,' he laughed. His rough paw covered one and squeezed painfully. 'Not worth looking at.'

She leapt away but he caught her and pulled her down on Tommy's bed, pushing his face into hers. His breath smelled of beer. She screamed again.

He was pulling at her knickers, the ones she'd been given for Christmas with lace at the knees. She kicked as he dragged them from her body. There were still her interlock knicker linings.

She could hear the bedroom door being kicked open. She knew it was Tommy; he wasn't even four years old and could barely reach the latch.

He asked in his piping treble: 'Dad? What are you doing?'

'Help me. Help me, Tommy,' Kate screamed. 'Don't leave me.'

She glimpsed him through her tears, slight for his age, glossy-haired, a worried look on his pert little face.

Mitch straightened up. She kicked out at him. She was still wearing her high button boots. She heard him grunt with pain and tried to repeat it but he caught her ankle and wouldn't let it go.

Kate fell back on the bed, crying, and gathered Tommy in her arms. 'Don't let him near me.'

Tommy was crying too. 'Get away from her. You're hurting her.'

'I'll tell Mam,' Kate spat at him. 'I'll tell her what you've done to me.'

Mitch's hand clamped round her neck and squeezed. She coughed and choked. She couldn't breathe; she panicked again.

'If you say a word to your mam, I'll flatten you. Don't you dare! Do you hear me?'

'I'll tell her.' Tommy was tiny, but he had plenty of spirit. 'You're hurting Kate.'

Mitch's other fist shot out to grab Tommy by the collar of his jumper. He pulled him closer.

'You too, Tommy. One word to your mam and I'll kill you.'

Kate wept and coughed as he loosened his hold on her. 'I hate you. Hate you.'

'I haven't touched you anyway. No harm done. No need to make such a fuss.' He gave Tommy a cuff with his fist that sent him flying.

'Don't you two forget. I'll kill you if there's a peep out of either of you.'

Kate lay huddled with Tommy until he grew restless and pulled away. Then she got up and washed herself again. She felt sick. Slowly then, she dressed herself in the clothes that weren't torn.

'Bring me a needle and cotton,' she bade Tommy. She mended her bodice, since she had no other with her. Then she combed her ginger hair and put her hat on top. There was shopping to get.

That secret had drawn her and Tommy together over the years, though they never spoke of it. Neither of them told Mam. They were too frightened to do anything. But anyway, Kate felt Mam had to be protected. She thought the world of Mitch. Her hand would go out to touch him, her soft voice could control him.

When he belched noisily after a meal, she'd say: 'Please don't, Mitch.'

'A sign of satisfaction, love. It was a good meal.'

'It's not a habit I want the boys to pick up.'

Kate never had been able to see what it was her mother liked about him.

Chapter Three

Kate finished putting the shopping away and started to tidy up their one living room. Usually it looked bright and homely, with a rag rug in front of the hearth and geraniums in pots on the windowsills. There was no separate kitchen and what had been intended as a parlour was used as a bedroom by the older boys.

Tom carried in a bucket of water to fill the boiler in the range. Brought in another to stand in the corner so that they had cold water on hand too.

As Kate started to chop up the meat to make the stew, the voices upstairs grew louder. Tommy perched on the edge of the stool beside her; his eyes kept going anxiously to the ceiling.

They heard a bellow of rage from Dad.

'We've got to go up.' Tommy's voice was an agonised whisper.

Kate put down her knife, wiped her hands on a cloth and headed for the stairs. She knew he was one step behind her.

'Mam!' At her bedroom door Tommy leapt forward and threw his arms round her. Kate could see she was crying. Somehow she found the courage to turn on her father.

'Leave Mam alone. Can't you see you're upsetting her?'

Kate had never got over her fear of him. She'd never spoken of it to anybody, not even to Tommy. She did her best to hide it from Mam, but Mitch knew. His aggressive eyes stared into hers and pinned her down by force of will. She bristled with resentment. She knew it was his way of showing his power. Power over his family and particularly over her.

'So you're here again?'

She was worked up enough to answer pertly: 'Somebody has to be at a time like this.'

'Less of your lip, you.'

Mitch hair had been glossy and thick when he was young; now it was growing sparse on top and hung round his head in greasy rings. His nose was not quite straight, having been broken in a pub fight in his youth.

He'd come over from Ireland to get work blasting out the railway tunnel between Liverpool and Birkenhead. As a child, Kate had listened to his stories about the terrible conditions he'd had to endure. Water seeping into the tunnel so fast that many were drowned. Then the rock-boring machine they'd brought in dried the rock dust to such a degree that it filled the air so that they coughed and choked and could barely see what they were doing.

But when that tunnel was finished and the trains began to run, he had to go further afield to find work. The rail network had already spread across the country, but sometimes there was work building a new tunnel or laying another branch line, but mostly the work was maintenance. He handed over just enough of his wages to keep them in poverty and spent the rest on drink and tobacco for himself.

He turned back to leer at her mother and prod at the makeshift cot.

'How do I know he's mine? You've picked up some fancy man while I've been away.'

'No, I tell you.'

Kate stopped, appalled. How could he say such a thing?

'I've never sired that baby.' Dad was blustering. 'It's got slant eyes, it looks Chinese.'

Mam was scrubbing at her eyes with the sheet. 'Course you have. You never leave me alone, do you?'

'I'm not staying here to be cuckolded.' Her father was heaving at the drawers in which he kept his own clothes and tossing their contents into a bag. 'You only want me because you know I'll tip up my wage every week. I'm going and I'm not coming back. I've had enough.'

Kate wanted to ask if he was leaving because he had another woman. She had to bite the words back, afraid it would upset Mam more to know what they'd seen. She was sure Dad was using the baby as an excuse.

She stood watching him pack his possessions while Mam's face screwed up with tears she made no attempt to hide.

'You've got to stay,' Tommy entreated. 'You've got to stay, Dad. Mam wants you here.'

'Where've you put my new bowler hat?' Dad was demanding. 'Where is it, woman?'

'In the box at the top of the stairs,' Mam sobbed.

'Get it for me,' he snapped at Kate. 'Help me get packed.'

He expected her to wait on him hand and foot. He bossed them all about, shouting his orders. The older boys no longer leapt to his will, but if Kate didn't he'd turn nasty. Sometimes he'd let his fists fly, particularly if he'd had a drink or two. She resented it, resented the affection the boys showed him, resented the way Mam relied on him.

'Go on, get a move on, you surly bitch.'

It dawned on Kate then that he was packing his things in Josie Oaks' carpet bag. She felt the heat rushing up her cheeks as she leapt at him.

'You can't take that. It's not mine. I borrowed it to come home.' She snatched up the bag and tipped all his things out on to the bedroom lino.

He let out another bellow of rage and his great paw slapped against her chin, sending her reeling. Kate staggered back against the wall, but she wasn't having this.

'Where are my things? What have you done with them? The things that were in it? You've no right to help yourself to this bag. I have to take it back.'

Mitch stepped forward to snatch it. Little Tommy, puny in comparison, was pushing himself between her and his dad. His fists were up to defend her.

'Don't you hurt Kate. I won't let you.'

Mitch went off into peals of cruel laughter. Kate snatched up Josie's bag and escaped to the back bedroom, her mind whirling. She'd never have dared to thwart Dad if she'd given it a moment's thought. She stuffed the bag under one of the two rickety iron bedsteads. She could feel tears of desperation in her eyes, but she was not going to let him take it.

Her clothes had been tipped out in a heap on Tommy's bed. All the time she'd spent ironing her blouses had been wasted. The door crashed back.

'I've got to have a bag,' Dad stormed. 'How can I get my things together otherwise?'

'You've got a bag. Use that.'

'I need another. I'm going for good. That isn't big enough.'

'There's shopping bags downstairs, Dad. Take them if you must.'

'Get me one,' he ordered.

Kate was reluctant to go. She didn't want to leave him in the room with Josie's bag.

'I'll show you . . .' She led the way downstairs, and gulped with relief when she found he was following her. Down in the living room, she dared to say more.

'We saw you with another woman. Me and Tommy, you can ask him. We saw you coming out of the pub. That's why you're going, isn't it?'

Mam had good canvas shopping bags with rope handles. If he took one away she'd miss it.

'Why do you have to upset Mam by saying that about the baby? He looks like Fred when he was small. And Tommy, he's got the same colour hair.'

'But Chinese eyes,' Dad spat back. 'Or Japanese. That fellow down in the market.'

'Don't say such things,' Kate stormed. 'You're just saying that to excuse yourself. Mam wouldn't do such a thing. You know that. We're all your children.'

He straightened up to his full six feet. His Irish eyes confronted hers aggressively.

'Well, Miss Hoity-Toity, you aren't for a start. And that's a fact. You're nothing to me.'

Suddenly Kate felt she couldn't breathe. Her legs felt weak with shock.

'You were two years old before I set eyes on your mother.'

She didn't doubt it for one minute. Hadn't she always been listing the ways in which she was different from the rest of the family? Then there was the four-year gap between her and Joe. She cringed in revulsion. She understood now why he didn't love her.

'You're lucky to be alive, you little bitch. You know what usually happened?'

Kate stared back at him, mesmerised. she shook her head.

'It was always happening. Servant girls like your mother getting themselves in trouble and trying to hide it. Often they gave birth alone, so they did. They'd kill the child, so they could carry on as though nothing had happened.'

Kate felt the hairs lift on the back of her neck. 'Is that what happened? Was Mam alone when . . .' Her tongue was dry with agony. No wonder her mother didn't love her either. She'd brought her terrible trouble.

He shrugged. 'Just saying it, I am. Before my time. It could have happened like that, often did.'

Kate pushed the shopping bag over to him and moistened her lips. She had to know.

'Who was my father?'

His hand closed on the bag. 'How would I know? You'll have to ask your mother about that.'

Mitch McGlory went bounding back upstairs to finish his packing and Kate collapsed on the sagging basket chair.

How many times had she tried to recall her earliest years? She could remember when there was just her and Mam. She could remember

25

Mam crying and being very sad, but she didn't think there had been any other man in their life.

Long ago, she'd guessed Mitch wasn't her father. The way he treated her, his whole manner had told her that. There were all the other reasons too that had made her come to the conclusion that Mam had had her before she was married.

She'd been thirteen when she'd first plucked up enough courage to ask her about it.

Mam had flared up straight away. 'Not your father? What's the matter, isn't he good enough for you?'

Kate had tried to explain. 'It's not that . . .'

'Of course he's your father. He's my husband and father of you all. You can forget your silly ideas. Put them right out of your mind. You're not any different to the rest of the family. That's the truth. Don't you dare suggest such a wicked thing again.'

Kate had believed her. She'd put it right out of her head, just as Mam had ordered her to. Now, as she listened to the sounds of Mitch McGlory leaving for good, she wanted to weep with disbelief to find she'd been right all along.

Freddie and Duncan were rolling about on the rag mat in front of the fire; fists were being raised. She pulled Freddie up on her knee to protect him, without saying a word. Mitch came heavily downstairs. She heard her mother cry out after him:

'Mitch, don't go. Please don't go.'

He slammed through the back door without so much as a glance towards his sons.

Kate knew it wasn't a good time to talk to her mother, but she couldn't wait any longer. She went upstairs to the ornate brass bedstead in the front room. Her mother's face was turned into the pillow.

She asked: 'Why did you tell me Mitch McGlory was my father? I asked you, and you said he was. I believed you. You were telling lies!'

Mam sobbed and the words came out slowly.

'He made an honest woman of me. He was a hard worker, a good man. He turned over his wages . . .'

'Who was my father? Mam, I've got to know.'

But Mam wouldn't say another word. Kate tried to press her but it only upset Mam more. In the end, she went downstairs none the wiser.

She set about tidying up the living room again, banging things about while her curiosity grew and grew. Why shouldn't she know? Why was Mam acting so strangely? She'd kept it a secret all these years, insisting Mitch was her father. But now Kate knew that wasn't the case, why not

26

tell her the truth about what had happened? She felt now that she was grown up, she had a right to know.

By four o'clock, Harry, who was six, was home from school. The great cauldron of scouse that had hung on a chain simmering over the fire for hours, was ready and filling the kitchen with mouthwatering scents.

'I'm hungry,' Tommy said. Kate felt ravenous; she'd had nothing to eat since breakfast.

'I want to take some up to Mam. She's exhausted and she won't rest until she's eaten. I'll dish up for the rest of you, if you'll keep an eye on Fred.'

'Course I will.' Tommy was sitting Freddie up at the table . . . The others were old enough to look after themselves.

Kate was really worried now. If Mitch had left for good, there'd be no more money from him and she couldn't see how Mam could manage. She took a big plateful of scouse up on a tray for her.

'Come on, Mam. You'll feel better when you've had something to eat.' She helped her up the bed, set the tray across her knees.

The new baby was mewling softly. Kate picked him out of his drawer. He was wet, so she set about changing his napkin. She was a dab hand at caring for babies, having had so much practice with her brothers. Then she picked him up to give him a little cuddle. Took him nearer the window to look at him more closely.

Her mother croaked: 'Is he all right? What d'you think?'

Kate didn't want to discuss this with her mother now. They were all too emotionally charged, and Mam looked exhausted. Her own mind was still churning after the row with Mitch. She couldn't get over the shock that he'd walked out for good. She'd always believed Mam inspired undying devotion in every member of the family.

She said carefully: 'He does have almond eyes, but he doesn't seem much different to the others.'

She wanted to be honest, no point in doing otherwise. After what Mrs Potter had said, they were bound to speculate, but Mam had had all she could stand for one day. Kate felt fearful about the baby herself.

'Before I go back, we'll take him to see the doctor. See what he says. It'll put your mind at rest.'

'I can't afford . . .'

'I'll pay.'

'With your dad going . . .'

Kate wasn't going to argue that he wasn't her dad. Not now, not today. Though she was burning up about that too.

27

'How am I going to manage without his money?'

Kate thought that a more urgent matter. 'I'll be able to give you a little more.'

They both knew that most of what she earned already came to the family one way or another.

'And our Tommy will be old enough to work soon. Things will get better as they all get older.'

Her mother blew hard into her handkerchief. 'I need you here to look after me. I can't manage everything by myself.'

'Mam, I can't. I'd be another mouth to feed if I stayed at home.'

She didn't want to stay here. She wanted to go back to the relative peace of the shop. Yes, she had to get up early and work hard, but she didn't have worries like this. And besides, there was Jack Courtney.

Her mother scraped her plate clean. Kate could see her eyelids closing.

'You'll need to suckle the baby before you go to sleep.'

Kate could see from Mam's face that she didn't want to. For a moment she thought she'd refuse. The she moved the tray and the plate to the other side of the bed.

'Give him here then.'

Kate put the baby in her arms. He was sleepy and slow to feed. Mam had to keep tickling his toes to keep him awake. It seemed to take for ever, but they both knew the babe had to get enough to grow. Tommy brought up a cup of tea and took the tray away.

At last Mam said: 'That should do him for his first day.'

With baby Billy tucked back in his drawer and her mother ready to drop off, Kate went downstairs. She felt very hungry indeed.

'You're a good boy, Tommy.'

He'd started to wash up in an enamel bowl of hot water, turning the dishes out on a tin tray to drain as soon as he'd cleared enough space for it on the kitchen table.

'Had to, no more clean plates.'

Joe came in from work before they'd got the dishes dry. He saw Kate there and asked straight away: 'Is it a girl this time?'

They'd barely finished telling him the news when Charlie appeared and they had to go through it all again. She divided the rest of the scouse between the three of them and sat down to eat feeling that she'd drop if she didn't.

Noisy and excited, all her brothers swirled round in the confined space. Kate had to ask them to be quiet because Mam was asleep. There was little rest to be had when the meal had been cleared away,

28

between making the fire up and keeping peace amongst the younger ones. Joe lit the oil lamp and she did her best to darn their socks and the elbows of their jerseys.

She got little Freddie ready for bed, but as his cot was in Mam's room she let him play downstairs until she heard the new baby whimper again. Then she crept up and put Freddie in his cot and brought Billy down to the fire. Joe took him from her.

'He looks all right to me.'

Charlie took him from Joe. 'The spitting image of Freddie when he was born. Perhaps we're worrying for nothing.'

Kate tried to give the baby a drink of boiled water. He hadn't wanted his mother's milk but he wanted the water even less.

When she took Billy back to his drawer, Mam was awake again, so she heated a cup of milk for her. Kate felt exhausted; the only place where there was room for her to lie down was in the double brass bed beside Mam.

To Kate, the soft whimper seemed a long way away. She lay still in the darkness trying to remember where she was. Then she heard the snore beside her and she knew she was in Mam's bed at home. Freddie's cot was close beside her; he was breathing deeply, fast asleep. Another whimper, louder this time, and she knew the new baby needed attention.

She got out of bed and the room seemed icy. There was light coming under the heavy curtains. She'd washed them some years ago and they'd shrunk so that they swung an inch short of the sill. In the half-light, she reached for an old coat she'd thrown across the foot of the bed and pulled it on over her nightie. Billy let out a wail of protest that was loud enough to wake her mother. Kate changed his napkin and brought him to the bed.

'I'm glad you've woken up,' she whispered. 'I think he wants another feed.'

Mam was slow to unfasten her nightie and put him to the breast. Billy let out an impatient wail.

'Shush.' Kate tried to soothe him, rocking him gently. 'Come on, Mam, before he wakes Freddie up.'

'Nothing will wake Freddie.' She sounded half asleep. 'I hate broken nights, I don't know how I'll cope with them again.'

Kate could hear the infant starting to suck. She tidied up his bed in the drawer.

'Would you like a cup of tea, Mam?'

Downstairs, she found the fire had gone out. Should she relight it now? It would be lovely to come down at six to find the fire in and the room warm, but it would be a waste of coal.

She lit the Primus instead. While she waited for the kettle to boil, she set the table for breakfast and checked on the porridge she'd made last night and left in the hay box.

She took two cups of tea upstairs. In the half-light she could see Mam sitting up in bed with the babe over her shoulder, trying to wind him.

'He's ready to go down now,' she whispered, handing him over to Kate to settle back in his drawer.

Back in bed, it seemed the height of luxury to be sipping hot tea. It was three o'clock in the morning and Kate was far from sleep now. They were alone in the night and she wanted to know who her father was. It seemed a good moment to talk to Mam. She heard her slide the cup and saucer on to the floor and settle back into her pillows.

'Mam? I want to talk.'

Silence. There was no invitation to go ahead.

'You heard what Mitch said to me downstairs? Before he left?'

'No.' He'd raised his voice to her; Kate didn't know how she could have failed to hear.

'I told you yesterday afternoon. He said he wasn't my father, that I was two before he met you.'

Mam let out a strangled sound.

'You've never admitted that.'

Kate waited but Mam said nothing.

She went on: 'It's true, isn't it?

Mam let out a gusting sigh. 'Yes – well . . .'

'Mam, I need to know.'

'I wasn't – married to your father.'

'I was assuming that. Who was he, Mam?'

Another loud sigh. Kate wanted to get her to talk. Surely here in the darkness it would be easier? But she was finding it harder than trying to light the range downstairs when the wind was in the wrong direction.

'He was a gentleman.' Mam's voice quickened. 'He had a silver-headed cane and a silk top hat.'

Kate didn't believe her.

'I'm sure every daughter born the wrong side of the blanket is told her father was a gentleman.'

'Yours was, Kate.'

'Tell me about him.'

'There's nothing much to tell.'

'Well – did he have a job?'

'He went to business.'

'What did he do?' Another heavy sigh. 'How did you meet him?'

'I don't remember.'

'What was his name? You must remember that?'

'No, I don't.'

Kate was astounded. 'This is my father we're talking about!'

'It was a very long time ago.'

'You can't have forgotten his name! I don't believe it. I don't want Mitch McGlory to be my father. I've always known he couldn't be. He treats me differently from the boys. So do you.'

Kate heard a sniff from the pillow. She was angry now.

'I need to know, Mam. He's provided one half of me. Do I look like him? I certainly didn't get my red hair from you or Mitch.'

'Mitch wanted us to be wed and his money helped feed you. He wasn't a bad man.'

Kate was shaking, hardly able to control her frustration. 'I don't want to talk about Mitch McGlory. I want to hear about my father. Did he have red hair?'

'He did. It's better if you don't know too much about him, Kate.'

'Why? Why won't you tell me? I'll never rest,' her voice shook, 'until I know everything. If you won't tell me, I'll find out somehow.'

'If you've any sense you won't try.'

'Why not? You must have loved him.'

'Yes, I loved him.'

Mam turned over noisily, bashing her pillows into shape. 'Now I need to get to sleep, and so do you.'

Kate heard the deep and heavy breathing start up a moment later. She knew her mother was only pretending to sleep. For her own part, she found sleep impossible after that. She wanted to know more. She had to know.

Lena turned over and silently wiped the tears from her eyes. Her head ached, her breasts were hard and sore, her nipples tender. The years and repeated childbirth had made her lose her looks.

She mustn't make a sound, mustn't let Kate know she was crying or she'd start asking questions all over again. She'd had nightmares about this; she didn't want those again.

Kate was so like her father. Lena had only to look at her to be reminded. She had the same determined line to her chin; the same straight nose and strong features. On a woman, they were a little too

31

strong for beauty. She had the same green eyes; sometimes jade green, milky and opaque, sometimes clear emerald in colour. They were eyes that seemed to know more than they should. She had her father's flame-coloured hair too.

Lena had loved him more than anyone else in her whole life. To be reminded of what she'd lost still hurt. His going had changed her life for ever. Everything she'd held dear had gone like a bubble burst in the wind.

She opened her eyes to look at Kate. She couldn't possibly tell her what she wanted to know. All this on top of Mitch walking out for good. She felt confused, couldn't think clearly about anything.

Kate meant well. She was very good to her. Lena ought to be grateful, because she couldn't manage without her. But she'd never been able to reach out to Kate as she had to the boys. The distance yawned between them however much she wanted it gone. Kate was tied up with such painful memories, it drove them poles apart. She wished she knew how to get closer to her.

Now Kate was making things worse by asking about Benedict. She'd sworn to find out and she had all his persistence; she'd not give up until she'd ferreted out what she wanted to know.

There was no way to stop her, though it wouldn't do her any good to find out. Lena had always tried to hide it, dreading the outcome. If she did find out, Kate would never rest easy again. It would worry her that she might take after her father in that way too.

Lena mopped her eyes with the sheet again. She wouldn't want Kate pointed out and taunted as she'd been. Poor Kate, her father had done her no favours.

The night hours dragged, she couldn't sleep. She heard Kitty Watts' cockerel crow at dawn. Every nerve in her body seemed on edge and her mind whirled with tension. She heard Kate get up and watched her draw back the bedroom curtains.

'You go back to sleep, Mam. It's what you need now.'

'I can't sleep,' she sighed. 'I'm worried.'

Kate was dressing quickly.

'About the baby? I am too. Look, Mam, we don't know. It's only Mrs Potter's opinion. We mustn't let her upset us. He looks all right.' She paused at the door. 'I'll bring you a cup of tea, as soon as it's made.'

Lena pulled herself up on her elbow to look at her new son. He was fast asleep, cocooned in a sheet, only a thatch of silky brown hair showing.

Mrs Potter had frightened her. Not right, she'd said, and nothing could be done about it. But Kate had said he looked all right, and anyway she couldn't think about more trouble coming her way. One baby was very like another. Billy would be no different from the others for years. Time to worry about him when she had to. She didn't want to hear what any doctor said. She wanted to push all that under the carpet and forget it.

There wasn't room in her mind for more when Mitch had left her. Gone for good. She found that hard to take in. She'd known that Mitch had been second best when she'd married him, but she'd grown to love him and he'd said he loved her. His boys too, he certainly loved them. He was proud of them. Surely he hadn't meant he was going for good?

The tears wouldn't stop coming. She didn't know what she'd do without him. She needed him, the boys needed him. Though if he stayed away there was one blessing she could count on. There would be no more babies. Billy would be the last.

Chapter Four

Kate had no difficulty getting up early; she was used to opening the shop at six. The work was harder here. Joe and Charlie were wage earners and had to be up and out first. She knew Mam got up to get them breakfast and cut sandwiches for their lunch, and felt she had to do the same.

The fire wouldn't catch and the water was slow to boil for tea. Poor Charlie was yawning and couldn't wake up. He had to carry hodloads of bricks up ladders on a building site. He worked from seven in the morning until six at night, six days a week for ten shillings. It was heavy work, and being on the go for so many hours, he needed more food than he usually got. She cut his sandwiches but there was only jam to put in them. She added a generous slice of Josie's cake.

Things were easier for Joe; his work wasn't so physical. He came to the cemetery quite often and knew everybody who worked there. Sometimes he popped into the lodge there for a cup of tea while a funeral took place.

Kate sighed as she saw them off. Her wage and theirs were all Mam had now, a mere pittance when it came to feeding a family of their size. It was time then to get the younger ones up. Harry had to go to school.

'You ought to go too, Tommy. Really you should. You'll want a good job when you leave.'

'Will school make any difference?' His big brown eyes stared into hers. Katie was afraid it wouldn't. All her brothers were destined for manual labour like Joe and Charlie. It hurt that Tommy seemed to know everything was stacked against him.

'I can read and write and add up the pennies when I go shopping. Not that I ever have many to count.'

'All the same, you're only nine and . . .'

'There's so much to do here. Mam says she needs me at home.'

Kate didn't approve of that. Mam used to say the same to her, and then Joe and Charlie in their turn. Kate thought they should all have gone to school more regularly, been given the best possible chance.

She said: 'I'm here now, I can manage.'

'There'll be plenty for both of us to do.'

Tommy's smile was lopsided. Mam had this effect on them. They strived to do all they could for her. It made them grow up before their time. Tommy knew what was needed. He trimmed the lamp wick and polished the glass, then made up the fire.

When Kate took up her mother's breakfast, her eyes looked red and puffy.

'Mam! You mustn't upset yourself like this. We'll manage somehow. Don't cry.'

'I'm not.' She sounded short. The puffy eyes examined her. 'Your hair! It's got a mind of its own. Can't you do something with it?'

Kate's hand went up to her bun. It was more wobbly than usual.

'Such as what?' She was tired of battling with her hair. Mam must know she'd spent less time than usual on herself this morning.

'Wear a cap,' her mother retorted. 'Cover it. I would, if it were mine.'

Kate felt a stab of hurt. She didn't want to wear a cap. Only old people wore them. Mam made it obvious she didn't like her ginger hair and wanted her to hide it. Mam didn't seem to like anything about her. She didn't hug her as she did the boys. It made Kate toss her head and another hairpin fly out.

'Why are you always sharp with me?'

'I'm sorry.' Mam's tears were coming again now. 'A bit on edge, I suppose. I've a lot on my mind.'

Kate picked little Freddie out of his cot and went downstairs again as quickly as she could. There was a lot on her mind too.

Kate felt overwhelmed when she saw the washing waiting to be done. The birth had provided plenty, and there were always dirty napkins by the dozen.

'I'd better make a start on this.'

It was a job Kate didn't like because it had to be done out in the wash house. It was bitterly cold out there at this time of the year, and steam from the hot water condensed on the tin roof and dropped on her head.

'I'll carry the water for you.'

Tommy fetched the bucket and went to the standpipe. He lit the fire under the boiler, rinsed the sheets and put them in to boil. Kate could understand why Mam wanted him at home. Later he turned the mangle for her and helped peg the things out on the line. They were in the middle of this when Mrs Potter came round to see her mother. Kate led the way upstairs.

'How's the babe feeding?' Mrs Potter looked into the drawer.

Kate said: 'A bit slow to get it down. Keeps dozing off.'

'Wake you in the night, did he?'

'Only once.'

'He slept well then.'

'Yes, he hardly ever cries.'

'You must wake him for feeds. Don't let him sleep through.'

'Have I ever done that?' Her mother was testy. 'He'll be all right. I can't see much the matter with him.'

'Get the doctor to explain . . .'

'No need,' Mam fired back. 'We'll manage all right. He's no different from the others.'

As soon as Mrs Potter had gone, Kate saw her mother swing her legs out of bed.

'Why don't you stay where you are today?' Kate asked. 'Nurse Potter said you should. Rest will . . .'

'What does she know? Or the doctor? They'd have me lying in for six weeks.'

Kate knew she wouldn't change her mind. 'All right. There's a good fire going, it's nice and warm downstairs.'

'She's always on about something, that woman. You mustn't let the baby go all night without a feed. Don't forget to register his birth, you only have six weeks.'

'She's only doing her job, Mam.'

'Well, I wish she'd stop telling me Billy isn't right. As though we haven't got the message.'

'Perhaps you should take him to the doctor.'

'No point in wasting money on what he thinks. For the likes of us, it isn't going to make any difference.'

Kate had to help her dress and get down the narrow stairs. The basket chair creaked as Mam sank heavily into it.

The kitchen was looking more cheerful. Yesterday Kate had swept the stone floor and shaken the handmade rag rug that went in front of fire. There was a dresser on which their cups and plates shone in the firelight, and a large scrubbed table set up against the settle, with a bench for the other side that was pushed underneath when not in use.

'I'll make a cup of tea for us.'

Kate's mind was only half on what she was doing. Mam was testy because she'd been asking about the man who was her father. Almost as though Mam felt she was prying into her past. Nothing was going to

36

stop her finding out about him. When Mrs Potter had been going on about registering Billy's birth and getting his birth certificate, it had given her a pointer about where she could start.

Her birth certificate would tell her something. She couldn't remember ever seeing it, but she knew where Mam kept all her important papers. She was pouring the tea when Ada Catchpole from number one came to the back door.

'Hello, Kate. How are you, Lena? I've come to see the new baby. Another boy, I hear.'

Ada was her mother's closest friend. Stout and podgy-faced, she was a few years older than Mam. She too had a large family. Kate had been friendly with her daughters when they were all growing up, but now, like most girls, they were away in service. There were three sons still living at home who were working now. There was also a toddler, a little younger than Duncan, who called Ada Mam, but everybody knew he was her grandson. Betty, her eldest, had been deserted by the man who had got her into trouble. Betty had gone back to being a parlourmaid and Ada was bringing him up.

Kate went up to fetch Billy down, but before she could put him in Mrs Catchpole's arms, a bird could be heard pecking at the putty in their kitchen window. Ada leapt off her chair and went to thump on the glass to scare it off. It swooped off in panic.

'Horrible things,' she stormed. 'Destructive. It's Flossie Jenkins' fault. I keep telling her. She's always putting crusts out for the creatures. Attracts them here in droves.'

'Don't worry about them, Ada. The landlord will put more putty in when it's needed.'

Kate knew Ada disliked Flossie Jenkins at number four as much as she disliked birds. Ada smiled down at the baby.

'Isn't he lovely?' It was her automatic response to the newborn.

'Do you think he's all right?' Mam was asking. 'Nurse Potter reckons he isn't.'

Kate decided this was the opportunity she needed.

'I'm going to make your bed, Mam.' she said, hoping she'd be fully occupied downstairs for the next few minutes.

Up in her mother's room, she could feel her heart pounding. She knew Mam would be even more upset if she caught her doing this. She could hear the rise and fall of voices below; she'd have a moment's warning if one of them brought Billy back.

She quietly eased open the top drawer in the chest and lifted out the tin box in which all the important family papers were kept. It had a picture of the old Queen on the front and dated from the time of her Jubilee. Once it had held biscuits.

Now it was half full of documents. She opened it on the bed. There were several birth certificates, some still in their envelopes. Kate riffled through them quickly. Hers was not amongst them. There was the insurance policy into which Mam paid a penny a week. Her marriage lines to Mitch McGlory. A photograph of Mam looking incredibly young and pretty, with stars in her eyes. It must have been taken before she'd had any children.

Kate put everything back and clipped the lid. Nothing to help her there. She'd drawn a blank.

Kate was already back in the rhythm of life at Cemetery Cottages. Ada was still with her mother, so she went along to number six to pay what was owed to Kitty Watts. Number six was the only cottage that had a bit of land to it. It was a smallholding of six acres that supported a cow, a couple of pigs, ten ewes and a flock of chickens.

Mam bought milk and eggs from Kitty, pork too when she killed a pig. She allowed Mam to have what she wanted on tick, but it was the first bill that had to be paid because she was such a close neighbour.

Kitty was mucking out the three hen houses in a corner of a field when Kate found her. She readily dropped her shovel to walk back to the cottage. She needed to consult the book in which she wrote down what customers owed her.

She always wore a misshapen brown tam about the house and farm, pulled well down over her head to cover her metal curlers. Kate could see the small bumps sticking up under the felt. A donkey grazing nearby caught her eye. 'How's Dolly?'

'Fine. Day of rest for her today.'

Dolly pulled the cemetery lawn-mower used to keep the grass verges trimmed. Kitty provided her stabling.

Although Kitty was friendly enough these days, Kate remembered how she'd waged war against her and the other children in the cottages. Dolly had been the attraction. They'd gone into the field to ride her whenever they thought Kitty's back was turned. Kate could remember running into the woods to escape her ire.

She also knew nothing had changed. Kitty waged war against the present generation of children, including Kate's brothers, but she never complained officially to Mam because she valued her custom.

'How's your mother, Kate? She's got her hands full, poor love. Another little boy, I hear.'

When she gave Kate her change, she put an extra-large egg into her hand.

'Give it to Lena for her tea. It's a double-yolker. Do her good. Tell her I'll be along later to see the new baby.'

Kate headed back along the cart track behind the houses. Ada Catchpole was shouting over the picket fence at Flossie Jenkins who lived at number four.

'Always feeding them dratted birds. You ought to have more sense.'

Ada had carried on a hate campaign against Flossie Jenkins for years.

'I like birds, Mrs Catchpole. I like to hear them sing in my garden. Most people do.' Flossie Jenkins thought herself socially superior to Ada because her husband was a police officer.

As Kate drew abreast, Ada turned to her. 'Look what she's got now, Kate. A ruddy bird table, as if she didn't attract enough without that.'

Kate didn't want to be drawn. 'I saw it yesterday.' She smiled and passed on.

'I don't like what birds do to my washing,' Ada stormed. 'Filthy creatures. Very unhealthy.'

Every cottage in the row had a washing line strung the length of its back garden. A huge elm overhung the garden of number one and the birds perched in the branches over Ada's line and let their droppings foul her newly washed sheets.

Flossie retorted: 'It's that tree. You ought to get your old man to cut it down.'

Kate smiled; they all knew that was impossible. Not only would it be beyond Mr Catchpole's strength, but it grew outside his garden.

She was about to turn into her own garden when Septimus Ratcliff, their neighbour at number two, called to her:

'Hello, Kate, how's your mother?'

He was an elderly widower who had retired after working in the cemetery for fifty-two years. His shoulders were bent and his legs bandy, and he now spent much of his time working in his garden. The rest of it was spent either in the cemetery talking to the men he knew who still worked there, or leaning on his front gate watching what they were doing. He always knew exactly who was being buried.

'Mother's fine, Ratty. It's another boy.'

'So I heard. I've got some vegetables for her. Come and get them.'

'Thank you, that's very kind.'

He was opening the door to his old pig sty, which was now full of

39

gardening tools. He'd put together a box of carrots and onions, winter cabbage and leeks, parsnips and swede.

'That's wonderful. I'll be able to make vegetable soup. Thank you very much.'

'I grow more than I need these days and your Charlie's very good. Helps me dig. Tommy too.'

Kate felt grateful as she carried the box indoors. She knew the tenants of Cemetery Cottages believed in helping each other. Ada Catchpole took a hot meal into Ratty's cottage every day. He kept her and Mam supplied with vegetables grown in his garden.

But they didn't all pull together. Mrs Jenkins in number four and Gladys Fry in number five kept themselves apart and would have nothing to do with the others. Quarrels over the picket fences frequently broke out. Neither side counted Kitty Watts as being their ally; she kept a foot in both camps.

Through the back window, Kate saw two pre-school children race along the cart track, hotly pursued by two others, one of whom was her brother Duncan. The first two shot screaming into Gladys Fry's garden shed, and Duncan and Lennie, Ada's grandson, ran off into the woods.

It was a wonderful place for children to grow up. Kate had roamed all over the hill and through the woods, a large tract of which belonged to the council and provided a pleasant public place. She'd played, as the present generation did, around the windmill and Bidston Observatory.

From the cottages there was little to see except the sandstone chapels and the cemetery, and in high summer even they could only be glimpsed through the trees. But higher up the hill it was possible to see over the Birkenhead docks to the Mersey and the Liverpool waterfront beyond. A breathtaking view on a clear day, but often it was masked by industrial haze.

After living at the shop in the streets of Wallasey it seemed a rural idyll, yet the Dock Cottages – not cottages at all but blocks of tenements, the most infamous slum in town – were only five minutes' walk away. There was noise from the ships on the river too, especially when visibility was poor.

Kate jumped as the one o'clock gun boomed close at hand. It was fired from the Observatory above so the ships in the river could set their chronometers before embarking on their voyages.

When the children came home from school in the afternoons the cottages rang with their shouts. Kate heard Mrs Jenkins next door sending them away. 'I can't put up with your noise.'

40

Kate went out to tell them to go up into the woods, but most were already swooping down the cart track.

'We're going to the dead park,' Harry told her.

'What are you going to do there?'

'Just weed our Liza's grave.'

Liza was their sister. Her grave was only a hundred yards or so from the house in which she'd spent her pathetically short life. At nine months she'd died of measles. They'd all had it. Joe was first; he brought it home from school. It gave Liza terrible earache and she'd never recovered.

'Don't make a noise there.'

As a child, Kate had spent a good deal of her time in the cemetery too. The groundsmen stopped to chat. They gave them little jobs to do, sweeping the paths and picking up leaves. They were paid with a barley sugar or a humbug.

Kate used to help the caretaker dust and polish in the chapels. It was a peaceful place. There was drama too, when the hearses came, pulled by big black horses with black plumes on their heads. The children kept out of sight then behind the bushes.

After a big funeral where there were lots of flowers, they were often piled up outside the chapels before being taken down to the Borough Hospital. Kate knew her brothers helped themselves to these and put them on Liza's grave. She used to do it herself.

In the following days, when her brothers came home from school, she took them and their friends up to Taylor's Wood to collect morning sticks for fire-lighting. When they had filled Mam's pig sty, they piled them into Ada's, and then into Ratty's. They even collected sticks for Kitty Watts. Mam received so much help that Kate felt she had to do something in return, and there wasn't much else that the McGlorys could do.

She enjoyed doing it, it got her out in the fresh air. Today, Tommy had discovered a large branch beginning to rot in a ditch. It was covered with moss and leaves and must have been there for a long time. They'd dragged it back to eke out their coal. It felt dry, so she took two good-sized pieces inside and put them on the fire.

Mam had been cutting slices of bread for their tea. Kate watched her flop down on a chair, put her head back and close her eyes. Her mouth drooped at the corners; Kate thought she looked depressed.

'Mam! You don't look well. Have your tea and go back to bed.'

'I feel awful.'

'It's only four days since Billy was born. You're doing too much.'

'I haven't felt well for months.' Kate saw a tear ooze from under her eyelid. She made up her mind.

'I'm taking you to the doctor tomorrow.'

'What can he do? It's a waste of money.'

'It'll set my mind at rest.'

'I wish you didn't have to go back. Everything's against me, Kate. How am I going to manage?'

Kate didn't know. She hadn't much money left, but she thought it would be well spent at the doctor's. They always went to Dr Weldon on Upton Road. It was only a short walk, and Kate insisted on taking Billy and her mother to his surgery as soon as they'd got Tommy and Harry off to school. Ada Catchpole offered to look after Freddie and Duncan.

They had to wait a long time, and Kate could see her mother wilting on the bench beside her. All round them, fellow patients were coughing and scraping their throats. When at last it was their turn, there was barely room for them all in the tiny surgery. Dr Weldon looked old and not much healthier than his waiting patients. Kate listed her mother's symptoms and he listened to her chest. He gave her a bottle of cough mixture and a bottle of tonic.

'Would you take a look at the baby too.' Kate lowered her arms and opened up Billy's shawls. 'Mrs Potter says he isn't right.'

He gave the baby one cursory glance. 'Down's syndrome,' he said.

'What can we do that will help?'

'Nothing,' he sighed. 'Nothing.'

She could see Mam panicking. 'What's caused it? Is it my fault?'

'It's just your age, Mrs McGlory. Just your age.'

Kate felt her week at home had passed very quickly. She was tired, having been on her feet from morning to night every day. She was torn in two about returning to the shop; for herself it was what she wanted, but she was worried about leaving her family.

'Don't go.' Mam sat by the fire looking pitiable. 'Mr Halliday won't mind if you take another few days off.'

'I have to go. He expects me to be there to open the shop at six in the morning. He's relying on me to do it.'

'He's a Quaker. He wants to be kind to people. He'll understand.'

'It would be taking advantage.'

'But what about me? Don't you ever think about how I'll manage without you?'

Mam was up and able to look after herself and the new baby. She'd done that for the last few days.

'I'll stay home and help you, Mam,' Tommy comforted.

The toddlers Duncan and Freddie were boisterous and noisy and a bit of a handful. Mam would never be able to manage them, let alone the shopping and the carrying-in of coal for the fire.

Mam ignored Tommy. 'There's always washing waiting to be done. I can't do everything.'

'I've done the washing,' Kate protested. 'I've boiled the nappies, everything's nice and dry.'

'I need a clean one now.'

Tommy tugged one down from the pulley over the hearth, and gave it to her.

Yesterday, he'd come home with a huge grin on his face. 'I've got myself a Saturday job,' he crowed.

'Where? What doing?'

'At Hamlyn's the butcher, on Hoylake Road. Delivering the orders. He's got a bike for me to ride.'

'Sounds grand,' Harry told him. 'I'd like to do that when I'm big enough.'

'I have to help clean up the shop too,' Tommy admitted.

'How much are they paying you?' Mam wanted to know.

'I'm to be paid in kind: a large joint for Sunday, big enough to provide cold meat for Monday, and all the bones and offal and bits we want to see us through the rest of the week.'

Mam beamed at him. 'That's grand. Excellent. I can make broth if I can get bones. You're such a good boy, our Tommy.'

'A wonderful help.' Kate smiled.

'Hearts and liver too, and he said small scraps for stews.' Tommy glowed with pride that he was able to provide the family with meat. They'd rarely had enough of it, up to now.

'All the same,' Mam said, 'I'll never manage. I'll have to apply to the Poor Law for help.'

After the evening meal, Kate packed her things into Josie Oaks' bag and carried it downstairs. Mam was nursing baby Billy by the fire. Kate could see her face crumpling; she was afraid Mam was going to cry.

'I hate leaving you, Mam. But I have to go. We need what I can earn.'

'I know that. I'm sorry, I shouldn't ask you to stay. It's just that . . . when I look to the future, it frightens me. I need somebody to lean on.'

'I'll help all I can.' Kate kissed her cheek. 'That goes without saying.'

Charlie walked down to the tram stop with her to carry her bag. It was lighter going back, without the fruit cake.

When the tram came, Kate sank down on the nearest seat. She was looking forward to seeing Josie Oaks again and catching up with the gossip. The journey was slow and she was tired. She almost dozed off. They stopped and started and passengers climbed the steep outside stairs to get on to the top deck. The shop was at the top of Rake Lane, in Liscard, a district she'd come to know and like in the six years she'd worked here.

The stop before hers, she heard a passenger coming down the outside metal stairs. It seemed he was holding the tram up for a moment, having a word with the conductor. She turned in her seat to look, and was in time to see Jack Courtney step inside to ride further. He came to stand by her seat. She felt her heart turn over.

'Good evening, Miss McGlory,' he said, raising his top hat. 'May I have the pleasure of escorting you to the shop? That is where you're going?'

Her cheeks were suddenly on fire. She realised Jack Courtney was riding beyond his stop so that he could talk to her.

'A pleasure? Would it be that?'

'A very great pleasure.'

Kate felt tongue-tied. She didn't know how to talk to a gentleman like him. 'Very kind.'

His shoes were of soft leather and highly polished. Kate wore high button boots and thought herself fashionable. Most people she knew wore hobnails. She'd worn them herself when she'd been growing up. Mam thought they were the only practical footwear.

'Your mother? Is all well? They told me in the shop.'

'Safely delivered. Another son, I'm afraid.'

He smiled down at her. 'Surely a son, another brother for you, is the best possible outcome?'

'No.' Kate told him why not. Then added shyly, 'I didn't realise you used the tram. I thought a carriage . . .'

'Our carriages are always much in use. Others in my family seem to have prior claim.' He smiled, but his manner suggested dissatisfaction with this. 'It's a lovely night for a walk, though.'

'Lovely.'

It was dry and frosty. The night sky was bright with stars. On the tram, Kate had thought it uncommonly cold and had buttoned up her coat at the neck. Now she didn't care how cold it was. A fire was blazing within her.

The tram was drawing to her stop before she was ready for it. He carried her bag the short walk to the shop. The lights were on inside and spilling out on to the pavement. It hadn't yet closed for the night.

'Thank you for escorting me back.'

'It can't be safe for you to walk about alone after dark.'

Kate smiled. 'I've never come to any harm.'

She slowed her step. Their meeting seemed to have given them no more time together than selling him his morning paper. It pleased her when he paused by the window of the hardware shop next door and lowered her bag to the pavement.

His gentle eyes met hers. He seemed shy, then with diffidence he said: 'May I take the liberty . . . I know it's very forward of me . . . I mean, would you care to walk a little further? Down to the promenade?'

'I'd love to.'

'Oh, good!'

'I'll just take my bag in and let Mr Halliday know I'm back.'

'You must bring a friend if you want to. To chaperone you.'

She laughed. 'Girls like me . . . we don't have chaperones. I'll be five minutes, all right?'

He beamed at her. 'We did say it was a lovely night for a walk.'

Kate ran through the shop and met Mrs Halliday on the stairs.

'I'm back.' She told her she had another baby brother and had had a good holiday. 'I'm going out again, just for an hour or so to see a friend.'

She flung her bag on her bed, picked up a warm scarf and ran down again. She'd meant to spend the evening in the kitchen exchanging news with Josie, but that could wait until tomorrow.

Jack was stamping his feet on the pavement. As they headed down Magazine Lane, he took her hand and placed it round his arm.

'You've forgotten your gloves.' He took off his own and his warm fingers closed round hers. He pulled her hand into the pocket of his overcoat. 'Too cold to be out without them tonight.'

Kate had no gloves. She'd lost the only pair she'd ever owned and had meant to buy another, but all her money had been needed by the family. She knew from the books she'd read that no lady ever went out without gloves and so didn't like to tell him.

He said: 'This is where I work.'

Kate looked up at the modest two-story building. It seemed a solicitor shared the premises. 'I supposed you worked in your family business.'

'I do.'

'This is a Courtney Line Building? I know your Liverpool office.

45

Everybody does.' It was on Water Street and very grand.

'This is our Wallasey office. Not so important now, but our business started here.'

She couldn't keep her eyes away from his face. He was older than she was, a lot, and he wasn't quite at ease either. He was making a big effort to talk to her.

She asked: 'Was this once an important business district?' It seemed to Kate to be something of a backwater, a suburb of New Brighton.

'My family were connected with the magazine – before they went into shipping.'

She glanced at him again, not understanding. 'There are so many places with magazine in their name round here: Magazine Brow, Magazine Esplanade.' But the magazines she was familiar with were sold over the newsagent's counter.

'This is Magazine Lane.' He smiled gravely down at her. 'A couple of centuries ago gunpowder and ammunition was stored near here. All ships carried an arsenal to defend themselves against attacks from pirates and privateers.

'When they came into port, ships' masters were required to unload their high explosives. Nobody trusted them not to fire at each other in the Mersey. To begin with, the magazine was in Liverpool itself, near Brownlow Hill. But as the city expanded, it was considered dangerous to cart high explosives through the busy streets and keep them there. So a piece of land was bought here.'

'An arsenal, of course.' Kate was amazed. 'Magazine Park. I've been here before and it does look as though it could once have been used as an arsenal.'

'Underground chambers were constructed to house the gunpowder, with spaces between filled with earth. This was surrounded by a high wall and trees planted all round it.'

The moon was up now. It was nearly full and bathed everything with sharp silvery light.

'I saw the remains of a fort here somewhere,' Kate said.

'Just here on the next corner. We'll come to it in a moment.'

She looked up at the sandstone gateway and could just make out the words above: 'The Battery 1858'.

'To defend the arsenal – should there have been need. It's too cold to stand for long.' As he drew her down the hill towards the slipway and the promenade, he told her more about it.

'It was considered safer to have the arsenal here near the mouth of the Mersey. Ships docked here before going into the port and called again on their way out to reload their gunpowder. The place became known as Magazine Village and it expanded because of the trade. Hotels and shops were built.'

'Was there ever an explosion?'

'No, never. But everybody was afraid there might be, because huge amounts were stored here.'

'I never knew that.' Kate was enthralled. 'And you said your family worked in the magazine?'

He smiled down at her again. 'Distant forebears of mine.'

There was no one else on the promenade. The wind off the river sliced through her coat like a cut-throat razor. Jack pulled her closer. The tide was full in and splashing against the promenade railings. The lights of Liverpool winked on the far bank. Ships were coming up river; she could hear the thump of their engines.

'Too cold down here tonight.' Jack shivered and led her back up into the streets behind, where they were out of the wind.

'This is Magazine Brow, the heart of the old village I was telling you about. Such pretty cottages, most date from the eighteenth century.'

'But the date on the fort was the nineteenth.'

'Yes, but by the time they built that, the people of Wallasey were protesting about the danger, and the gunpowder was eventually housed in hulks, old ships moored in the river between New Ferry and Eastham.'

Kate said: 'So this place became a sleepy backwater again.'

'Yes, I'd love to find lodgings here, in one of these charming cottages.'

Kate was surprised. She judged them to be bigger than Cemetery Cottages, and they were not all joined together, but they were not so very different.

'It's wrong of me to keep you out in the cold like this,' he told her. 'I'll take you back, it's high time you were indoors.'

'I've loved every minute of your tour.' Kate laughed out loud with the joy of it. 'I've walked round here by myself before, but you made it much more interesting.'

The shop had closed now. Kate took out her key to the house door.

'Could I take you out on another occasion? I know it's very forward of me . . . but I do feel I know you. After all, I've seen you every morning for the last year or so.'

Kate felt another wave of heat run up her cheeks. She'd thought a lot about Jack Courtney. It seemed he might have been thinking of her.

His soft grey eyes smiled down at her. He seemed to genuinely like her, be concerned for her.

'Saturday then?' he asked. 'Four o'clock?'

She shook her head. 'I have to be back by four thirty, but I'm free from half one.'

'Half one then.' He smiled. 'I'll meet you here.'

He raised her hand to his lips; she thought that very romantic. Then she put her key in the lock and let herself in.

It was only when she was tucked up in bed, unable to sleep for the excitement of walking out with Jack Courtney, that she realised he'd told her nothing about himself. Nothing at all.

Jack Courtney strode home with a spring in his step. Kate McGlory had intrigued him the first time he'd seen her serving behind the counter.

He'd been at a very low ebb at that time, having just had the rift and moved out of his family home to live in his present bachelor rooms in Beech Grove. He'd felt lonely and adrift and in need of something new in his life, but he hadn't had the energy to do anything about it.

That first morning had been dark and the shop lights had been shining on her glorious flame-coloured hair, highlighting it to gold. Her strong features had reminded him of somebody. Somebody he'd known well in the past.

The next morning when he went into the shop, he found he was searching her face, trying to put a name to that person. He felt so teased by the resemblance, he told her about it and asked her name. That sent a pink blush running up her cheeks, covering her faint freckles, but it didn't help his memory. He'd never known anybody called McGlory before.

'You're Irish?'

'No, I come from Birkenhead. Never been to Ireland in my life.' She'd smiled.

Within a few days it didn't matter. Jack knew he was going into the newsagent's to see her. Her green eyes fascinated him. He bought other things apart from his daily newspaper, just so that he could talk to her. He struck up inane conversations about the weather, but he always had to give up because other customers came in to be served.

He was a fool, he knew. She wasn't much more than a child. Eighteen, perhaps, when he was thirty-five. She seemed very capable and confident, but she was much too young to be any good to him. Besides, he shouldn't, it wasn't fair to her. Not the way things were.

His life was an empty mess. A young girl would bring more trouble, and he had plenty of that already. All the same, he was searching for another woman in his life, though he had no right to do it.

He wanted what every man wanted: a lover – that went without saying – a lively companion, a good conversationalist. He needed a woman of his own age, possibly a little older, the motherly type who would look after him. Cushion him from the hurts of this world. It was all a dream. It wouldn't happen.

Kate McGlory would not do. His parents would disapprove, she wasn't their class. They'd be rude about her and ask: did she ever go to school? Can she read and write? Jack could imagine it all. It would give his family another reason to point a finger of scorn at him.

It didn't stop him calling into the newsagent's shop every morning to see her. He'd been doing that every day for over a year and they hadn't got much further than the weather and what she wrote on the placards. He fantasied about getting to know her better. He thought Kate beautiful.

It had seemed a miracle to see her sitting on the tram tonight as he'd clambered down the stairs. For once, he hadn't allowed himself to hesitate. He'd stayed on and spoken to her, and he was so glad he had. Kate might look young but she seemed more mature than her years. Now he must think of how he could entertain her on Saturday afternoon. He felt quite dizzy with success, because for once he'd acted forcefully. He must do nothing to spoil it.

Chapter Five

Kate had spent all Friday and most of Saturday morning trying to decide what to wear for the outing. She did have two hats, but she'd been wearing the better of the two on the tram. Should she wear the other? She had only one coat fit to be seen in, so that was it. She pressed her best green skirt, looked out her good cream blouse and borrowed a pair of gloves from Josie. Jack Courtney would not expect a lady to go out without gloves.

Kate couldn't believe her eyes when she came out through the shop at one thirty on Saturday afternoon. He was getting down from a smart governess cart. It had immaculate black paintwork picked out with red lines. The brass headlights gleamed and so did the chestnut mare that pulled it. He raised his top hat.

'It's a fine day, I thought perhaps you'd like a ride.' He smiled.

'Lovely! Nothing I'd like more.'

He handed her in through the rear door and tucked a rug over her knees.

'What a treat! I thought your family always had prior claim to the carriage? I've never ridden in one before.'

'This is just the tub trap, a governess cart.' He sat down beside her. 'It's thought safe for children because it has inward-facing seats.'

'Your mother used to drive you round in it?'

'No.' He gave her an uneasy look. 'My mother never drove herself. Always been a bit of an invalid. My brother's wife uses it.'

'Your family has more than one?' She thought perhaps she shouldn't have asked that. It sounded too probing.

He nodded. 'Yes, both my brothers and their families live up at the Grange too. A family of that size needs more than one. But Father's bought himself a car. He's very proud of that.'

'A car! Can you drive a car?'

Again he looked at her strangely and she sensed he didn't like the question.

'Never tried,' but he made it sound as though he wouldn't have the

50

slightest difficulty given the chance. 'Father wouldn't let me borrow it.'

He was silent and she watched him drive. She thought he did it well. She wished she knew what to say.

'I don't live at home any more,' he volunteered. 'I have to make a special journey up there if I want to use this. It's easier to hire a cab or go on the tram.'

Kate stole a glance at him. She thought his face handsome. Soft grey eyes, a straight nose and a mouth that smiled often. His blondish hair curled naturally. His manner was diffident, rather disarming.

'What made you leave home?'

'I don't get on with my brothers.'

'That seems a shame,' she said. She couldn't imagine not getting on with hers. 'Tell me about them.' This time, she was determined to find out more about him and his family.

'There's Lionel. We call him Leo at home. He's company chairman. Then there's Oscar, he's fleet captain. They more or less run the business between them.'

She thought they sounded very grand. 'What about your father?'

'He's seventy-four, more or less retired now, though he still holds the purse strings.'

They bowled along the Esplanade at a cracking pace. Kate could see the sunlight sparkling on the water and the ships scudding against the tide. She wondered what her customers would think if they could see her now, being driven in such style.

When Jack Courtney handed her down to the pavement outside the shop at four fifteen, she'd accepted another invitation from him. The exhilaration she felt lasted right through the evening shift that night.

Kate often went home during her afternoons off. One day she arrived to find Mam jigging Billy up and down on her knee.

'There, I told you.' Mam seemed so much better, almost triumphant. 'Nothing much the matter with him. He's smiling at me.'

Kate thought she might have seen a fleeting smile, but wasn't entirely convinced. Mitch McGlory, Mrs Potter and the doctor had made her see Billy through their eyes, as a terrible tragedy. But the weeks were going on, and she had to admit he wasn't proving one, not yet anyway.

Billy never seemed to cry as her other brothers had; rather she heard him gurgle and coo. Her brothers couldn't stay away from his crib. Mam became besotted with him much sooner than she had with Freddie and Duncan. His very existence seemed to bring joy to all the family.

Kate watched Mam holding him up in the air, twirling him round to make him laugh.

'Isn't he a love?' she asked 'Isn't he beautiful? A real ray of sunshine.'

It hadn't taken her long to start calling him 'Sunshine'. Kate knew Mam loved all her babies, but she loved Billy with a fierce, protective, all-encompassing love.

She asked now: 'Have you been down to the Town Hall to register his birth?'

'Not yet.' Mam was always late with things like that.

'Why don't we go down on the tram and do it now?' Kate knew the six weeks allowed had passed. 'You could get fined if you leave it much longer.'

'I sent our Tommy to school. There's nobody to look after Freddie.'

'Ada will, if you ask her. I expect Duncan's round there anyway.'

Kate wanted to go with her. If she had half a chance, she meant to ask if it was possible to get a copy of her own birth certificate.

'I'll carry Billy for you,' she said smoothly.

As it happened, Mam didn't leave her side for a moment, but Kate saw a notice about getting copies of certificates, so she'd found out that it was possible. She'd have to come back by herself. It would upset Mam if she knew what she was doing.

Registering Billy's birth was routine, and afterwards they caught the tram home again. Mam hadn't the energy to walk round town.

'Another job done,' she said when they got back home. Kate went upstairs with the baby. He'd been asleep most of the time and she put him down in his drawer.

She could hear Mam poking the fire back into a blaze and moving the kettle over it to make a cup of tea. When she went down, Mam was studying Billy's birth certificate, which she'd spread out on the table.

At that moment they heard the knock on the back door, and Mr Ratcliff's voice:

'Lena? Do you want a cabbage? I've got some leeks here too.'

Kate watched her mother fold up the certificate, ram it back into its envelope and push it behind the clock on the mantelpiece before going to the door. Mam liked nothing better than a gossip with her neighbours, especially when they brought round little gifts to help her out.

Kate decided not to wait for the tea. She straightened her hat in the mirror before going for her tram. She didn't want to be late getting back to the shop.

Kate had never had a boyfriend. Most of the young men she knew living near Cemetery Cottages, or those who came into the shop, were too much like Mitch McGlory for her taste. She felt she'd rather end up an old maid than be involved with one of them.

Jack Courtney was different. He was taking her out once or twice each week during the afternoons when she had time off. They went to quiet little cafés not too far away, or for walks or carriage rides along the promenade.

'Don't you have to work in the afternoon?' she asked him when he'd suggested meeting her again on a weekday.

'Yes, but I can make the time up by working on during the evening.'

Kate smiled. She was forgetting he worked in the family business. Sometimes he spoke of it and his family. She felt she was getting to know him a little better, though she was finding it hard to get him to talk about himself. She was dreaming about him at night, romantic dreams in which he fell in love with her and wanted to marry her.

She knew his family circumstances were very different from hers and didn't want him to get an unrealistic picture of her background. She was half afraid it would put him off, but better he find out now than later.

Now she'd got over her shyness, Kate told him all her family secrets without hiding any of the sordid details. She told him about McGlory abandoning her mother, about how he'd denied being her father, about looking for her birth certificate and failing to find it.

The following morning, when Jack came to the shop for his newspaper, he asked her if she'd meet him that afternoon.

For once she hesitated. 'I've set my mind on going back to the register office to get a copy of my birth certificate.'

He smiled. 'You don't waste much time. Can I come with you?'

'Do you want to?' Kate felt such a lift that he should ask.

'Yes, I know this is important to you. Anyway, it's no fun being left behind to work in the office.'

She warmed to him. This must mean he really liked her. She'd never met a man like Jack before. Most men thought themselves superior to women. They decided where they should go and what should be done. Jack was diffident; he didn't force his ways on her.

'I don't know how much you'll be able to find out.' He sat beside her on the tram and paid her fare. 'What was your mother's maiden name?'

'Hadley.'

'If your birth was registered under that, it probably won't show your father's name. If you were registered under McGlory, that won't help either.'

'Mitch said I was two before he met my mother. If that's true, it won't be McGlory.'

Jack seemed much wiser in the ways of the world than she was. Kate found it helpful to talk her problems over with him. He knew more than Mam did. More than Mitch McGlory ever would.

As they walked towards the Town Hall, Jack said: 'Don't be disappointed if you learn nothing.'

'No,' she murmured, but she knew she would be. When the clerk went to search, she felt fluttery with anticipation.

But no Katherine Mary Hadley had been registered on her birthday. No Katherine Mary McGlory either. Kate felt she'd been brought down to earth with a bump. She'd drawn a blank again.

'No,' Jack told her. 'You have found out something.'

'It confirms that I'm not a McGlory, but I knew Mitch was telling the truth.'

'Your birth must have been registered in your father's name.'

'I suppose it must. But how do I find out what that was if Mam won't tell me?'

'You can't. She's the key to this.'

Kate sighed.

'Let's go over to Liverpool on the ferry and then catch the boat back to New Brighton. It's more fun than the tram and you've plenty of time.'

She told herself it wasn't a wasted journey even if she'd found nothing. It had whetted her curiosity. It was bringing her closer to Jack. The day seemed a turning point. He began to talk of more personal matters.

Jack hung over the ferry boat rail and watched the brown waters of the Mersey being churned up by the screw. He filled his lungs with the smells of rope and tar, diesel and ozone. It was a cold, overcast afternoon and soft mizzle was dampening his face.

'You love the river, don't you?' Kate smiled. 'I can see it in your face.'

'Seafaring is in my blood.' Jack strained his eyes through the mist up river. He could just see HMS *Conway* anchored in the Sloyne off New Ferry. He pointed it out to Kate.

'The black and white timbered ship? It dates from Napoleon's time, doesn't it?'

'Yes, but now it's a school. I was sent there when I was thirteen to learn about ships and the sea. In my family, all the boys go there.'

Kate knew it was the route that sons of gentlemen took to learn seamanship. They were trained to be ship's officers in the Merchant Navy.

'I remember John Masefield sitting beside me in the class room.'

'The Poet Laureate?'

'He made his name as a poet afterwards.'

'When you left, you joined your family firm?'

'It was taken for granted that I would.'

'So you went to work in their office?'

Jack said nothing. When the time had come for him to leave the *Conway*, he'd been given the option of administrative work in the office or going to sea. He thought paperwork a little dull and chose to go to sea, as Oscar had before him. He looked down into Kate's eager face. He couldn't go into all the difficulties he'd had then. Not yet. He wanted her to think well of him.

The ferry drew into the landing stage on the Liverpool side. He took her arm again and led her along to where the Egremont ferries berthed. They watched one come in and tie up while a flock of seagulls swooped overhead.

'I want you to tell me more about your family's business. I've heard of the Courtney Line, of course, everybody has,' Kate said as they climbed to the top deck. 'But I don't understand what the connection is between it and the Wallasey Magazine.'

'There isn't one, Kate. My family come from Wallasey, some of my forebears worked in the magazine and others went to sea.'

Jack knew the history of the business by heart. It had been drummed into him as a boy. He was supposed to be proud of his family.

'It was founded by my great-great-uncles Thomas and Oscar in 1851. Thomas had started as a clerk with the Orient Line, and Oscar had gone to sea, rising to take command of a sailing vessel by his late twenties.

'They wanted to go into business for themselves and they created the Courtney Line by raising fourteen thousand pounds of capital.'

'Where did they get the money?'

'They sold shares at ten pounds each. Mostly to friends and members of their own family. They used the money to buy a ship they called the *Pensicola*. She carried all manner of manufactured goods – boots and shoes, raincoats and clocks – to the West Indies and brought rum and sugar back to Liverpool, picking up any other available cargo on the way.

'Thomas Courtney became the manager of the line, and to start with, Oscar captained the *Pensicola*. They made a profit right from the beginning, raised more capital by the same method, and went on to build a fleet of ten vessels.

'By the time I was born, the Courtney Line had expanded to twenty-three modern iron vessels, powered by steam. Our name became well known in shipping circles and we earned a reputation for efficiency and good management.'

'You must be very proud of your family.'

Jack sighed, That was what everybody said. A family business it might be, but he felt himself excluded from it as well as from the family. All his life he'd been a failure, a disappointment to them and to himself.

He strained his eyes out to the Irish Sea. A ship was coming in. He was almost certain it was one of theirs. Yes, as it came closer he could see it was painted slate grey. Its tall funnel was yellow with two red stripes and two black ones, the company colours. He could make out the name on the bow now. *Pensicola III*. Flagship of the line.

To start with, Kate didn't mention Jack either at the shop or at home, but one afternoon, Josie Oaks saw him waiting outside for her.

'He's a real toff. Who is he?'

'His name's Jack Courtney.'

'Of *the* Courtney family?'

Kate nodded. She thought Jack was wonderful and had to talk about him to somebody. 'He's a real gentleman, so courteous and polite.'

'Does he want to marry you?'

'I don't know. He hasn't said.'

'Is he likely to? I mean . . .'

'I don't know, Josie.'

'Does he kiss you?'

That made her feel shy. He'd started by kissing her hand, which she'd thought wonderfully romantic. He kissed her cheek now, and last week he'd kissed her fair and square on her lips. 'Yes.'

'You take care now. Don't let him take any liberties.'

'He wouldn't he's too much of a gentleman.'

'I suppose you'll marry him if he asks you? He'd be able to keep you in comfort for the rest of your life.'

Kate had thought about little else. That was definitely what she wanted.

'You'd get away from all this drudgery; have a wonderful life. What a chance he is for you.'

'He hasn't asked me yet,' Kate said, determined not to lose sight of reality. 'And then there's Mam. She's getting a bit from the Poor Law, but she really needs what I give her. I'd have to go on working.'

Josie laughed. 'The likes of him won't want his wife working in a shop. He's rich enough to pay a bit out to your ma. Enough to keep her out of debt.'

Kate frowned. She didn't know; he'd never talked about his income. He was a good talker, always interesting, but it was usually about books or plays or his hobbies, of which photography was the chief.

Jack never told her enough about his own concerns. There was so much she wanted to know about him: about his work, about why he'd quarrelled with his family. She'd tried to ask, but his replies were as brief as politeness allowed. She didn't know what he thought, and his reticence was making her nervous about finding out.

Josie laughed again. 'Forget your mother. You have to think of yourself sometimes.'

Kate didn't want to think of anybody but Jack. He was very kind and generous. He brought her little gifts, such as a bunch of violets or a block of chocolate. She thought he was being thoughtful. He realised she wouldn't want to accept gifts of any value, not until things were on a more definite footing between them. She thought he was wonderful and knew she was in love with him.

The future seemed exciting. It was opening up for her. Jack came from a rich family and he was showing an unusual interest in her. Kate hoped she was going to enjoy a very different life from her mother's.

Kate made no conscious decision to tell her mother. She didn't have to.

'You're walking on air, aren't you?' Mam asked, the next time she went home. 'What's happened?'

Kate stared at her silently.

'You've met somebody?'

'How did you know?'

'Your eyes are shining and you never stop smiling. I'd say you're in love.'

Kate laughed. 'Is it that obvious?'

'A comely girl like you, it was bound to happen sooner or later. Aren't you going to tell me about him?'

'He's a lovely person, Mam. You might think he's a little old for me. He's thirty-five, but so kind and gentle.'

'So where did you meet him?'

'He comes into the shop every morning for his newspaper. *The Times*. A real gentleman, he is.'

She could see Mam straightening up with disapproval. 'I don't think he's for the likes of you. How does he earn his living?'

'In an office. The family business is shipping.' Kate took a deep breath. 'You've heard of the Courtney Line?'

'Kate! No! He won't want to marry you. You're too innocent.'

'He hasn't asked me.' She sighed. 'We haven't got that far yet.'

'He won't!'

'I hope he will. He seems to like me very much.'

Lena's face was suddenly fierce. 'Have some sense. What would a man like that want of you?'

Kate was taken aback. 'No, Mam, he's not like that.'

Mam's laugh was harsh and disbelieving. 'You be careful. You watch that fancy man, that's all, or you'll be in big trouble.'

'Jack's always very concerned. For my welfare, I mean. My reputation. He wouldn't do anything to harm me.'

Mam spat back at her: 'Don't you let him touch you. I know the sort, he'll get you pregnant then drop you like a hot brick.'

Kate felt her cheeks burning. 'There's nothing like that, Mam. Nothing at all. He's a gentleman.'

She could see her mother's face red with anger now. She seemed to be gasping for breath.

Kate thought she understood. 'Is that what happened to you? Is that how I was born?'

'You know you were born on the wrong side of the blanket. Don't let it happen to you. You won't find happiness that way.'

Mam slammed out of the house, crashing the back door with such force that baby Billy woke up and began to cry. Kate cuddled him closely, swallowing back the hurt. Why couldn't Mam speak of it quietly? Tell her calmly what had happened? She wanted so much to know.

Lena knew she had to get away from Kate. She didn't want to quarrel with her. Hadn't she had countless rows with Mitch that had only served to drive them further apart?

Kate was changing. Once she'd been like the boys, wanting to please her. Now she was in open revolt, demanding to be told about her father.

Even more painful was the news that she had a boyfriend. Lena knew she'd be nervous of any man friend Kate might have. She knew what men were like, but if he'd been an ordinary boyfriend it would have seemed normal. She had been pleased to see Kate looking so happy.

58

But this! It seemed almost a mirror image of what had happened to her. Lena's heart raced at the very thought. She hoped and prayed that Kate would drop him now before any damage was done.

But she knew she wouldn't. She was already dazzled by him, just as Lena herself had been dazzled. She squeezed her hands together. What if Kate should get herself with child? To start with, Ben had promised Lena he'd never leave her, never let her down, but . . .

She shook herself. Perhaps it wouldn't be quite like that after all. Ben had been married to someone else. If Kate's Jack was single, things could be different. He'd have no reason to do what Ben had done.

She sighed. She could understand how Kate felt. She thought a new and exciting future was opening up for her. A future in which she'd leave poverty and penny-counting behind for ever.

When the light summer evenings came, Jack suggested meeting Kate after the shop had closed for the night. Often it was only for a quiet walk, but he'd taken her once or twice into New Brighton to a concert on the pier, and last night they'd caught the ferry over to Liverpool, and gone to the Empire Theatre. Kate had laughed all through the variety show and told him how much she'd enjoyed it. She'd never been to a theatre before.

'We'll do it again,' he said now as they walked down to the promenade. 'What about Friday night?'

'I don't think I'd better.' She sounded subdued. 'I'm expected to keep early hours. Mr Halliday was in the hall when I went in last night and said I was coming home very late.'

'It was only eleven when I left you at the door.'

'But I have to get up at six to to open the shop. He doesn't approve, and he's very good to me, Jack. I don't want to upset him.'

'All right, we'll stay local when you're going back to the shop.'

Kate smiled. 'Saturday nights I mostly sleep at home. We could do it then and I can sleep in the next morning.'

Lena wanted to weep over Kate. She'd come home again this afternoon and helped her change the sheets, and yet again they'd parted on bad terms. She'd never been able to treat Kate right. They were never on the right footing.

The knots in the laces of her corsets were digging in her now she was lying back. She'd asked Kate to meet her in Birkenhead tomorrow and help her buy new corsets. These were worn out and she was getting too

59

fat for them. Corsets she couldn't make for herself. She'd joined a piece of string to the laces to let them out, and it showed through her skirts as well as digging into her flesh. She'd been into town with Billy last week, but it was difficult to look after him and try on corsets.

Kate knew the best shops for everything. She managed to keep her underwear nice.

'I can't come tomorrow, Mam. I've said I'll meet Jack in the afternoon.'

But instead of asking her nicely to make it another day, Lena had turned aggressive. Even now she didn't know what had got into her.

'Always Jack has to come first with you. I don't know how you find the time to come home at all.'

Kate had bristled up, and Lena couldn't blame her. 'I come to help you, Mam.'

'Well, you do a bit for the boys but precious little for me. Never much sympathy or support. I get more help from Joe, but I can't ask him to help me buy corsets.'

Lena blinked the tears away. That had upset Kate, and it was the last thing she wanted to do. Kate tried so hard. There was something within herself that made her hard on Kate.

Thank goodness for little Billy. She'd been right to take no notice of Nurse Potter, who'd looked on his birth as a tragedy. She'd not seen it like that. Not after the first weeks; not once she'd got used to him.

Kate weighed out half an ounce of dark shag for old Mr Dennis. She took pains to get the exact weight, because his glittering eyes watched every strand of tobacco go on the scale.

She knew he was poor and over eighty. He came in for it every Saturday morning, it was his weekend treat. Mr Halliday said his money would be better spent on food. This morning, Mr Halliday was here in the shop, replenishing the stock on the shelves and making notes of what he needed to reorder.

Miss Fisk was in a jolly mood. She'd been to a picture show the night before and had seen film actually shot from an aeroplane in flight. She was full of it. Wilbur Wright had taken a cameraman aloft in his biplane after giving a demonstration flight for the King. Mr Halliday didn't approve of the cinema, but because it was a documentary and had a royal connection, he allowed himself to smile.

There was a steady stream of customers, and Kate moved behind the counters serving them as quickly as she could. She was looking forward to seeing Jack Courtney at half past one.

Mr Halliday closed up his notebooks. He was about to leave. Kate scarcely noticed. As he passed behind her, he said quietly:

'Could I have a word, Miss McGlory?'

It seemed he expected her to follow him out. Kate hesitated, suddenly made nervous. This wasn't routine. If he had anything to say, he always did it in the shop. She sensed this wasn't to do with her work.

He led her into his own parlour. Kate felt her heart begin to pound. This was unheard of in all the six years she'd worked for him. Staff didn't use the parlour. It was his territory, his and his wife's. The horsehair chairs and Axminster rugs were not unfamiliar to Kate, because once it had been her job to clean in here. All the same, every muscle she had was tensed. This must be a serious matter. She was searching her conscience, but she didn't think she'd done anything wrong.

Mr Halliday took up a position with his back to the fire, feet well apart on the hearthrug. He didn't ask her to sit down.

He had a benign expression; a soft voice too, that was more likely to compliment his staff on what they had achieved than complain of their mistakes. But should they make them, he gave the impression that he had enough compassion to forgive wrongdoing.

He had very little hair left; his pale scalp was easily seen through thin, mousy strands. He had a straggly beard in the same shade.

'I feel I have to speak to you, Miss McGlory. You have been with us for six years and I've always been very satisfied with your work and your conduct.'

Kate began to quake. She had tried to give good service.

'However, I can't help but notice you are keeping company. He comes quite brazenly to my shop door, where my wife and my staff can't help but notice.'

Kate felt the heat rush up her cheeks.

'I feel I must warn you most strongly against keeping company with Mr Courtney. He is not a suitable person for a young girl like you.

'I feel responsible for your well-being, Kate, since you are young and live under my roof – particularly as he is a customer of mine and you met in my shop.

'Do your parents know you are keeping company with him?'

She choked out: 'My mother does.'

'And does she approve?'

She whispered, 'No.'

He rocked back on his heels. 'For the same reason I don't approve. He comes from a station in life somewhat above that of both of us. I

61

fear he is leading you astray. Putting wrong ideas into your head. Encouraging you to think things may be possible when they are not.'

'No,' she protested. 'He isn't.'

'You do not have experience of life. I must ask you to be guided by me in this matter. Please tell Mr Courtney that you don't wish to meet him any more.'

Kate felt the bile rising in her throat. She couldn't do that! She wanted to please Mr Halliday, but he was asking too much.

'I hope you'll do as I ask. It's for your own good. In my life, I've known young girls who get into trouble. When it's too late they wish they'd been more careful. They always regret it.'

'Yes, Mr Halliday.'

For the first time, she noticed a hint of steel in his eyes. Back in the shop, Kate hardly knew what she was doing. She served customers mechanically, hardly heard what Miss Fisk said to her. She felt rebellious. Jack wasn't like that. Mr Halliday didn't understand.

By dinner time she'd calmed down a little. She'd always done what he asked before. To refuse could put the job she enjoyed and needed at risk. But she'd made up her mind that for once she couldn't bow to Mr Halliday's request.

She loved Jack too much to give him up. Yes, she did have expectations from him, but she believed he wouldn't let her down. She loved Jack and believed he loved her.

Kate had arranged to go home to see her mother the following afternoon. When she let herself into the living room, she found a big pram there.

'Kitty Watts gave it to me,' Mam told her. It was shabby and very old. 'It's been up in her outbuildings for years. Since her daughter grew out of it.'

'Just the thing. You can take Billy to the shops now.'

'I wish I could get it upstairs for him to sleep in. Ratty's oiled the wheels for me.'

Kate looked inside. Billy wasn't sleeping. His almond eyes had grown bigger and browner and lit up with joy when he saw her. His smile grew into a wide, unwavering grin.

Billy started to chuckle. He cheered her up. Kate stepped back where he couldn't see her, then leaned over the pram to tickle him. His chuckles grew louder; he liked playing games. She turned back to her mother, who was sitting by the fire peeling vegetables for a stew.

'How are you managing?'

'We're rubbing along. The meat Tommy brings home is helping and the parish is paying the rent.'

'And you've only Freddie and Billy home all day.' Duncan had started school.

'Billy's no trouble.' Freddie was asleep on a cushion in the corner.

With the pan of stew set on the trivet, Kate picked up the hearthrug and took it out to the garden to bang against the wash house wall. Clouds of dust rose from it and the onion skins Mam had dropped flew in the breeze. Then she took a damp duster to the mantelpiece. It was ages since this had been done. Billy's birth certificate was still here.

'Mam, you ought to put this away somewhere safe.'

'I should. There's a lot of things I should do. Billy's too big for his drawer, I've had to put it on the floor these last few weeks. Freddie will have to give up his cot.'

'Shall I help you change things round?'

'Yes.' Mam picked up Billy's birth certificate and Kate followed her upstairs. While Kate tipped Billy's bedding out of his drawer and slid it back in its place at the bottom of the oak chest, Mam opened a drawer higher up and took out the tin box in which she kept the important documents. She sat back on her own bed to open it and began reading through some of the papers she kept there. Downstairs, Freddie let out a wail of protest.

'He doesn't like being left alone,' Kate said.

Mam sighed. 'If I don't get him, he'll set our Billy off.' She went heavily downstairs as Kate finished making up the cot.

Kate collected up the documents Mam had left strewn across her bed and tidied them neatly into the box. She was about to return it to its place in the drawer when she noticed a slight ridge in the faded newspaper that lined it. There was something underneath. Another envelope?

Her fingers shook as she drew it out. Some sixth sense told her she'd found her own birth certificate. Yes, she had! She wanted to whoop with exultation but dared make no noise. How like Mam! She kept even her birth certificate apart from those of the rest of the family.

She was choking with triumph as she opened it out. Her name had been given as Katherine Mary Rotherfield. Her father's name was Benedict Rotherfield. She'd wanted so much to know that! His trade or profession was given as wholesale fruit merchant. She could hardly believe that. A wholesale fruit merchant?

She'd been holding her breath. Downstairs, Freddie had stopped crying, and she could hear Mam crooning to him. She now knew something about her father. He'd been thirty-four, old compared with Mam's twenty-three. She had the address; it was in Wallasey, not far from the shop where she worked. She could go and look at the house in which she'd been born!

Her mind whirled with what she'd discovered. Wholesale fruit merchant! Why would Mam not want her to know that? Surely she'd expect her to be proud of having him as her father?

She went down to the living room holding the document out between her finger and thumb.

'Look what I've found, Mam. My birth certificate. Let me jog your memory: my father's name was Benedict Rotherfield.'

Mam collapsed back on the basket chair with Freddie in her arms. She looked as though she'd seen a ghost.

'Why hide it? Why pretend you couldn't even remember his name?'

Kate was angry. She paced the length of the room. When she turned back, her mother's cheeks were greyish-white.

Mam choked out: 'You've no business to go poking through my belongings.'

'Your belongings? It's my birth certificate! Why didn't you want to tell me? Why keep it a secret?'

Mam was hiding her face in Freddie's cardigan.

'I want to know about him, Mam.'

'No. It's better if you don't.'

'I'm a grown woman. I need to know. It's my father we're talking about.'

'No, Kate. Don't ask me.'

'Who else can I ask? You can tell me. I've a right to know, haven't I?'

But Mam wouldn't budge. In the end, Kate felt so exasperated she snatched her hat and coat and went out. She almost ran down the road, though there was no need. She was back in Liscard an hour earlier than she had to be. She spent the time striding along the promenade, seething inwardly.

Chapter Six

Lena clutched Freddie so tightly he began to whimper and struggle to get free. She put him down on the floor and lay back. Her heart was thumping. She'd been dreading this for years.

Trust Kate to nose it out. Kate thought she had a right to know, but it wouldn't do her any good. How would she feel when she really got to the bottom of it?

Lena had been meaning to find a more secure hiding place for Kate's birth certificate. That afternoon, when they'd gone to the register office, she'd seen her reading the notice about getting copies of certificates that had been lost. She half expected Kate to ask for a copy of hers there and then. She knew she'd been thinking of it. Kate would be sorry she'd pried into the past.

Lena had trained herself not to think about those far-off days. She'd lived in a very different world, and Kate was opening the floodgates. She pulled herself to her feet. She must busy herself with something, anything.

She set out a meal on the table. The boys would be back from school soon and they were always hungry. It didn't stop the memories dredging up.

Lena could see Benedict Rotherfield before her now. A large, handsome man in his mid-thirties with a head of bright-ginger hair, and a pointed beard and pencil moustache in the same shade. He used to wear a cutaway coat and top hat to go to his office, with a gold half-hunter on a chain across his waistcoat.

He'd been a fruit wholesaler in business in a big way, supplying retailers throughout the north-west of England. He'd imported oranges, grapes and tomatoes from Spain, buying shipping space on the small freighters that plied the Mediterranean routes. He bought more fruit at the auctions in Liverpool.

She'd been sixteen when she'd first gone to work at East Brow House in Eleanor Road. She could feel the years falling away from her. Her body was taut and slim again. She could move with grace and speed. She'd been pretty then with curly brown hair that reached to her waist when she let it down.

It was not her first job. She'd spent three years with Mrs Fulmer Scott, assisting her personal maid and learning the job. Mr Fulmer Scott had been about to retire, and there was a rumour going round that they intended to sell this house and move to their lodge in Scotland. All the staff were unsettled as a result.

One afternoon, Lena had been sewing lace on to a nightgown when Mrs Fulmer Scott sent for her. She was giving a luncheon party that day and there were six other ladies in the drawing room when Lena went in.

She expected to be asked to put a stitch in a hem or fetch a few hairpins. Instead she was introduced to Mrs Amelia Rotherfield, a tall lady in a tight blue dress with leg-of-mutton sleeves.

Her imperious blue eyes slid from Lena's head to her toes. Then she pulled herself to her feet and looked at her from a different angle.

'This is the girl?'

Lena drew in an anxious breath and wondered why she'd been picked out.

'Yes, Lena Hadley.'

Her employer beamed at her. 'I've been telling Mrs Rotherfield how good a hairdresser you are. Good with the needle too; she can dress-make from scratch. Honest and clean. I can recommend her.'

'If you're sure you no longer have need? How can I say no, after that?'

Lena was shocked. Her mind whirled. It sounded as though . . .

'By special arrangement. You'll go to my friend Mrs Rotherfield.'

Lena would have liked to tell them it was the last thing she wanted. She had her friends here.

Mrs Rotherfield said in an imperious manner: 'As assistant to Perkins, my personal maid. Same salary as you get now. Pack your things. I'll take you with me.'

'Now?' Lena was horrified. She'd been hoping to go to Scotland with Mrs Fulmer Scott. She definitely didn't like this woman. She was thin-faced, and there was a supercilious look on it.

'Yes, now. Hurry and pack.'

'There's no rush.' Mrs Fulmer Scott smiled. 'We haven't had our coffee yet. Ah, here it comes, at last. Thank you, Lena, just make sure you're ready for when Mrs Rotherfield wants to leave. About an hour, shall we say?'

Lena was shaking as she ran back upstairs. Nobody had asked her if she wanted to go. She felt she'd been treated like a slave. It had happened too fast; she couldn't take it in.

'It's a job you can walk into.' Molly, the parlourmaid, tried to calm her. 'You might as well try it. She's younger than Mrs Fulmer Scott, you might like it better than here. At least you know you've got a job.'

Lena was ready when the hansom cab came to the front door for Mrs Rotherfield. The driver put her two brown paper parcels under his seat.

'Goodbye,' Mrs Fulmer Scott said from the steps. 'I'm sure you'll be delighted with her, Amelia.'

Lena was about to climb up beside the driver. 'In here,' Mrs Rotherfield ordered. 'Tell me about yourself.'

As they moved off, Lena tried. When she dried up, the questions started.

'You have brothers and sisters?'

'One older sister, ma'am.'

'In service?'

'Yes, a personal maid in London.'

Lena hadn't seen her sister for four years. She'd made up her mind that if she couldn't go to Scotland, she'd see if Dora could get her a job down in London.

'What does your father do?'

'He's a monumental mason.'

'What? Gravestones, you mean?'

'Yes.'

'Your mother?'

'She was a dressmaker. She's dead now.'

Lena was glad she didn't have to tell Mrs Rotherfield that her father had married again very quickly and had started a new family. That she and Dora wouldn't be welcomed back home now. The cab seemed to be taking her a long way.

'May I ask, ma'am, where I shall be living?'

'Wallasey. East Brow is the name of the house.'

Lena liked the look of the place even before the cab drew up at the door. It had been recently built in the Tudor black and white style, and was set in large grounds well shielded by trees, and just off the Egremont Promenade. Inside, it had high, ornate ceilings and big rooms. It was very grand.

Perkins, Mrs Rotherfield's personal maid, showed her to a small room in the attic and helped her make up the bed. She wasn't pleased to see her and was rather frosty as a result.

'I don't need no assistant,' she insisted. 'She's said nothing to me about getting one.'

Within two weeks, Perkins was sacked for using too hot an iron and putting singe marks on Mrs Rotherfield's favourite blouse. That threw Lena into a fluttery state, terrified to put the iron on anything. Expecting the same fate if her work should be found wanting.

Those first days had been long and the house had been filled with sunlight. She'd been nervous of Ida Blundy, the parlourmaid, and Mrs Belper, the cook, and downright frightened of Mrs Rotherfield.

'The master's all right though,' Blundy told her. 'Treats us like human beings. He's used to getting his own way with everything and, as you'd expect with that flame-coloured hair, likely to blow up if he doesn't. Blows up at the missis sometimes. Does us all good to hear him rage at her.'

It was Blundy who told her that Mrs Rotherfield had threatened to sack Ena Perkins some weeks earlier. Blundy reckoned that had been her intention all along, but she didn't want to inconvenience herself by being left without a maid. Blundy said she was that sort.

Mrs Rotherfield was gaunt and prided herself on her very small waist. One of Lena's jobs was to lace her corsets very tight to emphasise it. She was very fussy about everything, especially her own appearance.

Lena had never been afraid of Benedict Rotherfield though. She'd seen him for the first time when he'd come into his wife's bedroom as she'd been dressing her hair.

Amelia's head had twisted round to look as he'd come in. 'What's that you've brought me, darling?'

'Bananas.' He'd laid a whole hand of them on her dressing table. 'You've seen them before?'

'Yes, at Langridge's, you must remember? You never stopped talking about them.'

From the first, Lena knew he was watching her. She went on rolling up the thin strands of soft brown hair streaked with grey, and pinning them in curls on top of Mrs Rotherfield's head. Lena had never seen bananas before and kept eyeing the yellow fingers of fruit.

'An exotic tropical fruit from the Canaries,' Rotherfield said, as though to her.

'The West Africa mail boat stops there for bunkering and has started importing them to Liverpool as deck cargo. I bought two hundred hands at the auction today. This is the sample.'

'Bananas are quite the thing,' Amelia trilled. 'Everybody seems to like them.'

'Your new maid has a talent for arranging your hair,' Rotherfield told his wife. 'It suits you like that. What is your name, girl?'

'Her name's Hadley.' Amelia gave a snort of contempt. 'Bananas need peeling, don't they? They were in a pudding when we had them that first time.'

'Yes, but it's easy.' He showed her how, stripping down the peel halfway. Lena noticed his soft white hands and immaculate fingernails.

'Do you want to taste this?'

'Not now.' Amelia's voice was irritable. 'It'll spoil my dinner.'

Lena had finished. She lifted the hand mirror to show her employer how she'd drawn her hair up at the back of her head.

'Yes, all right, that'll do. Benedict, why don't you get changed? We shall be late for dinner. I'm ready now.'

'I won't be ten minutes.' He turned to Lena with a smile. 'Perhaps you'd like to try one of my bananas?' He handed her the fruit he'd half peeled.

'Thank you.' Lena accepted it with pleasure. She warmed to him.

His wife corrected sourly: 'You must say "Thank you, sir." '

A few days later, Mrs Rotherfield reprimanded her.

'Hadley, this won't do. This is my favourite dinner dress and I can't wear it like this. Just look at the creases in the skirt, and this ribbon needs a stitch before it comes right off. Press it again, and make sure you do it properly this time.'

'Yes, ma'am.'

Amelia insisted on being called ma'am. It was only then that Lena saw Mr Rotherfield in the doorway behind her. To this day, she could remember his sympathetic smile, the amused green eyes under raised brows. It made her feel he was on her side.

Lena felt Mrs Rotherfield's reprimands came more often than her work warranted. But to be a ladies' maid was a good position. A scullery maid had to get up earlier and do dirty work. She felt she was fortunate to have such pleasant duties.

She enjoyed sewing. Mrs Rotherfield bought one of the new treadle sewing machines for her to use. Lena had always had a talent for dressmaking. She thought she must take after her mother.

Mr Rotherfield didn't have a valet to look after his things, so pressing his suits and cleaning his shoes was considered to be Lena's duty too. He was always courteous and thanked her for what she did. He always called her Lena, which she thought more friendly. She liked him and found him easier to work for than his wife. All the staff did. He was popular with them, while Amelia was not.

Lena worked closer to her employers than did the rest of the staff, and soon knew their marriage was not a happy one. She heard her mistress complaining about Mr Rotherfield's behaviour. Heard real quarrels as she went about her duties. Blundy and Mrs Belper furnished plenty of similar incidents to confirm it.

There were no children, but Lena gathered from what she overheard that they would like to have them. Mrs Belper said Amelia was disappointed and soured because babies didn't come.

'But how can they come when they have separate bedrooms?' Blundy let off screams of raucous laughter.

'He goes to visit her, of course.'

Lena's room was up in the attic immediately over Amelia's bedroom. She could hear their voices clearly in the summer when they all had their windows open. Benedict Rotherfield's had been raised in anger.

'Not feeling up to it? What do you mean?'

She'd only just caught Amelia's answer: 'A headache.'

'I thought you wanted a family? Amelia, we'll never have a child at this rate. I want a son to inherit my business.'

Lena thought she heard Amelia say: 'Not tonight.'

'Yes, tonight. Now.'

Amelia said something she didn't catch, then he was raving at her.

'Don't you call me an animal! I'm a normal man and I hoped I'd made a normal marriage. I had hoped for some affection from you. I see I was wrong. You're a damned cold fish and a rotten wife. I wish I'd never set eyes on you.'

Amelia's bedroom door slammed shut with such force Lena felt the floor vibrate. She held her breath, hardly daring to move and so betray to Amelia that she had heard so much.

After ten minutes, the adjoining door between the two bedrooms opened again.

'I apologise, Amelia. I should not have said what I did.' His voice was a little frosty.

'Look, we can't go on like this. Don't cry now. We have to talk things through. I'll not allow you to deny me my marital rights. Where else can I decently go for them?'

Lena could hear Amelia weeping. She thought Benedict had got into her bed.

Lena had been working there for six years when, just before Christmas, Amelia brought home a dress length of burgundy satin and told her she wanted an evening dress made to wear on New Year's Eve. Lena had never seen such rich material before and took infinite pains to get the style and fit exactly as her employer wanted it.

There were yards and yards of material in the skirt and she really enjoyed making it. While she did so, she day-dreamed about wearing it herself, except that she'd never be invited anywhere where she could.

After two fittings Lena went on to finish the dress, and was very pleased with her work. She thought it was really lovely. She took it along to Mrs Rotherfield's boudoir, holding it across both her outstretched arms. She thought Mrs Rotherfield looked sour as she went in.

'Not now,' she snapped, and almost waved her away. 'Is that my ball gown?'

'I've finished it, ma'am. I wondered if you'd like to try it on.'

'Perhaps I should.'

Lena helped her into it and thought it looked beautiful. It was very ornate, with a bustle at the back in the very latest style, and had lots of ruffles and tucks down the front of the bodice. Lena was pleased with the fit; she thought it was perfect.

'Find my dance slippers,' Amelia ordered. 'They've got high heels and the length must be right with them.'

She walked up and down in front of her cheval mirror. 'Just as I thought, it's not long enough,' she complained.

Lena had been expecting praise for a job well done; instead Amelia gave her a dressing-down for turning up the hem too much and pressing it with an iron before the skirt had been tried on and passed as satisfactory. Now there would be a visible line from the iron when it was let down again.

'I'm sorry, ma'am. I'll damp it, press it well. It won't show, if I'm careful.'

'But you aren't careful enough, Hadley,' Mrs Rotherfield had barked at her. She was impatient then to get out of the ball gown and threw it at Lena.

'Get the hem down half an inch, and in future, you'd save yourself a lot of work if you let me try things on first. It's not up to you to decide such matters.'

'I measured the length against your black ball gown, ma'am. I understood that to be the right length. I didn't want to trouble you.'

Lena went back to the sewing room, which was under the stairs going up to her attic bedroom. She was disappointed herself. She'd thought it absolutely perfect. The tears started to her eyes.

71

She was sitting at the table with the burgundy satin spread out before her when Mr Rotherfield came to the door.

'Would you sew a button on for me?' She glimpsed his overcoat over his arm before she turned her face away so he wouldn't see her tears. 'Came off in the office. I still have it.'

'Of course.' Her voice sounded strained, unnatural.

'What's the matter, Lena?' He came closer. 'Come on, you're upset. What's happened?'

She sniffed, blinking hard to make the tears go. How could she complain about his wife?

He put a hand on her arm. The gesture of comfort made the tears rush to her eyes.

'I'm sorry, I'm being silly.'

'No you're not. The next moment his arm was round her shoulders. It was meant to comfort her, Lena was sure of that, except that his touch seemed to set her whole body on fire.

'Don't let Amelia upset you,' he said gently. 'Not worth it.'

Lena turned to him then, clinging hard, burying her face in his soft white shirt. His arms tightened round her and his lips came down on her cheek.

'Was it about this dress?' His fingers plucked at the burgundy satin.

She tried to pull herself together. 'Yes.' She lifted the dress to show it to him.

'It's beautiful,' he told her. 'Amelia will look wonderful in it.'

She told him about having to let the hem down half an inch.

He smiled. 'Will half an inch make much difference?'

'Not a lot.'

'Just tell her you've done it. I don't suppose she'll know the difference.'

'I daren't!'

'I would if I were you.'

After that Lena couldn't stop thinking about Benedict Rotherfield. Although she pressed his suits, she felt he treated her as an equal. She thought she was falling in love with him. She wanted him to love her. Amelia didn't make him happy but she was sure she could. He'd divorce Amelia. She fantasised about the life they would live together.

She knew it was day-dreaming and she knew it was wrong – Mrs Belper was full of tales about men who took advantage of the servant girls who worked for them – but Mr Rotherfield was keeping his distance and made no further move towards her. Yet she knew she attracted him. He'd sided with her against Amelia. She was flattered about that, but she wanted more. Much more.

On New Year's Eve, Lena had helped Amelia to dress for the ball and was doing her hair when her husband came in wearing his white tie and tails. She took one glance, then kept her gaze averted. He looked very handsome and she was afraid Amelia would sense her interest in him.

She heard him say: 'That's a beautiful dress, my dear. Very flattering, shows off your fine figure. You'll be the belle of the ball.'

'Does it seem a bit short? I'm not happy with the length.'

Amelia stood up without warning just as Lena was about to fasten a pin curl in place; she had to let it fall back. Amelia twirled in front of a cheval mirror. The burgundy satin fluttered gracefully.

'Seems just right to me. Shows off your smart shoes and neat ankles.'

He smiled at Lena behind Amelia's back. She'd taken his advice and not touched the hem.

Lena spent the evening with Blundy and Mrs Belper. They had a specially good supper of roast pork, and kept the kitchen fire roaring up the chimney. Blundy poured each of them a glass of Amelia's sherry as midnight approached.

They heard the horses outside shortly afterwards, much sooner than they'd expected. Mrs Belper hurried to get the sherry bottle out of sight, but no one came to the kitchen. Moments later, Amelia's bedroom bell set up a frenzied jangle.

'My, she sounds in a bad temper,' Blundy said. 'You'd better watch yourself.'

Mrs Belper cut a slice of cheese from the piece still on their table. 'Eat this so she doesn't smell sherry on your breath.'

Lena did so as she ran upstairs. She knew immediately they'd not enjoyed their evening. Amelia was boiling with rage. She could barely stand still long enough for Lena to take her gown off. When she'd slid Amelia's silk nightgown over her head and guided her arms into her dressing gown, she had to take down her hair and brush it.

'Will you want a drink tonight, ma'am?'

'Yes, of course. Hot milk.'

When Lena went down to the kitchen, Blundy was already heating the milk.

'Mr Rotherfield wants brandy and hot milk. I thought I might as well heat enough for the missis while I was at it. Will you take his up at the same time? I'm dropping. I want to go to bed.'

Lena felt a jerk of pleasure. 'Of course,' she said as she set up the tray.

Mrs Rotherfield was already in bed, sitting up against her pillows, when Lena took the milk in. Her husband was not. He was pacing the floor of his bedroom, wearing a maroon silk dressing gown over his pyjamas. She could see from his face that he was feeling very down.

'It hasn't been a good evening.' He shuddered. 'Amelia and I had a real set-to. In front of all my friends too. Now it's public knowledge that we don't get on. What a way to start the new year.'

Afterwards Lena couldn't remember what exactly she'd said: a few words of sympathy, that was all. In return for the comfort he'd given her when she'd been upset.

She put his hot milk down and reached for the brandy bottle. He reached for it too at the same moment and his hand brushed hers. She felt the tingle run up her arm, but it was as though she'd set a torch to his emotions. The next moment she was in his arms and his lips were against hers.

Lena felt she was very daring. That was the night she became his mistress. He didn't press her; she knew it was as much her doing as his.

Benedict came to her room many times after that; sometimes just to talk, sometimes to make love. Lena welcomed him and did all she could to make him love her. When he said his wife was cold, she set out to be warm and loving and giving. She felt very much in love, but she was uneasy all the same.

'What if Mrs Rotherfield finds out?' She was frightened of that.

'She won't, we won't tell her.'

'But there are others in the house.' Mrs Belper and Ida Blundy both had rooms up here on the attic floor. 'They might hear.'

'Their rooms face the front and the landing separates your room from them. I don't even have to come along the landing.'

Lena sighed. That was true. Her room was at the top of the stairs. The attic bedrooms at the front of the house were bigger, but the only other one had been occupied by Ena Perkins when Lena had first come here. She'd thought of moving into it when Ena left, but by then she'd settled into her little back bedroom and it was too much trouble.

'You can't be afraid they'll tell Amelia?' He was smiling down at her, his brows raised in disbelief.

She wasn't. 'I don't want them to know.'

'They won't. The house is very solid. Didn't I have it built to my own specifications?'

It was Lena's turn to smile, and she told him what she could hear in the summer when bedroom windows were open.

'Really? So you know all our secrets?'

'Those you discussed in your wife's bedroom.'

'Surely not!'

'I know you wanted a child. A family.'

He laughed, half embarrassed. 'I was disappointed when the sons didn't come. Amelia was too. Things might have been different if we'd had a family.'

'What if I have a baby?' Lena asked.

'You won't with me. If you don't know that, you haven't heard everything.' He was teasing her, she knew. 'Amelia went to her doctor several times, and he told her there was no reason for her not to conceive. The fault is mine. She taunts me often enough about that.'

Lena smiled up at him. 'At least I don't have to worry about getting into trouble.'

'Not with me.'

'It's a load off my mind to feel certain about that.'

His green eyes smiled back at her. 'My room then? The bed's bigger. Would you feel safer there?'

'No! Not with her in the adjoining room! And there's a direct door.'

'Amelia keeps it shut. She never comes into my room. Hasn't for years.'

Lena shivered. 'It would put me off, knowing she's just the other side of the door.'

'Can't have that. I want you to stay just as you are.'

Lying in his arms one night after they had made love, she whispered: 'Love is everything, isn't it?'

'Between us, you mean?'

'No, for everyone.'

He kissed her. 'There are other things in life, Lena. Business, and . . .'

'But you had all those things and you weren't happy.'

She held him tight as she tried to make herself more comfortable in her narrow bed. 'You had everything else you could possibly want.'

'I wanted you. You caught my eye when you first came to the house. How long ago was that?'

'Six years.'

'I can't imagine a time when you weren't here.'

'I could always feel your eyes on me. I felt you were watching every move I made.'

'I was making a conscious effort to keep out of your way. I resisted temptation for as long as I could.'

'That makes me very happy. I thought it was useless to hope . . .'

'Lena, I've loved you for years.'

'That's what I mean. You needed love in your life too. So did I. Now we've found it, we'll both be happy for ever.'

Benedict sighed. 'It doesn't always work like that. There'll always be other things we need.'

'What sort of things?' Lena wanted to hear him say he wanted more of her company, more of her love.

'Lots of things,' he said.

He was getting out of her bed. Feeling for his slippers and dressing gown in the dark. When the door had closed behind him, she snuggled down under her blankets.

She hadn't been able to explain exactly what she meant. Not properly. To say that love made the world go round made it all sound so trite. Of course she wanted him to divorce Amelia and marry her, but it only meant she wanted to be more bound up with him, have more of his love.

Lena thought it was an impossible dream, and she didn't really expect it. She was a maid in his house and people in her position never did get the best. Marriage was the absolute pinnacle of her hopes. Now she had his love, she felt she could be very happy with that.

A lesser dream, but still a dream, was to have a little place of her own where Benedict could come and visit her. A place where she could relax and not have to worry about every little sound they made. Where she could live without the fear of being discovered. Benedict had talked of it as a sensible step to take, but he did nothing.

'If you find me a place, I'll get another job,' she told him. 'One where I don't have to live in. I don't want to sponge on you.'

He laughed and said: 'I don't want you to work somewhere else, I want you there waiting for me.' But he still made no move to make it happen.

Lena didn't like being so close to Amelia, attending to all her personal needs while at the same time carrying on with her husband. She knew she'd be sacked instantly if Amelia discovered what was going on, and she was afraid that sooner or later she would. It felt to Lena like an axe suspended over her head ready to drop. She was surprised when things drifted on this way, month after month, for another year.

Her first job in the morning was to take Amelia's breakfast to her room. She wanted that at eight thirty, which gave Lena time to have her own breakfast first. By then, Benedict had left for his office and the house was settling into its morning routine.

Usually when she went up, Amelia was a mound under the bedclothes and her room was in darkness. This morning, the curtains were already drawn and the room was filled with the cold light of a winter's day.

'Good morning, ma'am.'

Amelia was sitting up stiffly against her pillows, her face grey-white and sour. Lena set the breakfast tray across her knees. Amelia picked it up roughly and moved to the other side of her bed, out of her way.

'I'll give you an hour to pack your things and get out of this house,' she snarled. 'And don't expect a reference.'

Lena went cold with shock. She knew Amelia had found out, but couldn't think how. Benedict had been up to her room last night but they'd only talked. He'd lain against her pillows while she'd curled up at the bottom of the bed. There was nowhere else comfortable to sit. He'd brought some chocolate and they eaten most of that. He'd gone down about eleven. All had seemed as usual then.

She felt rooted to the spot, not sure what to do next. She mustn't admit anything. Not to Amelia. She mustn't land Benedict in more trouble than he was in already.

'Ma'am, is my work not up to standard? I'm sorry if . . .'

'Don't pretend you don't know why. Don't stand there looking as though butter wouldn't melt in your mouth. I know what's been going on. Do you think I can't hear the stairs creak, doors opening and closing in the middle of the night. I've suspected it for a long time.'

Lena didn't think she could have heard much last night, but she didn't feel she could argue about that. Her heart was racing.

'I'm entitled to my pay,' she choked.

'You'll be paid for the time you've worked. Now get out. I want you out of the house within the hour.'

Chapter Seven

Lena ran up to her room in the attic. Her knees felt weak and tears were blinding her. Yes, she'd half expected this to happen, but that didn't mean it was any less of a shock when it came. Suddenly, her orderly life here had come to an end. She didn't know what to do. She was panicking. She couldn't think straight.

Her mother was dead and her father had married again, but she'd never got on with her stepmother, who was only four years older than Dora, her older sister. She'd had little contact with her family over the seven years she'd been working here. Lena knew they wouldn't want her back living with them, though her father might help. It wouldn't be all that easy to get another job without a reference from Amelia. She'd have seven years she couldn't account for.

She began to put her things together. She didn't have much, and no bag in which to carry them away. Some of her clothes were downstairs in the wash, and she ran down to get them. Blundy was dusting the hall.

'I've got the sack,' she said as she passed.

Blundy followed her to the kitchen. 'When?'

It was only minutes since they'd had a companionable breakfast together.

'Just now.'

'Why? Surely she hasn't found out?'

Once in the kitchen, Mrs Belper's shocked face made her predicament seem worse.

'You've done it this time, young lady,' she told her. 'How are you going to get another job after this?' The fact that they knew was another shock for Lena.

'We thought you were heading for trouble.'

'How did you know?' Lena demanded.

'He's not exactly quiet when he comes up, is he? Slams the door in the middle of the night when he goes.'

'Oh, Lord! I must get packed. What am I going to do?'

Blundy was sympathetic. She found Lena a big basket that had held tomatoes.

'Not very strong, I'm afraid, you'll have to be careful.' She added some brown paper and string.

Mrs Belper was putting some food together for her: a piece of pork pie, some cold sausages, a bread roll and a tomato.

'You'll be hungry by dinner time. You'd better have these two bananas too. Remind you of Mr Rotherfield. I don't expect you'll get as much fruit at the next place you go.'

Their kindness brought the sting of tears to her eyes again.

'He'll be in trouble too,' Blundy said. 'Bet she waited until he'd gone off to work before sacking you. You'll be safely out of the way by the time he finds out.'

Lena straightened up. That started her thinking normally again. She felt calmer now she'd talked about it. Ben would help her. He'd want to. She gathered up her possessions and ran back up to her room. At the very least he'd give her a reference, though it would look odd coming from him, since she was a lady's maid.

She knew what she'd do. She'd go in to Liverpool and see him at his office. He wouldn't want her to disappear without trace. He loved her, he'd told her so only last night.

She dressed in her best. Made herself look as neat and tidy as she could. She didn't want him to feel ashamed of her in front of his office staff. He'd talked about his business from time to time. She knew he made a lot of money from it.

She packed up everything she wanted. Her bundles were heavy and carrying them made her look like a homeless waif. She couldn't go into his office with all her worldly goods packed in a flimsy tomato basket, especially one that had his name painted in red on both sides. Benedict Rotherfield, Fruit Importer and Wholesaler.

She'd never been to his office but she knew it was in Queen's Square in Liverpool. The full address was printed on the tomato basket too.

She decided to leave her belongings here. She could hide them in the hedge at the end of the garden. But no, it looked as though it might rain. The gardener had a shed; she'd leave her things in there. That would be the safest.

With one final look round the room that had been her home for the last seven years, she went down to the kitchen and said goodbye to Blundy and Mrs Belper. She let herself out into the back garden and ran past the flowerbeds and lawns down to the shed, hoping that Mrs Rotherfield wasn't looking out of her bedroom window. A six-foot wall cut off the vegetable garden from view of the house. Lena felt safer once she was behind it.

She was passing the big greenhouse when she saw Ted, the gardener, working inside. She went into the steamy warmth and told him she'd got the sack and that she meant to leave her parcels.

'I'll be back for them,' she said. 'Just leave them alone.'

'I don't want to know about them. Put them out of sight.' Ted had never been that friendly with any of them. She went on to the shed where he kept his tools, piled her worldly possessions on the floor under the dusty window, and covered them with a sack. She took the food with her; she knew she'd be hungry.

She walked down to Egremont Pier and took the ferry over to Liverpool. Ben had told her that was what he did. She had to ask the way then to Queen's Square. The buildings seemed so high and the roads so busy. When she found his office, it was bigger and grander than she'd imagined. Benedict Rotherfield was a more important man than she'd realised.

She felt a nervous wreck. Perhaps he wouldn't want to help her? Perhaps he wouldn't want to see her? She stood wavering in the street for a moment, watching the traffic hurtle past. But she had to go in and find out; she had no alternative.

She took a deep breath, pushed open the frosted-glass doors and went into a marble-floored hall. There was ornate plasterwork on the ceiling and carving on the heavy doors.

There was no one at the reception desk, but a notice invited her to ring the bell for attention. She did, and asked the clerk who came for Mr Rotherfield. She was directed upstairs and along formidable passages to a small office. A middle-aged lady got up from behind a typewriter and enquired the nature of her business.

'It's personal.'

She knew immediately she'd answered too quickly. Too briefly, too. She gave her name.

'Mr Rotherfield knows me. I'd like to speak to him on a personal matter.'

Seconds later the door to his office swung open and she was being ushered inside. He looked astounded. He closed the door carefully behind them.

'Lena! What brings you here?'

'Amelia's found out. She's sacked me.' Her voice was not much above a whisper. 'She gave me an hour to pack my belongings and get out.'

He put his arms round her and led her to a chair. 'Sit down, let me ring for a cup of tea. You look as though you need it.'

'I'm all right.'

The tears were beginning to prickle again. She was blinking hard, telling herself it was just the shock and the emotional turmoil.

'Thank goodness you had the sense to come here and find me.' He gave her a reassuring hug.

Lena knew from that moment that everything would be all right. She knew Benedict Rotherfield had spoken the truth when he said he loved her. She sipped the hot, soothing tea and told him what had happened, while Benedict strode up and down his office.

'I'm sorry, I should have guessed Amelia would do this. It did cross my mind . . .'

Lena choked. 'What caused it? Out of the blue . . . I don't understand.'

'I caused it, it was my fault. When I left you last night, I went downstairs. I fancied a nightcap. I poured myself a glass of brandy and sat down. I wanted to think.

'I dropped off in the chair, Lena. That's what happened. It was after two in the morning when I woke up. I was cold and stiff and cross with myself. I'm never much good if I don't get a proper night's sleep. I went up to my room then. I wasn't thinking straight. I switched on the lights and started to undress.

'Amelia came in. She accused me . . . Well, you know what of. I told her I'd fallen asleep in the chair downstairs, but she didn't believe me, even though I was telling the truth.

'She said she'd suspected it for a long time; she'd left our adjoining door ajar several times and listened for me. We had a row. I'm sorry, I should have known she'd go for you. I should have warned you.'

'It doesn't matter,' Lena said. 'Not now. I can put it behind me. But what am I to do now, that's the point?'

There was a tap on the door and his secretary's head came round.

'Not now, Miss Cummins,' he said impatiently.

'Mr Langford's arrived, sir. Your appointment for eleven o'clock.'

'Oh! Tell him I'll be another five minutes, would you?'

Lena gasped. 'I'm sorry. I've come here and you're busy.'

'Yes, and I must go to an auction after this. Then I'm meeting somebody for lunch.

'Don't worry, Lena. We'll rent a small house for you. I should have done it long ago. It'll have to be a hotel for tonight, or even a few nights. The Exchange?'

'The new Exchange? I've heard it's awfully grand!'

'Perhaps the other side of the river would be more convenient. The Woodside, then?'

He lifted the telephone on his desk and asked the operator to connect him with the Woodside Hotel. Lena heard him book a double room for Mr and Mrs Hadley.

'I must give you some money.' She heard the clink of coins as he took them from his pocket. Saw the flash of gold guineas as he put them into her hand and closed her fingers over them.

'Go to the shops here and get yourself what you need for a night or two. And a bag to pack them in. Then settle yourself into the Woodside. I won't be able to get away from here until about four, but I'll come as soon as I can.'

Lena found herself escorted out to the street again, but she was relieved. Benedict Rotherfield had been rushed, but he'd wanted to help. He'd kissed her cheek. He'd been kind and tender. She'd never been inside a hotel in her life and she felt bemused and fuddled, but she'd do it. Everything would be all right. She wasn't going to be turned out on to the street with only two pounds three shillings between her and starvation.

Lena discovered that Ben was used to taking snap decisions and quick action in his business. He came to the hotel at half past four.

'We need to find you a small house. I've phoned an estate agent, he's going to take us to see what he has on his books. The sooner we find somewhere the better, now it's come to this.'

He'd sent for his own carriage to meet the Woodside ferry, and it was now outside. He handed Lena in, in the way she'd seen him do with Amelia. It filled her with delight to be riding here beside him. She knew George Copple, the groom, because he'd been working at East Brow for two years and they both ate their meals in Mrs Belper's kitchen. But embarrassment made her pretend she didn't, and he did the same.

They called at Mayfield's estate agency in Liscard and were shown the list of small houses for rent in the district.

'What do you think, Lena? Which ones appeal to you?' She couldn't get over the fact that he was happy to defer to her wishes.

Together they picked out details of three houses, and then went back to their waiting carriage with the estate agent to visit them. Lena had not expected more than rooms in a respectable house. She'd have been satisfied with just one. True, Benedict had spoken of a small house, but just for her it seemed too much.

'Not rooms,' he'd said. 'I don't want a landlady poking her nose into my business.'

Lena liked the first house they looked at, but the second was the one she'd picked out from the list. It didn't exactly overlook the river, but it was very close to it, in St Vincent Road.

Ben referred to it as a small terraced house, but to her it was bigger than anything she'd imagined she'd have. It was newly painted and decorated inside and out. Everything looked clean and fresh.

'We'll look no further,' Benedict said. 'I can see this delights you.'

'Don't you like it?'

'The rooms are small. Isn't it a bit cramped?'

'No, it will be cosy in winter and it has a real bathroom.' Lena was thrilled with it.

'Since we're so close to East Brow, we might as well call in and get your things now,' Ben said.

Lena felt her toes curl up. 'I couldn't! Riding in your carriage like this! What will everybody think of me?'

'It doesn't matter. They'll hear of it anyway.' He nodded at George Copple's back. 'If I'm going to stay with you, I'll need a change of clothes. Come and show Amelia how badly she's misjudged things.'

'No! Couldn't I wait here? Sit on the prom?'

'If you'd rather. It's a bit cold, though.'

'I'd rather.'

'Tell George where you put your things; he can get them while I get mine.'

It was cold, too cold to sit for long. Lena stamped her feet and walked back and forth, and wished she'd been brazen enough to ride to the door in his carriage. It came back quite quickly. She could see the tomato basket and her brown paper parcel under Copple's seat.

'Here we are then. We'll go and have a slap-up dinner now. I've said nothing to Amelia except that I won't be back tonight.'

The following day, Ben took her to Bunnies department store in Liverpool, one of the best shops in the city, to buy what they needed to furnish the house. Lena felt she couldn't choose so many things at once.

Ben laughed at her and made a list of what he thought were essentials. He picked out one or two things before he had to go to his office, leaving her to choose the rest.

It took another day to get the curtains up and the carpets down, then Lena moved in. Ben wanted to hire a live-in maid for her. That made her laugh.

'Ben, I don't need a maid. I know what they're like, we'd have no privacy. A woman to do the heavy work and the washing would be the height of luxury to me. Just to work mornings.'

She looked round her new house with satisfaction. It wasn't grand, nothing like East Brow, but this was all for her. She was mistress here and could do as she wished.

Lena had been frightened when Amelia had sacked her without notice, but now it seemed she'd done her a good turn. She'd pushed Benedict into providing this lovely house for her.

Lena had enjoyed her three-night stay at the Woodside Hotel. Ben had spent those nights with her. He was showing his love for her. She could see it in his eyes, in everything he did. They seemed closer.

On the day she moved in, he stopped off on his way home to tell her that he'd been invited out to dinner at the house of a business colleague and thought he ought to go.

'With Amelia?'

'Yes.'

She felt lonely in her little house without him. The following evening he brought some of his clothes and books and some of the wine he liked. He stayed to have a drink with her and persuaded her to take a glass of sherry with him.

Lena said: 'I do wish you'd stay and have dinner here. I'd love to cook for you.'

Benedict laughed. 'How often does a man get an invitation like that? What about tomorrow?'

'Lovely. What do you like to eat? Ah, I remember, Mrs Belper used to make you steak and kidney pudding.'

'Still does occasionally.'

'I watched her make it once. I could do it.'

He praised her cooking. He came again for dinner the following evening and didn't go home. Soon he was spending all his time with her and rarely going home to Amelia.

Lena was happy. Ben bought her a wedding ring and suggested she wear it.

'We know nobody here. Better if they think we're an ordinary couple.'

She was getting to know her neighbours. She didn't feel they accepted her.

'They know you've much more money than they have,' she said to Ben.

'Does that matter?'

'No.'

Lena spent her time keeping the house spotless and preparing his meals for him. For her, life had changed completely, and she found it wonderful. It was like playing house. Ben was very generous with money for housekeeping. She thought she had everything she could possibly wish for.

She knew Ben had enjoyed a busy social life with Amelia. When she'd been at East Brow they'd always seemed to be going out. She hadn't expected him to take her out in Amelia's place, but soon he was suggesting little outings at the weekend. A carriage ride round the park. An evening at the music hall.

'You don't seem one whit abashed to be seen out with me.' She smiled.

'Why should I? You're a very pretty girl and I've made no secret of leaving my wife.'

'I don't have the right clothes. I don't look like a lady.' She had only one coat and hat. She had to wear them every time she went out.

'Better-looking than most of the ladies.' He smiled. 'Buy what you need to make yourself feel comfortable. Make yourself look like a lady if that's what you want.' He gave her money.

The next day she went into Birkenhead on the bus and bought herself another hat. It was very different to the one she already had but she could wear it with the same coat.

'Do you like it?' she asked, putting it on to show him when he came home.

He stroked his ginger beard. 'You must choose things of better quality, spend more money on them.'

'I can't.' She laughed. 'I can't spend on luxuries like that!'

'I want you to. Get yourself something suitable to wear to the theatre and then to supper afterwards.'

'I don't know what is suitable.'

'Of course you do. You made clothes for Amelia. Go and choose something tomorrow and I'll take you out.'

'I've never been in a shop that sells clothes like that.'

He met her in town that afternoon and took her to an expensive shop in Bold Street. He told the assistant what he had in mind and helped pick out two or three outfits. Then he sat down and waited while she tried them on. He chose a dressy blue costume, with a velvet hat and cape in midnight blue to wear with it. The price horrified her.

'I could make many of these dresses,' she said to him looking round the shop, 'if only I had a sewing machine. My mother taught me how; she was a dressmaker.'

'Amelia was pleased with the clothes you made for her,' he said. 'I'll have the machine brought down. If you're happy to sew for yourself.'

'I'd like that.' Lena knew she'd enjoy doing it. 'But isn't it Amelia's machine?'

'She went to the shop and ordered it, but I paid the bill. She wanted it so that you could sew for her. She doesn't know how to use it herself.'

Ben had bought tickets for the Playhouse the following evening.

'I have to work late,' he told her. 'Dress yourself up and come to my office. Take a cab from the Pier Head. Get there well before seven. We'll make a night of it and have supper afterwards.'

Lena dressed carefully. She stood in front of her mirror and knew her fine clothes transformed her. She looked every inch a middle-class lady, a fitting companion for Benedict Rotherfield.

But she didn't feel any different as she went up the stairs to his office. She still felt like nervous Lena Hadley, personal maid to Amelia Rotherfield.

'You look wonderful,' Ben told her. She relaxed a little. It helped to be with him. He'd changed in his office. With his red hair and beard, Ben was a striking figure. He was taller than most and stood out in a crowd.

In the foyer of the Playhouse Theatre, Lena stood back as he bought programmes. They were surrounded now by well-dressed theatre-goers. She saw Ben look up and smile at a nearby couple.

'Good evening, Charles – Marion. Should be a good play. I'd like you to meet . . .'

Lena felt their hostile eyes rake her from head to foot, then they turned their backs on Ben without a word. She froze in embarrassment for him. Understanding why they'd cut him dead.

'Oh dear!' He took her arm and led her towards the dress circle. 'It seems I'm not as popular as I used to be.'

'It's me,' Lena choked.

'No.' He laughed. 'They were Amelia's friends. They've taken her side. It's of no consequence.'

Lena thought it unsettled him all the same. It certainly unsettled her.

The next week, a cart brought the sewing machine Lena had used at East Brow to St Vincent Road. She was delighted to see it again, and knew she could make all the clothes she needed.

'Now,' Benedict said. 'Only buy top-quality material.'

She did, and spent several hours each day making the sort of dresses that Amelia would have liked. She bought some silver-grey silk and made a dinner dress. Lena was aiming to have a wardrobe to cover every occasion to which Ben would want to take her. He bought her a leather handbag and a warm coat of soft silver-grey wool. She'd never had so many expensive things.

'You're beautiful,' Ben told her, running his fingers through her long hair, and miraculously, she felt more beautiful. She'd always had neat, well-balanced features in a small face. Now her eyes shone and her cheeks were pink and a smile was never far from her lips.

'You're blossoming,' he told her. She could see it herself in her mirror. Love had put gloss on her looks.

She could see love in Benedict's eyes too. She counted herself the most fortunate woman in the world. One afternoon he came home later than usual and threw himself into the chair before the fire.

'I've been up to East Brow,' he told her. 'I've asked Amelia for a divorce.'

Lena stood stock still, unable to breathe. This was much more than she'd expected.

'What did she say?' Her voice was squeaky with anticipation.

'She said no. She said she doesn't want to be a divorced woman, she'd be shunned by society.'

He sighed. 'I've been to see my solicitor too. It seems she has to agree to it. I have no legal grounds to divorce her. I'm the guilty partner. I've committed adultery; she's blameless in the eyes of the law.'

Lena moistened her lips. What she wanted above everything else was to be Benedict Rotherfield's legal wife. She'd thought that to be beyond her wildest dreams, yet here he was talking about it. It seemed to bring it nearer, and yet it didn't.

'There's no hope then?'

'There's always hope, but she's not going to be easily persuaded.'

Lena went to sit on the arm of his chair. 'It would be wonderful if she would, but . . . I'm happy to be with you here. I love everything about my life now. I feel almost . . . as though I shouldn't ask for more.'

'Why not, Lena? In this world, we have to go after what we want.'

'I've got what I want.'

'You're more easily satisfied.'

'I'm very happy. I love you and I have your love, that's what's important to me.'

'This little house . . . It's only a stopgap. It's too small. I meant it for you, Lena. I meant to live at East Brow. That is the house I designed for my own needs. A house to reflect my success. I meant only to visit you here from time to time.

'But I haven't been able to stay away. I love you more and more, and I keep bringing more of my possessions here until this little house is crowded out.'

'I love it.'

'But it is too small for us both. I'd love to move you into East Brow.'

'Ben! How would Blundy feel?'

'She'd rather have you as her mistress than Amelia, I'm sure of that. But Amelia doesn't want to move out. Perhaps we should start looking for something more comfortable than this.'

Lena looked round her parlour. Most of the people she'd known in her life would think this wonderful. She did herself. She had everything she could possible want.

'There's always something more to strive for,' Ben told her.

Lena could think of only one more thing she wanted, and that was to be his wife. His legal wife.

He tried to explain. 'It's a time of change for me and I want to get things sorted. I won't feel settled until I do.'

Chapter Eight

Two months after moving to St Vincent Road, Lena got up as usual to make breakfast for Ben. She didn't feel well, and halfway through dressing, she had to run to the bathroom to be sick. Ben was sympathetic and led her back to bed.

'It must be something you've eaten. Stay here until you feel better. I'll bring you a cup of tea.'

Lena got up an hour after he'd left for work and felt perfectly all right. The following morning, the same thing happened.

'Do *you* feel all right, Ben?'

'Yes, I'm fine. I'll get my own breakfast, you go back to bed again.'

She lay listening to the clatter of crockery in the kitchen below and wondered if she could be pregnant. After what Ben had said about being unable to have a child, she decided she must be mistaken. When he came up with a cup of tea for her she told him what she'd been thinking.

'Definitely mistaken,' he laughed.

But as time went on, she found it was no mistake. She didn't know whether to be pleased or afraid; she was apprehensive. Having a child to bring up would change everything for her, just when things were going so well. Ben refused to believe it until she went to see a doctor. When it was confirmed, he was astounded.

'Amelia and me, we tried for ten years without any sign of one.'

'A barren woman.' She smiled.

He laughed. 'She blamed me. Said her doctors had told her there was absolutely no reason why she couldn't conceive.'

'Now you know it wasn't your fault. You have proof.'

He laughed again, lifting her in his arms and spinning her round.

'I've always wanted a family. A son to carry on my business. It makes everything so much more worthwhile. I'll have to marry you now. We don't want him born the wrong side of the blanket, do we?'

Lena was reassured. She knew she could rely on Ben. He truly loved her and wouldn't let her down. She was thrilled about having his baby and felt on top of the world.

He said: 'I'll go and see Amelia tomorrow afternoon, before I come home. She's got to agree to a divorce now.'

Lena prayed that she would. It seemed a long-drawn-out day of waiting. She had oxtail soup and a casserole prepared for their dinner. The table was set. There was nothing else she needed to do. She sat over the fire in the front parlour, wishing she knew what was going on, one minute afraid Amelia would refuse, the next full of hope.

She knew as soon as she saw Ben's face that Amelia hadn't agreed. He was angry.

'I offered to buy her a house and make over six hundred a year to her.'

'She refused?' Lena felt downcast.

'She said she'd be shunned by society. That divorce is a stigma.'

'It is.'

'Not as great a stigma as being born out of wedlock. I don't want my son to be illegitimate. I want him to have a good life.'

'We'll be able to give him a better life than most, Ben. Don't worry. He'll have two parents who dote on him.'

'I'll see my solicitor, get him to offer her more money. I really want a divorce now.'

Ben came home from his office a few days later and propped an invitation card on the mantelpiece.

'To a reception at Cammell Laird's,' he told Lena.

'A ship's being launched?'

'Yes, we've been invited by William Courtney, an erstwhile neighbour of mine. He lives close to East Brow. The Courtney Line, you've heard of it?'

'Yes.'

'He's had the *Jemima Courtney* built for the trans-Atlantic trade. It's being launched on Friday's morning tide. I'll take the morning off.'

Lena had never been to a launch before. There was a party atmosphere in the yard, and crowds had gathered near the slipway. Children waved flags. The *Jemima Courtney* surprised her. It was dressed overall in coloured bunting, which was flapping in the breeze, but it didn't look finished.

'The hull's complete,' Ben told her. 'It comes off the slipway and is then floated back into dock to be finished off.'

A brass band was playing sea shanties. It seemed like a carnival to

Lena. Seats had been reserved for them in the stand, but Ben seemed to know a lot of people and stopped to chat with them. She was introduced to William Courtney himself.

Then Ben led her to her seat, which gave her an excellent view. She watched Mr Courtney take the Mayor and Mayoress of Birkenhead to the dais, and after a short speech, the Lady Mayoress pressed a lever that released a bottle of champagne to crash against the hull. Lena thought that wasteful.

'It's traditional,' Ben told her. 'It's thought to be unlucky if the bottle doesn't break the first time.'

'It did.'

A cheer went up from the crowd as very slowly the hull was seen to begin its slide. The tide was full in, and waves were crashing against the bottom of the slipway in the boisterous wind. Lena had to hold on to her velvet hat. For the first time she felt at ease in this well-dressed crowd.

She watched the *Jemima Courtney* gathering pace. It hit the brown waters of the Mersey. The bow dipped and righted itself, and another cheer went up. Tug boats were waiting for it, lines were being attached.

'There'll be plenty more champagne at the reception,' Ben said, leading her towards the boardroom. It was only then that Lena saw Amelia Rotherfield striding furiously towards them. She positioned herself in front of Ben.

'What do you mean by bringing *her* here?'

'Let us pass, please, Amelia.'

'It's embarrassing enough to have my husband abandoning me to go off with a common servant. To bring her here, amongst my friends, is overstepping the limit. Do you think they want to meet a slut like *her*?'

Lena could feel Amelia's hate directed at her. People were turning to look at them.

'I didn't know you'd be here.'

'You knew Jemima was a friend of mine! You must have known.'

'I didn't think of you at all.'

'Well, do so now. How will I ever live it down if you bring your floozy to the reception? I am still your wife.'

Lena was gripping Ben's arm. She could feel the tension running through him, see the scarlet flush rushing up his cheeks. He looked as though he was going to explode.

'Let's go.' Lena tugged at him. 'Leave her to her reception.'

She thought Ben was going to insist on going to the reception, and taking her too, but suddenly he relaxed and allowed himself to be led away.

'It wouldn't do us any good,' she whispered. 'Not to have a public fight. You're asking her for a divorce to marry me. She hates me, she doesn't want to do either of us any favours. Ben, she's looking for revenge.'

He stumbled, and she held tightly to his arm. 'You're right, of course. I've got a terrible temper. I mustn't let it run away with me.'

Ben set out to work in the mornings before the postman came. Lena always propped his mail on the mantelpiece in the parlour to await his return. One morning, a week later, a letter came for him from his solicitor. Lena eyed it all day, hoping it contained good news.

Ben ripped it open moments after coming home. Lena watched his face. She saw it fall and felt a stab of disappointment.

'Amelia's refused again.' His green eyes were agonised as he looked at her. 'I didn't dare tell her you were having a child. Do you think I should?'

Lena sighed. 'It wouldn't make her change her mind.'

'But it makes the divorce imperative.'

'No, Ben. She's not going to give you what you want. I'm happy as we are. We're together, aren't we?'

'I want it for you and I want it for the sake of my child. I want us to have a decent life together, not be shunned by people I know.'

Lena shivered. She knew Ben had set his mind on divorce and he expected to have his way. He went back to his solicitor and offered Amelia more money.

'Everybody has their price,' he said grimly. 'I'll keep on until she agrees.'

Time went on and Amelia showed no sign of changing her mind. Lena grew heavy with child. She had a wardrobe full of beautiful clothes she could no longer wear. She felt fat and frumpy, but Ben laughed at her when she said that.

'You're more beautiful than ever.'

He wanted to employ a proper cook-general to work all day instead of the skivvy who came alternate mornings to do the heavy work.

'It's too much for you now. I don't want you worn out.'

Lena didn't think it was too much, but she agreed. 'Providing she lives out. I want us to have the house to ourselves.'

Ben no longer wanted a social life. He was happy to stay by the fireside with her in the evenings. He was thrilled about the coming

Lena jerked upright in her chair as Duncan, Harry and Tommy came bursting in from school, boots scraping on the stone floor. All were talking at once, shouting rather than talking. Lena came back from the past feeling disorientated.

Freddie had gone to sleep on the rug; now he woke up and started to snivel. This was her reality. Hard work and poverty. Kate, the baby, had grown up and left home, but there'd been plenty more to take her place. Benedict Rotherfield had given her a glimpse of heaven, but it hadn't lasted.

She lifted Freddie to the table. It was easiest to feed the brood as soon as they came home from school. If she didn't have their dinner ready, they'd only want bread and jam first and she'd end up having to provide more food. She usually had a pan of mince stew simmering for them; that was easiest, because even the tots could eat it.

Tommy was tickling little Billy to make him laugh. It wasn't hard. The boys wouldn't leave him alone and his chuckles cheered her up.

The buzz of triumph would not leave Kate, and she couldn't wait to tell Jack that she'd found her birth certificate. She would have liked to go round to his lodgings to see him when the shop closed that night, but she didn't dare.

She'd walked with him along Beech Grove and he'd pointed out the house, but he hadn't invited her in.

'Would ruin your reputation,' he'd said gravely. 'I can't do that.'

Young girls of good character simply didn't go to a man's lodgings. And it would be seen as much worse if she went alone and knocked on his door, especially after dark. Kate had to wait until the following afternoon when she'd arranged to meet him in the shelter on the Esplanades.

As she hurried down the road past the park, she saw him standing on the corner watching for her. He seemed almost as eager to see her as she was to see him.

'It's a fine day for a walk. We'll go along the Esplanade, what do you say?'

Kate didn't mind what she did as long as she could be with him. She took his arm as they set out and couldn't wait to say: 'I've found out who my father is. His name is Benedict Rotherfield.' She felt heady with success over that. 'A wholesale fruit merchant.'

She was glad she was not the daughter of a common labourer; now Jack would regard her as more his own class. She saw that as a plus to their relationship.

Jack's reaction took her by surprise. The colour left his cheeks, and his mouth fell open.

'Benedict Rotherfield?'

He sank down on the next bench they came to, and pulled her down beside him.

She had to ask: 'Do you know him?'

He seemed almost to choke. It took him a moment to make up his mind. 'Ye-es.'

'Where is he now?' Little flurries of excitement ran down her spine. It seemed the most tremendous stroke of luck. 'I do so want to find him.'

'No, Kate . . . I didn't mean . . . No, I'm afraid he's dead.'

The cold of the seat was penetrating her clothes. She told herself it was silly to hope for too much after all this time.

'But you did know him?' Some of the excitement was still there; this was another step forward. 'How did he die? You must tell me everything you know.'

She noticed then that his manner had changed. Even his voice had, and he was being ultra-careful.

'The Rotherfields were neighbours of ours . . .'

'Friends too?'

Nearby, a small boy was throwing crusts of bread for the birds, while an armada of seagulls swooped and fought over it. Jack seemed bewitched by them. It took him time to reply.

'Perhaps of my parents. He was older . . . I haven't thought about him for years. I'm sorry . . .'

She squeezed his hand. 'Will you ask them about the family? My family? I'd be grateful for anything they know.'

Jack gulped. 'Give me a little time . . . I'll try to find out . . . What exactly do you want to know?'

Jack Courtney felt his head was spinning as he strode in the direction of his rooms. He'd found it a difficult afternoon. For once, he was glad to deposit Kate back on the shop doorstep.

He'd had to get away from her without saying too much. He couldn't think fast enough, not with her eager eyes searching his, pleading for any scrap of information.

Benedict Rotherfield! The name told him everything. He knew in an instant why Kate's mother had kept it hidden from her. Why she didn't want her to know anything about her father. He knew now who Kate resembled. Her strong features were so very much like her father's. And now that he knew, he couldn't understand why the name hadn't come to him. It was all so obvious.

Of course, it had all happened a long time ago. He'd been only fifteen or sixteen at the time, but it had been such a red-hot scandal it had remained engraved on his mind. He wouldn't be the only one who remembered. Half the population of Merseyside must know. Not all the sordid details, not after all this time, but many would remember the general outline of the story.

Jack reached his rooms. As the only lodger, he was well looked after by his landlady. She cleaned and cooked for him, but otherwise left him alone. He was content here.

He let himself into his parlour; sat down in his comfortable armchair and poked the fire into a blaze, watching the yellow flames flicker up the chimney. He felt awash with love and pity for Kate. This altered everything, but it wouldn't make her any more acceptable to his family. Not that any alliance with Kate was possible anyway. He was in an impossible situation, and this was just an added complication. He wanted to protect her, help her, though he didn't know how he could.

Suddenly a thousand questions hammered at his mind. He wanted to know more about Benedict Rotherfield. He wanted to know every detail of what had happened.

Today was his mother's sixty-sixth birthday and he'd been invited to a celebration dinner. It would not be a party, because his mother was an invalid. She spent her good days lying on the sofa in the drawing room, and her bad ones upstairs in bed. It would be a family gathering of the sort he disliked most, and he hadn't been looking forward to going.

But now he saw it in a different light. He knew he could find out all he wanted to know about Benedict Rotherfield there.

He got up to wrap the book he'd bought for his mother. It was Marie Corelli's *Under Two Flags*. He'd heard her praise the author, and there was little else she could do these days but read.

It was seven o'clock when his father's car, driven by his chauffeur, drew up outside his rooms. Jack was ready; he'd dressed carefully so as not to attract the wrong sort of attention from his brothers. A plain boiled shirt stiffened with starch, no frills. He'd pushed his new dinner suit to the back of his wardrobe, and put on the one his mother had chosen for him some ten years ago, in the days when he was living at home. He was pleased he could still get into it. He struggled for ten minutes with his tie, and even now he didn't think the bow would please his mother.

At home, everything had to be traditional, that was the way they liked it. Nothing had changed since he was a boy. Minnie, the parlourmaid, let him in and took his coat. She was almost as old as his mother, and he'd known her all his life.

'You're looking very well,' he told her. He crossed the marble-floored entrance hall where the model of the SS *Pensicola*, the first ship in the Courtney Line, was displayed in a glass case. There were pictures of other ships all over the house.

Jack found the family had already gathered in the drawing room. It was a vast room with paintings of his forebears hanging on both sides of the fireplace and a lot of heavy mahogany furniture. His mother, stout now and seeming fatter in her prune-coloured dinner dress, lay on the sofa, exactly as he'd expected. He took her gnarled hand in his when he kissed her.

'How are you, Mother?'

'Just the same, dear.' She sounded world-weary, but she smiled. Her face was crazed with fine lines that made her look older than she was, and her head had a thin covering of faded brown down. Her hair had been cut short last year when she had an acute fever and it had never regrown. She wore it in a girlish Alexandra fringe that didn't suit her.

'Happy birthday.' He gave her the book and watched her unwrap it. He expected her to be pleased.

'Oh, darling, I've read it. Leo bought it for me last month.' Her tone was full of disappointment.

'Seems I beat you to it.' His eldest brother, taller, more handsome and with a condescending manner, was standing with his back to the fire. 'Sorry, old chap.'

'I'll take it back and change it.' Jack jammed it back in its wrappings. 'Is there any other title you'd like?'

'I don't know, dear. I'll have to think.'

'Get her Somerset Maugham's latest.' Leo beamed at him. He knew so much more about Mother's tastes. It showed how much closer he was to her; made Jack feel more of an outcast.

His father, still slim and upright, came in with Oscar, his other brother, and his two sisters-in-law, Ottilie and Constance. Champagne was poured to drink Mother's health. They did it every birthday, but her health never improved.

The ladies were discussing the latest gowns available in Liverpool. Constance, Oscar's wife, looked dumpy and frumpish in blue. Leo's wife, Ottilie, was tall and big-boned, and smarter in red silk.

'We haven't seen much of you recently, Jack.'

She was one of the reasons he'd left. Her hostility was scarcely veiled now. A state of aggression had existed between them from the moment they'd met.

Ottilie had blonde plaits wound into a coronet on top of her head, with a sprinkling of grey across her temples. Her face was square, with Germanic features. Her family had originated there, but Ottilie was second-generation English. Her father had made a fortune importing cotton from America. She thought herself one of the upper crust.

Jack tried to picture Kate here with them. Her looks were more striking than either of his brothers' wives, though he knew she didn't own a dinner gown.

His father and brothers talked business, about what had taken place in the Liverpool office that day. Jack felt he'd been pushed into the quiet backwater of the Liscard office where he wasn't in the way.

Father no longer went to the office every day, but no decisions were taken there without his approval. He was thinking of having a new ship built, and started talking about the latest ideas in ship's architecture. Jack knew his opinion wouldn't be asked; it never was. If he offered any, Leo would somehow manage to hold it up to ridicule. They went on talking as though he wasn't there. He felt pushed out.

The meal was slow and formal. He sat facing a painting of the SS *Jemima Courtney*, a vessel named after his mother and still in service with the Line. They always had roast chicken, because that was what Mother liked. There was a huge confection of fruit and cream, as well as a birthday cake.

When it was time for the port, his mother got up to return to the drawing room, supported on each side by her daughters-in-law. Jack got up and went to the library. He'd been able to think of little else but Benedict Rotherfield since Kate had left him. He knew he could find out all he needed to know without discussing him with his family.

When he was young, his mother used to amuse herself by keeping scrapbooks about everything that interested her. It was the business that had made her start. She saw it as her duty to keep every newspaper article that mentioned the Courtney Line.

Her old scrapbooks took up a vast amount of shelf space now. They were large books with thick paper made thicker with glue and added newspaper, and bound in leather.

He knew she'd made a scrapbook about Benedict Rotherfield's fall from grace. She'd followed up his case and kept every detail. At the time, he'd thought she'd never stop talking about it.

Jack found what he was looking for and opened it on the table. Perhaps not such a fat book as some of the others, but there was plenty to read. He felt a chill go down his spine as the first headline screamed out at him: *Benedict Rotherfield Charged with Murder*.

Jack could feel his heart pounding. Kate would be horrified if she knew. He couldn't concentrate here in the library. He was afraid one of his family would come looking for him, and he didn't want to be seen with this book open. Questions about his interest in Benedict Rotherfield would be impossible to answer.

He put the book under his arm and went quickly upstairs to his old bedroom. Nothing had changed here either. His bed was no longer made up, but the same green counterpane covered the mattress. Jack sat on it, opened the book and read: *Prominent Liverpool Businessman caught in Love Triangle*. The cutting was dated December 1891. Another named Rotherfield as the infamous Mersey Murderer.

Jack read the articles devoted to Rotherfield's lover very carefully. This was what he wanted to know most. Lena Hadley was described as a common working-class girl, who'd stolen her mistress's husband.

Rotherfield had wanted to marry her and had had several quarrels with his wife about divorce. She didn't want it. He'd lost his temper and killed her with a knife. He'd been hung as a murderer in August 1892. Jack let his eyes skim down the columns of print. He remembered much of it.

His family had known the Rotherfields. His mother used to invite them to dinner and to her bridge parties. Benedict's business had eventually been run by his brother, but nobody would invite relations of the Mersey Murderer to their home. The family had never recovered from the scandal. Jack didn't think the business had recovered from it either.

Half the population of Merseyside would immediately recognise the name Rotherfield. It had been a scandal that had held the headlines for weeks on end. Kate had been only a baby at the time; she wouldn't have known anything about it.

Jack wanted to peruse every detail but knew he mustn't absent himself too long from his mother's birthday celebration. He'd take the scrapbook home and read it at leisure.

He opened his cupboard and found an old bag, put the scrapbook at the bottom and covered it with a few of his boyhood books. If she asked, his mother would believe he was taking some of his old things.

He wanted that scrapbook out of this house. If Mother ever discovered his interest in Kate, he didn't want her mind refreshed on these gruesome details.

*   *   *

Jack had arranged to meet Kate on the promenade the next afternoon. By then, he had the facts all fresh in his mind and had decided how much he should tell her. She was eager to find out what he'd learned.

'Benedict Rotherfield's wife was a friend of my mother's. She came one afternoon each week to make up a four for bridge. I think my mother went regularly to her house for the same reason.'

Kate's hand clamped itself on his wrist. 'His wife? He was married then?' The colour was draining from his cheeks. 'Married to someone else? That's why . . .'

'Yes. He was Amelia's husband. That's how we knew him.'

'You knew him well?'

He shook his head. 'He was younger, quite a lot younger than Amelia. He came for dinner once in a while. When my parents had company I usually had my dinner on a tray by myself, though my brothers, being older, ate with them.'

Jack shivered. It was too cold and miserable to walk about for long, though Kate was so upset she hardly seemed to notice. He took her to a small café just off the front, where they could sit over a pot of tea and a plate of scones for most of the afternoon.

'What did my father look like?'

'You. The imprint of his face is in yours. He had the same red hair.'

'Ginger.'

'Ginger if you must. Lots of it, and a small pointed beard, ginger too. His eyes were green like yours. I'd never seen anybody with green eyes before. They seemed to see more than they should.

' "How's school, Jack?" he'd say to me. He had a habit of rubbing his hands together. "Don't you worry about it. I never did well at school. Definitely not the best years of my life either." I wasn't doing as well as my brothers, you see, and he knew that.'

Kate looked perplexed. 'But how did he know my mother, if he knew yours . . . ?'

'She'd worked in his house for seven years. She was Amelia's personal maid. Of course, I didn't know anything about this at the time.'

'You asked your mother last night?'

'No, there was a bit of a scandal. My mother kept cuttings from the newspapers. I read through them. It seems your father badly wanted an heir for his business, but in ten years of marriage to Amelia no children came.

'She wanted them too, and consulted her doctor. He could find no reason for her childlessness. She told Benedict it was his fault.

'Benedict fell in love with your mother. He set her up as his mistress in a house of her own. Very soon she found she was expecting you. Benedict wanted a divorce so that he could marry her and make the coming child his legal heir.'

'But he didn't?'

'His wife wouldn't agree to it. So he gave you his name on your birth certificate.'

'But what happened . . .'

'He was killed suddenly.'

'How awful for Mam!' Jack drew in a rapid gulp of air. He hoped she'd never know how awful.

'How?' Her green eyes were shining up at him. 'How was he killed?'

'A riding accident. Thrown from his horse.'

Jack prided himself on being honest, but sometimes a lie was justified. If Kate's mother didn't want her to know her father had been a murderer, he wasn't going to tell her.

Nobody knew better than he did how a family name could affect a child. The Courtneys were successful. People looked up to them and expected them to lead in business. Their success had affected him. He couldn't lead anybody. He didn't want Kate to be affected by her father. For her the pendulum would swing the other way. He was sorry she knew his name.

'So now you need look no further. You know about your father's family. He was middle class, therefore you are middle class.'

'Poor Mam. He died too soon.'

'Too suddenly to make the provision for you that he'd have wanted.'

'You mean I might have been rich?'

'Comfortably off. If things had turned out differently.'

'I wonder why Mam married somebody as uncouth as Mitch McGlory after that.'

He could see her sucking at her lip. 'She must have wanted a husband badly. Well, she had me. I've always thought . . . Well, she hated all the bad language and the fights he got into. She must have found Mitch very hard to live with.'

Chapter Nine

April 1912

Kate hummed a tune as she got dressed. It was a fine spring morning; already at ten to six the sun was shining.

She knew Mr Halliday was pleased with her work. She enjoyed it and felt she was making progress. During the autumn, the manager of their New Brighton shop had suddenly been taken ill. She'd been asked to fill in for him and she'd run the place for the best part of eight weeks. Then she'd stood in for the manager at their Egremont branch when she went on her annual holiday.

Miss Fisk, the manager here, was sixty-three and finding the work too heavy. She'd been saying for some time that she wanted to retire. Kate was hoping Mr Halliday would offer the job to her. She wondered as she buttoned up her blouse if she should ask for it. She decided she would when Miss Fisk had set a date to leave.

As she ran downstairs to open the shop, the clock in the hall was striking six. She heaved the parcels of newspapers from the doorstep to the counter just as she did every morning. As she read the headlines she gasped.

Titanic sinks with terrible loss of life. Greatest ever peace-time disaster at sea.

The ship had sailed on its maiden voyage with such pomp and ceremony. It had been heralded as the greatest and safest liner ever built, yet it had struck an iceberg near Cape Race and sunk. She wouldn't have to think of anything else to write on the placards this morning. It was the lead story in every newspaper. Almost every customer who came in commented on it.

When she went for her breakfast at nine o'clock, Mr Halliday asked her to step into his parlour for a few minutes first. He'd also mentioned the disaster; she'd put his *Manchester Guardian* on the hall stand before seven as usual.

Then he said: 'How would you feel about taking over Miss

Fisk's job? You know she wants to retire?'

That brought a rush of satisfaction. She felt the heat run up her cheeks.

'I'd be very honoured, Mr Halliday. Delighted.'

'You're very young to be a manager, but I'm sure you'll do it well. With an increase in wages, of course. Shall we say a pound a week?'

Kate was thrilled. A pound a week and all found was good. Even in the face of a disaster like the *Titanic*, all was well in her private world.

Even Mam was on an even keel again. And so she should be. Billy was thriving, and nobody in the world was more wrapped in love. Kate wasn't going home as much as she used to. The boys seemed to worship Mam; once that had made her feel jealous.

But not any longer, she was spending more and more time with Jack Courtney, and was getting the love she'd craved from him. She didn't talk about Jack to anyone. Certainly not to Mr Halliday who thought she'd taken his advice and sent him packing. Not to Josie, not to Mam either, though Mam knew she continued to see him.

Kate felt she was growing closer to Jack. She admired him; he was soft-spoken and kindly.

Yet she sometimes felt impatient with him. He was slow to tell her more about himself. Slow to advance their relationship. Almost as though he was unsure of how she felt about him.

Jack was pleased for her when she told him about her promotion.

'How clever you are, Kate. I'm proud of you.'

'I have an assistant now, her name's Millie. She's come from the New Brighton branch and she's only fifteen. So I'm still opening up in the morning, until she's more used to things, but I can have two evenings off each week.'

Jack took Kate to the Liverpool Playhouse on Saturday night as a celebration and watched her face in the semi-darkness as she sat enthralled.

Dear, sweet Kate. He felt at ease with her in a way that he did not with his own family. He'd passed the stage of wondering if he was in love with her; he knew he was. He believed she loved him, and the way he saw things, it followed that if they loved each other they would eventually be married.

He thought Kate wanted it; he certainly did. But there was a hindrance he'd never so much as mentioned. He had to do it, clear the air. What would she think of him when she found out?

He made up his mind he'd do it tonight. At the end of the show he

104

told her he'd see her safely home. That would give him the opportunity. It would be dark, they'd walk slowly and talk.

She smiled up at him. 'Jack, it'll take you miles out of your way. You could take the Egremont ferry, instead of coming with me to Birkenhead.'

'I can't let you go home alone. Not at this time of night.'

He insisted, and sat silently beside her on the tram, wondering how to start. He should have told her months ago. Even on the stroll through the late-night streets the words wouldn't come. He looked over the cemetery wall and saw the gravestones in serried rows stretching into the darkness.

'Aren't you afraid of coming this way at night?'

'The cemetery? No, I'm used to it.'

'It's eerie, all those obelisks and marble statues over there. Spooky.'

He'd never seen a graveyard in the dark. In the shadows, it seemed misty, atmospheric. It filled his mind, and he didn't get round to telling her after all.

The months passed and November came. It was much more difficult to find somewhere close at hand to spend a comfortable hour or two. Jack wanted to ask her to his rooms. He very much wanted to entertain her there, see her sitting in his own armchair by his fire, drinking tea from his cups.

They wouldn't get to know each other any better if they met only in public places. In the afternoons, there was very little entertainment to be had around Magazine Village, and none at all once the shop had closed.

Jack wanted things to move faster but didn't know how. And really he shouldn't. He shouldn't let things go one inch further without telling her there was a problem. He was afraid, though, that if he did, she'd never want to see him again.

He wanted to see more of her, not less. He knew she expected more from him and he wanted very much to give it. One Monday afternoon that he'd hoped would be fine enough for a walk along the front turned out to be very wet indeed. The rain was bouncing up from the pavement and there was a slicing wind coming off the river. He waited for her in the shelter on the Esplanade at the corner of Magazine Park. He was there too early as usual. The tide was out, and he could see vast areas of mud and rocks covered with green seaweed. The Liverpool bank was lost in mist. He thought longingly of the comfortable parlour he'd just left, but respectable young ladies couldn't go unaccompanied to a gentleman's rooms.

Kate came hurrying towards him, huddled under an umbrella, and sat down beside him in the shelter. There was nobody else about; they had it to themselves. He kissed her cheek, it felt cold. He took her hand in his, that was cold too.

'It's a bleak afternoon.' He'd thought of an afternoon visit to the cinema – there was one in New Brighton – but Kate had to be back at the shop before four thirty, which meant they wouldn't be able to see the programme through.

They often went to a tea shop in Seabank Road. They'd been in so often they were beginning to draw questioning looks from the proprietor.

'The tea shop or . . . ?'

'Or what?'

'I shouldn't take you to my rooms. It's wrong to ask you, but I know of nowhere else on a day like this. You could catch your death of cold out here.'

Kate's big green eyes were smiling at him. 'So could you.'

He asked: 'Would you come?'

'I've often wondered what your rooms are like. I'd very much like to see them.'

He brightened up. 'I promise you, I'll give you no reason for concern.'

She smiled again. 'Jack, I know that. You're aways the perfect gentleman.'

That made him straighten his lips. He knew it wasn't true. He knew he'd have to tell her. He couldn't go on like this, it was on his conscience. He'd have to tell her and risk the consequences.

He wanted a cab but there were none about. He held her umbrella over her and tried to shield her from the driving rain.

'There's something I have to tell you, Kate,' he said urgently. 'Something I have to say. I want everything to be open and above board between us.'

There were raindrops on her face when he turned to look at her. He brushed them away with his hand. He thought she'd never looked more beautiful.

This was it! Jack's tender concern was telling Kate he was going to commit himself at last. She felt heady with love for him. What she wanted above everything was for him to say he loved her and wanted to marry her.

She thought he was exactly right for her. If she had one small complaint, it was that things between them were standing still. Many times she'd imagined herself as his wife. It was what she wanted most, and now at last it seemed he was about to ask her.

The rain was still blasting along the road when they turned into a narrow street behind the Marine Terrace. They'd walked before past the house where he lodged; he'd pointed it out and it had surprised her. It was nice enough but one of many very similar ones in the district: terraced, with two bay windows, one above the other, with the front door only two steps from the street. She'd imagined his home to be grander than this. Much grander. This wasn't the home of a rich man.

Inside, Kate was met by a wall of warmth, and she liked it better. He shook the rain off her coat and took her into the front parlour, a comfortable room made bright by a good fire. He seated her in a velvet armchair beside it and busied himself piling on more coal.

'Is that your camera?' It took up a sizeable amount of space on his table. The tripod was folded in the corner of the room. He'd told her about it. She knew he was keen on photography; he often talked of his hobby.

He said: 'I'd like to take your picture. May I?'

It took a bit of courage for Kate to say: 'I'd rather hear what's on your mind.'

'Oh!' He seemed embarrassed, ashamed even. 'I fear, Kate, I'm trying to put off the moment.' His grey eyes were sad as they looked into hers.

Kate shivered. This wasn't going to be what she'd supposed.

'I'm a bit of a cad. I should have told you long ago . . .'

'What? What should you have told me?'

He couldn't look at her now. 'I have a wife and two boys . . .'

Kate gasped. It was the last thing she'd expected him to say. 'You mean you're married?'

'Separated. But not divorced. I should not have monopolised your time. All these months, without telling you that. I have tried, Kate. I have wanted to. I was afraid you'd not want to see any more of me. I couldn't have borne that.'

She couldn't take it in. Could hardly believe . . .

He caught at her hand. 'I do love you dearly. You must believe that. I've been wanting to tell you for a long time.'

Kate was blinking hard. She felt as though she'd had a bucket of cold water tipped over her. All her hopes dashed in seconds. What a fool she'd been to think it was possible. She stood up.

'Oh, Kate, love, don't say you won't see me again. I know it was wrong not to tell you. I want so much to have your love, to have someone of my own.'

Then she saw the pain in his eyes. He did love her, she couldn't doubt that. She hesitated for one more moment, then threw her arms round him. It was what Mam always said she should do. Show her love. She whispered against his cheek: 'What can we do about it?'

He let out a great choking breath. 'I'll ask Philomena for a divorce. We'll get married. Don't leave me, Kate. I love you.'

She tightened her arms round him. Told herself it would be all right. She loved him enough to wait. But the thought kept coming into her head. Why, if he loved her so much, had he not already asked his wife for a divorce? If he was prepared to do it now, why not earlier? It didn't make sense.

Kate felt the sting of tears. She'd believed that if only Jack would declare his love there would be nothing else she could possibly ask of life. Now that he'd done it, it left her feeling as though the bottom had dropped out of her world.

'Tell me about her. About your wife.'

He was tight-lipped. 'We didn't get on.'

Kate felt another chill run down her spine. It seemed there were a lot of people he didn't get on with. And yet she was quite sure he'd get on with her.

Jack felt restless. 'Kate, I'd like to take your portrait. I've wanted to do it for a long time.'

'Now? I don't feel ready. I'd like to be . . . more composed.'

'If you aren't pleased with it, I can take another some other time.'

He knew she was upset; he'd expected it. How could she be otherwise?

'You look beautiful.'

'My hair?' She was trying to smooth it into shape.

'It's fine, Kate.'

He needed to busy himself with something. He took his time setting up his camera on its tripod and getting everything adjusted. He fed in the glass slides and covered his head with the dark cloth. He could see Kate trying not to look downcast. This was giving her time to think things over.

Her green eyes came right into the viewfinder. Her tone was accusing. 'I've always felt you didn't tell me much about yourself.'

He was glad she couldn't see him. 'I'm sorry. Some things are hard to talk about.'

'I've told you all there is to know about me. It wasn't easy to tell you how poor we are. Not when you're rich.'

108

'I'm not rich either.'

'By my standards you are. You have a camera.'

'It was a birthday present from my family.'

He had to rush upstairs with the plates. He'd had a darkroom made in a walk-in cupboard off his bedroom. He did his own developing here. He'd take another picture, in case this one didn't do her justice.

Back in the parlour, he moved her chair to the other side of the fireplace and positioned her carefully. He gave her an open book to place on her lap. He was going to get this artistically right.

'Lower your left arm a little. That's fine, now turn your face more to me. Excellent, just keep still.' His grandfather clock would be in the background. It always looked well.

He came out from under his black cloth to find he hadn't deflected Kate's mind. Her eyes were fixed on his.

'I've told you plenty of things about me I'd rather have kept hidden. Things that pride makes me hide from most people. Why aren't you open with me?'

Jack swallowed hard. That was a definite complaint. 'You're a much nicer person.'

'Come on. I even told you I was born out of wedlock.'

'That's not your fault.'

'It carries a stigma. I was afraid you'd be put off.'

'Never! Nothing could put me off you.'

'Jack, don't you think I feel the same? I won't be put off whatever it is you tell me.'

He didn't entirely believe that. She'd told him about her circumstances, but there were things about him, about his personality . . .

'Tell me about your wife and children.'

'Edward is seven and Henry is nine. I miss them . . .'

'Your wife?'

'Philomena. We were very young when we married. It didn't last. We've been separated for six years now.'

'Why?'

How could he explain that she considered him a failure? Without damning himself in Kate's eyes?

'I didn't come up to her expectations. She wanted me to be a powerful force in the business, like Oscar and Leo.'

Kate was screwing up her face in thought. 'She expected you to earn a lot of money and you didn't?'

'Yes.' He felt relief wash over him. 'I disappointed her.'

'Do you still see them?'

'The boys, once in a while. My... Philomena doesn't like me taking them out, but I do occasionally.'

'But a separation rather than a divorce? What made you do that?'

'It was what she wanted. I didn't think I'd ever be lucky enough to find somebody else who'd marry me.'

She smiled up at him. 'Well, you have.'

Later that afternoon, he walked Kate back to the paper shop, holding tightly to her arm, the umbrella she'd borrowed from Josie Oaks held at the best angle to protect her from the rain.

'You will let me see you again?' he pleaded. 'I couldn't bear it if you ...' He wanted her.

'Of course. You know I want to, Jack.'

'I'll see Philomena and press for a divorce. I promise it'll all turn out well in the end.'

He watched her disappear into the newsagent's and wished she didn't have to work. He wanted her with him, all the time. He felt too restless to go straight back to his rooms. He walked along the promenade in the rain. He was thoroughly wet when he did get home. Then he sat down to write to Philomena.

Kate felt low. She knew she was serving customers like a robot. To find that Jack had kept this from her had really churned her up. She'd known all along he didn't like talking about himself. She should have guessed there was something he didn't want her to know. Some secret.

She wondered if there were others. There must be lots of things she still didn't know about him. She must try and draw him out, satisfy her curiosity about his family. Not allow him to keep things hidden. It wasn't as if he was shy.

He should have told her about his wife much sooner. She wished he had, right at the start, then at least she'd have known where she stood. It wouldn't have made any difference; she'd still have fallen in love with him.

Mam would be horrified if she knew. She'd say he hadn't treated her right. And he hadn't. Mam wouldn't want her to go on seeing him, but she couldn't stop now.

Kate spent the evening with Josie in the kitchen talking about everything but never once mentioning Jack. She was late going to bed but couldn't sleep. During the long wakeful hours, she tried to imagine a future without him. It looked bleak.

She loved Jack, and she couldn't turn her back on him, whatever he did. She knew it was very wrong for her to keep company with a married man; very wrong to have gone with him to his rooms, but if she was going to go on meeting him, they might as well be comfortable. Far better to make up his fire and relax in front of it than spend three hours sitting in a tea shop drinking tea and eating cakes they didn't want.

She understood now why their relationship had seemed to stand still and make no progress. It couldn't because he was married. He'd been holding back because of that. But why hadn't he told her? Her way was to tell him everything.

If she'd stopped to think, she might have guessed that by the age of thirty-seven he'd have been married. If not, then he wasn't the marrying kind and would be unlikely to marry her.

He'd said everything would be all right, that he'd get a divorce, but things were not straightforward any more. It wasn't going to be as easy as she'd thought.

Even the next morning, Kate's mind wasn't on what she was doing in the shop. A customer pulled her up for giving the wrong change. She could think of nothing but Jack. She wondered if he'd been to see his wife, and if he'd managed to persuade her to give him a divorce.

She was glad when one o'clock came and she was free to meet him. She'd told him she'd go round to his rooms. The open shelter where Magazine Lane joined the Esplanade could be rainswept and cold, and since Mr Halliday had asked her not to see him, he didn't come to meet her outside the shop.

As she walked down Beech Grove, she saw him at his parlour window, watching for her. His face lit up when he saw her coming. He opened the front door to her before she reached it.

'I shouldn't let you come here like this,' he worried. 'Quite improper. What if the neighbours should see you? Working where you do, lots of people could recognise you. Your reputation . . .'

'I came yesterday. So why not today?'

She got no further than the hall, and the front door remained ajar while he put on his overcoat. 'Shall we go for a walk?' he asked, and led her back into the cold, grey afternoon.

Kate had been on her feet all morning and would have preferred to sit by his fire, but if this was what he wanted, she was prepared to go along with it. She took his arm and couldn't wait to ask: 'Did you manage to see your wife yesterday, Jack? Did you ask her?'

She felt him stiffen.

'I wrote to her.'

'Oh!' She was sure he'd said yesterday that he'd go to see her.

'She's living with her parents, took the boys there. The far side of Liverpool. Quite a journey.'

Kate bit her lip. It wouldn't be too long a journey for her. Not for such an important matter. The river came into view. It was low tide, and the Liverpool bank was shrouded in heavy mist. There was a strong smell of seaweed and mud.

'Her parents are rich, I suppose?'

'No, no. There's one of our ships.' Jack pointed his silver-headed cane out across the Mersey. 'The SS *Egremont*.' Kate could just make out the shape of it coming out of the grey murk. At any other time she'd have been interested, but now her mind was on more important concerns.

'Jack, we can't go on like this. I've got to be sure where we stand. There are things I need to know. You're hiding them from me.'

The murk had been coming steadily closer, Kate felt the first drops on her face. The next moment the heavens seemed to open. She took his arm and hurried him back to the shelter. 'Never mind your ships now. I want to hear about you.'

They almost ran the last few yards, but even so got wet. It was the biggest shelter of its kind that Kate had ever seen, but half the floor was running with water and the drumming on the roof made it impossible to talk.

'We can't stay here,' Jack said. 'And we're too wet to sit about in tea shops. I'll have to take you home again.'

'It's easing off.' Kate shivered. She felt really cold. 'Let's go.' The rain had stopped before they reached his rooms.

'We should have come straight here,' Jack said, 'as soon as the rain started. We've really got wet.'

Kate said nothing. She was grateful for the wall of warmth that surrounded her in his parlour.

Chapter Ten

Jack shook Kate's hat and coat very carefully and set them to dry near the fire. He built that up; he wanted it to roar up the chimney. He found a towel and patted her face dry, and then the heavy fringe of straight red hair. He finished by mopping round the bottom of her dress. He knew he was fussing.

'You're soaking!'

He insisted she take off her boots, which were sodden, and wear a pair of his slippers. They were much too big for her. She laughed up at him, and her beauty brought an ache to his throat. With her lovely rich red hair glowing above her dress of pewter grey, she was like a flame against his hearth.

'Tea?' he asked, and put his kettle on to boil. It was lovely to have her here in his home, but he felt guilty enough about what he was doing to her without adding this. 'I shouldn't bring you here.'

She laughed at him. 'Should we still be sitting out in that shelter, dripping wet?'

'We mustn't do it often.'

He'd developed the two photographs he'd taken of her, and was pleased with the result. She looked a little taken aback in the first, but in the second she had a vulnerable smile and such haunting beauty in her eyes. It was a flattering portrait. He'd made two enlargements and had them framed; one was to be a present to Kate, the other was for himself. He'd set them up on his table. Kate saw them now.

'Jack! It's lovely. You're really good at it.'

He felt a glow of pleasure. Nobody else praised anything he did. 'The one in the silver frame is for you. The other I shall keep by my bed.'

'Thank you. You've made me look handsome. I shall be proud to show this off. You've a real talent for photography.'

The warm feeling came again. 'It's a hobby. I enjoy it.'

'Do you have any other pictures you've taken?'

That was what he liked about Kate. She was interested in everything. He had albums of photographs.

113

'Lots.' He got them out of his cupboard.

Kate picked one up and sat herself down by the fire to look at it.

'I don't think you took these. Isn't this you as a child?' She was laughing up at him again.

'Oh, yes. That's a very old album. My mother took those. Here, let me have it.'

'No, no, I want to look at it. I want to see what you used to be like. Didn't I say I wanted to know everything about you? Come and tell me who these other people are.'

Jack leaned over the back of her chair. 'Yes, that's me.' He saw himself as a four-year-old boy, flaxen-haired and timid. 'With my two older brothers. This one's Leo, and this is Oscar. There's only thirteen months between them, whereas I'm six years younger than Oscar.'

Jack's brothers were very able and vied with each other. Oscar had no fear of challenging Leo; he was so sure he had the better brain and probably the stronger body. They had both grown tall and broad in adult life. Whereas Jack had remained slight and slim.

'You've hardly mentioned your brothers – tell me about them.'

'They were noisy and boisterous.' Too boisterous for him. 'They were good friends.' He was excluded on account of his age. Too young to climb the many trees in the huge garden. He had no companion. His brothers wouldn't play with him and he had no friends of his own. He been known as 'the baby' until he was eight years old. Mother had feared for him, said they mustn't be too rough with him.

'These were taken in your garden? It looks very grand.'

There was a tennis court, but three couldn't play. They allowed him to be their ball boy.

She turned the page to a whole collection of pictures. 'All three of you in sailor's uniform.'

'On the *Conway*. We all went to school there, though Leo had left before I started.'

'Did you go to sea?'

He didn't want to admit that, but Kate had been saying he was secretive and told her as little as possible about himself, so he had to. 'Yes.'

Jack felt his career at sea had been touched by ill luck. As a midshipman on his first ship, the SS *Elutian*, he'd fallen from the rigging and spent much of the voyage in his bunk with a sprained ankle and terrible bruises. Mother had thought him lucky not to have broken his back.

His second ship, the *Mary Courtney*, had sailed from Marseilles without him, and he'd had to travel overland to Livorno to catch her up. His father had accused him of being too long in a bar, but the truth was that he'd fallen asleep in the sun sitting on a seat in a park.

Being a Courtney, these minor difficulties hadn't slowed down his rapid promotion. His real disaster had come shortly after he'd been given his first command.

'But you gave it up? You didn't like life at sea?' Kate's green eyes looked up into his. He had to be honest.

'I don't think I was cut out for it.'

'Why not?'

'My first command, and my ship went down. Waiting for the pilot . . .'

On a voyage from Baltimore to Liverpool, he'd run his ship aground in thick fog off the coast of Anglesey. She'd been carrying a cargo of horses. Jack knew that a story had gone round the office that he'd saved himself by hauling himself up on the back of a horse as it swam ashore. The truth was he'd clung to a box of butter and was lucky enough to be washed up on a gentle beach. The *Caroline Courtney*, almost a new ship, named after his aunt, was a total loss.

And worse, thirteen of the crew of nineteen had been drowned and the Welsh coast line was bombarded with boxes of cheese, butter and bacon, as well as horses both dead and alive.

Jack sucked in his cheeks in agony as he remembered the enquiry in Liverpool. He'd had his master's certificate suspended for six months and was never given command of a vessel again. He didn't want it; he'd lost his nerve. It had all been very public, with accounts of his shame appearing in the newspapers.

His father had said that as master he'd shown bad management and bad judgement and had brought disgrace on their name. A Courtney who let his ship sail off course and founder on rocks with such a loss of life was a failure. The Courtneys were sailors and shipowners and had a responsibility for those who sailed on their ships under their command.

Jack couldn't remember his father ever being so angry with him.

'You're a disgrace to the Line. A disgrace to the Courtney name. I don't want you working for us. You're a liability. I'm going to cut you off without a penny. You don't deserve anything after this.'

Jack pulled himself together. 'It was in a terrible storm, but my father blamed me. He didn't want me to carry on.'

Kate's eyes were full of horror. 'You blamed yourself too, I'm sure. You didn't want to go to sea again?'

'Father relented; he usually does. He arranged for me to sail as first officer on the *Francis Courtney*. I didn't get on with the captain – he found fault with everything I did – but I stuck that out for two years.'

He'd hated it. He hadn't wanted to go to sea in that capacity either.

'It was during this time that I met Philomena. She was the daughter of an employee of the company, a seagoing captain who'd been in command of the *Courtney Crest* for ten years, and was well thought of by my family.'

Nevertheless, they hadn't entirely approved. Philomena hadn't the right social background. They'd gone along with it because they'd already dismissed Jack as a person of no importance.

'Once married, I didn't want to go to sea.'

Once married, Philomena had expected the lush lifestyle of the Courtneys. She'd wanted the latest Paris fashions, and he couldn't afford them. He'd taken her to live at the Grange. She didn't get on with his mother and was prepared to cross swords with her. Philomena had a quick mind and a sharp tongue; she could run circles round Jack and always had the last word. They'd had terrible rows.

'Do you have a picture of her?' Kate's voice trembled. She was keeping her eyes down on the album.

He'd taken countless photographs of Philomena when he'd been enamoured. There were all those wedding pictures.

'No, not here.'

'She hasn't replied? To your letter about . . .'

'Not yet, Kate.'

Jack's conscience jabbed him. He hadn't posted it yet, hadn't finished writing it. He must do that today, as soon as Kate had gone.

'That's when you decided on office administration?'

He hadn't actually decided on anything. Father had found him a desk in the office but he'd got on no better there. He knew he was working at the level of ordinary clerk on twice the salary because of his family connections.

It was deadly dull work, but he'd stuck at it for nine years now. He'd been so fed up at one stage that he'd sought work with other companies. Father had been furious with him.

'Is this all the Courtney Line means to you? You'd rather work for another shipping line? Where is your loyalty? You don't deserve a penny from the business. I hope you aren't expecting to inherit part of it?'

'No, Father.'

He'd had to try his luck elsewhere, but had only been offered routine office jobs that were lowly paid. He'd found it impossible to get a job commensurate with his social status and had had to swallow his pride and ask if he could work again for the Courtney Line. Father had pursed his lips. 'I suppose you can, you are a Courtney, but this time I expect more loyalty from you.'

How his brothers had crowed at that.

Kate's green eyes were staring up at him, full of questions. She'd turned another page in the album, to where the handsome ivy-clad façade of the Grange was portrayed several times.

'Why do you live in two rooms when the rest of your family live in luxury?'

'I told you, I don't get on with them. I prefer to be on my own.'

How could he be on good terms with his family when they saw him as a failure and made him see himself that way too? His mother had been a semi-invalid all her life, and her health had always been her main interest. His father had lost patience with him. He was now seventy-six, and although he said he hadn't retired, he did very little in the office. Leo and Oscar were running the Line between them. They were increasing the profits; they were successful.

'But why cut yourself off from them?'

She must have seen him shy away from that, because she added: 'I want to see things as they really are, Jack.' She was serious, she meant it.

How could he tell her? Kate saw him as a worthy person, and he wanted that to go on, even though he felt he was already letting her down.

At four fifteen, Jack walked with Kate back towards the shop. The rain had cleared but the wind was cold. She held on to his arm until they reached the top of Magazine Lane. There she pulled him to a standstill, afraid someone from the shop might see him.

'I loved looking at your photographs,' she said. 'I feel I know you better now.'

That made his conscience stab at him again. He hadn't told her one half of what he should. He couldn't, if she was to think well of him.

'Thank you for my portrait.' She carried that as though it were the Crown Jewels. 'I've never had one taken of me before.'

'I must take more.'

She left him a hundred yards from the shop. He watched her hurry to the door. She gave him a discreet wave and a smile before she disappeared inside.

He felt lost without her. Lonely. He couldn't get enough of her company now. Dear, sweet Kate. She wouldn't understand him, she was so strong and capable herself.

He needed to go home and finish that letter to Philomena, but first he ought to look in to the office. He felt he was neglecting his duties there. No, not exactly neglecting, because Williams was doing what was needed. As the office was in Magazine Lane, he'd pop in on the way home and see that all was well.

It was the original office, opened when the Courtney Line was established in 1851. Liscard was a backwater now, and most of the business went through their Liverpool office.

Jack let himself in. There were only three clerks working here. All three heads were bent over their desks. The only sound was the scratching of pen nibs. He walked through to his room at the back, hung up his coat and hat and sat at his desk. His desk drawer was slightly ajar. He didn't think he'd left it so.

Mr Williams, the most senior of the clerks, appeared in his doorway.

Jack asked: 'Has someone been in my office?'

'Yes, sir, your father came with Mr Lionel.'

His heart sank. They would come while he was out. They'd complain about that the next time they saw him.

'Mr Courtney asks that you call on him. At your convenience, sir.'

Jack had no doubt the last had been uttered with heavy sarcasm. 'Did he say what he wanted?'

'No, sir.'

'What time did they come?'

'About two.'

Jack's heart sank further. He opened his desk drawer to see what Father had seen. Nothing out of the ordinary, apart from the mint imperials and barley sugars he'd bought over the counter from Kate before he got to know her properly. The barley sugars were melting into a sticky mess. He dropped them in his waste-paper basket.

'Was he going home? Do you know?'

'He didn't say, sir.'

'I'd better go and see. If there's nothing else?'

Jack walked to the Grange. It put off the moment when he'd come face to face with Father. He wondered what he wanted; it was a long time since he'd come to the Liscard office. His route took him past Kate's shop again. He paused for a moment to see her serving a customer.

The house seemed very quiet as Minnie let him in. The glass case round the model of the SS *Pensicola* gleamed. It had obviously been polished that day.

'Is Father in his study?'

Jack felt tense. He must appear strong or Father would say he was like a limp lettuce. He rapped hard on his study door and went in. Father's grey head turned stiffly from his desk.

'Oh, you've got here then?'

'You wanted to see me, Father?' He was relieved to find no sign of Lionel.

'I wanted to see you at two o'clock. I brought Lionel to have a word with you.'

Jack sat down by his desk. 'What about?'

His father's tired grey eyes searched into his face. 'We've decided to close the office in Liscard.'

Jack sucked in his breath.

'It's not worth keeping it open any longer. Not enough business coming in. The expenses outweigh the profits.'

Jack roused himself. 'I think the focus of business has changed. It's all being done through the Liverpool office.'

'It is, because you make no effort to attract it. You're never in the office, you take no interest.'

'I do my best.'

'It isn't good enough, Jack. You're a bad influence on the clerks. They do what they like while you're out. We need two more in Liverpool. Which are the best two?'

'Williams, and I suppose Hardy.'

'They can have jobs there, if they want them.'

'What about me?'

'What indeed, Jack? I really don't know what to do with you.'

He couldn't look at his father. He wished he didn't have to listen to this.

'What have you got to say for yourself?' Jack knew better than to think that was a direct question. It was Father's usual way of starting a diatribe against him. At thirty-eight, he was too old for this.

'I've given you every possible advantage.' His father sounded severe. 'You went to a good school. Your brothers did well there. Where did I go wrong?'

Lionel and Oscar had both excelled academically, at games and at seamanship. Jack was no good at anything. He felt he couldn't compete with them, but his problems had been building up long before he reached school age.

119

'Will there be a job for me in Liverpool?' He dreaded having to go there. He'd be under permanent surveillance.

His father's manner was weary. 'What if I just gave you an allowance, Jack? How would you feel about that?'

That shook him rigid. 'An allowance?'

'Yes, then you'd be free to do what you want.'

Jack felt a wave of anger. They really had given up on him! 'What d'you mean? What I want?'

'You're out every afternoon. You must be doing something.'

Jack hesitated, knowing this was the moment to tell his father about Kate.

Father gave a gusty sigh. 'I should have known it was too much to hope for. You haven't found some way of earning your own living?'

A wave of heat washed over him. 'Was this Lionel's idea?'

'We've talked it over from time to time. It's been on the cards for years. You know that.'

Jack shuffled his feet; he hadn't known. Hadn't even thought about it.

'There's been very little business coming through, and it's declined year by year.'

Jack felt numb inside. He had known that.

'I just wish you could stand on your own feet.'

Another pause, followed by another sigh.

'Is there anything you'd like to do? If you can think of some way to earn a living, I'd be glad to help. I'll continue to pay the allowance to Philomena and the boys, and I'll see you don't starve.'

'Thank you, Father.'

He had to tell him about Kate. He'd need a bigger allowance if he was ever to support her.

'Right then, think about it, Jack, and go and see your mother while you're here. She worries about you, you know.'

Jack felt knocked sideways. It had never occurred to him that the Liscard office might close. It had always been part of the Courtney Line. That his family wanted to close it seemed like another stab at him.

When he thought of the future, he felt apprehensive. He wanted to divorce Philomena. He'd go over to Liverpool and see her now. Ask her to her face. Tell her he was in dire straits.

He wanted to marry Kate and set up home with her, in a house that was halfway reasonable. Father had offered help; he'd meant help with some sort of business, of course, not the sort of help he needed. Jack didn't understand what had made him freeze up. He should have told his father about Kate, it would have cleared the air. He'd know where he stood and Father might have offered help.

He hated seeing Philomena. Her home in Wavertree was better than the one he was living in. Her father was away at sea, so she shared it with her mother and the boys. They had a live-in maid, a tired-looking girl of about fifteen. She opened the door to him and left him on the step while she announced him to her mistress.

Philomena took her time coming. 'Oh, it's you.' Her dark eyes flashed contempt. 'Do you want to come in?'

That made him bristle. Of course he wanted to come in! It had taken him over an hour to get here.

'I want to talk to you.'

She led the way into an empty sitting room and sat herself down. She dressed expensively; she was still a handsome woman and looked very much in command of herself.

'What about?'

The look in her eyes said she despised him. That she knew him for what he was: a total failure. He tried not to look at her, choosing to sit on a chair well away from her. He'd had plenty of time to prepare himself for this, and he wasn't going to beat about the bush.

'I want a divorce.'

She didn't answer immediately. When he stole a glance at her, she was studying her wedding ring and the fine sapphire engagement ring Father had paid for. The next second, her dark eyes were peering into his.

'Separation is no longer enough? That means you've found someone else. You want to marry again?' It had always disconcerted him, the speed with which she went to the root of things.

'Yes.' There seemed no reason to hide that. Just talking about it seemed to bring it closer.

She tossed her head. 'Well, Jack, I don't want a divorce. I don't see any advantage to me in that.'

'Why not? We aren't husband and wife any more, we rarely see each other.'

'I've had an absentee father all my life. An absentee husband suits me well enough. I like things as they are. I want to keep them this way.'

Jack felt the blood rush to his face. 'I don't. I want to marry again.' He never had been able to deal with Philomena.

'Why should I give you what you want? All I've ever had from you is trouble. No, Jack, the answer's no.'

She was squaring her shoulders, looking aggressive. He didn't know what to do next, even though it was what he'd expected.

'Don't just dismiss it. At least say you'll think about it.'

The room overlooked the road; he saw his sons and his mother-in-law coming to the front door.

'I suppose you want to see the boys.' Philomena got up and went out to the hall.

'Come in here, darlings, there's someone to see you.'

Their coats were half off when they came to the door. They'd been toddlers when Philomena had left him. Now Edward was seven and Henry nine. Their eyes met his, dark like their mother's. He saw momentary blankness there.

'Your father,' Philomena prompted.

Jack realised they hadn't recognised him. The room swam round him. What sort of a father was he that his children didn't even know him?

'How tall you've both grown,' he said, as they gave him dutiful kisses. 'Almost young men now.' But they didn't seem like his flesh and blood. They were not close. He ought to love them, yet he felt nothing.

He tried to ask them about school, while his mother-in-law pursed her lips with disapproval. He couldn't get out of the house quickly enough. To stay would have added to his humiliation.

Chapter Eleven

Saturday was always the heaviest day of the week in the newspaper shop. It stayed open late, but at least Kate could look forward to her day off on Sunday, when she'd be able to sleep in until eight o'clock. At a quarter to nine that evening, the shop was empty and Mr Halliday said they might as well close.

Supper was laid out for her in the kitchen after that, but Kate wrapped up the pork pie on her plate to eat on the tram going home so that she could get away quickly. She'd already put together the few things she needed to stay at home overnight.

She was tired. The tram seemed slower than usual, and walking up past the cemetery, the hill seemed steeper. Her feet dragged as she went up the cart track and her eyelids were ready to close. She hoped her mother had put the little ones to bed.

It was almost dark, but Duncan and even little Freddie were still playing outside. She could hear them shouting to each other as she drew nearer. Her spirits sank. Charlie and Joe would have gone out by now, but Mam could have got Tommy to call them in. What was she thinking of?

She scooped Freddie up into her arms before going indoors, calling to Duncan to follow. Blinking in the light, she saw Billy curled up asleep on the hearthrug and all her other brothers arguing round the living room table.

'What's the matter, Joe? It's Saturday night, I thought you'd have gone out.' She lowered Freddie to the floor. 'Where's Mam?'

Tommy turned round, his impish face serious for once. 'Dad's come back,' he gulped.

That brought a stab of fear that took Kate's breath away. She stood there trying to take in what it would mean. Mitch had been gone for more than two years. Mam had had to manage without any help from him in all that time. She didn't need him now. Kate didn't want him back.

123

'He's upstairs,' Joe said wearily. 'He's been hurt at work.'

Kate was choking with anger as she rushed up to Mam's bedroom. Mam, white with exhaustion, was leaning against the windowsill.

'What did you let him in for? You should have sent him packing.'

Mitch McGlory was taking up more than half of the double bed, the space Kate had expected to occupy tonight. He'd used all the pillows to prop himself into a sitting position.

'Your mam wants me back,' he smirked, then sucked his breath in in pain. 'It's not up to you, thank goodness.'

'He's not well.' Mam sounded shocked. 'Caught in a rock fall at work. Tunnelling, for a new branch line. Crushed.'

Mitch had aged since Kate had last seen him. His face was flabby and the colour of putty. He'd shaved recently, but a dark shadow covered bluish jaws. His hair was sparser than it had been and hung in greasy whorls. He looked uncouth. Kate could see it was hurting him to breathe.

'Broke me ribs, I have.' Dirt-ingrained hands twisted at the sheet.

'And his arm,' Mam added. It was in plaster inside a sling.

Kate hardened her heart. 'Your young lady friend doesn't want you? Doesn't want to take care of an invalid? Not her sort of fun?'

'I couldn't turn him away, could I?' Mam asked. Her eyes were dark with apprehension.

'I would have done.'

'As I said, it's not up to you, Miss Hoity-Toity. You can make me a cup of tea now you're home. And something to eat. Is there any of that broth left?'

'I don't think that's up to me either,' Kate said, and marched downstairs.

'Another mouth to feed,' Joe said miserably 'He had some of our dinner. There wasn't enough to go round.'

'He's been signed off work. Won't be able to go back for months, not the state he's in,' Charlie fumed. 'Just when we were getting on our feet.'

'When did it happen? The accident . . .'

'Wednesday. He's been in hospital. An ambulance brought him to the door.'

Kate felt tears prickling her eyes. She was scared of being under the same roof as him. She'd felt this dread since that awful day when he'd attacked her.

'There's nowhere for me to sleep. Not with him here. I'm going.'

'No, don't,' Tommy pleaded. 'We want you.'

She gave Mam seventeen shillings every week out of the pound she earned. She handed it over to Joe now.

'See he doesn't get any of it,' she told him. 'Get the babies to bed, Tommy. I'm going, I've had enough.'

She turned to find Mam had followed her downstairs. 'No, Kate!' There were tears in her eyes too. 'Don't go. Be reasonable. It won't hurt you to sleep on the armchair for once. You can take the old eiderdown, I'll put my coat across our Duncan's bed.'

'It's not just the bed.'

'I want you here tomorrow. I need you. I wish you weren't always spoiling for a fight. Dad wants . . . Mitch wants you to stay too.'

'I don't want him to . . .' Kate caught herself just in time. She'd almost let slip what Mitch had done to her. She knew she mustn't; Mam would be the one who was hurt. She must keep that a secret.

'I'm going,' she choked. 'I can't stay here with him.'

It was pitch dark now; there was neither moon nor stars. She strode furiously down the cart track, almost tripping in the ruts she couldn't see. She was cross with her mother. Over the last year or so, Mam had looked to her for help and support. Now, Mitch was back, she was afraid that would end. She'd be pushed out in the cold again.

When she'd first gone into service with the Hallidays, Mam had said she was sorry to see her go. She was always glad to see her when she came home. Kate felt valued for the help she could provide rather than for herself. On the tram going back to Wallasey, it occurred to her that she was jealous because Mam still loved Mitch, and that made her crosser than ever.

The lights on the tram made the suburban roads seem darker. It was getting late. If she went back to the shop, Mr Halliday would ask questions. Kate wondered if it was too late to go to Jack's rooms. She was no longer tired. The shock of finding Mitch reinstated at home had shaken off any sleepiness. She needed comfort now.

She got off the tram at the stop before her usual one. She could walk past Jack's rooms to see if the light was still on downstairs. If it was, she would knock. If it wasn't, she'd go on to the shop.

As she turned into Beech Grove, she could see the red glow shining through his parlour curtains. He hadn't gone to bed. Even so, for a girl to knock on a man's door at this hour would be considered very daring. Kate didn't care. She needed him.

Jack felt useless. He'd screwed himself up to see Philomena, gone all that way and achieved nothing. Worse, it seemed to put Kate out of his

125

reach for ever. He felt he'd led her to believe marriage was possible when clearly it wasn't. That, on top of seeing his family and hearing his father's opinion of him, had driven him into a black hole.

He was disgusted with himself. He'd come back on the ferry and felt so miserable by the time he reached Wallasey that he'd stopped at the nearest hotel for a drink. It hadn't helped, and by then it was past the time that his landlady served his supper. He knew she'd be cross because she'd have cooked a meal for him and he wasn't there to eat it.

He had a meal out; it wasn't very good. When he eventually got home, his fire was out. He had to relight it himself.

Then he'd sat back and compared his lonely parlour with the fine house his family lived in. He thought of Kate. She was the only worthwhile thing in his life, and he was very much afraid she'd realise what a failure he was and have nothing more to do with him.

The tap on his window made him sit upright. It came again. He lifted the curtain and was surprised to see Kate's worried face close to the glass. For a moment, he thought he was imaging things. He'd been thinking of her and here she was. He shot quietly to the front door.

'Kate!' She was the solace he needed, her company the one thing that would help.

'It's awfully late for me to come,' she whispered.

'No, it's fine. Come to the fire and get warm.' Even he could see she was upset. She was telling him then that Mitch McGlory had returned home a broken man, unable to work for weeks, yet another burden for her mother.

Jack tightened his arms round her, though he thought her problems minor compared with his. It allowed him to offer comfort to her and thereby comfort himself too. He told her something of his problems but he made light of them. He didn't mention how ineffective and useless he felt. He didn't need to. Having Kate in his arms chased that away.

'Stay with me tonight,' he urged. He'd heard his landlady retire to her room an hour back. He could take Kate upstairs without her being seen.

'I shouldn't,' Kate whispered, with her head on his shoulder.

'It's very late. Too late for you to go back. Stay here with me.'

He knew she was wavering. 'Mr Halliday will be cross if I get him out of bed.'

'Come on, let me take you upstairs.' For Jack, having Kate with him made him feel a man again.

* * *

126

Kate was in the habit of waking early. On Sunday morning she woke Jack before his landlady was up and about.

'Let's get up,' he whispered, 'I must take you out.'

They went for a walk along Magazine Promenade in the grey light of dawn. The boisterous wind buffeted them and hurried them along, making them hold on to each other.

He was apologetic. 'What have I done? I shouldn't have let you stay the night. I'm sorry.'

She felt euphoric, on top of the world. 'I didn't give you much choice. I came to you. didn't I?'

She'd dared to share his bed, the ultimate sin, and he'd lifted her from the depths of depression to unimaginable heights. She didn't think anybody could make her feel as Jack did.

'It was wonderful,' Jack smiled. 'Best thing that's ever happened to me.'

At nine o'clock he took her back to his lodgings to share his breakfast. His landlady even made extra toast for her.

'I'll have to have another go at Philomena,' he told her. 'I'll have to change her mind. Nothing is going to stop me marrying you.'

Kate glowed. It was what she wanted.

'We're right for each other, Kate. I wish we could get married straight away.'

Kate didn't go home for a whole week, then she began to worry about how her family were managing. She went on Monday afternoon.

Her mother looked ill and exhausted and the house was a chaotic mess. Once again, Tommy hadn't gone to school.

Kate said: 'There's no change then? You're all running round after Mitch?'

'He's not at all well. Go up and see him.'

Mitch was sitting up in bed sipping beer. There were four empty bottles on the floor beside him and his pipe lay against a paper of tobacco.

Mam said by way of excuse, 'He does his best to help. He's good with our Billy.'

Kate didn't think Billy was much trouble. Mam had been given a playpen for Charlie and it had done duty for all the others since, being permanently erected in the corner of the living room. Billy was happy to sit in that, watching through the bars and chuckling at them. He was late learning to walk, and though almost able to do it, he seemed to prefer crawling on his hands and knees.

Kate set about the huge pile of washing that was collecting in the wash house. With Tommy's help, she filled the lines that criss-crossed the back garden before giving up. When she came back indoors, Mam was making a pan of soup and the playpen was empty.

'Where's Billy?'

'Upstairs with Mitch. I told you, he likes to play with him.'

Kate was astounded. 'After what he said about him when he was born?'

'Our Billy's turning out all right, isn't he? A real ray of sunshine. Everybody takes to him. Bundle of fun, that's what he is.'

Kate heard a distant chuckle and Mitch's deeper rumble of mirth. It hardened her heart.

'Why did you have him back, Mam? Why do you run up and down stairs for him? You've enough to do looking after the boys.'

'He's my husband.'

Kate was indignant. 'He was ready to forget that. He stayed away for over three years. You never even heard from him.'

'I thought about him often. I missed him.'

'Or missed his wages? You should have told the hospital he didn't live here any more. You shouldn't have had him back.'

'I love him. You don't understand what love is, Kate.'

Kate thought she did, though what she felt for Jack Courtney was very different from what Mam felt for Mitch. She admired Jack, she didn't think he'd let her down. He was very careful, always considered what was best for her.

As the week wore on, Kate tried to discuss the coming weekend with Jack. She wanted to spend Saturday night with him, but she knew he wouldn't ask her. He was afraid it would be taking advantage. On Friday, she got round to suggesting it herself.

'Everybody at the shop will think I've gone home, and Mam will think I've stayed at the shop. That makes it easy, and even if we can't marry yet, we can be together, enjoy each other's company.'

Jack had beamed at her, she knew he wanted it as much as she did.

On Sunday night, Kate was back at the shop by nine thirty. After spending twenty-four hours in Jack's company, it had been hard to tear herself away. She felt full of fresh air and sunshine. It had been a bright dry day and they'd spent it on the beach at New Brighton. Kate felt they'd had a wonderful weekend.

Monday morning when she had to open the shop at six brought her down to earth. It was on her conscience that she hadn't been home to take Mam the money from her wages. She took the tram home on Monday afternoon. The weather had broken and it was drizzling again. Nobody was outdoors as she approached Cemetery Cottages, but she could see smoke ascending in spirals from the row of chimneys.

She let herself in to number three. Mitch was dozing on one side of the fire and Mam on the other. Tommy was rolling on the floor with Billy; they were laughing together. Tommy leapt to his feet.

'Hello, Kate.'

She put the best part of her wages on the arm of Mam's chair. Mam stirred and smiled. 'Bless you. We've no bread left.'

When Kate looked up, Mitch's intense gaze had fastened on her.

'Thought you'd forgotten where you lived. Your mam was worried about you.'

Kate said: 'She doesn't need my company when she has you.'

'She needs you to give her a hand. You know she's got too much to do. You're her daughter, no reason why not. The wash house is full again.'

'It's raining.'

'You could get it washed for her.'

'I put it to soak in hot water and soda this morning.' Tommy sounded defensive.

Mitch turned on Tommy then. 'You, get down to the shops. Two loaves, and a few beers for me.' He leaned over and scooped Kate's money into his fist.

'No!' Kate spat out. 'Tommy's not buying beer with my money. Give it back.'

'A drop o' beer does me good.' He smirked at her. 'I'm out of tobacco too.'

'It's to be spent on food,' Kate protested. 'Only food. Heaven knows, that's needed in this house. Tell him, Mam.'

'I'll get it myself then. I can walk as far as Upton Road now.'

'No! Give me that money back. It's mine. I earned it, I say what it's to be spent on.'

'Come and get it then.' He pretended to lunge at her and then backed off.

Mam was saying evenly: 'Don't tease her, Mitch.' She ended in a panic-stricken screech. 'Look where you're going.'

Billy was still lying on the floor, smiling up at them. Mitch tripped over him, making the child scream out. Trying to avoid Billy, he twisted and fell sideways over the playpen, catching his chest against the corner. He bounced back and fell across Billy's chubby legs, making him howl even louder.

Kate said: 'You shouldn't play silly tricks. Now look what you've done.'

The coins fell from his fist and rolled across the floor. One half-crown ended up at her feet. She stepped across and pushed Mitch over to free Billy's legs, then picked the child up.

'Where's it hurt, then? Poor Billy.'

She felt his leg, had to prise Billy's fingers away to do it. Tommy was grovelling on the floor after Kate's money.

'Better pay the bill at number six first and bring more milk,' she told him. 'Then get down to the shops for the bread.'

Mam croaked: 'Mitch! Mitch? Are you all right?'

It was only then Kate realised he hadn't moved. His face had gone grey and there was froth in the corner of his mouth. That made her freeze. Her heart was thudding as she thrust Billy into her mother's arms. As she went to him, she heard a gurgling sound from his throat. His eyelids fluttered and opened. Kate started to breathe again. He wasn't dead.

'Help me get him in the chair, Tommy.' She tried to keep her voice calm; she was frightened. Mitch looked really bad and he wasn't breathing properly. He couldn't help himself, but he was a big man and was more than they could manage. Mam had to help too. Tommy brought the chair nearer.

Mam looked panic-stricken. 'What can we give him?'

'Brandy's the thing,' Tommy said. They had nothing like that.

'Tea,' Kate said. 'We all need a cup.' But when Mam held the cup for Mitch, he took only two sips before waving her away.

His eyes fastened again on Kate. His voice was little more than a whisper. 'Your fault . . . Silly bitch. Always crossing me.'

Mam was wringing her hands. Within minutes Mitch seemed barely conscious. His breathing was getting worse. Kate felt on a knife edge. 'Perhaps we should get the doctor. What d'you think, Mam?'

'What good does he ever do?'

When after an hour Mitch didn't look any better, Tommy was sent to fetch him.

Kate could see her mother shaking. Mitch was going blue round his mouth. It was time for her to go back to the shop, but she didn't feel she could leave Mam to cope with him. It bothered her that there was no way she could let Mr Halliday know what had happened. He praised her for being reliable, but this was one time she was going to let him down.

By the time the doctor came, the boys were home from school and squabbling over their tea. He took one look at Mitch and said:

'Hospital. That's the only place for him. I'll arrange for an ambulance to fetch him.'

It was three more hours before it came. Kate was very relieved to see it. Mitch's breathing seemed worse and Mam had worked herself up into a state about how they'd pay for the hospital.

Once he'd gone, and the boys were all ready for bed, Kate said: 'I've got to go back to the shop now, Mam.'

'Oh, Kate! It's late, stay here with me.'

'I've got to, I'm expected to open it at six in the morning. It's my job. I'll come back tomorrow afternoon.'

It was late when Kate reached the shop. The lights were on above it in the Hallidays' parlour. With her heart in her mouth, she knocked on the door and went in. They were drinking cocoa.

'What's this, Kate? Coming in at this hour?' Both looked displeased with her.

'I'm sorry I wasn't back for half four.' She felt overwrought and upset. 'I know I've let you down.'

She told them something of what had happened, referring to Mitch as her father. Just that he'd tripped over the baby and fallen on the corner of his playpen. Mr Halliday's face softened.

'Millie worked on till seven in your place. Thank you for coming back tonight. I was worried about you – afraid something had happened.'

'How is your mother?' Mrs Halliday asked.

'Very upset. I didn't want to leave her. I had to stay. Dad was in a terrible state, and my brothers . . . the older ones were at work.'

Kate went to bed but she couldn't sleep. Mitch's last words were on her mind. He was blaming her for the accident. She kept telling herself it wouldn't have happened if he hadn't taken her money.

'He was only playing with you,' Mam had said. 'Teasing you.' She seemed to blame her too.

Kate had asked: 'Has he been out yet? To the shops?'

'He's been to the pub,' Tommy said. 'He wasn't teasing about that.'

She sighed. 'He asked for all he got, Mam. It's not right to blame me. Why should I buy beer for him when the boys aren't being fed properly? You shouldn't have done it last week, it makes him expect it all the time.'

'He had a little bottle of whisky too, last week,' Tommy piped up.

Mam mopped at her eyes and blew her nose hard. 'He was feeling low.'

'Well, we're all feeling low now.'

Kate was on tenterhooks all morning in the shop. Jack came to buy his newspaper as usual, and was sympathetic when she told him what had happened, but she only had a few minutes with him. He always went when other customers came in. She couldn't talk in front of them anyway.

She was anxious; she wanted to know what was happening. When she went home after dinner, her mother wasn't there, but the washing was blowing on the line. Ada Catchpole was looking after Billy and said: 'Your mam's gone down to the Borough Hospital to see Mitch, and Tommy went to school.'

She saw most of her money still in two little piles on the mantelpiece and took some. She wheeled Billy in his ancient pram down to the shops and bought liver and onions for their dinner. She came back and peeled potatoes and chopped cabbage. She didn't know what else to do that would help.

She hoped Mam would be home before she had to catch the tram back to the shop. She kept going to the window to look down the cart track. At last she saw her coming, her shawl-covered head bent against the wind. She was walking very slowly.

'He's no better.' She looked really downcast as she eased off her boots. 'Can't breathe. On oxygen now.'

'He's worse?'

Mam lowered herself on to the old basket chair. 'I think he's failing.'

Kate swallowed. 'Going to die, you mean?'

Mam was nodding slowly. 'I'm afraid he is.'

Kate put an arm round her mother's shoulders and hugged her, but she could find no words of comfort.

The following morning, Jack pressed four guineas into her hand when she was giving him his change for his newspaper.

'I hate to see you worrying about hospital bills,' he told her. 'This will help.'

'I don't know whether we'll have to pay or not. Mitch had something deducted from his wages to cover the doctor, but he's had him a lot and been in hospital recently, and . . .'

'I want you to take it. Your mother can spend it on other things if not the hospital.'

Kate went home to give Mam the money that afternoon and found her sitting in the basket chair with her apron over her head. Billy was curled up asleep in his playpen.

'Mam?'

The apron came down. Mam's face was woebegone.

'How is he?'

'Died in the night, he did.'

'Oh my goodness!' She lifted her mother's cold hand between both of her own and squeezed it. For herself, she felt shock but not grief. Mitch wouldn't be a trouble to any of them ever again.

'I've already been down to see him and collect the things he had with him.' She was tearful. 'There's going to be a post-mortem.'

Kate put the four guineas Jack had given her into Mam's hand. Her fingers closed round it.

'Where'd you get this?'

'From Jack. He wants to help.'

Mam sniffed. 'Him? I told you what I think of him. He scares me.'

'He's all right, Mam. Don't worry.'

'I'll not say no to his money. There'll be the funeral to pay for now. Thank him for me.'

Kate went back to work in the shop but she visited her mother every afternoon. Mam talked of arranging a fine funeral for Mitch: a hearse and two carriages, each pulled by four black stallions wearing black ostrich plumes on their heads.

Kate added testily: 'I'm sure he'd like the best oak coffin that money can buy. Brass handles too.'

'And ten of those mutes,' her mother said dreamily. 'You know, those professional mourners.'

When it came to the point, she chose the cheapest coffin she could get, and said it was to be a walking funeral.

'We've got a grave already.' Mam was looking better now. 'We bought one when baby Liza died. There's room for him in that. Room for me too, when my time comes.'

'Mam! Don't say such things.'

'I'm only telling you, so you know. No point in buying another plot, is there?'

For Kate, it made everything harder because Mam was so testy with her.

The post-mortem showed that a rib, broken in the accident when the tunnel collapsed on him, had not knitted together sufficiently when he fell on it again. This time it had pierced his lung.

The Hallidays spent a good deal of their time at the Quaker Mission Hall, where, amongst other things, they strove to ease the burdens of the poor. Mostly this meant poor Quakers, but over many months the congregation had collected mourning clothes that were too fancy for a

133

Quaker to wear, and these were now offered to Kate.

'People give them to us because they know we only wear only black.' Mrs Halliday's fingers caressed a black satin bow. 'But there's too many pin tucks and frills on these.'

There were two black crêpe and bombazine dresses for deepest mourning, and a black silk for half-mourning that was meant to be worn after eighteen months. Everything was of good quality and quite fashionable, and there were even black silk underskirts with frills. The Hallidays meant her to wear the clothes to show decent respect for her father.

Kate wasn't going to grieve for Mitch McGlory and didn't want to wear them. She had black skirts to wear in the shop and wore white blouses with them as a compromise. She made the excuse that the mourning clothes fitted her mother much better than they did her. In them, Mam looked smarter than she had for years. She was very pleased with them.

Mitch's body was brought from the hospital mortuary to the chapel of rest in Flaybrick Hill Cemetery. It was very handy that they lived so close.

Kate was given the afternoon off for the funeral. She'd never seen all her family looking clean and tidy at one time. Apart from the neighbours, there were very few other mourners. She found the funeral hard to bear. To see Liza's grave opened up and Mitch's coffin being lowered into it caught at her throat. She lifted her eyes to the Cemetery Cottages, so near, but lost in the trees on the other side of the wall.

The funeral tea was easier. They were all relieved to have the worst behind them. Apart from family, only Ada, Ratty and the Wattses came. They rarely had such a good spread on the table: ham, tongue and pickles, blancmange and good rich fruit cake. They all did it justice.

Kate wished Mitch McGlory hadn't come back. If the accident hadn't left him in need of nursing, she doubted he would have done, but she didn't want to say that to Mam. It would have upset her more. His return and death had churned them all up. They were all a bit weepy and more emotional. Even Kate was.

Kate went on spending her weekends with Jack. She felt she needed to if she was to get back on an even keel. He was used to seeing her in his rooms now, and they both accepted that it was the best place to spend wet afternoons and evenings.

It was Jack who advised her: 'Go with your mother to see his employers. If he had an accident while he was working, they have some responsibility to her. Get an extra copy of his death certificate and give it to them.'

Kate did so. They immediately paid over the week's wages they always kept in hand for their employees and said there might be compensation when their insurance claim was settled.

When Mam calmed down a little, she remembered she had a paid-up insurance policy on Mitch's life. That eventually paid twelve pounds, and another thirty-five came as compensation from his employers. Lena was delighted, and provided another good ham tea.

'A nice little nest egg from Mitch after all.' She smiled. 'It should see us through until our Tommy can get a job.'

Chapter Twelve

1913–1914

In the last months of 1913, Kate found herself beset with problems.

Mitch's death had left her family feeling unsettled and on edge, and it had taken many months for things to settle down.

She knew that for her, it was easier because she was engrossed in her job. Mr Halliday was leaving the ordering of stock to her, and she felt she was doing well.

And of course, she had Jack. Lying in his arms helped her forget everything, but Jack had problems that wouldn't go away. His problems became hers.

He'd told her that his father had been giving him an allowance since the Liscard office had closed, that was over a year ago. But Kate didn't think it reasonable to think of marrying again on just an allowance.

Jack didn't seem to care how much he spent. He said money was to be used and he lavished gifts on her: an elegant coat, far too smart for a shop assistant, then a soft leather handbag and some gloves. Kate had been brought up to think money must be made to stretch as far as possible. When he wanted to buy her a silk umbrella she tried to stop him. He insisted. But she couldn't see any sort of a normal life for them unless he had a job.

When he told her his allowance was five hundred a year, she couldn't believe her ears. It seemed a prodigious sum.

Her mouth opened. 'That's far more than . . .'

She'd been about to say: *you could ever hope to earn*, but she understood enough of Jack now to know he'd find that belittling.

'More than what?' He was looking at her anxiously.

'More than I expected. That's ten pounds a week.' She was earning twenty-two shillings now and thought that good.

'It doesn't go all that far,' Jack sighed.

Then one afternoon when he was walking her back to the shop, he spoke of resenting the time they had to spend apart.

'I hate leaving you on the doorstep,' he told her. 'I've too much time on my hands now I have no job. I don't like being on my own, I'm bored.'

Kate couldn't imagine Jack doing an ordinary job; he didn't seem cut out for work. It started her thinking about the things he might do.

'You're keen on photography, good at it too. You'd enjoy doing something with that.'

Jack perked up. 'If only I could.'

'Newspapers use photographs now. More and more. Hardly any drawings. Just the job for a gentleman like you.'

Jack pulled her to a halt. She could see from his face that he was interested.

'But here in Liscard? I'd have to go where the news is being made. London perhaps? I wouldn't want to, not leave you. I couldn't do that.'

Kate smiled, flattered that he didn't want to leave her. 'Could you make postcards from local views?'

'Yes.' He puckered his forehead in thought. 'But where would I sell them?'

'To shopkeepers. I've seen them in newsagents in New Brighton.'

'I'd need a lot of shopkeepers to do it. To make any sort of a profit.'

'I could ask Mr Halliday. He has five shops.'

But Jack was pursing his lips.

Kate thought hard. Part of the problem was that what she would consider a good living seemed a paltry amount to Jack.

'What about running a photography shop?'

'I don't know anything about shops.'

'You could sell cameras, develop other people's films. You know all about that sort of thing.'

'How clever you are, Kate.'

'Where do you buy what you need? For taking photographs?'

'A shop in Liverpool.'

'But there aren't many. What about one this side of the water?'

'It's a good idea.'

'It's a great idea.'

It would give him something to do that would interest him. Kate thought that without that, there could be no self-respect for a man. She thought the allowance he had from his father very generous. If he were to hand that over to her, she knew they could live very well. But he was used to having money, and he didn't think five hundred a year was a lot. A shop would add to it.

Jack said slowly: 'But I'd need capital to start a shop. I don't have any.'

Jack had terrible twinges of conscience. He knew he wasn't treating Kate fairly. He'd told her he'd see Philomena again and really press her about the divorce. Things like that were so easy to say, and he did mean them. It was just that when he was eating his breakfast in the cold light of day, he couldn't see any reason for Philomena to change her mind. She'd just humiliate him again, so he put off going to see her.

Recently, he hadn't been so careful about what his landlady saw. Kate was coming to his rooms more often and staying for meals. They were spending the weekends together. She'd said several times she didn't feel comfortable with his landlady, that she thought Mrs Gilley considered her a fallen women.

This morning, Mrs Gilley had referred to Kate as his paramour. He hadn't liked that. He knew he shouldn't let Kate come, but what was the alternative?

He thought his best plan would be to change his lodgings. Other rooms would not be impossible to find. He could buy Kate a wedding ring and introduce her as his wife. She could give Halliday some story about getting married and stay with him every night. That wouldn't be a problem if he took rooms within walking distance of the shop.

Just to think about it made Jack feel better. He talked about it to Kate. He even suggested she might stop working for Halliday, since the pay hardly made it worthwhile.

'I can't stop working.' Kate was aghast. She felt she was lucky to have such a job. 'Live on you? Not unless I was your wife.'

Jack did get as far as looking at the lodgings advertised in the local paper, but the rooms he had were very comfortable. Somehow he didn't get round to moving.

During the first days of 1914 he noticed that Kate wasn't looking well. She seemed quiet, had less to say. They were spending more time walking along the promenade and visiting New Brighton. He wanted to buy tickets for the Floral Pavilion, but she turned the outing down.

He was afraid Kate was growing tired of his company and didn't know how to tell him. It went on for another two weeks before he plucked up the courage to ask:

'What's the matter, Kate?'

He could see her lip trembling. Her eyes wouldn't meet his. She looked really washed out. 'I think I'm having a baby.'

It had happened! Jack felt the strength drain from his legs. He'd been telling himself for months that he was a fool to risk this. It was a shock all the same. Guilt poured over him like a waterfall. He'd taken advantage of Kate. It was she who would have to bear the brunt of this. He could see she was worried stiff about it.

He hadn't realised he'd covered his face with his hands until Kate was lifting them away. He could see utter terror in her green eyes. He reached for her, folded his arms round her.

'Kate, love!' She felt stiff, resistant. Usually her body moulded itself to his. 'What can I say?'

Her voice was stiff too. 'You're upset it's happened? You don't like the idea?'

'I'm upset for you. I shouldn't have let it. You've known for some time? You didn't want to tell me?'

'I was afraid to.'

'Why? Why, Kate?'

She was whispering into his shirt. 'Afraid you'll walk away. Want no more to do with me.'

'Oh, no!' His arms tightened round her. 'I love you, Kate. I want you here with me all the time. I blame myself for this.'

'No . . .'

'I pressed you . . . I'm older, more experienced, I should have had more self-control.'

'You mustn't blame . . .'

'I should have known it would happen, sooner or later.' He felt anguished. He loved Kate, and wanted her to have the best of everything, but instead he'd brought this trouble on her.

'I've let things drag on for years . . . done nothing. How long have we known each other?'

'Four years since . . . the tram.'

'Five or more since I started coming to the shop. You've been so patient with me. What are you going to do?'

He saw the tears start to her eyes and corrected himself: 'What are *we* going to do about it?'

Kate shook her head. He gave her his handkerchief, sat her down in his best armchair. Poured her a glass of sherry and put it beside her. It gave him a moment to pull himself together and think.

'You can't go on working now. Getting up at six in the morning.'

'I'm all right at the moment.' Kate blew her nose. Her eyes were red and frightened.

'I want you to come and live with me. I'll look after you.'

'Come here, you mean?'

He had meant that, but he thought of Mrs Gilley's attitude.

'We can find somewhere else. You can help me choose.' He had to put Kate's welfare above his own convenience now.

'I'll take care of you as well as any husband, I promise. I'll be a good father when the time comes.'

'I wish it hadn't happened like this.'

'You should have told me the moment you knew, not worried yourself.'

'I wasn't sure, you see . . . I just thought that perhaps . . . I've had visions of . . . Well, you know, Mr Halliday putting me out. Of being sent to the workhouse.'

'Oh, Kate! You mustn't worry like that, you'll make yourself ill. I'm sorry it's happened.' He really wasn't. He knew he'd never have changed anything if this hadn't forced his hand.

'We'll be a happy family, you'll see. It's what I've always wanted.'

Kate washed her face and he took her out to stroll along the prom. She was very anxious that her eyes shouldn't be red and puffy when she went back to the shop.

For once, Jack refused to leave her thirty yards from the door.

'No point in hiding the fact that we're keeping company any more.' He went in behind her and bought an evening paper. He felt forced into action. He'd find new rooms. Rooms where Kate would be happy.

He took the paper back to his rooms and read all the advertisements for lodgings and rooms to rent. He ticked three that sounded hopeful and then went out to look at them. He was going to change. He was going to be a man of action. He didn't want Kate to be disappointed in him.

The first one, in Zig Zag Road, was what he was looking for; he needed to search no further.

'For myself and my wife,' he told the landlady. She was younger than Mrs Gilley, gentler in manner, with soft brown hair. He hoped Kate would take to her. She would provide three meals a day for them and clean their rooms.

'I have to give a week's notice on my present rooms; we shall move in next week.'

He paid two weeks' rent in advance. They were to have three rooms and a bathroom, the whole of the upstairs of a terraced house that was within ten minutes' walk of the shop. The furnishings were of reasonable quality. The biggest room had been turned into a parlour and the other two were furnished as bedrooms.

Jack felt better. He'd achieved something. The other thing he should have done long ago was to see his father. Tell him about Kate and see if he'd offer a somewhat larger allowance so he could afford to keep her. Perhaps he'd be prepared to help him set up as a photographer? He had to find out now if the offer Father had made was still open.

He should have done that long ago too. He couldn't remember how long it was since Kate had suggested the idea. Jack turned round immediately, deciding to go and see his father straight away. He stepped out briskly, not allowing himself time to think, in case his courage should fail him. He had to do it for Kate's sake now.

The Grange looked beautiful in the last of the evening sun. Square and solid in the Queen Anne style, it looked gracious and comfortable. The rooms he'd thought adequate half an hour ago seemed impossibly poor and cramped by comparison.

Oscar was the first person he saw. 'What a surprise! To what do we owe the honour of your company?'

'Is Father in?'

'Yes.'

All the family had gathered to have a pre-dinner drink in the drawing room. Jack said when he went in: 'I'd like a word with you, Father. If you don't mind.' His mother was stretched out on the sofa as usual. He went over to kiss her cheek.

'How are you, Mother?'

'As well as can be expected, dear. We're just going to have dinner.'

His sister-in-law Constance asked: 'Have you eaten? Would you like to join us?'

Jack had forgotten it was dinner time. 'Yes, if it's no trouble.'

She got to her feet and gave the bell pull a tug. When Minnie, the parlourmaid, came, she said, 'Set another place at the table for Mr Jack.'

He preferred Constance to Ottilie. Neither went out of their way to be kind to him; it was hunger or greed that had prompted Constance to act. She was fond of her food and her figure showed it. Ottilie, Leo's wife, had cold, hostile eyes and the lines round them were becoming more noticeable.

'Do you not change for dinner these days?' She was looking down her nose at his flannels.

Jack noticed for the first time that they'd all changed. It made him feel uncomfortable. Leo's hair was still damp from his bath.

He felt even more uncomfortable when, over the soup, his father asked:

'What is it you want, Jack?'

He had to say: 'I'd like to speak to you alone. If that's all right.'

It made them stare at him, but he couldn't admit at the table, in front of them all, that he'd got Kate pregnant.

There was a long silence, nothing but the chink of knives and forks. He was relieved when Leo started talking about the business. It was what they always did, and it had the usual effect of making him feel out on a limb and a complete ass. All the get-up-and-go he'd had earlier in the evening melted away like butter on hot toast.

Father thought of this as an informal meal, but to Jack it wasn't. It dragged on through four courses. He was beginning to feel mesmerised by the wine and the twinkling light from the chandelier. Father suddenly threw his napkin on his cheese plate, poured himself another glass of port and stood up.

'Come on, Jack, we'd better go to my study for this talk you want.' Once there, he stood on the hearthrug, legs apart, his back to the fire. 'I'm glad you came to see us. Ottilie has come up with something you could do.'

Jack felt his spirits sink. He didn't expect to be pleased with anything Ottilie suggested.

'You tell me what's on your mind first. What's brought you here?'

Jack felt he'd lost the impetus he'd had when he'd first arrived. It was only the memory of Kate's tear-stained face that got him going.

'I'm in trouble.' He told his father about Kate expecting his baby.

'Jack! We can't have a scandal. Bad for the business. Who is this woman? Is she someone we know?'

'She's Benedict Rotherfield's daughter.'

'Benedict Rotherfield? Yes, I remember now.' Jack saw his father's eyebrows go up. 'You mean by that lover he had? The one he murdered his wife for?'

'Yes, Father.'

'Good Lord! You can certainly pick them. Wasn't she a housemaid?'

Jack ignored that. 'Kate doesn't know what her father did. If you ever meet her, you mustn't mention him.'

'Good gracious! How did they keep that from her?'

'She's a lovely girl. You'd like her, Father.' He took a deep breath. 'I want to marry her.'

His father grunted with displeasure. 'Jack! You can't, you've already got a wife. I hoped you'd come with some ideas about how you could support yourself. And here you are in another mess, wanting to take on more responsibilities and . . .'

'I have ideas too, Father. I've been thinking very carefully about that. Of course I want to support Kate and the baby. I've decided I'd like to be a photographer. I want a shop where customers can come to have their portraits taken. I'd make my own postcards of local views, develop amateur film, sell cameras, that sort of a thing.'

Jack could see his father looking at him with more respect. 'I'm glad you don't want to stay a remittance man for the rest of your life. Photography, eh? You might make a success of that. Yes, I'm pleased . . . I'm glad you've thought of something. You won't make any fortune, but I needn't be ashamed of what you do.'

Jack knew he was offering Kate's ideas as his own. It didn't matter, Father need never find that out. The main thing was to get him to help.

'I'll need capital to set it up,' he began.

'I'd be prepared to find that for you if . . . Jack, you know your mother has this idea about Baden-Baden?'

It was the first Jack had heard of it. He said so.

Father's patience went. 'Well, what do you expect? You hardly ever come near us. Only when you want something for yourself. Your mother's got it into her head that it's the only thing that will improve her health. She wants to take the waters there.'

'It might help,' Jack said.

'So might Buxton, or even Bath, but she won't hear of those. She's set her mind on going to Baden-Baden. Ottilie thought you might like to escort her there.'

'Me?'

'She can't go alone. One of us will have to go with her. It's a man's job, Jack, and the rest of us have work to keep us here. What about it?'

'She'll want to stay?'

'Yes, of course. She's thinking of two to three months.'

'But Kate is . . . I don't want to leave her when . . .'

'It can be fitted round that, I'm sure. Look, I'll provide you with the capital you need in return for this.'

'All right then.' What else could he say? Father had always been generous with money. 'Thank you, Father.'

'We all want to see you make something of yourself. I wouldn't let you starve, you know that, but it's better for us all if you stand on your own feet. Where were you thinking of having this shop?'

'Liscard . . .'

'No! Centre of New Brighton. Better still, centre of Birkenhead, or even Liverpool.'

'There is already such a shop in Renshaw Street.'

143

'Don't go anywhere near that, then. Look for a main road position. That's important for trade. You'd better see what's on the market.'

Jack watched his father rubbing his hands together. For once he was not displeased with him.

'So you want to marry this woman and set up as a photographer?'

'Well, yes, but Philomena's refused to give me a divorce.'

'Did you go to see her?'

'Yes, some time ago. I told her I wanted to marry Kate. Did my best to persuade her. She was adamant, said there was nothing in it for her.'

'For goodness' sake, Jack.' His father was impatient with him again. 'Why didn't you come to me and let me handle it? I'll let Philomena know what's in it for her; she'll have to agree. I'll write to her today.

'I'll tell her I'll stop her allowance unless she does. The law doesn't require me to pay her anything, I do it out of the goodness of my heart. The law requires you to pay, but as you don't have any money, she can't get blood out of a stone.

'I've been meaning to write to her. Henry will be due to start on the *Conway* in September. Did you see him too?'

'Yes, both the boys are well and growing up fast.'

'As long as she's not spoiling them. We'll have them in the business as soon as they're old enough. I hope she's talking to Henry about the *Conway*. I've had their names down for years.'

'I think she sees it as a good opportunity, Father. She wants them to go.'

'It'll weaken her hold once they leave home. I should have insisted on a boarding prep school for them long ago. I hope you're not making a mistake with this new lass.'

'I'm not, Father. I know I'm not.'

'No scandal now. We can't have anything like that, and you're to take your mother to Baden-Baden.'

Jack had a spring in his step as he set out to buy his newspaper the next morning. He had to wait a moment while Kate served another customer. He thought she looked quite strained.

'I've made good progress,' he whispered as he handed over his coins. He smiled, proud to be able to tell her he'd achieved so much.

'I've taken better lodgings in Zig Zag Road. Paid the deposit and given notice to Mrs Gilley. I'll take you to see them this afternoon.'

A radiant smile lit up Kate's face.

'And I've spoken to my father, He's willing to help set me up in a photography shop.'

'Wonderful.'

'On top of that, I think Philomena is going to agree to a divorce. I've got things sorted.'

'You certainly have.' Kate's green eyes were sparkling up at him. 'I'm absolutely delighted.

'That's the good news. Father wants me to take my mother to Baden-Baden, and that's not so good.'

Chapter Thirteen

For Kate, the rest of the morning passed in a whirl. She felt she was walking on air. She'd been desperately worried when she first found out she was pregnant. Now she knew she need not have been. Jack wasn't going to let her down. In fact, the news had fired him to achieve everything that was needed very quickly.

He was waiting at the shop door for her when she went out after her dinner.

'I want you to give in your notice here. You can't go on working now. Besides, I need you with me.'

Kate felt bubbly with excitement. 'I'll be able to help you run your shop when you get it. You'll have to teach me all about cameras and film, but I do know about shops.'

'I've already thought of that. Your expertise and mine, they'll fit together. We'll make a success of this.'

'Such good news today.' She took his arm, feeling his mood didn't quite match hers.

'Not all of it. I've agreed to take Mother to Baden-Baden for her health. It was a condition of Father giving me the capital for my shop.'

'That doesn't sound too bad.'

'I'd have to leave you, Kate. For around three months.'

Kate shivered. 'Is it to separate us? Is that why? Is it me they don't like?'

'No, nothing like that. Mother really wants to go. Believes it's the only way she'll get her health back.'

'I don't like the idea either, but you have to do things for your family too. It's only right.'

Jack was relieved. Philomena now, she'd have told him he should have refused. Constance had young children, but Ottilie's were at boarding school. There was no reason why she couldn't go. He'd have thought she'd want to. Jack wasn't sure he could cope with his mother or all those train connections.

'When?' Kate asked.

'Not yet. In the summer, when the weather's better. I'm to see about the shop first.'

'That's all right then.'

Jack smiled. 'Let's start by getting you a wedding ring. I want us to look like a married couple when we move into these new digs. I do hope you'll like them.'

He took her to the best jeweller's in Liscard, where wedding rings were brought to the counter for her inspection.

'Which one will you have?' Jack asked. 'These are all twenty-two carat.'

The jeweller slipped one on her finger. 'To get your size, miss.'

He sorted through his stock and arranged half a dozen in front of her, some narrow, some wider. 'These will fit your finger.'

Jack picked up the widest and the heaviest. 'I like this one. Try it.' He slid it on her finger.

Kate smiled. 'It's lovely.' It was the sort of wedding ring he'd choose for a real wife.

The jeweller took it from her finger, put it in a little box and wrapped it up. He seemed to think it would be put back on her finger in church.

Jack walked her a hundred yards up the road before taking it out again. He held her left hand while he slid it slowly on to her finger.

'I want you to know, Kate, that I love you very much.' He kissed her cheek in the street, in full daylight. 'I promise I'll make this legal as soon as I can.'

Kate looked with misty eyes at the ring on her finger. She was too full of emotion to speak. She felt she could push her fears behind her for good. Jack had been tested and had done more than she'd expected.

She was excited when they reached Zig Zag Road. She liked the look of the house; liked the look of Mrs Scott, the new landlady, when she was introduced. It was the first time she'd heard herself addressed as Mrs Courtney, and it sent a little quivers of pleasure down her spine.

When Jack led the way upstairs, she shot from room to room, filled with delight.

'We've even got a bedroom for the baby.'

'I don't think the parlour is quite as good as the one I have now.' Jack put his head on one side to consider. 'My own furniture will cheer it up. Mrs Scott has agreed to take some of her things out to make room.'

'The grate's very small.' Kate went over to the tiny Victorian iron fireplace. 'But of course, this was meant to be a bedroom.'

Jack stared at it. 'I hadn't noticed. I hope we'll be warm enough when winter comes.'

'It isn't just that . . . It isn't very big to cook on. Hardly room for one saucepan, and no trivet or oven.'

Jack laughed. 'You won't have to cook on it, love! Mrs Scott will cook our meals downstairs and serve them here on this table. She'll do the cleaning too. These are lodgings, not just rooms.'

'Jack! You don't have to pay for someone to cook and clean. If I'm coming to live here with you, I'll be able to do that.'

'No, I don't want you to work. Not if you're expecting a child. You can't possibly. Too much for you.'

Kate thought of what her mother had had to do, what most women had to do, but Jack came from a different class and he didn't expect his womenfolk to work.

'I won't know what to do with myself all day.'

'As soon as we're settled in here, you can help me look for the right shop. Then it will need setting up. You'll have more than enough to do helping me get that organised.'

'It's not just that,' she said quietly. 'I give my mother most of my wages. She couldn't manage without.'

'What, every week? I didn't realise . . .'

'I get everything found at the shop. The food is good, I don't need to buy much.'

'Clothes?' He looked surprised, shocked even.

'You're giving me so many things. More than I'd ever be able to buy with my own wages.'

Kate saw Jack's mouth tighten. 'Here am I, taking from my parents, while you're giving to yours . . . You're a much better person. Very generous.'

She smiled. 'But you do see why I have to go on working?'

'No, I don't. How much do you give your mother?'

'Eighteen shillings a week. I'm paid twenty-two.' She was proud of that. It was a good wage, seeing she was getting her keep too.

'I'll pay you an allowance of twenty-five shillings a week. You can continue to give your mother just as much.'

'That's, let me see . . . sixty-five pounds a year! You'll be paying my keep too.'

Jack wouldn't look at her.

'Can you afford it?'

'Yes.' It sounded like a confession. 'I told my father about you, and he increased my allowance.'

Kate drew in a long, slow breath. Things were very different for Jack.

'I do admire you,' he said, squeezing her hand. 'You're standing on your own feet. Helping your family too, while I . . .'

But she knew Jack found the amount she earned so small as not to be worth the effort she put into earning it. Money had a very different value for him.

They were back outside the Hallidays' shop. Kate sensed Jack's dismay as she removed her new ring.

He said seriously: 'I want you to stop working here. Tell Mr Halliday now, so you can work out your notice. I want you to keep that ring on your finger all the time.'

'What reason shall I give?' Kate wondered.

'Tell him you're going to get married.'

Kate thought it over all that night. The Hallidays would never believe she'd want to leave immediately to get married. They'd expect her to say she was engaged first, and then wait a year or so to collect her bottom drawer. If she was going to tell a lie, she decided it had better be a believable one. The following day, when Mr Halliday came into the shop, she was wondering how to broach the subject. Out of the blue, he asked after her family, and it gave her the opening she wanted.

'My mother's very low. Losing . . . Father suddenly like that. She's not over it, finding things hard.'

'Yes, I'm sure. It can't be easy for her.'

'She's not very well and not coping with the children. She keeps asking me to stay at home with her to help. Pleads with me. I've been thinking it over. I think I'd better give in my notice . . .'

'Kate, no! Isn't there some other way? I don't want to lose you.'

'I'm her only daughter. I feel I should. She's nobody else now.'

She watched him straighten up and accept it. 'If you're sure? I'd better start looking for a replacement then. Millie's too young. It won't be easy, Kate. I'll be sorry to see you go.'

Kate sighed. Millie had heard them talking, so she knew the situation, but there was still Josie Oaks. She'd tell her at dinner time. It came to her then, with a sting of guilt, that she'd have to tell her mother that she was leaving too.

She wasn't going home nearly as much as she used to, but she knew that if anything went wrong, Mam would send Tommy along to let her know. If she moved out without telling her and that happened, it would be embarrassing all round. Even worse, Mam would have no way of getting in touch with her.

She talked it over with Jack. He agreed that her mother would have to know.

'Get it over with as soon as you can. You'll feel better when you have. Do you want me to come with you?'

Kate shook her head. 'Better if I go alone.'

She made up her mind that on Friday, when she'd been paid, she'd go home and see Mam. She'd tell her she was moving in with Jack and that she was expecting his baby. Get it all over at once. She was dreading it, but she'd have to do it.

On Friday morning, Mr Halliday asked her if she'd work for a few more days. He'd found a man to replace her but he wasn't starting until Monday and Mr Halliday wanted Kate to show him what his duties were. Be with him for the first few mornings.

She had to agree; it would have been churlish not to.

Kate felt very much on edge as she walked up the cart track, trying to work out how she would break the news to her mother. When she let herself in to the kitchen, Mam's arms were covered with flour halfway up to her elbows. She was making a huge suet pudding.

'Got to have something to fill the boys up. This will stick to their ribs.'

She thought Mam was looking better. It was a long time since she'd seen her cooking like this.

'Make a pot of tea, Kate. The kettle's boiling. I meant it for this pudding but there's probably enough for both.'

Automatically Kate did as she was told. She was struggling for words that wouldn't come. Billy came rushing across to her to throw his arms round her waist. She bent down to kiss him and his arms went round her neck. He was four now, and heavy for his age. He snuggled against her. He was always happy and he followed Mam around all day.

Kate sat down and he climbed up on her knee. She wished there was an easy way to tell her mother. She had to get it over before the boys came home from school. She couldn't look at Mam, had to bury her face in Billy's shirt as she said:

'I've given in my notice at Halliday's.'

'What! What d'you mean?'

Kate stole a glance, Mam's mouth hung open, the pudding forgotten. 'I'm giving up work.'

'You can't . . . What on earth for?'

Kate went on quietly. 'I'm going to live with Jack Courtney. He's taken new lodgings. This will be my address from Wednesday.'

She took the slip of paper from her pocket on which she'd written it out. Slid it down beside the cups.

'Live with him?' Her voice was heavy with suspicion. 'Isn't he going to marry you first?'

Kate could hardly get the words out. 'He's already married. To someone else.'

She'd known her mother would be shocked, but she hadn't expected such a screech of horror. 'You never told me that!'

Kate swallowed, watching her mother struggle for breath. Lena turned on her furiously.

'Have you taken leave of your senses? You must think about it first. Think very carefully.'

'I have, Mam.'

'He'll get you into trouble. In the family way. Then what'll you do?'

Kate took a deep breath. 'He already has. That's why I'm doing it. Better before it shows.'

'Oh! Oh, Kate!' Her mother collapsed on the basket chair and threw her apron over her head. For once Mam didn't notice she was putting flour all over the cushions.

Kate felt desperate. 'It happened to you, I know . . .'

Mam snatched her apron away angrily. 'And it's the last thing I wanted to happen to you. You won't find happiness. Not this way, I've told you that before. Why didn't you listen? No decent man will look at you after this.'

'You don't understand, Mam. Jack and I love each other. I don't want any other man.'

'I understand all right.' Mam's face had gone purple. 'It won't last. Nothing is for keeps in this world.'

'Don't say that!'

'He'll get tired of you, find somebody else, and then what will you do?'

'He won't.'

'You'll have no security. He could leave you with a child to bring up on your own and you won't know where your next penny's coming from.'

'That can happen when you're married, Mam. It's happened to you.'

'All the love in the world won't do you any good then. It can turn to hate.'

'Jack won't leave me.' Kate was certain of that now. 'He really loves me, Mam. He's asked his wife for a divorce, and we'll be married once that comes through.' She'd added that to placate her mother, but her renewed ferocity made Kate draw back.

'Don't let him do that!' Mam pushed her face closer; it was ugly with fear. 'Don't let him ask for a divorce. That can makes things a thousand times worse.'

After what seemed an age, Lena got to her feet and poured the tea. She couldn't say that this had come out of the blue, because Kate had told her about Jack Courtney. Since then, she'd feared this. Not that it made it any less of a shock.

She was desperately worried about Kate. Wasn't this exactly what had happened to Lena herself? Swept off her feet by a toff. Kate was out of her depth just as she had been, and was following the same downward path.

Lena gulped at her tea and said: 'You think I don't know anything about love.' Kate's innocent young face told her she was right about that.

'Let me tell you, I thought I'd have your father's love for ever. He told me I would. Promised me he'd look after us both. Nurture, he called it. He used to say: "I'll nurture you both, always."

'I wanted him to get a divorce from his wife, Kate. I wanted to marry him more than anything else in this world.

'He said to me: "I want it too, for myself and for you, but most of all I want it for our child. I want her to grow up strong. I want her to have a stable and loving family. I want her to have the best from life."

'He smiled at me then. "She already had the best mother. I'll see she has the best teachers. She'll inherit my business. Perhaps I can teach her to run it. Most of all I want her to enjoy her life." '

'He said that about me?' Kate's face was soft with wonder.

'You looked like him then; your hair grew more flame-coloured each day. He used to walk round the house with you in his arms.

' "Love is the most precious gift for a child," he'd say. "Katherine needs to grow up feeling love all round her. But I know she will, I have only to open the door of this house to feel it. There's warmth, a feeling of happiness. You radiate love, Lena. That's it. You beam love all round you, in the way a lighthouse beams light.

' "That's your talent. You'll always have it, however old you grow." '

'Did he say that?' Kate had a look of wonder on her face. 'I feel like that about you too. And so do the boys . . .'

Lena collapsed on to a chair. She felt deflated. 'But it didn't last. I was absolutely certain it would, but I was wrong, it didn't. Oh, Kate, I'm so afraid it'll go wrong for you too.'

'Mam, he couldn't help leaving you. Not when he died in that riding accident. You'd have been all right if it hadn't been for that.'

Lena stiffened with dismay. A riding accident? Where had she got that idea? But anything was better than the truth.

'He did, didn't he?'

She didn't want to talk about Benedict's death. She felt for her handkerchief, blew her nose. What was the use of crying? It didn't help with troubles like these. When she looked up, Kate's green eyes were studying her.

'Tell me, Mam. Tell me about my father. I want to know everything about him.'

Kate didn't understand that she couldn't do that. There were things it would be better if she didn't know. And anyway, the pain had made Lena lock all that away inside her years ago. She simply couldn't.

Kate asked again, pleaded, demanded to be told about Benedict Rotherfield. Then, when the boys came home from school, she left early, full of frustration, saying they'd only go on like this, not getting any further. Kate had made up her mind about Jack Courtney, what they were going to do, and nothing Lena could say was going to change that.

Lena felt the rift between them widening. She was afraid it would get worse; already they were having less contact than they used to.

She said: 'Come over the weekend, Kate. Come and spend Saturday night with me like you used to.'

Kate shook her head. 'It wouldn't do any good, if you won't talk about my father.'

'I wish you'd come home for good. You'll be all right with me. What does one more mouth matter here?'

That got Kate's back up. 'You won't change my mind about living with Jack. Better if I don't come. We'll only go through all this again.'

Lena felt so bad, she left the boys eating their tea and came up to lie on her bed. She brought Billy with her. He was so much easier to cope with than Kate.

She wished now she hadn't told Kate what Benedict had said about love shining out of her. It was romantic nonsense. That hadn't stood the test of time either. She'd never been able to get close to Kate. Ben would have been disappointed that she'd done so little for her. Shown so little of what she felt.

Kate worked in the shop that evening like an automaton. She hadn't expected Mam to approve of what she was doing, but at the same time she hadn't expected her to flare up as she had. Mam had said enough to prove she remembered everything about her father very clearly, but then she'd clammed up and refused to say any more. Kate shivered. She'd sensed her mother was afraid. But afraid of what?

When the shop closed, Kate wanted Jack. She wanted the comfort of his arms. She walked up to the new lodgings in Zig Zag Road that would soon be her home. He'd told her he'd be moving in the last of his belongings and his furniture that afternoon.

She had a key and let herself in. It came as a shock to find he wasn't there, and neither was his furniture. Space had been made in the parlour for it; it looked half empty.

'He hasn't been today,' the landlady told her. 'I lit the fire this morning, but I let it go out when he didn't come. I had a nice bit of haddock for your suppers. Will you be wanting it now?'

'No,' Kate told her. She couldn't eat anything. Feeling even more upset, she almost ran back to his old lodgings in Beech Grove. She was relieved to see the light shining through his parlour window as she walked up the street. At least he was here. She tapped on his window as she usually did, to avoid seeing Mrs Gilley.

The curtain whisked up and she glimpsed his fraught face. The next second he'd opened the front door.

'Kate! Is it that time already?' She was drawn into his parlour and clasped in his arms.

'What's the matter, love? I can feel you trembling.'

'I was afraid something had happened to you. I was imagining the worst.'

His room was chaotic. There were boxes and crates open everywhere. 'I thought you said you'd move in this afternoon?'

'I did. I thought we could have supper in Zig Zag Road together. But there's more here to pack than I thought and I forgot to order the cart. When I did get round to it, the carter was booked up all day. Tomorrow morning was the earliest he could come. I've had a terrible afternoon.'

Kate shook her head. 'So have I.' She told him how upset her mother had been at her news. How she'd tried to dissuade her.

'I didn't expect anything else,' Jack said slowly. 'She's hardly likely to approve. You won't let her . . . ?'

'No. My mind's made up.'

'Come and sit down. Let me pour you some sherry.'

She laughed. 'Can you find your sherry and glasses in the midst of all this?' She waved her arms at the mess. 'I'm too restless to sit down anyway. I'd rather be doing something.'

'I've been packing all day. I had a darkroom upstairs. A walk-in clothes cupboard really. Had to empty the tanks. I'm mostly packed up there now, just my clothes. Then there's all this.'

'Let me help you. Are all the books here yours?'

Kate thought she was more practical than Jack, more used to getting things done. She organised him to stick markers on the furniture that belonged to him. Got him to stack the full boxes against the wall. She had his books packed in no time.

'Hadn't you better finish upstairs?' She opened his cupboard.

'Everything in there is mine. But not the ornaments on top.'

Mostly it was photographic materials. 'These could come in useful in your shop,' she told him. She dealt with them quickly, while he continued to fetch and carry for her.

There were countless photographs. Some in boxes, many loose. Some in albums. Her energy was waning, but she felt she was almost finished. She sat back on her heels and looked at some of his pictures.

'My family,' he told her. 'I took these years ago.' Kate had already seen photographs of the Grange, but here were people she didn't know playing croquet on the lawn. He pointed out his parents and his cousins.

'And that is Philomena, with the children.'

'I thought you said you didn't have any of her here.' She studied the picture closely.

'I'd forgotten. I hardly know what I have in there.'

'Your wife was very beautiful. *Is* beautiful – I'm sorry.'

'That was taken years ago. She's not as beautiful as she was. I didn't make her happy. There's a peevish look about her now.'

Kate sensed his discomfort, and knew he didn't want to talk about his wife. She closed the album, put it in the box and reached for another.

It was a heavy book with a cover of brown tooled leather. She knew the moment she opened it that this was different. It was a scrapbook not a photograph album. The pages were of thick parchment; the newspaper cuttings pasted to it were yellowing. Then, as her eye caught the headlines, she gasped.

'No, not that!' Jack's hands pounced, closing it up.

Kate hung on. She could feel the blood rushing to her head.

'Yes, yes. I want to see it.' She forced the page open to read again: *Benedict Rotherfield Charged with Murder*.

She could feel shivers of shock running down her spine as she took the book to the table, nearer the light.

'Kate, darling! I don't want you to read that.' Jack's arms came round her. She could see he was agitated.

'You knew?'

155

He was still trying to take it from her. 'What a fool I am, I'd forgotten it was there. You shouldn't . . .'

She folded both her arms across the book. 'I want to know. I've got to know. A murderer? Poor Mam!'

'I can't believe I've been so careless!'

Kate was only half aware of his anguish. She was taking a firm grip on herself.

'Please, Jack, go upstairs and pack your clothes.' She was fighting to stay calm. 'Then you'll be ready to move out first thing in the morning. I want to read this. It's important to me.'

'I can't leave you with that.'

'Please.'

He stared down at her for a moment, then the door closed behind him and slowly, with thumping heart, she turned the page.

She found it hard to believe. Almost impossible to grasp. Her father a murderer! She was battling with total disbelief.

Kate looked at the dates of the cuttings and tried to piece the story together. According to one article, on 8 February 1891, Benedict Rotherfield had gone to East Brow, the house he'd had built for himself and his wife and where Mam had been employed as lady's maid.

At that time he was living with his mistress, Miss Lena Hadley, and their baby daughter in St Vincent Road. The purpose of the visit was to ask his wife yet again for a divorce, which he very much wanted in order to marry his mistress.

But Mrs Amelia Rotherfield did not want a divorce. There was a quarrel, during which he stabbed her through the heart with an ornamental dagger, a gift from a relative who had brought it home from India.

Kate could hardly breathe. She had to read it through a second time. She'd have been about four months old when that had happened.

She turned the page and started to read another article.

Benedict Rotherfield appeared before a stipendiary magistrate on 18 February where Ida Blundy, his parlourmaid, gave evidence.

When shown the murder weapon, she said she'd dusted it frequently. She understood it was used as a letter-opener by Mr Rotherfield. It had been kept on his desk for the last year or two. No, it hadn't occurred to her that it was a dangerous weapon.

The prosecution said Mr Rotherfield, who admitted adultery, was noted for his quick temper. He could be violent if he didn't get his own way. Amelia Rotherfield was the innocent wife he'd abandoned. She was ready to forgive him and wanted him to come back. Rotherfield was committed for trial at Liverpool Assizes on 4 May.

The newspapers had carried many drawings and photographs of her father. Kate studied them all very carefully. He'd been a handsome man, with a beard. She shuddered. A man hanged for murder. The thought made her feel ill.

There were one or two photographs of her mother, looking so pretty and vulnerable and unbelievably slim. Kate was reminded that Mam had loved him, so he couldn't have been all bad.

Upstairs, Jack tossed his clothes into his cabin trunk and several leather bags. He was shocked that he'd allowed Kate to see that scrapbook. He should never have allowed it to happen. He couldn't believe he'd been so negligent. His fury at his own carelessness made him get on with the job with more speed than he had earlier.

When he went back down to his parlour, Kate was sitting quietly at the table, staring straight in front of her. He slid on to the chair beside her and gently took her hand. Her face was wet with tears.

'Poor Mam, what she must have gone through.'

'I shouldn't have let you find out like this. Such a shock.' He still felt agitated, blaming himself.

'It's better that I know, Jack. You shouldn't have kept it from me.'

'If your mother wanted it that way, it wasn't my business to tell you. She was trying to protect you. Stop you worrying.'

'Yes.' She sounded deflated. 'You were trying to protect me too, but how can I understand things if I don't know? I'd no idea that Mam had gone through all this.'

'We should burn the thing now.' His hands went to the scrapbook again.

'No!' Kate grabbed at it. 'I want to go through it again. I can't take it all in at once. Tonight, in bed.

'Then I must see Mam. Tell her that I know and that at last I'm beginning to understand. I'll stay with her tomorrow night, Jack. Spend most of the weekend with her.'

He didn't like that. It made the weekend loom in front of him, empty and lonely.

She was trying to smile; she understood him. 'You must come and meet my family. Sunday afternoon. I'll tell Mam, you're coming to tea.'

He didn't need persuading. 'I'd like that.'

Afterwards we'll come back early and spend the evening in our new place.' She frowned, looking round.

'I thought you'd given Mrs Gilley notice? That you were supposed to be out of here by today.'

'I was,' he sighed. 'I had to keep this place on for another week. Couldn't get out in time.'

Kate sighed. Jack wasn't one for making every penny count. She hoped he'd cope with running his own business.

Kate went back to the shop and got ready for bed before opening the scrapbook again. Propped up against her pillows in the quiet of the night, she looked at the same pictures, read the same text.

Her father a murderer? It made her confused and angry, and she found it hard to believe.

Mam had betrayed her. She should have told her, instead of hiding it like this.

Kate was frightened too. Had she inherited her father's temper? Could she have inherited the capacity to kill? The thought churned her up. So much of her had come from her father – her red hair, her green eyes. What if that had too?

Her father had gone to the gallows. That thought was chilling.

She couldn't be angry with Mam or Jack. What they'd kept from her had been done for her benefit.

Was this why she'd never managed to get on better terms with her mother? Mam had always talked of love, saying it was more important to her than anything else, yet somehow it had been beyond them both. She'd wanted to show Mam how much she loved her, yet to do so had evaded her all her life.

Kate wanted to cry; she wanted no more secrets.

Chapter Fourteen

By the time Kate had worked through the next day she felt calmer. She had to keep her wits about her because she was training the new manager. It was Saturday and she was finishing at five o'clock; he and Millie were going to work the late shift.

Kate had a leisurely tea with Josie Oaks and then packed an overnight bag. She knew Saturday night was always bath night at Cemetery Cottages, but usually it was over and all cleared away before she got home.

Tonight the fire was roaring up the chimney to make hot water, and towels were steaming over the fire guard. The hearthrug had been taken up and the tin bath brought in and put in its place. A clothes horse draped with clothes provided some sop to modesty.

The boys bathed in turn, strictly in order of age. Joe and Charlie started as soon as they'd finished eating, because they wanted to go out on Saturday nights. There were now too many for them all to bath on one night. The water got dirty and the towels too wet. Mam had her bath on Sunday, and those still in need of a bath followed then.

There weren't many clean clothes warming on the clothes horse now. Through the gaps, Kate could see Mam soaping Harry's back. She looked up to see who had come in.

'I thought you said you weren't coming?' Mam didn't look particularly welcoming.

'We've got to talk. I've found out about my father.'

Mam's voice was filled with irritation. 'Not again! We've been all through this. There's nothing . . .'

'I'm not asking you to tell me. I know, I know everything.'

'What d'you know, Kate?' Tommy asked. He was sitting on the bench beside the fire wearing a flannel nightshirt, his damp hair sleeked back.

'Never you mind, Tommy.' Mam's face was guarded, telling Kate not to say another word in front of the boys. 'Put your head back, Harry. I want to wash your hair. You next, Duncan, get yourself undressed, you'll be the last tonight.'

Kate took a damp towel and wrapped Harry in it as he stepped out of the bath. Took another and rubbed his hair dry.

'I want you to know, Mam, that I understand now why you wanted to keep it from me. I know you were trying to protect me and I'm touched, but I needed to know.'

Mam was emptying another kettle of hot water into the bath. She stopped halfway.

'Not now, Kate.' The stream of hot water continued.

Kate felt for a clean nightshirt for Harry. Those that remained were too small or needed mending. She chose the one with the smallest tear.

Charlie and Joe came out of their bedroom dressed in their best.

'Don't go until I've finished here,' Mam ordered. 'I want you to carry the bath out.'

Joe looked put out. 'Hurry up, then. We want to go.'

'It's a lick and a promise for you, Duncan. Put your head back, we might as well do your hair.'

'His knees are still dirty,' Kate said, starting to soap at that end too. At last Duncan climbed out, and the bath was taken out to the wash house. Kate followed with the wet towels and dirty clothes and put them to soak in the warm soapy water.

It was a routine Saturday night. Billy came and sat on her knee. 'Want my bath,' he said.

'Tomorrow, Billy,' Mam told him. 'We'll have ours tomorrow. You and me and Freddie.'

Kate wanted her brothers in bed and her mother to herself. The boys resisted; they wanted to stay up as late as possible. At last Kate succeeded in getting them all tucked up. Then she went to Mam's room; she was already in bed, and her eyes were closing.

Kate reached for her overnight bag. Took out her nightdress and the scrapbook with the tooled leather cover. She opened it on the bed. Mam was wide awake in an instant, her attention captured by those dreadful headlines.

'Where did you get this?'

Kate told her while she got undressed. Told her, too, that Jack's mother had collected the cuttings. She saw her mother shudder as she turned the pages, but she said nothing. The colour had gone from her cheeks.

At last she looked up. 'Why are you showing it to me?'

'So you know there's nothing left to hide. There are no secrets left.'

Kate got into bed beside her. 'When I first saw it, I was overwhelmed that this had happened to you. I wouldn't have been any comfort to you, not then, when I was only four months old.'

'You were, Kate.'

She could see Mam's eyes misting up. She watched her slide the book on to the floor and blow out the candle. Kate wanted to know how her mother had fared through that trauma, but she stayed silent.

'I went to look at the house in St Vincent Road where I was born. It's not far from the shop.'

'I loved that house.' Her mother started to speak at last. 'It was very handsome inside, though Benedict thought it small.'

After a moment's silence, Kate urged: 'Please tell me, Mam.'

'Ben wanted to take me to live at East Brow as the mistress. Would have done, except he couldn't get his wife to move out. She refused point blank.

'He wanted a son, but you were what came. He loved you all the same. It upset him to think his only child would have the stigma of being illegitimate. He was determined we should marry and put that right. He registered your birth in his name, not knowing that it would soon be infamous.

'We loved each other, Kate. Nobody could be more in love than we were. Not even you and your Jack.

'Everything was wonderful. I thought I was going to have a marvellous future, but then it turned into a nightmare.'

Kate put an arm round her mother and hugged her. 'Go on,' she whispered. 'You've never mentioned this before, but I've felt it between us. It's a secret that's kept us at arm's length.'

She waited, but heard nothing but her mother's heavy breathing. She prompted: 'We were living in that house in St Vincent Road. I was four months old . . .'

Lena turned on her back and sighed. She'd tried so hard to put Benedict Rotherfield out of her mind. She'd thought that was the only way she could stay sane. Even now the disappointment, the horror of the scandal and the ache for Ben were impossible to bear.

She had thought of it as a dreadful secret. She could feel it inside her like a heavy weight that she had to carry round, like Bunyan's burden. She hadn't dared open her mouth about it to her neighbours or family. She'd locked it away inside her all those years ago, and though she'd told Kate she'd forgotten, she hadn't. Every detail was etched on her memory in indelible ink.

'Mam . . . ?'

Kate had wormed out all the awful facts. She wouldn't be shocked. Perhaps now it was better for her to hear her side of the story.

161

'I thought I had the world at my feet.' Lena's voice was little more than a whisper. 'I'd risen from being a maid at Amelia Rotherfield's beck and call, to living in what seemed luxury to me. I had Ben, who loved me dearly, and we had a beautiful baby daughter. It all disappeared like a puff of smoke.

'Ben had been at work all day. I had a woman, a cook-general, who came in every day. Can you imagine me with a servant, Kate? I had you for company, but without him, the day seemed long. I always looked forward to his return, I planned meals for him. He liked three courses every night. Three or four courses. The evenings were the wonderful part.

'Then, one evening he came home and I found he'd ordered his carriage to take him to East Brow. Usually he walked back and forth to Egremont landing stage and took the ferry over to Liverpool. It was only a short distance and he had no need of a carriage. He left that for Amelia's use. The horse was stabled at East Brow, the coachman lived there.

'Ben told me he wanted to see his wife again. He was determined to get her to agree to a divorce. He'd tried many times and offered her increasing amounts of money. He was going to offer to put East Brow in her name. He thought that would do it.'

Lena sighed and pummelled at her pillow. 'I didn't want him to go.'

'But you wanted the divorce, Mam.' Kate's arm tightened round her waist.

'I didn't think Amelia would agree, whatever he offered. She was a hard woman. I thought I knew that side of her better than he did. I thought she was playing with him, like a cat plays with a mouse.

'And I thought we could be happy as things were. But Ben couldn't accept anything that was less than perfect. He said he'd be back in a couple of hours at the most.'

Lena shivered. 'We had dinner and he went. I was up and down to the parlour window. Once or twice I went to the door and listened, hoping to hear his carriage coming back.

'I fed you and put you down for the night. You were a beautiful baby; we both adored you. Still he didn't return. I was worried because he was away such a long time. I sensed in my gut that something terrible had happened. It would have to be terrible to stop him returning to me.

'I didn't know what to do. I was tempted to go to East Brow to find out. Blundy was still working there. I knew she'd tell me what was going on. Even find out for me if she didn't know.

'But I couldn't leave you alone. I thought of lifting you and taking you there in your pram, but it was getting late and it was cold.

'I went to bed but I couldn't sleep. I was out of my mind by the next morning. I knew Ben wouldn't go straight to his office without calling to tell me. He'd know I'd be worried stiff. He knew I was worried when he was setting off.

'When Martha Hoole, my cook-general, arrived to make breakfast, I asked her to look after you while I went to East Brow. I was feeding you first, up in the bedroom, when two policemen come to the door. I panicked when I saw them.

'Martha answered the bell. I heard them ask: "Does Mr Benedict Rotherfield live here?"

'Then they were asking for me by name and insisting on coming in to look through his things. I've never been so frightened in all my life, but I had to find out what had happened to Ben. I crept downstairs, still holding you like a shield in front of me.

'They told me they'd arrested him last night for the murder of Mrs Amelia Rotherfield.

'I sank down on a chair, clutching you to me. Stayed there as though carved in stone until you woke up again. I moved round like a zombie all that day. I was in a state of shock. Murder? Yes, his temper could boil up fast, and I knew he felt more hate than affection for Amelia. But I was sure Ben wasn't a murderer.

'None knew better than I that Amelia had always been a difficult woman. It had to be her fault, not his.'

She felt Kate writhe in agony beside her. 'Mam! How awful . . .'

'I couldn't believe it was happening. It seemed like something out of one of the plays we used to see at the Playhouse. Murder? That's a fantasy thing. I even questioned my own normality.

'I couldn't sleep, I couldn't eat, I couldn't do anything. I couldn't even look after you. It was heart-wrenching. I'd look at you, knowing he'd been set on that divorce for your sake. He hated the thought of you being illegitimate.'

She felt Kate stiffen. 'You blamed me?'

Lena used the sheet to wipe a tear from her cheek.

'I wasn't thinking straight in the days that followed. I'd have been satisfied as things were. Without you, he might have been too. But having a child drove Ben to insist on a divorce. It ruined everything. Even the relationship between you and me.

'Grief and fear are terrible to live with. I couldn't bear to hear you cry. My milk went because I wasn't eating properly. I had no patience

163

with you or anything else. I was in such shock and despair I wanted to die, and I was terrified.'

Kate was making her turn over to face her. She was cradled in her arms.

'Oh, Mam! I've always felt it there between us though I didn't understand. You always showed such love for the boys. All of them. But for me . . .'

'Forgive me, Kate. It was nothing you did. It was the circumstances . . . It was my fault.'

'I can understand now. Perhaps it's normal to feel like that.'

'I don't know. I thought life had twisted me. I should have got over it in all these years, but I never managed to. I loved you in my way, Kate, I really did. I just couldn't show it.'

'Of course. I feel better about it now I know.'

'So do I.' Lena felt the confidences she'd shared had drawn them together.

'Go on,' Kate whispered.

'We ought to go to sleep.'

'No, I want to hear the rest.'

Lena sank back into those painful memories.

'I missed Ben terribly. He'd given shape and meaning to my days. I'd had such huge expectations for our life together. Nothing seemed real any more.

'I couldn't stop loving him. Whatever he'd done, I couldn't do that. It had a crippling effect on me. I had no control over anything and I was running out of money.

'Martha was the only support I had, but I couldn't pay her wages. I knew I ought to move to a single room as quickly as I could and sell all the nice furniture, but I couldn't get moving to do anything. I just sat about crying.

'I felt numb. Could no longer take anything in. I had plenty of time to get over the shock. I didn't know how to deal with Ben now he was in prison. I went to see him. It was the only way I could convince myself that what the police said was true.

'What did he say? Did he admit doing it?'

Lena sighed. 'No, he said Amelia was expecting him, and that she had her parents with her when he arrived at East Brow. They were hostile towards him, full of animosity. He couldn't say what he wanted in front of them – they were haranguing him – so he asked her to go with him to his study.

'Ben said she was no less hostile, having been influenced by her parents. He claimed that Amelia picked up the dagger and attacked him. He had scratches on his hands where he'd tried to ward off her attack, and a cut on his arm that needed nine stitches. He said he'd forcibly taken the dagger from her in self-defence. That she'd come at him, trying to snatch it back, and had impaled herself on it.

'She'd screamed and her father came rushing in. They'd carried her out to his carriage and driven straight to the Borough Hospital. He thought she died almost immediately. Certainly before they got there.'

'Surely, Mam, that wasn't murder? It was an accident.'

'That's how Ben saw it. He told me not to worry, that he'd be all right. But it was causing the most terrible scandal. The newspapers were full of it. I saw my face up on the hoardings together with Ben's and Amelia's. I was scared of being recognised in the street. I hardly dared go out.

'I went to his trial at the Liverpool Assizes in St George's Hall. I couldn't bear to stay away. Ben looked ill standing in the dock.

'I found it all stomach-turning. There was evidence from a forensic scientist. The dagger had gone through the wall of her chest between the ribs at an angle, and had penetrated the heart itself. There was blood everywhere within minutes.

'There was more evidence about Ben's good character. Blundy said he was a thoughtful employer. Somebody from his office said he was highly thought of. I really thought . . .'

'I read that he'd pleaded not guilty,' Kate put in.

'I don't believe he was.' Lena couldn't prevent the sob. 'Amelia's father stood on the witness stand and said he'd seen Ben attack his daughter. That it was vicious and that she'd not been expecting it and hadn't stood a chance. Her mother supported that.

'It made things look suddenly grim for Ben. He was in the witness box for two and a half hours. I believed every word he said. Ben was the most honest and truthful of men.

'I'm sure Amelia's parents were out for revenge. They blamed him for leaving Amelia for me, a servant. And because of the trial, it was all very public.

'Oh, God, Kate, the last day, it was dreadful, I still can't get it out of my mind. The summing-up . . . I couldn't sit still. The jury were out for only an hour, and then returned the verdict of guilty. The judge placed the black cap on his head, and I'll never forget what he said: "The sentence upon you is that you be taken from this place to a lawful prison, and from thence to a place of execution, there to suffer death by hanging, and that your body be buried within the precincts of the prison in which you were last confined before your execution, and may the Lord have mercy on your soul." '

Kate couldn't sleep after that. As she tossed and turned, she heard her mother doing the same and knew she couldn't sleep either. It had been harrowing to listen to her story, and Kate felt very moved.

Poor Mam, she couldn't be the same person after an experience like that. It would alter the way she thought about everything. It would alter the way she thought of her baby, the way she treated her.

Kate felt the air had been cleared between them. It wasn't that her mother didn't love her. She'd been trying to protect her by keeping the truth about her father hidden.

It hadn't been the right thing to do. Kate felt she'd needed to know the full story to quench the awful curiosity she'd felt. But Mam had kept it hidden for her sake. Just as Kate herself had remained quiet about the way Mitch had groped her when she was fourteen. They'd both kept secrets, and for the same reason. Kate felt better about things. Mam did love her after all.

She had a sudden urge to tell her mother how she felt.

'I've always loved you, Mam,' she whispered. 'I've always been jealous of the boys or anyone you seemed to love more.'

Lena's hand felt for hers. 'You were my first-born, my only living daughter. I've loved you since the moment you were born, and wept inside because I couldn't reach you. And I've felt jealous of your Jack, because you spend more time with him than with me.'

From that moment Kate felt the wall between them had been swept away. It brought her relief and great satisfaction.

Lena was up early the next morning. She wanted the house clean and tidy when Kate's gentleman friend came to tea. She had to bake cakes. She wanted to make a good impression. She didn't want him to think they were poor and starving.

It surprised her that Kate felt she could bring him to Cemetery Cottages, and even more so that he'd agreed to come. She wouldn't have taken Benedict to meet her family. She'd have been afraid he'd be put off.

Lena felt better now she'd told Kate about Benedict. To have talked it through after such a long silence brought a feeling of freedom. It was a weight off her mind.

'You don't have to turn the place inside out,' Kate said as she saw her taking out the hearthrug to shake.

'I don't want him to think it's dirty.'

'He won't. Probably won't notice if it is.'

'Of course he will.'

Lena wouldn't let the family sit on round the table once Sunday dinner was eaten. She wanted the washing-up done and the table reset.

'More important to make yourself look your best,' Kate advised. 'Wear that black dress with the jet bugle beads on the collar that Mrs Halliday gave you. You look nice in that.'

'It's mourning.'

'Black's smart any time. Specially on older women.'

Although Jack knew where Kate's home was, having escorted her there one evening after their trip to the Playhouse, he had never travelled these from Liscard. He didn't know how he managed it, but he got confused with the tram routes and had to walk from the Laird Street depot. The way up Lansdown Road was pointed out to him by the conductor and he set off at a great pace, glad that he'd set out on this expedition earlier than was necessary.

'You can cut through the cemetery,' he was told. 'That's the shortest way.'

He felt puffed with the uphill walk by the time he went through the great ornamental iron gates and paused at the cemetery lodge. Ahead of him, the main avenue led straight uphill. At the top of the rise, a dignified façade topped with a clock joined the two sandstone chapels of rest. It was easily the most handsome cemetery Jack had ever seen.

Like most places of rest, it had a calming and tranquil atmosphere. As far as he could see, amongst the trees were headstones, obelisks, chest tombs, spires and Celtic crosses, in stone and marble, black, white and grey. He read the inscriptions on some. There were Brasseys and Vyners and Wilmers and Prices, and even a Laird or two. Familiar names because they'd had the streets in town named after them.

Charmed, in spite of himself, he turned down a narrower path edged with bushes to see more. The land rose and fell, so that although the cemetery covered many acres, it seemed small and intimate because so little of it could be seen at any one time.

There were gracious flights of steps up and down, some with low walls bordering the walkways. There were many paths, wide and narrow; many trees and bushes, though holly predominated; and it was all immaculately cared for. Here and there a gardener worked, and a few mourners were setting flowers on the graves.

He saw a great sandstone wall and thought it was the remains of an old fort until he walked round it and found it was just a supporting wall. On top, the land was level and covered with more gravestones. Kate had told him that once there had been an old sandstone quarry here, and he thought this was it.

He could hear mechanical sounds now as well as the singing of birds. He went on until he saw a donkey pulling a lawn-mower along the grass verges. The man in charge of it doffed his cap. 'Afternoon, sir.'

The lower end of the cemetery was the newest, and here there were fewer headstones. Jack turned back, heading for the gates behind the chapels of rest, and went out on to the road.

He recognised the cart track that ran up to Kate's home. He hurried now; he'd dallied longer in the cemetery than he'd intended. It had given him an inner calm that made him feel at peace with the world.

He could see the row of six cottages. He thought them very attractive eighteenth-century dwellings. For a long time, he'd imagined her home to be in one of the red-brick terraced houses that filled so many of the streets here near the docks. By anybody's standards, she lived in a lovely position. It seemed almost rural, even though the town was so close.

Lena was uneasy, one minute feeling a thrill of anticipation that she was going to meet Kate's gentleman friend, and the next fighting a sinking feeling that her family would put him off. Or he might have a big opinion of himself, or she wouldn't be able to take to him.

She'd told the younger boys they must be on their best behaviour and not let Kate down. They seemed more boisterous than usual. Harry was tearing round the cottages on a home-made scooter. Duncan had climbed a tree and torn the clean jersey she'd dressed him in.

The older ones, Joe and Charlie, were as edgy as she was. They wanted to be out with their friends but they'd dressed in their best and were waiting restlessly for their guest to arrive. Only Kate seemed calm.

Billy was excited and keen to eat the spread on the table. She'd sent him out to the garden gate to watch for Jack Courtney. Now the front door crashed back as he came rushing in.

'Mam, he's coming. He's coming.'

Kate took Billy by the hand and led him out to meet their guest. Lena watched from the front window, keeping well back behind the lace curtains and the pots of geraniums.

He looked a fine gentleman. Tall and slim, he swept off his hat as they met and leaned forward to kiss Kate's cheek. Then, formally, he offered his hand to Billy. But Billy stood on tiptoe, threw his arms round Jack and kissed him. She watched him jerk back, and even from a distance she could see his face working with surprise.

Lena could see Billy was upset. She wanted to console him, but Kate took his hand in hers and drew him to her. When Billy kissed people with such joy, they usually responded with kisses and hugs. Jack looked lost, as if he didn't know how to treat him.

Kate brought him in. He had to stoop to get through the door. His highly polished shoes were muddied from the cart track. He was not used to unmade roads, and though he wiped his feet on the doormat, it was a polite wipe and not nearly enough to get them clean. There were footprints on the flagstones. Lena would have complained loudly to Joe if he'd made them.

'I'm very pleased to meet you, Mrs McGlory.' He was soft-spoken and kindly. He put out a hand to her. Such an age since she'd seen a man's hand so white, with such neatly manicured nails. Much whiter than her own.

Tommy came rushing in with Duncan to be introduced, and the older boys stood up awkwardly and shook hands. Jack turned back to Lena.

'I was going to bring flowers for you, but Kate said not. That you always keep your vases full.' He looked round. There were fresh roses on the dresser.

'I thought you might prefer a portrait of your daughter.'

'A portrait?' The package was neatly wrapped. Lena undid it carefully so she could use the paper and string again. Kate smiled up at her from the framed photo.

'Oh! Thank you. I'd much rather have this. It's lovely, you've made her look beautiful.'

'She *is* beautiful. I've shown her as she is.'

Billy took it from her fingers. 'It's our Kate!'

'It's a photograph,' Jack told him.

'What's that?'

Jack tried to explain. Lena knew Billy couldn't understand, that he'd never seen a camera.

'Want picture of me.'

'Can't today,' Jack said gravely. 'I haven't brought my camera. I will next time I come.'

Lena couldn't take her eyes from him. He was much older than Kate, just as Ben had been much older than her, but in every other way Jack was very different. His dark-blond hair waved round his head and his grey eyes were kindly and diffident, yet he couldn't unbend with Billy.

He wasn't a worker and he wouldn't push for what he wanted as Ben had done.

But he had the same middle-class polish, the expensive clothes and a gold watch chain across his waistcoat, and it was enough to make her nervous and a little scared for Kate.

Harry and Freddie came crashing in. Kate went on with the introductions. Lena lowered the kettle on the fire to make the tea. The sooner they all sat down at the table, the better; the room seemed so crowded now all of them had come in.

Usually they only washed their hands before a meal if they were particularly dirty. Today they must do things properly. She ushered the young ones towards the bowl of water Kate had set out. There was a stampede to get it over with, so they could sit down and eat.

Lena had borrowed Ada Catchpole's best linen tablecloth. The starched folds could still be seen. She had a small posy of primulas on it. There'd been no stopping Billy bringing them, though Tommy told him off for doing it. That had made her smile. Tommy had brought home more flowers than anyone else when he was younger.

They were handing round the beef sandwiches with unusual politeness. A pity about the cups and saucers; Lena didn't have a matching set. They were all oddments bought in the market, but Kate said that wouldn't matter.

Harry meant to whisper to Joe, but it was heard all round the table.

'Isn't he old, Kate's young man? He's as old as Dad.'

Jack swallowed what was in his mouth and said gravely: 'I'm afraid I am a lot older than Kate. Can't help it, though.'

'Will you die soon?' Freddie asked. They all laughed.

'I hope not,' Kate said.

'Our dad died.'

'But Jack won't.'

'Why not?'

Kate exploded. 'Because I shall be looking after him.'

'I don't have a dangerous job like your dad,' Jack tried to explain. 'I'm not going to die, not just yet. I've too much to live for.'

The look he gave Kate twisted at Lena's heart. It made her worry even more that Kate was treading the same path she had.

Chapter Fifteen

On Wednesday, Kate served behind the counter in the newsagent's shop for the last time. Now the time had come, she was sorry to go, but having a baby meant she'd have to leave sooner or later. Much better to go now before the Hallidays knew. They would be horrified.

Everyone was asking after her mother. Each time it brought a rush of guilt. Kate left with their good wishes, one of Josie's plain fruit cakes and an extra week's wages.

'If you ever want to work again, get in touch,' Mr Halliday told her. 'With five shops, I'm always looking for reliable staff.'

'Thank you.' Kate shivered, hoping she'd never need to. She was starting a new life. 'I shall miss everybody here.'

Jack was waiting for her in their rooms in Zig Zag Road. 'It feels wonderful,' she told him, 'to be here with you and not have to go to work. Not tomorrow or the next day or as far ahead as I can see.'

'I want you to start your new job tonight,' he teased. 'We need to work out where to buy this shop. I want to support you and our child.'

'I was thinking about it at work today. I think New Brighton's the best place. It's a holiday town. In the summer, people come to stay and there are throngs of day trippers from Liverpool and Birkenhead. You could take their photos on the promenade; they come with money in their pockets to indulge themselves. Those who haven't a camera of their own will happily pay to have their picture taken.'

'What could be nicer than spending a summer's morning on the prom?' Jack smiled. 'I could take the film back to the shop to develop and the customers could collect their pictures from there.'

'A good place to sell postcards too. All holiday-makers want local views to send home.'

'What good ideas you have, Kate.'

'Tomorrow we could see if there are any empty shops we could rent.'

'We'd have to lease property like that, I think.'

'On a main road. Right in the centre of town.'

Kate had never seen Jack so keen She went to bed feeling they were poised at the beginning of a new way of life.

The next morning Jack was still in high spirits. His father had given him the address of an estate agent in New Brighton who specialised in business premises. That seemed the best place to start. They got up early to go in on the tram.

It was cool but sunny when they got off in Victoria Road, intending to walk through to Hope Street. Jack tucked her hand through his arm and strode out. Kate enjoyed being out and about, looking at the shops from the outside.

Suddenly she brought Jack to a halt, unable to believe her eyes. She was looking at a photography shop much as she'd envisaged for Jack. The window was full of cameras and other photographic equipment. There were two customers inside; another edged past them and opened the door. They were in the main shopping street in the town. Kate felt weak with disappointment.

Jack had gone white. 'We can't set up here,' he whispered. 'This chap's well established. We wouldn't stand a chance. We've been beaten to it. No good going into competition.'

'There are other places,' Kate pointed out. 'Birkenhead or Liverpool.'

'But New Brighton would be best.' She knew Jack was bitterly disappointed.

'Not necessarily. We ought to go inside, talk to this man, see his set-up.'

'No, no, what's the use?'

Kate knew they both had a lot to learn about the photography trade. They needed to study exactly what stock they would have to carry. It was an unpleasant surprise to see Jack so ready to give up.

'Let's see what the estate agent has on his books, then.'

All Jack's happy anticipation had gone. 'Is it worth . . .'

'Of course it is.' She took his arm. 'We might do better in Liverpool or Birkenhead.

'There's one in Liverpool already. I go there a lot.'

'Liverpool's bigger. Much bigger. There'll be enough business for more than one photographer. There, you could do portraits in the shop. You'd probably like that better than walking up and down the prom.'

'Perhaps . . .'

'Don't lose heart, Jack.'

At the estate agent's office, they discovered there were leases available on two empty shops in Birkenhead: one in Grange Road and one in Market Street.

'We must look at both,' Kate said firmly. 'Market Street is the main shopping area and very busy, but Grange Road is up and coming. Higher-class businesses there. And we must make sure there aren't any other photographers near by.'

'Tomorrow,' Jack said.

'This afternoon,' she insisted. 'Let's make an appointment to see inside. It's the only way to find out if they'll suit us.'

They went home and had the dinner their landlady had prepared for them, then caught the tram to Birkenhead. From the top deck, Kate couldn't see the river, only the docks, factories, warehouses and railway sidings that lined it.

'Too far to travel backwards and forwards every day,' Jack said despondently.

'We're only in lodgings; we can easily move again. Probably have to in any case.'

'If we took a shop in Liverpool, we could go over on the ferry. I quite enjoy the boat.'

'Think of the time it would take up. Better to live nearer.'

The agent met them outside the shop in Market Street. There was an ironmonger on one side and a greengrocer on the other.

Kate didn't like that. 'Photography is a luxury,' she said. 'We need to be amongst shops selling antiques and perfumes and musical instruments and such.'

'It's too small anyway,' Jack decided. It consisted of one medium-sized room, with a smaller one behind it; a lock-up, without living accommodation.

The shop in Grange Road was much bigger. There was a high-class gentlemen's outfitter on one side and a subscription library and bookshop on the other.

'The position's good,' Kate breathed, as she felt a fizz of hope. 'This could be it.'

The shop had sold ladies' millinery before it went bankrupt. It was nicely panelled in dark wood and it wouldn't take much to convert it to sell photographic products. There was a small storeroom, a living room and a tiny kitchen behind the shop. Above it there were two big bedrooms, the third having been turned into a bathroom.

'We could live here too,' Kate said.

'No, we'll need a good-sized darkroom. We could have a lot of work in summer and the tanks take up space.'

'Upstairs,' Kate said.

'Couldn't work upstairs and look after the shop at the same time.'

Kate couldn't see Jack doing two jobs at once. Particularly not when one was developing film, which needed to be timed carefully.

'I'll look after the shop.'

'How can you, with the . . . ?'

'To start with, anyway. See how it goes.'

'And if I'm going to take portraits, I'll need a studio with proper lighting. And my lady customers will need a room with a mirror to take off their hats and comb their hair first. If we're going to do it properly . . .'

'We are,' Kate assured him. 'So we won't be able to live here as well?'

'There won't be room.'

They walked the length of Grange Road and Grange Roads East and West looking for another photography shop. There was a chemist who sold and developed film, but no specialised camera shop.

Jack was enthusiastic again, and Kate was hopeful that things would turn out right for them.

Jack felt jumpy. He knew he should be pleased that his plans were making progress and that his father would provide the capital he needed.

He said to Kate, 'I telephoned Father while I was out getting my newspaper. Told him we'd found a suitable shop. He wants us to go and see him. Supper tomorrow night.'

The thought of taking Kate home was making his guts turn to water. Leo and Oscar had changed Philomena's opinion of him almost over night. They'd humiliated him by telling her of his failures. He couldn't bear it if they started that with Kate.

And once they knew she was Benedict Rotherfield's daughter, they'd have a field day and be bound to upset her. Even Father had found that hard to accept.

'I'm to come too?'

'Of course, Kate. He said it was time the family met you.'

Jack could see that Kate was just as nervous at the prospect as he was.

'What do I wear? I haven't got a dinner dress.' Kate had worn her best things in the shop.

'It's informal.' Jack said. 'That frilly white blouse will be fine.'

'The one you bought for me?' Kate wasn't convinced it would. And her skirts were getting tight.

'Father wants to hear my business ideas. He's promised to help me set it up.'

174

Kate knew it wasn't the time to be fussing over her clothes. She'd need to keep her wits about her if she was to help Jack.

'He meant financial help, didn't he? He'll expect you to do everything else.'

Jack's mild grey eyes studied her.

Kate said: 'He's bound to say, "Exactly how much money will you need, Jack?" '

'It won't seem much to him. Whatever it costs, he won't mind.'

'Are you sure? He's a business man. Won't he expect you to be as careful as he is about putting capital into a business? You'll have to make a profit. I think we should work out exactly how much you'll need.'

Kate had learned a lot about retailing from Mr Halliday. She took out a pencil and a sheet of paper.

'Right, we've found suitable premises. We can have a twenty-one-year lease or buy the place freehold.' She wrote the figures down.

'Then there's the cost of setting up a darkroom. You'll need equipment and materials for developing and printing. Packaging for the finished photos too. And then we'll have to stock the shop. What with exactly? We don't want to buy a lot of stuff that won't sell.

'Before we go, we ought to work all these things out, and the likely cost. We have to seem businesslike about it.'

Jack was frowning. 'I don't know anything about running a shop. You'll have to help me.'

Kate said: 'I know nothing about photography. Not the first thing. You'll have to teach me that.'

'Of course, Kate. But there's a great deal neither of us knows . . .'

'We can find out. We could go to that camera shop we saw in New Brighton and make a note of what he's selling there. Talk to him, pick up what pointers we can. Be sure to tell him you're thinking of opening up in Birkenhead, that's far enough away. Perhaps he'll show you his darkroom. He understands the business, we don't. Not yet.'

'Then there's that place in Liverpool.'

'We should go there too,' Kate agreed. 'But there's only tomorrow. You go to one and I'll go to the other. First thing in the morning. Hopefully they won't be busy and will have time to chat. Then in the afternoon, we can get something on paper to show your father.'

'How do you know all these things?'

'I worked for Mr Halliday for ten years. He often talked about the business and how he ran it. Let's work out what questions we need to ask these photographers tomorrow.'

* * *

The following evening, Kate dressed very carefully. She was far more nervous about meeting Jack's family than she had been about visiting the photographer's shop.

Instead of walking, Jack ordered a cab to take them up to the Grange, so she wouldn't arrive feeling wind-blown. Kate looked at the ivy-clad walls, the line of tall oaks just coming into leaf and the daffodils growing in the grass that stretched into the distance, and was shocked.

She couldn't understand how Jack could leave these surroundings to live in ordinary lodgings with her. She wondered again what had cut him off from his family and driven him away from his home. And yet his father was on sufficiently good terms to offer help now.

'It all looks very grand. Overpoweringly grand.'

Jack took her hand. 'Don't worry. When I lived here, I took it all for granted. I hardly noticed what it was like. My family are like that.'

'I bet you noticed Beech Grove wasn't as good when you got there.'

'But that was all mine. I was comfortable enough.'

The front steps seemed as wide as those of the Town Hall. A parlourmaid with streamers on her cap let them in. Jack pointed out a model of the Courtney Line's first ship, the SS *Pensicola*, in a glass case. Kate thought it wasn't like a house at all; more like the entrance to a museum. And Jack had been brought up here!

She felt jumpy as she followed Jack to what he called the drawing room. She was afraid his family would look at her with critical eyes. He ushered her in. It seemed vast and full of sofas. Full of people, too. The men shot to their feet.

'I've brought kate to meet you all,' Jack said, and led her round. 'Let's start with Mother.'

She was lying on one of the sofas, propped up on several velvet cushions and wearing a dress of similar material. She offered Kate a plump hand sparkling with jewels.

'Jack speaks very highly of you. I hope you're not the sort to run off after a year or two.'

'No! Of course not.' Kate thought her older and plainer than her own mother.

'He needs to settle down. Have some sort of a home life.'

Kate quaked. What could she say to that?

His father seemed kindly, though a little austere. She felt she might be able to take to him.

'I've been asking Jack to bring you here for some time. I don't know why he wants to keep you hidden.'

176

'My brothers Lionel, known as Leo,' Jack said, 'and Oscar.' She knew they were both older than Jack, but they looked very much older. They stood up straight, with their shoulders back, proud men in command of their lives. Successful men.

'And Leo's wife, Ottilie, and Constance, who is Oscar's.'

They stood in a row, and Kate sensed four pairs of hostile eyes on her. She felt she was being inspected, quite sure that the women were taking in her clothes and checking to see if she looked pregnant yet. Jack said her figure hadn't altered at all, though she was over three months. She felt very young and inexperienced compared with these people.

A glass of sherry was put in her hand. She took a sip. It was a beautiful glass, but she didn't like the taste.

Jack was asking his mother: 'When do you want me to take you to Baden-Baden?' Kate knew the trip was hanging over him. He didn't want to go at all, but felt duty-bound to do it.

Leo said: 'You said in the spring, Mother, when the cold weather was over. It's the end of February now; shall we book it for next month? Jack can take you before he opens his shop.'

'I'm not well enough at the moment.' Her face puckered. 'I always feel low at the end of the winter. You know what cold weather does for my aches and pains.'

'You want to put it off?' She heard the note of hope in Jack's voice.

'Just for a month or two.'

'But that will mean you'll be there in high summer. Won't it be too hot for you?'

'The autumn might suit me better.'

Kate didn't think the autumn would suit her; she'd be on the point of giving birth. Neither would it suit Jack. He'd want to be with her, and besides, there was the shop to think of. He wouldn't want to hang fire for months. It could be open by the autumn, and somebody would have to look after it.

Jack was trying hard. 'Why don't you take the waters in Bath, Mother? So much less travelling, and you'd find the climate more to your liking.'

'Ottilie's mother went to Baden-Baden last year. She says there's nowhere to beat it.'

The parlourmaid came to tell them that dinner was ready. Kate looked with dismay at her sherry; the glass was still almost full. They were moving to the dining room, so she took one gulp and left it. Jack had called it supper and told her it would be informal. That was the last thing it was. A great expanse of starched white cloth stretched in front of her.

'So, Jack, you're about to turn into a businessman at last?' Leo asked sarcastically.

'Not before time,' Oscar put in. 'Life begins at forty, eh?'

'I'm only thirty-nine'

'So you are. But not a fast start, old man.'

'Tell us about your plans,' his mother said.

Jack sounded uncertain. 'I'm hoping to set up as a photographer. Take portraits, sell photographic materials, that sort of thing.'

'We'll come and have our portraits done, won't we, Constance?' Ottilie said.

'Hope you'll be able to keep on top of it,' Leo remarked. 'Be more successful than you were working for the firm.'

'Jack's very good at photography,' Kate said as firmly as she could. 'I think he has a real talent for it.'

'If he has, it's the only thing.' Oscar raised his eyebrows. She could see from Jack's face what he thought of that.

There was soup followed by a roast. Kate had already eaten one dinner that day. The landlady served their main meal at lunch time. She had no appetite.

They were waiting for their pudding when his father said: 'Come on then, Jack. Tell us about this business idea you have.'

'We've found a shop we think is suitable in Grange Road. We can have a twenty-one-year lease with a rent review every seven years, or buy the freehold.'

'Better buy it while you have the chance,' his father said. 'I've heard of people being caught on rent reviews; they put it up so high it's almost impossible to make a profit.'

'Hold on,' Leo said. 'It depends who's going to pay out. If it's the business yet again . . .'

His father put down his knife and fork. 'How much are they asking?'

Kate held her breath. She knew now that his brothers resented what their parents were doing for Jack. She could understand that: they were working in the family business and earning the money, and their parents were giving it away to Jack. Was this why he'd gone into lodgings?

'I've worked out some figures.' Jack looked tense and pale, and Kate saw his hand shake as he took a neat copy of Kate's workings out of his pocket. It went round the table. 'I've estimated . . .' He looked at Kate. 'We've estimated how much it will all cost to convert the shop, buy the stock and everything.'

'You've never got this far before.' Leo scrutinised it. 'It's a change, but you've got a nerve to keep coming cap in hand all the time. It's time you learned to stand on your own feet.'

Kate was horrified.

Oscar looked her in the eye. 'Jack's a remittance man,' he said insolently. 'The family business has supported him all his life. We run it; Jack's never managed to do anything useful. You're expecting too much if you think he'll change now. You'd better know what you're getting. He's not going to make any fortune for you, he's no great catch.'

That twisted Kate's gut. She could see Jack felt diminished.

'I think he is.' She was angry, but didn't want to show it and make matters worse. 'I don't expect him to make a fortune for me. I value his company and his love.'

There was a long silence. She looked round the table and nobody met her gaze.

'We'll make a living from this photography shop, I'm sure we can. I'll help him.'

'I'll buy the property outright for you,' Jack's mother said slowly. 'I have a little money of my own; it hasn't come from the business.'

'That's very kind . . .' Jack sounded at his wits' end.

'Too kind probably,' Leo added. 'You could be throwing good money after bad.'

Kate said desperately, 'I called at a similar shop to the one we want to set up – in Liverpool – this morning. The proprietor was very helpful. He gave me the names of his suppliers and some catalogues from manufacturers.'

She'd glanced through them and been shocked at the number of different films and cameras on the market. She'd imagined that that was all there was to it, but had now discovered there were lenses and filters and tripods and a hundred other pieces of equipment about which she was ignorant. She had bought a book which she hoped would enlighten her.

'The owner is about to retire and close his shop down, which is good news for us.'

'Couldn't you take it over as a going concern?' Jack's father asked as he summoned the parlourmaid to bring him more wine.

Jack said: 'We thought of that, but it's not in the main shopping centre and he hasn't much room. And there's another photography shop in Renshaw Street, bigger and better and not very far away.'

Kate added: 'But he's got a lot of equipment he wants to get rid of. He's offering it cheap.'

'It'll be old-fashioned,' Oscar said superciliously. 'No good.'

'We have catalogues from all the main manufacturers, and Jack can check what's currently offered in those. He'll see then what's out of date. His backgrounds, for instance, will be all right.'

'His what?'

'Painted backgrounds. For taking portraits. There are buildings with Doric columns, landscapes with trees and streams, all painted on canvas. There's a handle to wind up the one you want. Five on the roll. The customer sits in front of a picture and on the finished photo it looks real.'

'That's exactly what I'll need,' Jack told them. 'I'll go over and see him tomorrow.'

'You seem to have a bit more go about you than Jack.' His father was smiling at her.

Kate said quickly, 'Jack was doing the same thing in a New Brighton shop. We need to find out as much as we can about the trade.'

Ottilie looked down her Germanic nose at Kate. 'I hear you've spent years working in a shop? So you'll be used to all this?'

'Yes, but Jack will have to teach me all about cameras.'

'What sort of a shop did you work in?'

'A newsagent's and sweet shop.'

Constance was condescending. 'Didn't you find that utterly exhausting? Selling newspapers all day long?'

'No, I enjoyed it. Energy is not something I'm short of. Well, it shouldn't be, not at my age.'

She saw Jack smile at that.

'Most unsuitable. I wouldn't allow my wife to work in a shop. No lady should have to,' Leo grunted.

Jack was despondent on the way home. Kate knew why.

'You've got what you wanted,' she pointed out. 'Isn't that the main thing?'

'What must you think of me? My family makes their low opinion of me very plain.'

'They went out of their way to blacken your character.' Kate was indignant. 'Trying to take you down a peg every time they opened their mouths. My brothers are never so rude and bad-mannered as that.'

'You stood up for me. Thank you.' He sounded miserable.

'Are they always on at you like that?'

'Most of the time. It hasn't made you change your mind? About me?'

'No, why should it?'

'I think that must be why they do it. They worked on Philomena. Changed her opinion of me.'

'They won't change mine. I make up my own mind. I can see now why you wanted to leave home.'

'You were great. Gave them little digs back when they tried to pull you down.'

'I have brothers too,' Kate smiled. 'I'm used to holding my own with them. We'll make a go of this shop, I know we will.'

They'd have to. Jack wouldn't be given funds for another start, and she didn't want him to become a remittance man again. It was bad for him. It made him think he couldn't earn his own living.

'You've got more guts than either Ottilie or Constance. I don't know why they should feel so superior. You're much better-looking too. They won't like that.'

They had to wait a few weeks for the sale of the premises to go through. They made plans and lists and bought a lot of equipment and stock from the photographer who was retiring.

They went to Chester to see another shop there. On fine days they went out to take local views for Jack to make into postcards. They discovered that weddings were considered the most lucrative end of the business.

Kate learned all she could about cameras and took a couple of portraits of Jack. She was quite pleased with them, but he pointed out how they could be improved.

Then he gave her his camera and she went home to take pictures of her family. They were all very keen to sit for her. She was proud of the picture she took of Mam and Billy with their heads together.

But the real thrill came when they were given the keys of the shop and they were able to fit it up. They had made up their minds about what was needed and they hired help to do much of the work. Jack wanted to get everything right.

'I want us to have good working conditions. I think we should use all the bedrooms. The biggest, in the front, to be divided between darkroom and printing. The other room for taking portraits. We're lucky the bathroom is big enough to put in a dressing table and chair as well as a full-length mirror. So the ladies can titivate before having their portraits taken.'

'That still leaves the downstairs living room,' Kate said.

'We'll have a gas fire put in there and a couple of easy chairs. It's somewhere to sit when we close for lunch.'

'With two of us, we could stay open. First one has lunch, then the other. That's what we did at Halliday's. We don't want to lose trade, Jack.'

Kate had hoped there would be room for them to live on the premises.

'I don't like lodgings. They're fine for a single man – it saved you cooking and cleaning – but now, well, it costs twice as much because the charge is per person not by the room. And when the baby needs real food, there'll be three of us.'

It was a sunny spring day. As Lena propped her back door open, she saw Tommy digging in the next-door garden under Mr Ratcliff's close supervision. It brought a twinge of conscience, for she'd allowed him to stay off school again. Ratty had asked for Tommy's help; digging was getting beyond his strength. He was very bent now, and she could see quite a hump under his grey flannel shirt.

She knew Tommy found him a hard taskmaster. He was very fussy about his garden and everything had to be exactly right. She hoped Kate wouldn't come home today and catch Tommy here; she nagged at her for allowing it. Though Tommy would be leaving for good when school broke up for the summer holidays, and what difference did a few weeks make?

He'd been off all week. They were having a run of warm, dry weather and Mr Watts at the end cottage had scythed down an acre or so of grass to make winter feed for the sheep and the cemetery donkey. Kitty Watts had come round to ask for Tommy's help to rake and carry it to the barn. Kitty felt her need was more urgent than Ratty's because she had to get it all in before the weather broke.

Lena had been glad to have Tommy working for the Wattses for two days because they paid for his services with produce. Last night, he had come home with a dozen eggs and said Kitty had crossed three shillings off their milk bill too.

Whereas old Mr Ratcliff repaid favours with seedlings and garden produce when it was ready. Being early May, there wasn't much apart from lettuce, and the boys didn't care for salad.

She was watching Ratty, his unkempt grey hair tossing in the wind, and thought she saw him stagger.

'Lena?' Kitty Watts, with her curlers bulging under her ancient tam, was coming along the back path. 'Could I borrow a bit of sugar? I'm making a bread and butter pudding and I've run out.'

'Course you can.' Kitty gave her unending tick when money was short; she couldn't refuse her anything. 'I've just put the kettle on. Fancy a cup of tea?'

'Lovely. Could just do with one.'

Lena was pouring water into her teapot when she heard Tommy shouting.

'Mam! Mam! Come quick.' There was terror in his voice, and it made her heart thud.

Kitty reached the back door before she did. 'What is it?'

In the next-door garden, Lena could see the grey flannel shirt down on the newly dug soil. Mr Ratcliff had collapsed.

'Mam, help me!'

By the time she reached them, she could see the old man's eyes fluttering open.

'Did he faint?' Tommy's eyes were wide with panic. 'Or is it a heart attack or something?'

Ratty was groaning and trying to sit up.

'A blackout of some sort.' It was Kitty who helped Tommy get him to the garden seat. Farm work kept her physically strong.

Lena asked: 'What happened, Ratty?' His dark eyes looked out over a full set of facial whiskers that were almost white and badly in need of a trim.

'I don't know . . . Must have passed out.'

'You're doing too much,' Lena told him. 'You've been out here with Tommy all day.'

'Wanted to get my sprout plants in.'

'You're not well enough. Tommy, I've just made a pot of tea. Fetch him a cup. Bet you could do with that, couldn't you, Ratty?'

She thought he looked bone weary as he sat huddled on the wooden seat, his head in his hands.

'You've got to rest more.'

When he wasn't tending his garden, he'd be at his front gate staring out over the cemetery where he'd spent his working life. He called it 'God's acre'.

'Nearer thirty acres, I'd say,' Kitty Watts always corrected him. 'But it is beautiful.'

'Nowhere better to be put to rest. If it's good enough for the Lairds, it'll be good enough for me.'

'But not yet, Ratty? Not yet, eh?'

'I'm in my eighty-fourth year. Can't be that far off now, can it? I'll not be all that sorry to go. I'd like to be with Bertha again. Lonely without her.'

'You've got your daughter, Myrtle. She's very good to you.'

'Aye, she is.' He went to her house every Sunday for his dinner. She came every Thursday to clean his house through.

'Shall we let her know you aren't well? Our Tommy can run round and tell her.'

'She'll want me to go to her place. She's always asking.'

'Perhaps it's time, Ratty. Perhaps you'd be better off with her. She'll take care of you.'

Lena knew he'd only been able to manage alone this long because Ada Catchpole cooked him a hot meal every day.

'Look at my runner beans. I can't leave them.' He'd always grown vegetables for his family and friends.

'We'll send them to you when they're ready.'

'I don't want to be a burden to anyone.'

'Your Myrtle won't see it like that. You know she won't.'

'She hasn't got a garden. Just a back yard, and I'll miss the cemetery. It's not the same in a narrow street.'

'Don't you worry about missing the cemetery,' Kitty told him. 'You'll be there soon enough.'

That raised a smile on the old man's face.

Chapter Sixteen

Kate had never felt so busy. She'd expected to have more time for herself when she gave up working for the Hallidays, but the reverse was true.

She was really enjoying being involved in setting up Jack's shop. She could count this as her own, and she found it much more fun. Jack asked her advice about many things, and Kate was trying to learn all she could about photography.

As soon as the darkroom was ready, she persuaded Jack to teach her how to mix and make up the chemical solutions, and how to develop and print film. She practised under his supervision when she could.

She felt she could manage to take portraits if customers came in and asked for them, and she already knew more than Jack about keeping the books and buying stock.

At last the outside of the shop was painted and the name above the window was changed to read: The Camera Shop. Proprietor: J.J. Courtney. The stock was on the shelves and they were able to open for business. Kate was thrilled to be serving behind the counter. Jack kept telling her she should do less because of the coming baby, but her health was good, and she knew she'd feel bored and left out if she stayed at home in their lodgings.

The lodgings Jack had taken for them in Zig Zag Road were the one thing about her new life she didn't care for. The shop had taken all her attention, but she wanted to look for somewhere closer to live. The journey to the shop took too long and she didn't want lodgings where she was waited on. When her baby came, they'd need more space. Jack agreed, but his ideas of what was suitable were grandiose. He thought she'd need a live-in maid too.

She was not able to spend as much time with her mother these days, so on Thursday, when they closed at lunch time, she usually called to see her before going back to the lodgings.

As soon as Kate saw her pink cheeks and glittering eyes, she knew her mother was on cloud nine.

'What's happened?'

'How d'you feel about moving in next door?' Mam was ushering her to the basket chair. 'Ratty's gone to live with his daughter, and they're doing the place up a bit before looking for a new tenant.'

Kate could see a lot of advantages in living next door.

'I could give you a hand with the baby.' Mam was almost singing. 'It would be lovely to have you close. They're going to put piped water in for all of us. Water closets too, though they want to put the rent up. You won't know the place when they've finished.'

Kate felt her interest quicken.

'Do you reckon your Jack would come here?'

'Yes, he loves the cemetery and the grand buildings. Yes, I think he'd like this better than where we are.'

The more Kate thought about it, the more she was sure it was the right place for them.

On Sunday, she took Jack to have his tea at her mother's. It gave them a chance to look over number two. The workmen were not there, but they'd left the key with Lena when she asked for it.

Kate led him inside. It smelled of new distemper, and the walls were all bright white. It was a little smaller than her mother's house, with no downstairs parlour. When Ratty had lived here, the ground floor had been one room. A portion at the back had now been walled off to make a kitchen. A new sink with one cold-water tap had been installed by the back door. Outside, in the wash house, there was a bath and a water closet waiting to be fitted.

Jack stood on the back step. 'We'd have to go outside for a bath?'

'Only a few feet,' Lena said.

Jack wasn't pleased about that. 'Why not put it in upstairs? There are three bedrooms, and we'll only need two.'

'The rest of us have only two,' Lena pointed out. 'Somebody divided the back one in this house years ago. They're really too poky. The workmen say it's cheaper to put the lav outside.'

'We'll have the whole house for less than half what you're paying for our lodgings,' Kate pointed out. 'And I'll have Mam next door.'

'Perhaps we could get a porch built.' Jack paced out the distance. 'A big one to join the back door to the wash house. Then it wouldn't be so bad.'

'We'll take it then?' Kate asked, feeling a surge of pleasure.

'Why not, if you want it?'

'D'you like it, Jack?'

'Yes, it's very peaceful, like being out in the country. And those lovely sandstone chapels down there, much nicer than in a street. Yes, I think I could live here.'

'Let's do it then.'

Kate found he took as much interest in setting up the house as she did. All the other cottages in the row had floors of flagstones on the ground floor. Jack had theirs covered with plain linoleum and then bought a carpet to go on top. He did the same in the bedrooms. It made it cosy and comfortable.

He went out searching for furniture. He liked antiques, and only the best would do for him.

'I know where we can get second-hand furniture at a fraction of what you're paying,' Kate told him.

He laughed at her. 'Whatever we get now we'll have to live with for a long time. It might as well be something we like. Besides, the rooms are small, it won't take much to fill them.'

By the time Jack had finished, Kate was surprised how smart her new home looked. It was beautifully furnished and fitted up. Yet it felt homely and familiar, because she had her family next door and she knew all the neighbours. When they moved in she felt she had everything she could wish for.

'He's got taste,' Mam said, looking round. 'Knows how it should be done and doesn't care about the cost.'

Ada Catchpole saw the porch joining the wash house to the back door and employed the builder to do the same for her. Inside the wash house was the new water closet and the bath, but there was no hot-water system. The bath was plumbed in but with only a cold tap.

'Penny-pinching,' Jack complained. But they'd left the boiler there for washing clothes. When they wanted baths they had to light the fire under that. It heated both the wash house and the water, which could be scooped into the bath.

Kate was very happy to be back in Cemetery Cottages. It surprised her how quickly Jack settled down and how well he got on with her family.

'Your mother couldn't have been more welcoming,' he told Kate. 'Your brothers too . . . But poor Billy. I didn't realise at first . . .'

Kate had noticed that he wasn't at ease with Billy.

'Can't get down to his level somehow.'

'You will when you get used to him.' She wasn't worried; everybody took to Billy.

Every morning, Jack travelled with her to the shop. He bought *The Times* newspaper when he got off the tram, and while she opened up the shop, he turned on the gas fire in the back room and settled down to read.

If there was developing or printing to do, or if someone required their picture taken, Jack did that while Kate stayed in the shop. What he liked best was having a wedding or other function to attend. He set off happily with his tripod and his camera. He preferred to be out and about rather than pinned down in one place.

He mentioned this to Mam, who said afterwards to Kate, when they was alone: 'He's always lived the life of a gentleman and can't change. He expects to please himself, and he expects to be waited on.' She sighed. 'Your father was just the same.'

Kate was not unhappy about this. She'd known Jack a long time, and if she'd thought about it, it was what she would have expected. What came as a complete surprise was the depth of his love. She could see it in his eyes when he looked at her. She felt wrapped in its warmth. He doted on her and was always looking for ways to show it. He came back from his expeditions with little gifts for her: chocolate or fancy biscuits, flowers or an antique brooch that had caught his eye.

About a month after they had opened, Kate was serving a customer when the shop door bell pinged again. When she looked up, she found Jack's father staring at her in amazement.

When they were alone, he said: 'Is Jack here? Working upstairs in his darkroom?'

'No, he went out, I'm afraid. He'll be sorry he missed you.'

'He leaves you here by yourself?'

'I'm not alone. My little brother Tommy's here with me.' He was in the storeroom, unpacking some new cameras that had just arrived. She called him to be introduced.

'Tommy's just left school and wants to learn the business too.' Jack had said he could come to fetch and carry for her, save her legs on the stairs.

'With Tommy, I can manage.' She smiled. 'I'm not as good as Jack at some things, but I'm learning fast and I can cope.'

'Where's he gone?'

Kate didn't exactly know. He often went out for a drink just before lunch time. 'To buy some food, I expect.'

'I wanted to see him. To talk to him about the arrangements for going to Baden-Baden.'

Kate's heart sank. 'Is the journey booked now?'

'Not yet, but Jemima's made up her mind. She wants to set out at the end of July.'

Kate's baby was due in mid-August; for her, the timing couldn't be worse. 'And they'll stay for three months?'

'Yes. She wants to be home before winter sets in.'

'I'll tell Jack.'

'I'll take some film for my camera. I should buy it from you now.'

'We're glad of your custom,' she told him, as she wrapped up what he asked for. His sharp grey eyes were studying her.

'Should you be doing all this in your condition?'

Kate knew there was no hiding her pregnancy now. 'I have a stool here to sit down behind the counter, and Jack has fixed up a room where we can both relax in comfort.'

She thought he looked impressed, if a little shocked too. 'Would you like to see round the premises?'

'Is the shop not busy?'

'Not as busy as we'd like. It takes time to build up trade. People have to know we're here. I'll leave the dividing doors open so I'll hear the shop bell.'

Kate led the way into the back room. A copy of *The Times* had been taken apart and the sheets scattered round the armchair pulled close to the gas fire.

'It's easy to see Jack has used this recently,' his father said wryly.

'We both do.' Kate picked up the newspaper and tried to put it together. 'There's an article in it today,' she said, showing it to him. If she'd still been in the paper shop, she'd have written on the placards: 'Germany Re-arming for War.'

'I've read it.'

'The Austrians don't like their Archduke being murdered in Serbia. They sound aggressive. It even suggests we might . . .'

'No, Britain won't go to war about what the Serbs do. We've too much on our plate already with the Empire. The Irish are on the verge of civil war, then there's Moslem risings in India and Egypt and a rebellion in South Africa.'

'But is it safe to travel through Europe now?' Jack thought not. 'It's a powder keg. Germany wants to expand her Empire.' She knew it was the last thing he wanted to do.

'The papers were full of the same thing last year. Jemima's determined to go to Baden-Baden. She believes that to take the waters there will restore her health.'

Kate gave up. 'Come and see what we've done upstairs.' She took

189

him into the darkroom. 'You can't see a lot here in this dim light, I'm afraid. These pictures hanging up to dry were developed this morning. This is the room where we take portraits. We have daylight lights, and these are the canvas backgrounds I spoke about that night I came to your house.'

'Yes, I remember. I fancy having my portrait done.'

'Now? Wouldn't you rather wait for Jack to take it? He's better . . .'

'No, you do it.'

Kate told herself to keep calm. This was no time to have an attack of nerves. She had to appear capable of running this business, since he and his wife had given Jack the money to set it up. She took a deep breath and tried to look at him with a photographer's eye.

'Right. Off with your topcoat; you can hang it in here. Most of our customers like to comb their hair, but yours doesn't need it.

'I'd like you to sit in this chair.' She moved it so his shoulders would be at an angle to the camera. 'For the background we have a country scene with a Palladian mansion just visible behind you.' She wound the scenery into position and switched on the lights.

'A table beside you, I think. With your hat and gloves placed on it.' She turned them round for best effect, and then went under the black cloth that covered the camera. It looked quite good.

'Could you bring your right arm down a little, that's right, rest it on the arm of the chair. I can see your watch chain now. Are you ready? Keep still.'

She pressed the button and hoped she'd got it right. She would have liked to take another, but common sense told her she must get it right first time if they were to make a profit.

'When will it be ready?' His eyes were twinkling at her now.

'Tomorrow. We could post it to you.'

'Yes,' he said. 'Do that.'

Kate wanted his picture to be perfect. If it were not, he would think they weren't running a viable business. She was kept busy in the shop after that. Dinner time usually brought an increase in customers. When Jack returned he looked after the shop while she had her lunch. She could see he was upset about the timing of the trip to Baden-Baden.

During the afternoon, he developed his father's portrait. When Kate saw it, she was delighted. William Courtney looked out of the photograph, a slightly quizzical smile on his face. Every line of the picture was clear and exactly as she'd planned it.

'Excellent,' Jack told her. 'He'll not be able to fault this.'

* * *

Jack was dreading the trip to Germany. He didn't like foreign travel, he spoke only English and he liked people to understand what he wanted.

Ottilie kept phoning him at the shop, expecting him to rush home at a moment's notice to discuss the arrangements. They talked endlessly about whether it would be better to travel via Harwich or take the boat train from Victoria and go through France. He had no idea; both routes seemed complicated.

They'd argued for days as to whether Mother should use an invalid carriage or a bath chair. He was afraid an invalid carriage would be heavy and awkward to manoeuvre on to trains and ferries. Both Ottilie and Mother thought it would give her more comfort.

Then there was the fuss about passports, and getting bookings that wouldn't tire his mother too much.

'I must have a hotel bed every night, dear.'

'They have sleeping compartments on the train, Mother. I'm sure they do.'

'But I wouldn't be able to sleep if it was rushing through the night. All that swaying and bouncing. I must get my rest.'

Her tired eyes looked up at him, seeking sympathy.

'Mother can't be rushed in the mornings either,' Ottilie told him. 'She doesn't rise before eleven these days and it takes her a long time to dress.'

'I stiffen up so, but I could make a special effort. I could be ready to start by eleven.'

Jack was afraid the journey would seem endless. He blamed Ottilie for the whole idea. She had fired Mother's enthusiasm for going to Baden-Baden. Then, in her usual high-handed manner, and without further discussion, she had booked the trip to start on 28 July. The date hung over Jack. It seemed terribly close.

He felt rushed off his feet. He bought himself some matching luggage and new clothes. He knew it was important to hire more help in the shop. Tommy was keen, but he was too young. He looked even younger than his thirteen years. Kate would be unable to run the shop for a few weeks when she had the baby, and now he was reminded of that every time he looked at her. She was near her time.

He advertised the vacancy in the local newspaper and interviewed several men. He wasn't sure he could trust any of them and couldn't make up his mind. Kate put a card in the shop window; she said she'd see to it. But she too found that those who applied had only a vague knowledge of photography and couldn't be left to manage the business.

Kate said, 'I feel desperate about it, but Tommy's here to keep the shop open.'

'He's just a lad, he hardly knows what's what.'

'As much if not more than those who've applied. I've always been able to rely on Tommy. Perhaps for a few days . . .'

'Teach him to develop and print.'

'It's asking a lot of him. There's only a few days left.'

Kate was rushing to read Jack's newspaper every morning now, and the news from Germany seemed more and more threatening. Jack said Ottilie wouldn't listen when he tried to tell her, and Mother was so used to having her own way that she thought the Kaiser would continue to put off any war plans until they were safely home again.

At the last moment, without consulting Jack, Ottilie hired a trained nurse to go with them. It made Jack feel superfluous, as though she didn't trust him to see that Mother was comfortable.

He couldn't sleep on the last night he spent at home with Kate. He hated the thought of leaving her in her present state. She told him she was fine and still had plenty of energy; that she was sure she would manage and he mustn't worry. But she couldn't sleep either, and she clung to him, burying her face in his chest. He felt she needed him and he shouldn't be going at all.

It was only when she got up to dress in the morning that he realised his pyjamas were damp and that she'd been weeping. She was all right over breakfast, dishing up the porridge with her usual vigour. Then she had to leave to open up the shop. He hated having to say goodbye to her, and watched from the front door as she hurried down the cart track with Tommy.

Poor Kate was heavy with child now, ungainly. It made him feel terrible, as though he was abandoning her. Next time he saw her, she'd be slim and graceful again, and have his baby in her arms. The only good thing was that she was living here next door to her mother. At least she had somebody to look after her.

Jack took his time getting himself ready for the journey. Kate had suggested he take his luggage over to the Grange in readiness yesterday. Now said goodbye to Lena and Billy.

The nurse was at the house before him. They hadn't met before; it was Ottilie who had interviewed her. Jack didn't think he'd take to her. Miss Fosdike seemed fussy and elderly, and she wore her fluttering muslin headdress across the middle of her forehead. It covered all her hair.

The invalid carriage was cumbersome, a narrow bed on wheels, with leather covers to protect the bedding from the weather. Three hours before their train was due to leave, Ottilie dispatched it to the station in the care of a gardener. Then she and Father fussed round him with a huge number of tickets and timetables before the taxi arrived.

They were leaving from Lime Street and had to get over to Liverpool. Father came to the station to see them off.

'Your mother isn't at all well,' he worried to Jack. 'I hope this is wise.'

The train was waiting. They still had fifteen minutes before it would leave. Ottilie had reserved a first-class carriage for them, but Mother didn't feel comfortable on the plush seat. She thought she'd feel better if she could lie down in her invalid carriage.

'There isn't room in here for it, Mother.' Jack's eye told him that.

'I must insist, dear. I don't think I could sit up for four hours. That's how long it takes, isn't it?'

Jack was compelled to collect it from the guard's van. Two porters trundled it down the platform and tried to get it into the carriage, but it was too wide to fit between the seats, just as he'd known it would be.

'Yer can travel in it in the guard's van,' one porter suggested with a grin, but Mother was incensed at the idea and elected to sit in the window seat.

Father bought them a collection of newspapers and magazines from the bookstall. He seemed to find saying goodbyes difficult too. Half an hour into the journey, Miss Fosdike had to collect the pillows and blankets from the guard's van so that Mother could lie down along one seat, while he and the nurse sat one in each corner on the other. The news from Germany was bad.

Mother didn't enjoy the journey, he could see that. She was grimacing and groaning and clearly was in great discomfort. Nurse Fosdike fussed interminably.

Euston station seemed desperately busy. He helped to get Mother out to a seat and went in search of a porter. He now had to get them across London to Victoria. He'd never done it before, and moving Mother was like trying to move heaven and earth.

'I think we've come far enough for today.' His mother was looking at him with pitiful eyes. 'I really don't feel well enough to go further, not now.'

Jack was alarmed. 'You said you could do this. It's all booked. It's the boat train, much more comfortable, you'll be able to lie down. There's a wagon-lit booked.'

If they didn't go on, he'd have to alter the reservations for the rest of the onward journey, and they had no hotel booked here. He looked round at the invalid carriage and their mound of luggage piled high on a trolley.

'I couldn't face another train journey, dear, not yet. Tomorrow I'll feel better.'

Jack felt desperate. 'Mother, I insist. This is what you and Ottilie decided to do.'

'The invalid carriage.' She'd slumped down on the seat. 'That's why we brought it. I've got to lie down or I'll fall. I need the ladies, too.'

The nurse took her to the ladies' waiting room, and settled her in the carriage. He was grateful for her help, but they had only an hour and twenty minutes to get to Victoria, and neither of them shared his feeling of urgency.

Ottilie had said they must travel on the underground. Jack consulted a porter, who found him a lad who would travel with them and act as guide. They had to take Mother down in the lift, and between them the boy and the nurse managed to get the invalid carriage on to the train. The luggage had to come off the trolley and was stacked all round them. Jack knew time was getting short, and he was very much afraid they were going to miss the boat train.

It took an age to get them all out of the underground at Victoria and find porters to help again. When they and their luggage reached the platform from which the boat train left, it was already pulling out of the station.

Jack swore under his breath. He felt useless. How many times had Ottilie said, in her bossy way: 'You won't miss the connections, will you, Jack?' as though she fully expected him to.

Mother wasn't upset. Her wizened face looked up at him from the pillows.

'We'll have to go to a hotel after all. All this rushing about is not good for any of us. I don't feel at all well.'

Jack took his jacket off. He was hot, sweating from every pore. This was a disaster. It flustered him to be in charge of this party.

'Where's the nearest hotel?' he asked the boy who was acting as guide. The lad pointed to a big building only fifty yards from the station. Jack was filled with relief to see it so close, and left them waiting while he went to see if they could be accommodated there.

As soon as they had their rooms, Mother wanted to go to bed. Jack felt grateful for Nurse Fosdike's services.

From his own room, he telephoned Kate at the shop. She sounded pleased to hear his voice. He told her about the disaster he'd had so soon after setting out, but that they were safely settled in a hotel for the night. She told him he'd done the right thing and that it wasn't his fault, it was impossible to hurry with Mother in an invalid carriage. She reminded him that he'd have to make new reservations for the next day.

After he'd done that, he went down to the bar and tried to unwind. The word war was on everyone's lips. He couldn't bear it. Just to think war might be imminent terrified him. He finished his drink quickly and went back to his room.

He couldn't get to sleep; any problems like this churned him up. London was, after all, the easy part of the journey. What if this had happened at the Gare du Nord? He was dreading having to change trains there. He fell into a heavy sleep towards morning, and it was late when he woke up. He wasn't too bothered. The train didn't leave until midday and he knew exactly where to go.

He had a bath, then, picking up the newspaper he'd ordered, went down to the dining room for his last English breakfast. At the table he opened *The Times*. The headlines screamed out at him in thick black letters: Austria had declared was on Serbia yesterday.

He felt sick and couldn't eat the eggs and bacon he'd ordered. If Austria was at war, the last thing he wanted was to take his mother to the region. He rushed upstairs to talk to her. She was still in bed and just having morning tea. He pushed the newspaper in front of her.

'We can't go on, this is ridiculous. Austria is at war.'

It took her a long time to read the article. 'I don't see why, Jack. What difference will it make? England's always fighting distant wars in India or the Sudan or . . .

'This is different. Germany has re-armed. She'll declare war too. The paper says she's thirsting for it, greedy to gain more territory. I shall telephone Father, see what he has to say.'

He went to his own room; he didn't want Nurse Fosdike listening to every word. He hadn't meant to have any contact with his father until they were safely in Baden-Baden, but this altered everything.

Minnie, the parlourmaid, answered the phone and told him his father wasn't at home. He rang the office and he wasn't there yet either. He telephoned Kate instead, and it was balm to hear her voice. She agreed with him.

'You mustn't go on, Jack. It isn't safe to go there now.'

There was a frenzied hammering on his bedroom door. He could no longer hear what Kate was saying. He rang off as the door burst open. Nurse Fosdike was radiating panic.

'Come quick. Come quick. Your mother . . .' Her voice trailed off in a choking sob. 'I think she's dying!'

'She's what?' The blood was pounding in his ears as he rushed to her room. She was lying across the bed.

'Mother?' Unseeing eyes stared up at the ceiling. Her mouth was open. He stared down at her as shock waves broke over him. 'Mother?' She'd gone!

The nurse was beside him, her voice squeaky and breathless. 'She wanted to go to the bathroom. I was helping her back when she just went down on me. Heart attack, it must have been.'

Jack hung on to the rail at the bottom of the bed. He needed it to stay upright. His knees felt weak; he could feel himself trembling.

'My God!' They'd sent him to look after Mother and he'd let her die. It was unbelievable. What had he done wrong? Nothing! It wasn't his fault. Thank goodness for the nurse, she'd be able to tell Father he wasn't to blame.

Of course he'd missed the train yesterday, but that had worried her less than it had worried him. She'd wanted to stay over at an hotel. The whole trip had been her idea. Her and Ottilie's. Hadn't he pleaded with them to give it up?

Jack could feel the sweat standing out on his forehead. He couldn't believe this terrible thing had happened so quickly. He felt ill; bile was coming up his throat. He went to the bathroom and was sick. Poor Mother, to die like this away from home. None of the family near her; even he hadn't been.

He splashed cold water on his face and felt a little better. He wouldn't have to find his way across Paris to the hotel there. He'd been dreading that.

When he went back to his mother's room, the nurse was visibly trembling too. No doubt she blamed herself for losing her patient. She crept over to the bed and gently closed his mother's eyelids, then her mouth. It wouldn't stay shut.

'We . . . we need a doctor's certificate before we can move her,' she choked.

He shuddered. 'See to it, will you?' The nurse's face was grey; her eyes were blank. 'Are you up to it?'

'I don't know any doctors. Not here.' She was wringing her hands.

'The hotel manager. Ask him. I have to ring my father.'

He went next door to his own room. He couldn't do anything with his mother lying there on the bed. This time Ottilie answered the phone.

'Is Father there?' he asked, and remembered immediately that he wasn't. What was he thinking about?

'He's gone to the office this morning.'

'I'll ring him there. Ottilie? I have some terrible news. Mother's had a heart attack, she's dead.'

He could hear her gasping with horror.

'It happened this morning, a few minutes ago. I want you to cancel all the reservations for me. Easier for you at that end.'

Hadn't he had terrible trouble altering them yesterday? 'Do it straight away.'

'Are you in Paris?'

'London. Mother wasn't well enough to go on yesterday. I had to delay our crossing. We're due to catch the boat train at midday.'

'Thank goodness! Have you seen the papers today? Austria's declared war.'

'Yes, and it won't be long before Germany's in.'

For the first time it occurred to him that the fiasco in which he found himself was more Ottilie's fault than his.

'I kept telling you. You wouldn't listen. We should never have set out on this trip. A wild-goose chase from the start. Mother just couldn't stand it.'

He had to steel himself again to ring his father. He was the one who'd be really upset. The operator kept him holding.

Then Father's anxious voice came on. 'Hello, Jack, so worried about you and your mother.'

'Father, I have . . .'

'Where are you? In Paris? You mustn't go on . . .'

'I'm in London.'

'Thank goodness for that.'

'No, Father, listen. I've terrible news. Appalling, in fact. It's Mother.'

Chapter Seventeen

1914–1916

Kate had to run the shop and couldn't meet Jack's train when he returned to Lime Street. He was waiting for her when she got home that night. He looked drawn and very upset; he'd lost weight in the few days he'd been away.

'Such a shock, Mother dying like that. I still feel trembly when I think of it. Father's devastated. Guilt-ridden too, because he wasn't with her.'

Kate knew that Jack's happiness and peace of mind were tied up with his family, in the same way that she was tied to hers.

'I'm glad I'm not trying to cross Europe with Mother. Father said he was pleased I'd had the sense to stay put in England when Austria declared war on Serbia. I didn't tell him it wasn't quite like that.'

'I'm so relieved to have you home. So much sooner than I'd expected.' Particularly when the situation in Europe was going from bad to worse. Within days, Germany had declared war on Russia and France, and had violated Belgium's frontiers so that Britain was drawn into the war too.

'I'd be terrified if you were still in Germany now.' Kate was aghast when she heard that.

'We'd all have thought it was the stress of war that brought on Mother's heart attack. Everything happened so fast I hardly know whether I'm on my head or my heels.'

'At least you'll be here for the birth of our baby. There's a lot of good things to take your mind off the bad.' Kate smiled at him.

'Yes, we were thinking so much about the baby and the shop, we hardly noticed war was coming.'

Lena had been making preparations for the birth since Kate had moved next door. She was looking forward to this far more than she had to the birth of her own children.

'This time it'll be all the pleasure and none of the pain,' she told Kate. 'My turn to look after you.'

'I'll be well cared for then. Jack can talk of nothing else but looking after me.'

'Jack? We'll see. I could always rely on you to come home when I needed you. Now I'll be able to repay you for that.'

She thought Kate had not found pregnancy too trying. Her cheeks were rosy, her eyes shone and she'd not put on very much weight. Lena was glad Jack was back and going to the shop with her again. Now that Kate was near her time, she didn't think she should still be working, but Kate said she wanted to be there.

Lena had been down to admire the premises and knew Kate had somewhere to rest when she wanted to. The baby was due on the second Saturday in August. The night before, Lena had asked: 'You're not going to the shop tomorrow?'

'Yes, Saturday's our busiest day. There's no guarantee it'll be tomorrow. You were always a week or more over. I still feel fine.'

'I don't know where you get the energy. I couldn't do it.'

'You had other babies to look after, Mam. Jack fusses round me all the time, making me rest.'

Lena was chatting to Kitty Watts at the front gate when Billy pulled on her skirt to point at the cab coming up the cart track. When she saw Kate doubled up in pain and Jack half lifting her down from the cab, she turned back to her own house.

'Tommy,' she shouted. 'I want you to go for Mrs Potter. Kate's time has come.'

Mrs Potter, the midwife who had attended Lena herself, was still seeing to all the births and deaths in the district.

Lena had never seen Jack so nervous. He helped Kate upstairs and saw her into bed. He didn't want to leave her side. Lena knew what needed to be done. She lit fires in Kate's living room and bedroom. Went back to her own house to make sure there'd be plenty of hot water.

'You're young and strong,' she told her daughter. 'You'll forget all this as soon as it's over and you're holding your baby in your arms.'

Kate was squeezing Jack's hand when her pains came.

'Let him stay,' Lena said to Mrs Potter as she fussed about getting things ready for the delivery. 'Let him see what women have to go through.'

Jack was ashen. 'Will it be very bad?'

'Course not.' Mrs Potter was brisk. A baby girl was born just after midnight.

'Sunday's child is loving and giving,' Lena said. She couldn't wait to hold her. She'd always wanted another daughter herself. Now she felt blessed to have a girl as a first grandchild.

She cuddled her close, a healthy seven-pound baby. She thought she favoured Jack; she had his fair curly hair and was utterly beautiful.

The colour had returned to Jack's cheeks, and he was triumphant now, as though he'd given birth himself. 'We're going to call her Victoria Jemima Lena,' he announced. 'After her two grandmothers.'

'Quite a string of names,' Lena said, but she was pleased with them.

'Vicky for short.' Kate smiled. She looked thrilled with her new daughter, and it was easy to see that Jack adored them both.

Lena quaked inside. Things had been good for her too, up until the time Kate had been born. It was afterwards that her world had turned upside down. She hoped things would not turn sour for Kate, and yet she dreaded they would.

Jack spent most of Sunday sitting in the bedroom with Kate, marvelling at their new daughter. The only time he left her side was to walk down to the post office, which had a phone box outside, to telephone his father with the news.

His father offered congratulations and said: 'You must bring the baby for us all to see just as soon as Kate is well enough.'

When Monday came, Jack didn't want to go to the shop.

'You must,' Kate insisted. 'We'll lose business if you don't. And you must stay open during normal business hours.'

'What about you?'

'Mam will be in and out.' Lena had brought all their meals in yesterday. 'And Mrs Potter's coming to make sure we're all right. You needn't worry about us.'

'You're a hard taskmaster,' he told her. But he knew Kate expected no more of him than she did of herself. 'I wish we'd found a manager.'

'It's better that we haven't. It isn't earning enough yet. We need to get it established. Anyway, you'll have Tommy.'

Jack liked Tommy. His big brown eyes followed him round the shop. He asked all the right questions and was picking things up quickly. He carefully followed any instructions Jack gave him, and even showed deference. It made Jack feel more of a man. In fact, he felt he was getting on well with all Kate's family and neighbours, and even the customers at the shop. They didn't bring up his past disasters and were always polite.

Family and friends of similar social status to the Courtneys seemed to know instinctively that he hadn't made the grade and put him down. With Kate and her family, he felt he'd found sanctuary.

Already he'd come to rely on them. He went home exhausted that evening but he remembered to take his camera. Tommy had to help him carry the special lights on the tram.

He took portraits of mother and child, and, to please Lena, of grandmother and child, and several of Vicky in her cot.

'Never known a child to be so photographed,' Lena told him.

Jack printed a full set for Lena and another for Kate. He bought some fine silver frames for them and displayed them about the house.

The shop had seemed to run effortlessly when Kate was there, but without her he found it very hard work. Tommy referred everything he couldn't cope with to him. Jack had to do all the developing and printing, and often come down to the shop in the middle of it to explain technicalities to a customer.

But he told Kate they were managing fine and that she mustn't hurry back.

Lena was delighted with her new granddaughter, and also with Jack, though it bothered her that he was still married to somebody other than Kate. His clean white hands and formal good manners reminded her of Benedict. Her boys got on well with him, all except Billy. For some reason, Billy and Jack avoided each other when they could.

Jack was generous too. He rarely came back from the shop empty handed. He brought her joints of beef and pork so big she could hardly get them in her oven.

'If you're going to cook for me and Kate,' he said, 'I need to get enough for us all, and your boys have good appetites.'

Lena was pleased, it meant they could all eat well. She took generous portions next door and served them with as much style as she could, using a trolley in the bedroom until Kate was able to come downstairs.

Jack always thanked her and complimented her on her cooking. He even consulted her about what food he should buy. He brought grapes for Kate, and oranges, biscuits and sweets for the boys.

'I'm going to need a cot or pram in the shop.' Kate frowned as she nursed her baby. 'What did you do with Billy's bassinet when he grew too big for it?'

'Sold it to Kitty Watts for her grandson. Got four shillings for it.'

'Oh! I don't suppose you know of anyone else with an old pram for sale?'

'There's one in our shed. I don't know whether you'd want it, though, it's very old. Kitty didn't like it.'

'I just want somewhere to put the baby down to sleep. Let's have a look.'

Lena led her up the back garden path. She had to move spades and rakes and buckets before she could get it out.

'What d' you think?'

It was covered in dust and cobwebs; an old baby carriage made of wickerwork and shaped like a bath chair. It had three wheels, one of which was off but lying on the seat. It was pushed from behind.

'Good Lord!' Kate laughed and flicked a spider off it. 'It must be nearly forty years old. Where did you get this?'

'Charlie found it on a dump and brought it home when our Duncan was a baby and the one he had was beyond repair. He thought it would do him, but Mitch bought the bassinet from Ada Catchpole for me.'

'I don't know . . . It looks awful.'

When Jack came home and saw it, he thought differently. 'I had one like this myself when I was a baby,' he said. 'Wonderful, a real find.'

So Harry cleaned it up and Charlie fixed the wheel. Even after they'd greased it, it still clanked and squeaked when it was pushed.

Jack took it down on the tram and installed it in the room behind the shop.

Kate thought she knew all there was to know about babies. She'd helped with her brothers, fed them, bathed them and changed their nappies. But coping with Vicky was a different matter.

Vicky slept less than any other baby she'd cared for, and demanded twice the attention. At the same time, she pulled at her heart strings with twice the force. She was such a pretty baby, with Jack's fair curly hair and eyes of gentian blue.

Jack was her devoted slave within the first week, though she demanded a great deal from him too. It surprised Kate that he was willing to get up in the night when she cried and pace the floor with her.

Kate thought Jack no longer looked well. Coming on top of his mother's sudden death, he had all the extra work in the shop and the broken nights. She felt well enough to do more and decided she'd go back to work in the shop.

Lena didn't want her to. 'You're still lying in. It's too soon.'

'These days lying-in is only a fortnight.' She smiled. 'Not the six weeks it was for you. I'm on my feet again now.'

'What about the baby?'

'She'll have to come with me. I'll be able to feed her in the back room. I won't do too much to start with, Mam. Jack will be happy just to have me there. He needs me.' Lena didn't miss the look of love in Kate's green eyes.

'Vicky's not three weeks old yet.'

'I'm all right. You were always up and doing by this time.'

'Not for my first. Not for you. I'll help. I'll clean your place through once a week for you, and cook your dinners.'

'That would be a wonderful help. Thanks, Mam.'

Lena too felt the war had crept up on her almost without her noticing it. She'd been so involved with Kate and her boys, she hadn't taken much notice of the wider world. Now suddenly it was thrust upon her. It made her fearful for her sons. A huge wave of nationalism was sweeping the country. When she went into town she saw posters everywhere saying: 'England Needs You'.

Joe was nineteen, and Charlie's eighteenth birthday was next week. Just the age the Army wanted, and they'd been working long enough to feel bored with their jobs. They craved the excitement that war promised. They talked of enlisting.

'No,' she told them. 'Don't you dare do that.'

But nobody expected the war to last more than a few weeks.

'We don't want to miss the fun,' Joe said. 'I think we ought to go. We aren't married men, after all.'

'It doesn't mean to say you won't be missed,' Lena snapped. She was worried sick about them going off to fight.

Battalions of soldiers were leaving for France every week. Military bands played at their head as they marched through town to the railway station. Already the news from France was of fierce fighting and heavy losses. That didn't deter Joe and Charlie. They came home together at two o'clock one day, just when she was getting ready to go out with Billy.

'We've done it,' Charlie told her. 'Signed up. Volunteered.'

Lena went cold inside. She wanted to rail at them for being such fools, but it was too late to do any good now.

'All our friends are doing it.' Joe gave her a little hug. She wept a little when they'd gone back to work. Their papers came five days later, and they were in uniform within two weeks.

When she told Kate they were leaving for basic training, her face looked stark with foreboding.

'I'm glad Jack's nearly forty. He'll surely be too old.'

Lena said: 'He's got a business and a family to keep him here. They won't want Jack.'

'Not that I can see him wanting to join in any sort of a fight. His brothers are even older, above the age for volunteering. The Courtney family are safe.'

Lena found life went on much as usual for her. Her day was filled with cleaning and cooking for her family. She counted herself lucky that her other sons were safe because they were too young to join up. Tommy was only fourteen, and everybody said the war would be over by Christmas.

Kate was pleased to be back in her routine. She went to the shop every morning with Jack and Tommy. They wouldn't let her stand behind the counter all day as she used to. Jack did much more, and encouraged her to wheel Vicky out so that they both had some fresh air. When the baby needed feeding, she could sit down in comfort for half an hour to do it in the back room.

The following Sunday, Jack wanted them all to go and see his father. He carried Vicky wrapped in a shawl. Summer was over; it was a blustery October day and dead leaves were blowing about the grounds.

The big drawing room hadn't changed, but Kate felt the atmosphere had. She put it down to their recent bereavement. All the family were collected there to take tea. Constance's children were brought down by their nanny to see the new baby. Ottilie and Constance made a fuss of her too.

Old Mr Courtney didn't look well. He was sitting as close to the fire as he could get. To Kate the room felt too hot.

'Let me hold her,' he said, and Kate lowered Vicky into his arms. Her big blue eyes stared up, studying the old face while he studied her. 'A beautiful little girl.'

After two minutes he indicated that he wanted Kate to take her back. The parlourmaid brought in a trolley set with a silver tea service, fine china and several plates of cakes and sandwiches.

'Thank you, Minnie,' Constance said. 'Ask the nanny to bring a cradle down, will you? You can't enjoy your tea, Kate, with the baby in your arms.'

They talked of the war. It was a subject that occupied everybody's attention these days. Ottilie looked sorry for herself. 'I'm bereft. I'll have relatives fighting on both sides.'

'And it could mean the end for us,' Leo said. 'War is a disaster for any shipping line.' It was only then that Kate noticed their confidence had gone.

'Our ships will be sunk,' Oscar unbent enough to explain to Kate. 'We have a fleet of twenty-three up-to-date freighters at the moment, but the Courtney Line could be finished.'

'But it's very profitable,' Jack said. 'Won't war bring greater profits? Shipping space will be much in demand.'

His father shivered. 'Yes, freight rates have been picking up over the last few years, but the Germans will want to stop supplies coming into Britain. Their U-boats will hunt down our ships. What I've spent my life building up could be finished.'

Ottilie said: 'You're lucky, Jack. Your business won't be affected by war in the same way.'

When they were about to leave, his father said: 'Vicky looks very comfortable in that cradle. Do you want to take it with you?'

'I'd love it,' Kate said. 'She's sleeping in a drawer at home . . . until we get a proper cot.'

The old man smiled. 'Why don't you go up to the nurseries and see if there's anything else that would be useful? You might as well take the baby things from here. Eh, Constance? Your children have grown out of them now.'

'Yes, there are things there that generations of Courtneys have used as babies.'

'My pram,' her son put in. 'Let's go and see.'

'And toys,' her daughter added.

Constance took each of her children by the hand and led the way upstairs.

There were high chairs, cradles and cots of all description, some antiques and some quite new. Jack pointed out a baby carriage just like the one they already had. It made Kate see it in a very different light, but she preferred the newish one used by Constance's children. There were baby clothes and toys, and every manner of baby equipment.

Kate was thrilled to think she could have her choice, but she felt inhibited by Constance's stare. Not so Jack. 'What about this little rocking chair? I remember using it, and this, and this.'

Constance rang for the housekeeper and disappeared with her children. Jack made a list of what they wanted. Kate had to stop him in the end. 'We haven't that much space.'

He gave the housekeeper his address, and she said she'd have the things sent over on a cart.

Kate felt that she and Jack were settling down to life with Vicky and managing well.

One cold, dark January afternoon, Kate closed the shop and went home with Jack and Tommy as usual. She was always tired by the time they were climbing up the cart track. Jack held the baby in his arms, while she and Tommy carried provisions for the next day or two. She thought she glimpsed Freddie's face in Ada Catchpole's window as they went past.

Jack took Vicky into their own house while Kate went on to her mother's with Tommy and the provisions. Mam always had dinner ready for the family at this time. Kate's brothers were usually all there, jostling and teasing, but setting the table too.

Everything seemed quieter than usual. Kate had a sinking feeling that something was very wrong. Mam was sitting by the fire with Billy on her knee. She was crying and hugging him for comfort.

Tommy propped the shopping bags against the dresser. 'What's happened?'

Kate's eyes went straight to a yellow envelope on the table. Fear knifed through her. Half the families in England lived in dread of receiving one. 'Mam!' She shivered. 'Who?'

'Our Charlie. Our Charlie's copped it.'

Kate knelt down and threw her arms round Mam and Billy. Tommy pushed in too. It seemed all four of them cried together for Charlie.

'Only eighteen,' Mam wailed.

Charlie had signed up seeking excitement and a bit of fun. His letters had told of terrifying times in the trenches.

'I'm so frightened for Joe,' Mam wept. 'They're just boys, barely more than children. Pushed into the front line. And what are they fighting for? It's the politicians I blame; they took us into the war. I don't care what happens to the French or the Belgians. Charlie didn't either.'

When she felt a little better, Kate read the telegram. *It is with deepest sympathy that we have to inform you that Charles Edward McGlory was mortally wounded in battle . . .* The print swam through her tears. She couldn't see to read more.

Charlie's face was in front of her, rather thin but with boyish good looks. He'd been more like Mam than Mitch.

'Where is Compiègne?' Lena asked. 'They say it happened near there.'

Kate shook her head. She'd never heard of the place.

Old Mr Courtney came to the shop from time to time. He said he came to buy his photographic needs, but she didn't think he was all that interested in taking pictures now.

He brought peaches from his hothouse, and apples and pears from his orchard when they were in season. He seemed to be growing more hunched.

Jack was often out, but Kate invited him to the back room to see Vicky and he'd sit for a while holding her on his knee. Kate always asked after his ships.

'The *Jemima Courtney* was caught bringing meat from Argentina. She was torpedoed and sunk without warning forty miles west of Cork.'

'That's dreadful news!'

'The crew – only five were picked up alive, that's the worst part. Archie Bulloch, the captain, had been with us for twenty years.'

'Terrible.'

'There is some good news. The *Pensicola* was attacked by a gunboat in the Mediterranean but she managed to escape by making smoke.'

He usually asked how the shop was doing. Kate spoke openly about it and showed him the books she kept. He offered advice which she sometimes found useful. The profits were going up as they became known. She felt she was getting to know him better.

When Vicky learned to crawl and wanted to romp on the floor, it was no longer feasible to take her to the shop every day. Lena offered to look after her at home.

'It's an awful lot to expect of you,' Kate said.

'Aren't I used to babies? Haven't I always had one at heel? What will I do when our Billy starts school? I won't know how to get through the day if I don't have a baby clinging to my skirts.'

Kate knew her mother was getting older and no longer had the energy to run after toddlers, but she could see no alternative if she was to help Jack with the shop.

It was May when Kate first left Vicky at home with her mother. Alone at the shop, Kate realised that Billy would have been old enough to start school after Christmas, but her mother had done nothing about it.

Jack said: 'She wants to keep him with her. Doesn't want to part with him. Perhaps now she has Vicky, she will.'

Over dinner that night, Kate said: 'Really, Mam, Billy should be in school. What are you thinking of?'

She knew Mam didn't get on well with the headmaster. In the past he'd complained to her that Tommy in particular was not being sent to school regularly.

Mam shook her head. 'He'll say Billy can't learn, won't he? Refuse to take him.'

'He can't do that,' Jack told her. 'It would be against the law. The council must provide an education for every child between the ages of five and twelve.'

'You want to go to school with the others, don't you, Billy? You want to learn . . .' Kate wanted to say *to read and write*, but like Mam, she was afraid he wouldn't be able to.

'Want to go.' He beamed.

'I'll see about sending you then.'

'I think you should,' Kate said. 'He'll learn something.'

But Billy didn't like school. Every morning Mam took him there, pushing Vicky along in her pram. She hadn't done that for the others. Always after the first day, the new entrant had been put in charge of an elder brother and sent off from the breakfast table.

She hated to leave Billy at the school gates, and although he had his brothers with him, he made a fuss. Mam was tempted to keep him at home with her.

'It's what he wants,' she said to Kate. 'And the teacher just lets him play about. He isn't learning anything.'

'No, Mam, he'll learn to get on with other children. He needs to know that there are other places. He needs a chance to learn.'

So Mam persevered. It took the best part of the term before he settled down. It was such a relief when she could send him off happily with Harry.

'What's it like having just Vicky at home?' Kate asked.

'She's a lot more trouble than Billy ever was. She looks a little angel but she's a determined little minx. You were such a good little girl, Kate, and Jack's so gentle, I can't understand how you managed to produce such a rebel.'

Charlie had been killed early in 1915. In October of the same year they heard that Joe had died of wounds received in battle in Salonika. Mam spent a few days in bed after that. Tommy stayed off work to look after her and took over the cooking. He persuaded Mam to come downstairs to eat with them in the evenings.

'They shouldn't have volunteered.' Mam shook her head, toying with her food. 'I told them not to, but they had to go and do it.

They'd be alive now if they'd listened to me.'

'They had to go,' Tommy said, his face fierce. 'Men of their age who haven't, they're being sent white feathers. And have you seen the posters? They're all over town.

' "When the war is over and someone asks your husband or your son what he did in the Great War, is he to hang his head because you wouldn't let him go?" '

'Better than having no head to hang,' his mother said sharply. 'At least they'd still be alive.'

'I wish I could go. I'd give the enemy what for.' Tommy's face glistened with fierce anguish. 'Killing two of my brothers as well as all those other lads.'

'Count yourself lucky you're too young.' Mam turned on him. 'I'm very glad you are.'

'Perhaps the war will last until I'm eighteen.'

'Heaven forbid.'

Mam hated the war. It had robbed her of her two eldest sons, but she thought she was safe now; it could take nothing more from her. There were desperate shortages – food had to be queued for and was becoming more expensive – but she continued to cook dinner every night for Jack and Kate. Jack maintained in his gentle way that if she was going to do that, then the least he could do was to provide the ingredients, so she was cushioned from the cost. As if it was any trouble cooking for two or three more when she already had her own brood to feed.

Jack liked to take a walk about town and was often able to get her meat and bread and other things in short supply.

Every month or six weeks, Jack took Kate and Vicky to visit his family on a Sunday afternoon. Kate began to feel a little sorry for the Courtneys. They always had horrific stories to recount about their ships.

Ottilie had told them on their last visit that the *Charlotte Courtney* had been requisitioned for use as a 'Q' ship by the Royal Navy and renamed HMS *Fortescue*. From a distance, she still looked like a vulnerable cargo ship, but she'd been fitted with an arsenal of guns to protect herself.

'We've just heard she's been torpedoed by German submarine U103,' she said now.

'And sunk?' Jack asked.

'No, seriously damaged, though. She's been towed by tug to Airewell. They're going to repair her.'

'That's something.'

'And our own crew weren't on board.'

'She was on a crew training exercise off the Lizard.'

'There is really bad news, though,' Leo said. 'The *Spinola*'s been sunk off Ancona with all hands after striking a mine.'

Kate no longer felt in awe of him now he looked so downcast.

'I get nightmares when I think of all the men I know who are going down with their ships,' old Mr Courtney sighed.

'I read in the newspaper that freight rates are up again,' Jack said. 'So there's good news too.'

'No.' Oscar shook his head. 'There's to be a Ministry of Shipping now, and all ships will come under government control. Government freight rates will be lower than those on the open market.'

'I also read that the Government is compensating shipowners for their losses.'

'Yes,' Leo admitted. 'There is that. It's not a total loss when a ship goes down.'

'Handsomely compensated, according to *The Times*.'

Kate thought Ottilie and Leo remained frosty towards Jack, but Jack no longer felt they held the upper hand.

Kate had feared the war would affect the photography trade, but their suppliers continued to provide sufficient materials for their needs. In fact, the business was growing faster than before. She felt on top of it now, competent at developing and printing. They were doing many more portraits in the shop, as men joining up wanted to leave pictures with their families, and their wives and girlfriends came too so that soldiers might carry their likenesses with them. Kate sometimes went out to photograph a wedding as well.

Last year, they'd started a developing and printing service for amateur films that were handed in to chemist's shops all over town. One of them, either Tommy or Jack, went round collecting the films in the morning, and took the completed work back for the late afternoon. Jack said he was delighted with the way the business was going, and they were both beginning to feel quite prosperous.

Lena was going about her usual chores on a sunny May day in 1916. It was mid-morning when she went to Tommy's bedroom; he had the parlour to himself now. He'd made his bed, as he always did before going to work. On his pillow was a sheet torn from an exercise book.

Dear Mam,
I've gone to join the Army. I couldn't tell you to your face because
I knew you'd try to stop me.

She said aloud: 'Good God! Tommy, no! You fool! You stupid fool,'
then collapsed on his bed, horror shafting through her. All she'd gone
through with Charlie and Joe she'd be going through again with Tommy.
All the worry and anguish. It was five minutes before she could read
on.

It's something I just have to do. I want to get my own back on the
Germans for killing Charlie and Joe. Don't worry about me. I'll
take good care of myself. You know me, I'm a survivor.
Love from Tommy.

Lena swallowed back the cold panic that threatened to engulf her.
Tommy wasn't even sixteen until June; she'd thought he was safe for
two more years. She had to stop him. But how? The next moment she
was ramming her old straw hat on her head and easing Vicky, who was
asleep in her pram, out of the door.

She went straight to the recruiting office in Birkenhead. She knew
exactly where it was; she'd seen the flags flying above the doorway,
and there were posters all over town advising everyone of its address.
She'd expected to have to push her way to the desk, as Charlie and Joe
had told her they had. There didn't seem to be so many signing up
today.

'Nobody called Thomas McGlory,' the sergeant in charge told her.
She didn't believe him until he showed her his records. There'd been
only two that day, and neither was Tommy.

'Gone further afield to volunteer,' he said. 'He'd know you'd be
down after him.'

'He's not even sixteen,' Lena stormed. 'He's far too young.'

She didn't know where to turn next. Tommy had been a skinny little
thing at ten, but he'd been able to eat his fill these last few years, and he
was tall and strong now. He looked eighteen. He looked healthy too; he
wouldn't be one who'd fail his medical. She pushed the pram up Grange
Road to tell Kate and Jack.

'Mam!' Kate was aghast. 'I was wondering what had happened to
him. He went round the chemist's shops and I saw him take the films
upstairs, then he just disappeared.'

'He's under age, surely we can stop him.' Jack's brow was furrowed

211

with thought. 'He's wily enough not to do it near home. Where would he go?'

'Liverpool,' Lena suggested.

It was Kate who asked the telephone operator to put her through to the recruiting office in Liverpool. Lena watched her hanging on for what seemed an age, and then the answer came: no, he hadn't volunteered there.

Jack had taken Kate's place in the shop and was serving customers. Vicky woke up. Lena cuddled her on her knee and thought how short a time it seemed since she had held Tommy like this.

Kate went on telephoning. She tried Wallasey and Chester and a few small subsidiary offices, but drew a blank each time.

'Surely there's some office that co-ordinates all volunteers?' she asked each time. 'Can you tell me where that is? Give me the phone number?' but nobody could or would.

Lena had to agree when Kate said it was hopeless. That she couldn't ring every recruiting office in Britain.

'The silly boy,' Lena wept. 'He'll get himself killed. He must realise that.'

'Tommy's always been a daredevil. Nothing ever seemed to frighten him.' She knew Kate had always been very close to Tommy.

Two days later, Lena had a letter from him postmarked London. He said he'd had to do it this way. He still wasn't saying which regiment he'd be in, and he gave no address, but he said he had lodgings for a few days until his papers came through. He was all right. She mustn't worry.

Lena sniffed. There was no way she could avoid worrying, not when her little imp did things like this.

Chapter Eighteen

1916–1921

Vicky was two years old when Jack received a letter from his solicitor telling him that his divorce was now through. He knew he'd only have to wait a few more weeks for the decree nisi to be free of Philomena.

He stood holding the letter, alone in the room behind the shop, feeling as though he'd put down a great burden. He listened to the rise and fall of Kate's voice as she spoke to a customer, and felt a moment of pure joy.

They could be married at last! Not that he saw her as anything less than a wife already. He was closer to Kate than he'd ever been to anyone before. There was trust between them now, as well as love. She was giving him what he wanted from life.

There were other things he wanted, of course: he'd like to make more money from this business, for a start. But as soon as he mentioned that to Kate, she got out the books to show him that their profit was increasing all the time. It was just that it seemed slow to him.

Kate told him he was extravagant and didn't know how to handle money, and that he'd better let her look after the cash. He'd thought of asking his father for more funds to buy another shop in Liverpool and so double their income, but Kate wouldn't hear of it. In fact, that was the only time she'd been angry with him.

'We don't need further help. We need to be independent and stand on our own feet. We'll be perfectly all right. We're managing fine, aren't we?'

Yes, they were, but he didn't like to see her working so hard. She'd be behind the counter most of the day and working on the books on many evenings. Apart from that, he was very content with his lot.

He heard the customer leave and went out to show Kate the letter. He saw such radiance in her face as she read it.

'We can be married very soon,' he choked, and the next minute she was in his arms.

'I'm so happy, so happy.' She was wiping her eyes. He felt heavy with emotion and pulled her into the back room so that no customers could burst in on them.

'What sort of a wedding do you want?' He hadn't dared talk about it before in case it brought bad luck. At times, he thought he'd be tied to Philomena for life.

'Quiet,' she said. 'No fuss. We jumped the gun, and lots of people think that's very wrong. As quiet as possible.'

He remembered the big church wedding his mother had arranged when he married Philomena. They'd had four bridesmaids, two pages and a four-tier wedding cake. Most of their employees had been invited to the marquee on the lawn.

He said: 'It isn't so much the wedding I hanker for as the state of marriage. I want us to be legally bound together.' He felt euphoric.

As soon as Lena heard of Jack's divorce, she lost her fear for Kate. It was a huge weight off her mind. Kate had seemed to be following in her exact footsteps and she hated to think she was heading for a similar end. Marriage would make everything right for Kate, and Vicky would no longer be thought illegitimate.

The wedding was fixed for a Thursday afternoon, because that was early-closing day and they could shut the shop. It was to be at the register office, with just family members invited.

Kate bought herself a dress of fine blue wool with bands of dark-blue velvet round the skirt and on the stand-up collar. She saw a big hat in a matching shade with darker blue silk flowers covering the crown.

'It would be very extravagant to get that,' she sighed.

'You'll look smart in it for years,' Lena told her. 'Would Jack hesitate? Get it while you can.'

Lena said she couldn't afford a new outfit for herself, not if her boys were to look halfway reasonable.

'Nonsense,' Jack said, taking some money from his wallet. 'You take her out, Kate, and buy her something smart. I want to be proud of my mother-in-law.'

Together Kate and Lena chose a hat and dress of mauve silk.

'Your Jack's a very generous person,' Lena told her daughter. 'I'll be able to wear this afterwards for best.'

The wedding took place on a sunny but cool September afternoon. Lena kept all the boys off school. She spent the morning cleaning, and preparing a special dinner for the evening.

Jack and Kate took their wedding finery to the shop and said they'd change there and go direct. Kate wanted to have time to titivate.

'If you could dress Vicky for me and bring her down?'

'Of course, love.'

Kate had bought Vicky an ornate white dress with lots of lacy frills. Billy, smartened up in grey flannel knickerbockers, held Vicky's hand throughout the ceremony.

Lena was on edge, worried about meeting Jack's relatives. She could remember with awful clarity the day Benedict had taken her to the launching ceremony of the *Jemima Courtney*, and the fracas afterwards with Amelia. She'd been introduced to William Courtney and shaken his hand. The humiliation of what had happened afterwards must be as clear in his memory as it was in hers, the whole family must know who she was; must know she'd been Amelia Rotherfield's maid. She was nervous that they'd cut her dead; refuse to speak to her.

Kate said they wouldn't, that the Rotherfield name had never been mentioned to her, but all the same, for Lena it cast a blight over the preparations for Kate's wedding. All the McGlorys were down at the register office in time to see the Courtneys arrive in two very smart motor cars.

Jack introduced them. His father seemed kind and shook Lena's hand. His brothers were both haughty. Lena had to take a mental grip on herself not to call them 'sir', as had been expected when she was in service.

She didn't take to the womenfolk. She thought Constance looked like an overstuffed cushion in her fine clothes, and both women were arrogant, merely inclining their heads towards her when introduced, and treating her boys like stable lads.

They tried to make a fuss of Vicky. She looked demurely sweet with a red velvet band round her fair hair, but Vicky was clinging to both Lena and Billy and couldn't be enticed away. Lena felt loved and trusted. She had something these rich ladies wanted which money couldn't buy.

Kate looked so much younger and more attractive than they did. Today she looked stunning, with her flame-coloured hair shining brightly under her hat and her cheeks flushed with excitement.

The ceremony was formal. The wedding ring Kate had been wearing for years had been taken off and was now officially put back in place. Jack clung to her as though she were the giver of life itself. Lena approved of him, and thought he'd make a loyal husband. It was just a pity he didn't know what work was.

Afterwards, Jack's relatives wanted to take them all to the Woodside

Hotel for a celebratory drink. They'd even reserved a private room, but Jack insisted they all go to his shop first for a commemorative photograph.

'He's already taken two or three of me in my wedding finery, before we set off,' Kate told Lena.

Many more photographs were taken, and the Courtneys were shown over the premises. Kate made them cups of tea and offered them little cakes that Jack had bought that morning. The boys wolfed most of those.

Lena wanted to get home to the dinner she was cooking. Ada Catchpole had promised to put the leg of pork in the oven for her, but there would still be plenty she needed to do.

Jack had asked if he might invite his father to dinner. 'He's lonely now Mother has gone.'

'But not your brothers and their families?'

'No,' he'd said. 'No need. Constance will want to take her children home and put them to bed.'

'I'll have it ready for seven o'clock.'

Lena took all the boys home with her except Billy. Vicky was still hanging on to him, and Jack wanted to take his daughter to the hotel. She got the lads to carry her table and chairs into Kate's house, so they could all eat together. She was using both fires to cook for them.

Kate's living room looked very festive. Jack had provided the tablecloths; he didn't think the ones she'd made from bleached flour bags smart enough. They didn't have enough matching cutlery and china, but Kate said that wouldn't matter.

Lena put a wedding cake on each table. Her intention had been to make a two-tier cake, but when she'd gone to buy the pillars needed to arrange one cake above the other, they'd seemed outrageously expensive for something so trivial, so it was two separate cakes. She'd been very pleased with the baking. Ada had helped her ice them, but they hadn't made too good a job of that.

The wedding party returned home in good time. Old Mr Courtney, who was rather jovial by now, brought them in his motor car. The chauffeur sat outside and waited throughout the meal. Lena sent Harry out with food and drink for him.

They drank a toast to Tommy, who had sent a telegram of congratulations. Lena prayed that one day he'd return home safe and sound. She thought the wedding had gone off very well and was pleased with her efforts.

When the old man had left and the children were yawning, she got the boys to carry their furniture back home, because tomorrow it would be school as usual.

As she undressed for bed that night, Lena felt very satisfied. Kate was settled, and for her the future looked rosy. Jack's family had given them some wonderful wedding presents.

Kate thought that if only the war would end, they would all be happy. Jack kept telling her she was wonderful both as a photographer and as a mother, and she felt very content with him. They both adored Vicky, who was growing fast and would be starting school soon.

But the war raged on. Kate felt it dominated their lives. She'd lost two brothers, and now Tommy was caught up in the fighting. She'd loved them all, perhaps Charlie more than Joe, but Tommy was her favourite brother. She missed his cheeky grin and pushy ways, and none of them had done more for the family. It brought an edge of anxiety to everything else. She knew Mam was fretting about him.

It amazed Kate that with all the time Tommy had had off school he'd learned to read and write as well as he had. He wrote home often. Sometimes to her and sometimes to Mam. It didn't matter who he addressed his letters to; they were handed round the family for all to read.

He had come home on two weeks' leave when he'd been in the Army for nine months. He was shamefaced on arrival and said he was sorry for the anxiety he'd caused, but they couldn't tell him off then because he was about to embark for France.

He seemed to be thriving on Army life; he exuded strength and health and confidence. He'd already been promoted to corporal.

Kate knew he was serving in the trenches, but he mentioned none of the horrors of war. There were times when she wept for the brave front he put on for them. He wrote home of football matches played behind the lines, of swimming in the canals and rivers, and of the fact that the French cafés and bars were open for business close behind the front.

She talked about him to Mam often. They both agreed he seemed to be taking care of himself. He'd survived at the front for longer than either Charlie or Joe. He was promoted to sergeant. Even Mam said he was doing really well.

It was March 1918, and it seemed as though the war would drag on forever, yet Tommy still wrote home with enthusiasm. They didn't hear a word about the mud and rats in the trenches, the dysentery, the snipers and the continual bombardment by big guns. Kate was beginning to think he might come through.

She came home at lunch time one day because Billy was off school with mumps and Vicky hadn't been feeling well that morning. She was relieved to find Vicky had picked up and was playing happily, but Mam was worn out.

'Go and have a rest on your bed,' Kate told her. 'I'm home now, I can see to Billy.'

'He's asleep upstairs at the moment. I might as well join him.'

She watched her mother pull herself wearily up from the chair. As she was passing the window to go upstairs, she paused, and Kate heard her gasp.

'What is it?'

When she didn't answer, Kate got up to look. She saw a telegraph boy trying to cycle up the cart track. It became too steep for him. He dropped the heavy red bike against the hedge and came walking rapidly up, taking a yellow envelope from his shoulder pouch as he did so.

Mam croaked, 'Is he coming here?'

Kate's mouth went dry with dread. She couldn't take her eyes off the lad. He was whistling as he came on towards them. It was their gate he turned into. She went to the front door to meet him.

'Mrs McGlory?' he asked. Kate nodded and signed his book. She took a deep breath, closed the door and leaned back against it.

'It'll be about Tommy,' Mam said, her face sickly white. 'Open it.'

Kate did so and started to read: *It is with deepest regret that we have to inform you that Thomas Eric McGlory died fighting for his country on 4 March 1918 during a battle on the Somme. Please accept our sincere condolences.*

She felt stunned, bereft. She'd always been close to Tommy. His face, still sparky and pixie-like, danced before her misting eyes. She opened her arms to her mother, but was seeking comfort for herself.

Mam was in terrible floods of grief. Kate knew she too had been specially fond of Tommy. Hadn't he been home helping her more often than at school?

She took her mother up to her bed and covered her with her eiderdown. Vicky was letting off wails of protest now she'd realised she was alone in the living room.

Kate went down, collapsed on the old basket chair and pulled her daughter on to her knee. She rocked her gently, soothing herself at the same time. Poor Tommy, what a terrible waste of a young life.

Within ten minutes Vicky was falling asleep. She laid her in the pram and went back to her mother.

'Oh, Kate! I can't believe he's dead, not our Tommy. He was so full of life, and just a lad still. All those years of struggle to bring him up, and for what? He's had nothing of life. Nothing of the pleasures it can bring, just the awfulness of war. Dead and not yet eighteen. Killed by a bullet when he should have had all his adult life before him.'

Kate slipped off her shoes and got under the eiderdown beside her.

'What a senseless waste. I hate war. All those Kings and Emperors who want to fight, but it's families like ours who pay the price, not them.'

She put her arms round her mother, trying to find words of comfort for her. 'At least the others are too young to fight.'

'Who knows when it will end?'

'It's got to, before they're old enough. Harry's only fourteen.'

'Going on fifteen.'

'At least you left a good gap between him and Tommy.'

'Left a gap? You don't know what you're talking about.'

'Mam, there's years between . . .'

'I made that gap.'

'Of course you did. There's going to be a big gap between Vicky and the next. I'd like to have another baby, but it just doesn't happen.'

'What are you talking about? Kate, I killed three others. I killed three other babies.'

Kate shivered. She knew her mother was emotionally overwrought, that she hardly knew what she was saying. 'And how I wish now I hadn't.'

'Hush, Mam. You know that's not true.'

'It's true enough.' Mam pulled herself up the bed and out of Kate's arms, her face fierce and tear-stained.

'Don't think I haven't mourned for them. Three times I had an abortion. Mitch knew of this woman who lived in the Dock Cottages. She'd do it for ten shillings.'

Kate stiffened, appalled at what she was hearing.

'I had you and Joe and Charlie. Then Liza, who died at nine months, and Tommy. We hadn't enough money to feed any more. Couldn't feed those I did have properly.'

Kate felt sick. Mam had more secrets than she'd supposed. She'd thought she knew everything.

'So you see, Kate, your father wasn't the only . . .'

'Nonsense, Mam! Don't say such things. Better to try and limit your family. You had to.'

'It was what Mitch wanted and I thought it would be for the best . . .

I wouldn't have gone on to have Harry and Duncan . . .'

'And Freddie and Billy,' Kate prompted. She had wondered about that three-year gap but had put it down to the vagaries of nature.

'Except that I almost bled to death with the last abortion. I don't remember too much about it – I passed out – but it scared Mitch, I can tell you. They had to take me to hospital. After that I had the babies as they came. Even Mitch thought I should. And I'm glad now. At least I still have four.'

'Five,' Kate prompted. 'You aren't counting me. You never do.'

'Oh, Kate! It's because you're a girl and you're grown-up and so different. It's not because I don't love you.'

When the war was finally over, Lena felt drained. Jack felt they should celebrate. Wages had doubled in the four years of war and everybody wanted a camera. His prosperity was increasing.

Lena reflected that hers was too. Harry had left school and Jack had taken him on at the shop. He'd bought a bicycle for him, and Harry pedalled all over Birkenhead and its suburbs collecting films from chemist's shops. He swept up and made the tea and was learning to serve behind the counter. Jack said he was very willing, and when he was a little older, he'd teach him to develop and print too.

Duncan was twelve now, and it wouldn't be long before he was earning too. The years were passing quickly. Freddie was nine, and Billy, growing up plump and sturdy, had been going to school for nearly four years. All the other children went up a class at the end of the school year, but Billy never made the progress needed for that. Instead he stayed where he was and went through the same work again.

He'd spent two years in class one and two in class two, and now his teacher had told her he'd be staying with her for another year. Billy was twice the size of the other children in his class.

'It's what suits him, Mam,' Kate told her softly. 'He can't keep up with the others.'

His teachers liked him; he was helpful, looking after the younger ones. There was nothing he liked better than helping the teacher to clean the blackboard, opening or closing windows, and handing out slates, chalk or reading books to the class.

As Lena saw it, Billy was becoming less like other children. All her other sons had been quick at school work. Billy could sing; he'd learned a little poetry off by heart; he could make his letters on a slate. He wasn't much good at reading, and words defeated him when he was asked to write them. He was willing and obedient, and no trouble at all in class.

In a way, Lena found it a comfort. She'd never be without a child in the house. Billy would always be with her.

Vicky was quite the opposite.

'Rules the roost here, does your Vicky,' Lena complained to Kate. 'She's a little madam.'

'You've got to be firm with her, Mam.'

'She knows how to get round me.'

'Knows how to get round most of us. She twists Jack round her little finger.'

'But not you, Kate.'

'Somebody has to stand up to her.'

Lena couldn't help comparing Vicky with Billy, who was over four years older. In the early days, he'd looked after her, but by the time she was four she was leading him. He was happy to be her slave.

When Vicky was coming up to school age, Lena couldn't help but wonder how Billy would feel when Vicky started there and passed up the school, leaving him behind. She said as much to Kate and Jack one night after they'd put the children to bed.

'I don't think we'll send her to St Bede's,' Jack told her.

'It's a good school. All mine went there. I did myself, but it was called the Claughton Mission Room then.'

'I want Vicky to go to the High School.'

'The High School? You'll have to pay for that.'

'Yes, I know.'

It was several days after this that Kate told Lena they'd been discussing Vicky's education when they went to visit Jack's family. It was really his father's idea, not Jack's.

'He's offered to pay her school fees.'

'I thought the Courtneys' fleet had been sunk, that they'd lost their money.'

'They lost fifteen of their ships due to enemy action, but they've been handsomely compensated by the Government for that.'

'Trust the likes of them . . . and I thought they were losing everything.'

'No, his father's very frail now. It's really upset him . . . so many of their crew went down with their ships. He wants to sell up, get out of the business.'

'But what about Jack's brothers? They'll still have to earn a living.'

'They won't need to earn anything more, Mam. Leo's over fifty. I think he wants to retire and live like a gentleman. They'll each have an unearned income.

'The ships they have left are being sold off, and prices are sky-high now the war's over and there's a shortage.'

Lena sat back and pondered on how much more the middle class earned compared with their workers. She wondered if Kate would have been any different if she'd been able to go to the High School. Her father would have provided schooling like that if only . . .

Vicky looked very smart in her school uniform when she started. Kate took her there in the mornings on her way to the shop, but Lena collected her in the afternoons. It wasn't very much further away than St Bede's. She was proud of having a granddaughter at such a fine school.

On Saturdays, Lena looked after them all at home. It was her hardest day, though she told herself it wasn't as hard as it used to be. Duncan had left school now and was working at the shop for Jack. Harry had decided he wanted to go to sea and see something of the world. She now had only Freddie and Billy left at home, but there were fewer children in Cemetery Cottages these days, and they had no one to play with.

The only others of school age or under were the Jenkins children next door at number four, and those of Flossie Jenkins' friend Gladys Fry at number five.

Flossie Jenkins' son had married when she was newly widowed, and his wife and family lived with her. Lena had never got on with the Jenkinses and had kept her children away from theirs.

Now the Jenkins and the Fry boys played together in and out of the two houses. Each family had a boy of about twelve and another of about seven. They ganged up against Billy, shouting after him that he was threepence short of a shilling, or had a slate loose on his roof. Vicky returned insults on Billy's behalf, though she was younger than any of them. She had great fluency for a six-year-old.

It sometimes seemed to Lena that war waged around Cemetery Cottages even if there was peace in France. Freddie didn't often join in, unless Vicky appealed to him for support. He usually stayed about the house helping her, as Tommy used to.

It never ceased to amaze her that the children followed their parents' patterns of friendship. Usually in the afternoons, Lena took Vicky and Billy out to the shops, to the park or to the cemetery. Anywhere to get respite from the slanging matches and the fighting outside.

'Let's go to the park,' Vicky said. 'I'd like to feed the ducks.'

Lena didn't have the energy to go that far. 'The dead park,' she said. Vicky was pulling a face. 'I want to go to the real park.'

'No, the dead park. Come on, Billy, we'll weed your dad's grave.'

Billy was happy to carry the little gardening fork for her. He put his hand in hers and trotted beside her. Vicky moaned and groaned, but eventually followed ten yards behind.

Lena liked the cemetery. It was a peaceful place, quiet, except for the rooks cawing in the tall trees and the distant hum of the mowing machine being pulled by Dolly the donkey.

Billy helped her to pull up the grass that was spreading over the grave, while Vicky went off by herself. Lena knew she'd gone to look for some fresh flowers to replace those that had wilted in the marble vase. There had been several funerals this morning, and there were lots of flowers outside the chapels of rest. Lena sent Billy to the tap with the marble vase and sat down to rest for a moment. It didn't displease her to think that one day she'd join Mitch and Liza here.

Vicky fussed over the white gladioli, arranging them carefully. 'Aren't they nice, Gran? Billy's father will like them, won't he?'

Lena admired them too.

'Don't let's go home yet,' Vicky said. 'Let's walk round.'

It soothed Lena to saunter along the walkways bordered with holly bushes with Billy's hand in hers. She knew exactly where Vicky was leading them. The scent of new-mown grass was in the air now and the sound of the mowing machine much louder.

Now Vicky went whooping ahead. 'Please, Mr Watts, can I have a ride on Dolly?'

Archie Watts from number six sometimes allowed the children to ride on Dolly as a treat. Obligingly he lifted her up, and Vicky laughed with delight.

'Me too,' Billy said, 'Me too.'

'You're a hefty lump now, Billy. It would flatten poor old Dolly if I put you up too. In a minute.'

'I've got something for you, Billy,' the young lad who was sweeping up the grass cuttings told him. 'Been keeping it on one side till I saw you.'

'What? A present?' Billy clapped his hands.

'Sort of. Come on, we'll go and get it.' The lad's father also worked in the cemetery and the family lived in one of the lodges. 'Is it all right if I go home to fetch it, Mr Watts?'

'Be quick then, George.'

Lena trailed behind them, and had just reached the lodge when they came out. Billy was hugging an air rifle.

'A gun!' Billy chortled. 'I've got a real gun.'

Lena was alarmed. 'He can't have that.'

'It doesn't work any more, Mrs McGlory,' George told her. 'Wouldn't part with it if it did. I left it on the grass and Dolly stood on it. It's crushed here and I can't get the cartridges in any more. Ruined really, such a pity.' He showed her. 'It's no good now except as a toy.'

Lena hesitated. 'Lovely gun.' Billy caressed it.

'Thank you, George. It was kind of you to think of Billy.' The groundsmen were always giving the children sweets and little gifts. 'Say thank you, Billy.'

While Billy had his donkey ride, Vicky sat on the grass nursing his gun.

'You hold a gun this way,' George showed her. 'Broken open means it's not loaded. You fire it like this.'

Vicky drew back the trigger and made it click.

'Course, it would make much more noise if it was loaded.'

'It looks wicked,' Vicky said, stroking it. 'Really wicked.'

On her return, Lena stopped at Ada Catchpole's house. Betty, Ada's daughter, was home for a week's holiday from her job as a housekeeper. As a child, she'd been Kate's friend and much the prettier of the two. She'd been involved with a man who'd deserted her, and Ada had brought up her son. He'd started work now at the Co-op but still lived with her. For years, Lena had dreaded the same fate for Kate. She stayed to hear details of Betty's life, and couldn't help comparing it with Kate's. Kate's life was wonderfully better.

They were still sitting over the tea cups an hour later when they heard a scream of terror and shouting close by. Lena leapt to her feet, and they all rushed out to Ada's back garden.

Lena had recognised Vicky's voice. She saw her levelling the gun at the two Jenkins boys. Alec, the younger one, was snivelling with terror. Howard, the elder, was cringing back against the fence.

'Give Billy your toffee,' Vicky was demanding. 'And you, Howard. We want all of it, not just one piece. Go on, or I'll shoot you.' The gun waved threateningly. 'Get it, Billy. I'll keep you covered.'

Lena was struggling for breath as she watched Billy take greaseproof packages from unresisting hands.

'Right, bring it to me. We'll go in my house.' Vicky was backing away, keeping the gun trained on Howard Jenkins. 'Stay where you are or I'll kill you. One movement and I'll shoot.'

Once in her own garden, she burst into contemptuous laughter as

Alec ran home screaming at the top of his voice. His mother, Miriam, had already heard him and come rushing out; so had Freddie and almost everybody else living in Cemetery Cottages.

'She's taken our toffee, Mam,' Alec complained. 'Vicky Courtney's taken it off us.'

'Give it back this minute.' His mother stood with her hands on her hips. 'I've just made that.'

'No,' Vicky shouted, and popped a generous piece in her mouth. 'D'you want some, Billy?'

'She was going to shoot us.'

'It's only a toy gun.'

'That's no toy, Lena McGlory. Your kids are hoodlums. You let them terrorise the neighbourhood. I'll be glad to get away from here.'

'We shan't be sorry to see the back of you.'

Flossie Jenkins' son was rumoured to be retiring from the police force to buy a shop of his own. Going into business on their own account, they called it.

'You let that girl run wild.' Miriam was angry. 'And your Billy's no better. Doesn't know his own strength. He went for our Alec yesterday.'

'Billy wouldn't hurt a fly.'

'You've got no control over either of them.'

Lena ordered: 'Billy, give that toffee back to Howard. Go on. Both lots.' He obeyed slowly.

'I can't believe the cheek of her. Stealing the toffee I took the trouble to make.'

'It's not much good,' Vicky retorted, moving the toffee from one side of her mouth to the other. 'Not nearly as nice as toffee from the shops.'

'Wants a good hiding, that little savage. Dangerous, and you let her have a gun. It's lucky nobody's hurt. I ought to get the police to talk to you.'

Lena protested: 'It's just a toy!'

'Cowardy cowardy custards,' Vicky chanted from the safety of her own garden.

Lena took a deep breath. 'Couldn't your Howard manage to take a duff gun from a six-year-old girl? He's a big boy, for heaven's sake!'

'I thought it was real,' Howard said, heading for home. 'She said she was going to kill us.'

Lena was exasperated. 'It's all pretend. Surely you know that?'

She rushed Vicky and Billy into her own house, slammed the door and ran upstairs to hide the gun on top of her wardrobe. That was the last they were going to see of it.

Chapter Nineteen

1921–1929

When Kate arrived home with Jack that evening, they were both in a good humour. They'd had a good day at the shop and taken more money than usual.

'We're doing well.' Jack had self-congratulatory moments these days. 'Of course, business is booming everywhere, it's not just photography. We could afford that car, Kate.'

He'd been talking for some time about getting one, and had decided on a model T Ford. Kate had urged him to wait, but now she wondered if she was being overcautious.

'It would make it much quicker to get to the shop,' he urged.

'Right, let's do it,' she agreed, before breezing into her mother's living room.

Vicky and Billy were sitting side by side, quiet and subdued. She knew from her mother's face that something had upset her.

'Your daughter has been a naughty girl,' Lena said, with a grimness that wasn't all assumed.

Kate knew that Vicky was a handful, and looking after her was asking a lot of Mam. Jack's bubble of satisfaction was burst when she took Vicky home and told him she was upsetting the neighbours.

'Come along with me, young lady,' he said. 'Before you have your dinner you can apologise. First to your grandmother, and then to the Jenkins family. We can't have this.'

Dinner at Mam's house was eaten almost in silence. For once, Kate felt relieved when she'd tucked Vicky up in bed for the night.

She went downstairs. 'We're going to have to do something,' she said to Jack. 'That child's getting out of hand.'

Jack poked the fire into a blaze. 'We'd have such a peaceful life if it wasn't for her.'

'Who would have thought she'd turn out like this?' Kate worried. 'We love her so much, and yet . . .'

'She's like Leo. She wants to control everybody, bend them to her will.'

'She's only six.'

'Nearly seven.'

'No child could be more loved.'

'Love was what you wanted, Kate. Vicky's got all she needs of that. She wants power. Billy does exactly what she asks of him. She wants the same from everybody else.'

'What can we do about it? We'll have to do something.'

Jack shook his head. 'It's not just Saturdays; there's the school holidays to think of. We can't leave her here all the time for your mother to look after, not as we have.'

'She'll have to come to the shop with us then,' Kate said, 'and we can arrange for her to do more now she's getting older. Dancing lessons . . .'

'Or music? We could get her a piano,' Jack said. 'Yes, definitely a piano, she ought to learn to play.'

'Lessons on Saturdays, then, to fill up the day. And we can have her in the shop too, let her learn something about the business.'

'We'll buy that car,' Jack said slowly. 'It'll make it easier to get her around. And your mother would like it. We could take her out on Sundays. We ought to give her little treats. She does a lot for us.'

They sat quietly for a long time. Then Jack looked up and smiled at her.

'I feel very contented with everything else in my life.'

'With me?'

'You know how I feel about you, and the shop, and living here. Your mother and brothers, I feel they've accepted me into the family, all of them.'

Kate smiled and said nothing. All her brothers except Billy. Jack had never really taken to Billy.

Kate found the piano lessons were not a success once the novelty had worn off. Now, not only did she have to make sure that Vicky did her homework every evening, but there was piano practice too. Vicky preferred to do other things, and it became a battleground.

'If she doesn't want to do it, no point in fighting her,' Jack said. 'It's become a rod for your back. Let her have dancing lessons instead.'

Kate felt he was ready to give up too soon, but eventually she had to concede that he was right.

Vicky took happily to dancing lessons. She also enjoyed being in the shop with them. She understood from an early age what the business was about. Kate thought Jack was very patient with her, explaining all the technicalities.

The car was popular from the moment they bought it. All the family clamoured to be taken for rides. Jack loved driving, and it made it quicker and easier to get about.

Mam exclaimed: 'It's lovely to see you and Kate doing so well out of your shop.' On fine Sunday afternoons Jack took them for trips to the Lake District or to the seaside. 'Billy enjoys that. So do I.'

For Kate, the years began to pass more and more quickly. When the time had come for Duncan to leave school, Harry had announced that he wanted to go to sea and see the world. So Duncan had started work at the shop, but within a year or so had decided to follow Harry and go to sea too. Now Freddie came to work in the shop in his place.

They bought Vicky a bicycle and let Freddie take her round with him when he went to collect and deliver films from chemist's shops. It helped fill the holidays from school. On wet afternoons, sometimes Freddie took her and Billy to a cinema matinée. By the time Billy was old enough to leave school, Freddie was talking of going to sea like his brothers.

'Want a job.' Billy smiled at Kate. 'Want a job in your shop.'

She discussed it with Jack.

'No,' he said. 'He'll be more trouble than he's worth. We couldn't leave him on his own behind the counter, could we?'

'There's lots he could do.' Kate frowned. 'If we don't have him, he may never work.'

Billy said: 'Want job. Start tomorrow?'

'Tomorrow's Sunday,' Jack told him. 'We'll all go for a ride in the car tomorrow.'

'I think we ought to give him a try,' Kate said.

'Better if we don't.' Jack was adamant.

'All the same . . . I wish you could see Billy as the rest of us do. He'll try and try. He'll do his best to please.'

'I know, but he'll be a big responsibility.' It bothered Kate that Jack didn't rally round Billy in the way her own family did.

'I'm not for it.'

'All the same . . .'

'Be it on your own head, Kate, if you want to try him.'

'I do.' It upset her that she had to go against Jack's wishes on this. 'Nobody else will give him a chance if we don't.'

Freddie was supportive. 'I'll teach him to ride Vicky's bike. He can come round collecting films with me. Then when I leave he can take over.'

But Billy found it hard to manage the bike. Vicky tried to teach him too. The weeks were passing and he still wasn't safe on it.

Jack was alarmed. 'He could have an accident. The roads are busy in town.'

Kate was afraid of that too. She suggested that Freddie try to teach him a bus route round the chemist's shops, but that took twice as long and meant Jack was rushed with the processing.

Billy wasn't good at finding his way round town either, and he became confused in surroundings he didn't recognise. He'd almost mastered the bike and the route when another chemist's shop wanted to join their service and the route had to be changed.

Freddie took him round the revised route two or three times, but the first time Billy was entrusted to make the journey alone, he missed the new shop out. It upset him when Freddie had to rush out to do it for him.

Jack said: 'If he can't be relied upon to collect and deliver, Billy will be of limited use to us.'

'Want to work,' Billy insisted. 'Want job.'

'He'll manage it,' Freddie was quick to support him, 'I know he will. It's just that it takes him longer than the rest of us. We'll keep trying, won't we, Billy?'

'Don't like bike much.'

'I'm scared he'll have an accident on it,' Mam told Kate. 'Or he'll get himself lost. To be honest, I like having him at home with me. He's company, and a help about the house.'

Kate gave up, and thereafter Billy stayed at home with his mother. All Kate wanted was for her family to be happy. For her own part, she was content, though Vicky continued to cause difficulties.

For her tenth birthday, they gave her a Box Brownie and showed her how to get the best results from it. She started taking pictures, which she learned to develop and print herself. Kate thought she showed some of Jack's talent, and they were both very proud of her.

The business went from strength to strength. Jack kept telling Kate she was a marvel, and admitted to everybody that it was due to her efforts rather than his.

Often he said: 'I wish you didn't have to work so hard. I know you'd like to spend more time at home.'

Freddie was still with them, but he'd told Kate again that he wouldn't be making his career in the shop. Mam had been upset when he and

Duncan had announced their intention of emigrating to Canada. It seemed Duncan wasn't all that keen on seafaring and was looking for another change.

'We're off to Canada as soon as I'm turned twenty-one,' Freddie told them.

He served behind the counter when Kate made the usual cup of tea in the middle of the afternoon. She took tea for her and Jack into the back room.

'Plenty of time for Freddie to change his mind,' Jack told her, opening a packet of biscuits and offering her one.

'If we can keep Freddie here until he's twenty-one, Vicky might just be old enough to take over from him.'

Kate had grown used to Freddie; he'd learned to do most jobs in the business.

'She may not want to.'

'She will.' Kate was sure of that. 'She's learning all about photography now. She really wants to come here in the holidays. Can't get enough of it. She's always asking what this is for or how that works.

'When I went to work in the newsagent's I enjoyed it, but working in our own business . . . there's far more satisfaction. And there's much more to photography than there was to newspapers. More interesting. How could Vicky not want to come here?'

Jack stirred his tea. 'She might not take to it. Your brothers didn't.'

'Freddie thinks he might find a similar job in Toronto.'

'Harry and Duncan . . . all of them, just biding their time until they could move on to something else.'

'They liked cycling all over town,' Kate admitted. 'And we are easygoing. Not like most employers. But I'm sure Vicky will want to stay.'

'Kate! She'll not want to do what your brothers do, not after her education.'

Kate took another biscuit and thought about it. Jack could surprise her.

'I expect you're right. She'll want to take over and run it quite quickly. If she made up her mind to run the shop I'd be able to take it easier. I'll be happy to stay at home more and take a back seat.'

'Don't bank on it, Kate. Don't force her into it.'

'I won't if she doesn't want to, but . . .'

'But you want her to so badly. I felt compelled to go into the family business because my father wanted me to. I couldn't cope with it.'

'Vicky's very different.' Kate thought she could cope with almost anything.

With a glow of pleasure, Vicky turned over in bed. Today was special.

'Happy birthday.' Her mother bent over and kissed her.

'Fifteen.' Vicky gave a cat-like stretch. 'Almost grown up.'

'Not quite. Are you going to get up and have breakfast with us?'

It was the summer holidays, and she didn't have to go to school. A very special day. 'No.'

Dad was peering round the door, looking disappointed.

'There's a pile of presents for you downstairs. Don't you want to see what you've got?'

Of course she did. She leapt out of bed and went racing down.

'Put your dressing gown on,' her mother called. 'You'll get cold.'

She had one gift unwrapped by the time Dad came with her dressing gown and pushed her arms into it.

'Dad, it's wonderful! I love it. Thank you. And you, Mum.'

It was one of the latest lightweight Leica cameras. She'd longed for a more sophisticated camera for a long time. She'd been round all those displayed on the shop's shelves and decided that the most gorgeous was this Leica.

'I must take your pictures before you go. Oh, I can't wait . . .'

'Come on then, open up the rest of these packages.' Mam was getting impatient; she wanted to get herself ready to go to the shop.

Vicky gasped with pleasure. 'I should have known . . .' She had all the accessories she needed: a folding tripod, lenses and filters, and a whole pile of film. 'Thank you. thank you. I love it.'

'Careful with this.' Dad picked up the instruction booklet she'd dropped on the floor. 'You'll need to read it carefully.'

'I've done that,' she chortled. 'You saw me doing it at the shop last week. Isn't that how you knew what I wanted?'

'Sit down and eat with us,' Mum said.

There was porridge for breakfast as usual, followed by boiled eggs. Boring stuff.

'Don't want any.' Then she realised she was hungry. 'Yes, perhaps an egg and soldiers.'

She unwrapped chocolate from Billy. Lots of lovely chocolate.

As a toddler, Vicky could remember Billy pushing her round in a pushchair. As a young child, he'd always been there playing with her. Gran had trusted Billy to take care of her. He'd never have let any harm come to her.

Then, inexplicably, she'd found herself in charge of him. At the time, she hadn't understood how this came about, because he towered over her.

231

When Gran sent them to the shops, it was she who took charge of the money and remembered what they had to buy, and Billy who carried the goods home. If Billy was sent to the shops without her, Gran had to write down what she wanted and fold the money into the note so he wouldn't lose it. It confused him if she wanted goods from more than one shop too.

Vicky opened up Gran's present. She knew what it was. Gran had made her a dress; she was very good at sewing. Vicky had chosen the lavender-coloured cotton and the pattern and she'd had several fittings, so it was no surprise.

She held the dress against her now.

'What d'you think, Mum?'

Mum pushed her straight fringe away from her forehead. 'It's a bit short, isn't it?'

It was fashionably short. So beautifully short that Gran had whooped with horror when she'd first suggested it. Vicky had had to threaten to turn the hem up again if Gran didn't make it that length.

She laughed, and stood her birthday cards up on the end of the table. Then she put a film in her new camera and was ready to shoot.

'Right.'

Steam was rising from Dad's porridge, and his face was full of quiet pleasure. Mum was lifting a heaped spoon to her mouth. Mum always looked a bit rushed in the mornings, but today she was all smiles. Perhaps Vicky's birthday was a special day for them too.

'You'll come and give us a hand at the shop?' Mum asked as she usually did when they were ready to leave. 'You know how busy we are on Saturdays.'

That always irritated Vicky. She had had to make a real stand before they'd leave her at home. Dad thought it such a treat for her to be taken down in his car. He couldn't see that she'd rather have an extra hour in bed and go in on the tram. She was sick of the shop, it was all she ever did on Saturdays. Serve behind that counter.

'I don't want to work today,' she said. 'It's my birthday.'

Mum's face told her she wasn't happy with that. 'I know, love, but we could do with your help.'

Mum adored working in the shop and thought she should too. She didn't realise there were other things in life. Dad hung back when Mum was going hotfoot for the car.

'Do come, Vicky,' he pleaded. 'It'll please your mum.'

When the car had bumped off down the cart track, Vicky pushed her feet into her mother's slippers and went next door to see Gran and Billy to thank them for their gifts.

She took a picture of them sitting one each side of the old range with the kettle on the hob belting out steam. She took another close-up of Billy against a whitewashed wall, talking to him all the time to make him appear as handsome as she could. She did the same for Gran, but her face was all lines now. Dad would call it a character portrait.

Then she went back to bed and read all through the instructions for the lenses and things. That done, she was was bored. Always she thought she wanted a lie-in on Saturdays, but once she'd been up for breakfast, there wasn't much point.

She got dressed in the lavender-coloured dress. In front of her mirror she pulled on the new cloche hat Mum had bought her and thought it really made her look grown up. Eighteen at least.

The wind was gusting outside, so she pulled her best coat from her wardrobe and put it on. It spoiled the whole effect, and she wasn't having that. She tiptoed into the front bedroom and looked in Mum's wardrobe. Just the thing, the jacket of her best costume. It was a misty blue and toned in nicely. She felt a real fashion plate as she went down the cart track.

She turned back and raised her camera to take a view of Cemetery Cottages, getting all six in the picture. She wanted to go round the shops, but the best in Birkenhead were close to Dad's and she didn't want to be seen nearby.

She decided to go to Liverpool. She'd go over on the ferry and take pictures of the ships and the waterfront. Her new Leica had a leather case and was so wonderfully small and light it was no trouble to carry round.

She walked down to St James' Church to catch a bus to Woodside. Dad didn't like her coming down this way. He said the Dock Cottages, which were really blocks of flats, were the worst slum in town and she was to keep away.

As she went down the hill, she saw the bus she'd meant to catch go careering round the church. She stood at the bus stop and stamped her feet. It meant a fifteen-minutes wait for the next one.

She couldn't stand still, not here. She'd have plenty of time to walk on a couple of bus stops. She started to walk along Corporation Road, which was considered a respectable area. She could see ahead of her a youth bringing a wicker basket full of cabbages out of a shop to join one of cauliflowers already on the pavement. He put a card on each: one read: *Cabbages 3d each*; the other *Cauliflowers 4d each*.

'Hello, Vicky,' he said as she drew level. 'Don't often see you down here.'

It was Alec Jenkins. She hadn't seen him for some time. His parents had bought this general grocery shop some years ago when they'd moved out of Cemetery Cottages. Once in a while, she'd seen him when he'd come up to visit his grandmother. Alec always used to put his tongue out when he saw her, but recently he'd been more friendly. Not that Gran approved of that. She always said: 'I'd stay away from those Jenkinses, we don't want any more trouble.'

Vicky asked now: 'You working in your dad's shop? You always said you wanted to work in a cinema.'

'I'm the second projectionist at the Empire,' he said proudly.

She laughed. 'But you get roped in to help in the shop?'

'Bet you do too. Or are you working for your dad full time?'

'No, I'm a freelance photographer.' She pushed her camera under his nose.

'Gee! A Leica? Take my picture. Go on.'

Vicky tossed her blonde curls. 'I can sell my pictures to magazines and newspapers. This is professional equipment I've got.'

'Go on, take my picture, don't be mean.'

'You'll have to pay me. I don't want to waste good film on you.'

'How much?'

'Depends what you want.'

'My portrait. I want you to make me look handsome.'

'Handsome!' She laughed. 'You're just a kid.'

'I'm sixteen and I'm older than you, so there. Here's our Howard.'

Vicky turned. It was even longer since she'd seen Howard Jenkins, two or three years at least, and he'd really grown up in that time. Once she'd thought him a wimp, but now he was in uniform. 'You in the police?'

'Yes.' His dark eyes met hers. She could see she'd stirred his interest. She was working out how old he was. Six years older would make him twenty-one. A man now, and earning his living. He was tall and broad; unusually burly for his age, but the right build for a police officer.

'I might join when I'm old enough,' Alec said.

Vicky was reminded. 'I'll take a picture of you both together,' she said, getting her camera out. 'Right here, outside your shop.'

It had been newly painted and was the smartest in the road.

'Half a crown for three postcard-sized prints. It's what my father charges.'

Howard stood in the doorway, shoulders back, head up, proud of his uniform. He really was very good-looking. Alec was just a kid beside him.

'Take a picture of my mum and dad,' he pleaded. 'They'd love you to.'

'All right.' She smiled at Howard, wanting to show off her talent for photography. She mustn't stare at him; she didn't want him to think she fancied him.

While Vicky waited for Alec to bring his parents out, she pretended an interest in the contents of their shop window. Tins of Libby's cooked corned beef, Camp coffee and jars of jam and pickles were placed in three artistic groups. Behind them a wooden partition advertising Stephen's Ink and Zebra Grate Polish partly cut off the view to the shop, but tiers of shelves could be seen on the far wall loaded with other delicacies.

'Hello, Vicky. My, haven't you grown up?' Mrs Jenkins came bustling out to smirk at her. 'We're shopkeepers too now, with our own business. We've come up in the world.'

She'd never liked Miriam Jenkins. She hadn't spoken to her since the episode of the treacle toffee and the gun. Gran said the woman was a snob. Everyone knew a general shop like this was socially way down on a photographer's like Dad's. Mrs Jenkins started to remove the pinafore that covered most of her floral dress. She was obese.

'Leave that on,' her husband urged. He wore a green apron too, and a straw boater. 'It'll make a nice publicity picture.' He looked at Vicky and added: 'If it comes out.'

'It'll come out,' Vicky retorted. Gran was right, they were both pains in the neck, but she wouldn't be rude to them. She didn't want to upset Howard. Every time her eyes met his, she felt a tug of attraction.

She waited for the traffic to clear and then went out to the middle of the road to get the whole shop in the picture behind them. The gold lettering over the window would show up beautifully. It read: J.W. Jenkins, High Class Grocer.

'When will they be ready?' Alec wanted to know.

'Depends when I get round to developing them. I'll bring them round when I have.' Vicky was pleased she had a reason to see Howard again.

'Where are you going now?' His dark eyes smiled into hers. 'I've just come off duty.'

Vicky could feel herself tingling. It wasn't one-sided, what she was feeling for Howard.

'Why don't you come with me? I'm going over on the ferry. I've been commissioned to take some local photographs. To be made up into postcards and sold to tourists.'

235

'By your father?'

She had to say yes. He still seemed impressed that she could. Already, two of the cards in Dad's shop were of views taken by her.

'I'd love to. Well, I'm ready if you are.'

'Aren't you going to change?'

He pulled himself up to his full six feet. 'I'm supposed to wear uniform all the time. Even when I'm off duty.'

'Not when you're with me.' Vicky laughed. She went closer and whispered, 'I don't like you in that funny helmet.' She thought it looked a bit of a joke, especially the strap round his chin.

'It's traditional. The police have worn this since the force was founded.'

'You'd look much nicer without it. Go on.'

'Well, perhaps just this once.' He took her upstairs to wait in their living room. Alec clattered up behind them. It was all newly painted here too, very smart, with modern furniture. Dad wouldn't like it, it wasn't his style, but Vicky thought she did. She took what she hoped would be a really nice picture of Alec to fill the time.

When Howard returned wearing flannels and a sports jacket, she was totally captivated. He was a very handsome man, with the sort of looks that would make the girls at school sigh over him.

They went over to Liverpool on the ferry. Vicky snapped away with her new camera but she knew the results would not be used for postcards because they already had these views on offer. She took several of ships in the river.

'Which ones belong to your grandfather?' Howard wanted to know.

'None, he's retired. The Courtney Line is no more; its assets were sold to another company. A shame, really.'

Most of the photographs she took that morning were of Howard hanging over the boat rail with the wind ruffling his dark hair.

Vicky had a wonderful day. Howard took her to a café for lunch; nothing expensive, but it was a rare treat for her. He wanted to take her to the Argyll Music Hall that evening, and she'd really have loved to go, but as it was her birthday, Gran was cooking a special dinner for when the shop closed. She knew there'd be a row if she skipped that. These days she always seemed to be in trouble.

The time raced past while she was with Howard, and she was already late when they were getting on the bus at Woodside. He wanted her to get off at the shop with him and let him run her home on the back of his motorbike, but she wouldn't let him. Dad would have a fit if he saw her on a motorbike. She'd have to prepare the family for that first.

Instead, she promised to call for him the next day, and go for a run on it then.

'It'll have to be afternoon.' Sunday lunch was another fixture she dared not miss. The trouble with her family was that they expected her to be there with them the whole time. They didn't want to give her any freedom. If she did manage to get away for a few hours, they wanted to know exactly what she'd been doing and who with.

When she got home, Vicky felt the atmosphere immediately.

'We've had to keep dinner waiting for half an hour,' her father told her. 'You know how that bothers Gran. Especially when she's making a special effort for you.'

'That's the jacket to my best costume!' Mum was irate. 'I wish you wouldn't borrow my things. You didn't even ask.'

'You weren't here.'

'I'd have said no. You've got oil on it too. Where's that come from?'

'It must have been the ferry boat. It isn't very much.'

'It's new, Vicky. I've hardly worn it.'

'I'll get it off for you, Kate,' Dad said. 'We were disappointed, Vicky, that you didn't come to the shop.'

It continued all night. The questions: who had she been with? What had she done? She wasn't expected to have any life of her own. Some birthday dinner that was, a right dirge rather than a celebration.

Vicky had meant to get up early on Sunday morning, but when she went down, she found her parents had already finished breakfast.

She said: 'I'd like to develop the pictures I took yesterday. Can I go down to the shop?'

Her father was reading the paper. he looked up. 'Why not? I'll give you the key.'

'Will you run me down, Daddy? You know how difficult trams and buses can be on Sundays.'

She heard him sigh. 'I suppose so. When do you want to go?'

'Now.'

'Vicky, you've had no breakfast,' her mother objected. 'Eat something first.'

She cut herself a piece of bread. 'It's a lovely, lovely camera you gave me. I can't wait to see the pictures.'

'I'd better fetch you back too.' Dad refolded his newspaper. 'To make sure you're home in time for lunch. We don't want another débâcle like last night.'

'Thank you, Daddy.'

At twelve thirty, Jack looked down Grange Road, unfamiliar in the Sunday quiet, before letting himself into the shop.

'Are you ready, Vicky?' he called.

'Not quite.'

He went upstairs to see if he could give her a hand. 'We mustn't be late.'

Vicky was mounting some of her pictures. Others were still hanging up to dry. He looked at them with a critical eye.

'This one's really good.' He studied an enlargement of a young man with limpid eyes looking straight at the camera, and another of the same fellow taken at an angle, which was rather more flattering. He looked familiar, but Jack couldn't put a name to him.

'Who's this?'

'Howard Jenkins.' The way she said his name alerted him. He knew it had special significance for her.

'You've got a boyfriend?' He could see that as a source of more trouble.

'No, just Flossie Jenkins' grandson. Used to live with her, next door to Gran. You remember them?'

'Yes. You've taken a lot more pictures of that family.'

'They're paying me.' Vicky gave him a radiant smile. 'Makes me feel a professional.'

'You're taking business from me,' he joked.

On the way home he talked about her childhood clashes with the Jenkins boys and how pleased Gran would be that the fighting was over.

'We're all older now, grown up,' she said.

Jack was afraid Kate's mind would not be put at rest by the news.

Kate was surprised to see Vicky's pictures. 'This one of Miriam and John in front of their shop – they'll love it. Doesn't he look the proud proprietor? And there's so much detail – even the tins of corned beef in the window.

'You're going down there? To deliver these photographs? You'll be back for tea?'

'Maybe not.'

'Where will you eat then?'

'I don't know yet, do I? Perhaps I'll go somewhere with Howard. That's all right, is it? I'm allowed to have friends of my own?'

Kate sighed; she knew she'd pressed too hard. 'Of course you are.

But remember you must be home by ten o'clock tonight at the latest.'

'Right.' Vicky picked up the package of photographs and Kate watched her walk down the cart track.

Sunday was the only lazy day Kate had, and it seemed to flash past. Ten o'clock came and went, and so did eleven.

Kate got undressed and into her nightclothes. 'We can't go to bed until she's home.' She felt desperate. 'I couldn't sleep if I did. What is she doing? Vicky never gives a thought for anyone else.'

Jack said, 'It's adolescence, love. She's testing us, finding out how far she can go.'

'Not as far as this,' Kate retorted, 'and it's not adolescence; Vicky's always defied us.'

'Since she learned to say no. I think she was two.'

'But out till this hour with a boyfriend?'

'And only just fifteen!'

'But with Howard Jenkins? I thought she disliked the Jenkinses as much as Mam. Anyway, didn't she deny there was anything between them.'

'Secrecy is part of her technique.'

'What do you mean, technique?'

'For getting her independence. She wants a life of her own. She's pitting her strength against us, trying to break parental control.'

'She still needs it,' Kate retorted. 'She was quite aggressive towards me after lunch.'

'It's all part of growing up, love.' She watched Jack get wearily into bed.

'I was never like this when I was growing up. We've tried so hard with Vicky. I'm worried about her.'

'We always have been. Vicky's never been easy.'

Vicky couldn't get enough of Howard's company, and the wonderful thing was that he felt exactly the same about her. From the very beginning they seemed to be on the same wavelength.

She propped up the photographs she'd taken of him around her bedroom. She bought frames for the best. He wanted to take her out to cinemas and the music hall, to dances and for rides on his motorbike.

'Motorbike?' Dad had been shocked when he'd first seen that. 'Dangerous things. I don't like you riding around on the back of that.'

Vicky would have preferred Howard to have a car. The girls at school didn't rate motorbikes highly, but most didn't have boyfriends, and if they did, they were still at school or college. Just kids who hadn't started to live. Howard was a man, and he was working for his living.

'He's saving for a car,' she told everybody. 'It won't be for long, Dad. Don't worry, Howard's a very safe driver.'

'A police constable?' That didn't impress the girls in her form either. One of her friends said: 'My father's in the police, but he's a superintendent.'

'Howard's very clever.' Vicky assured them. 'He'll soon be promoted, he won't be a constable for long.'

She didn't like going out with him when he was wearing his uniform, it attracted too much of the wrong attention. People were always asking him the time or the way to somewhere. And once somebody had had their bike stolen and he'd had to do something about that.

Gran said: 'Never did like the Jenkinses. You can do better than him.' Vicky didn't want to. Howard was lovely.

But none of this really mattered. Not when Howard was loving and tender and said things like: 'I was head over heels from the moment I saw you.'

It left her breathless and starry-eyed, and feeling bound to Howard.

Chapter Twenty

1930–1932

Jack had never felt very close to his father, but he'd kept in touch over the years, visiting the Grange to see him every few weeks. By March, he could see that his strength was failing. Ottilie hired a nurse to take care of him. Jack went more often, fearing that his end was near.

It still came as something of a shock when Ottilie telephoned the shop and asked him to come. He and Kate had been up at the Grange only two days previously and they'd both thought he was a little better.

He died with his three sons round his bed and two of his daughters-in-law. Jack felt in an emotional turmoil. He knew it wasn't easy for anyone when a parent died, but for him it was more difficult. He'd failed to live up to his father's expectations, and though Father had eventually accepted him as he was, Jack had never told him how grateful he was. He'd been cut off from his family for a long time; still was from his brothers. It was Father who had befriended Kate and brought him back into the fold.

Ottilie and Leo took care of the funeral arrangements, but fate had it that it was a Thursday afternoon, early-closing day, so Kate was free to come too. Vicky stayed off school, and he took Lena and Billy in the car with them.

It was a big funeral. Many people remembered William Courtney. He was buried in Wallasey in the same grave as his wife.

Jack heard Billy ask: 'Why isn't he coming to our cemetery? Ours is much nicer.' Lena hushed him.

They all went back to the Grange afterwards. He saw Lena looking round with wide eyes, but Leo and Oscar were talking of selling it now.

'It's too big. Too old-fashioned. Expensive to keep up.'

'Can't manage here without a big staff,' Ottilie complained. 'I'm tired of trying to cope with it.'

Jack decided it would be the last time he would come. He went up to his old room to see if there was anything he wanted. There wasn't; he wanted no reminders of this part of his life.

The big shock of the day came when they were leaving. Leo said: 'You know you're a beneficiary under Father's will?'

Years ago, Father had flown into a rage and told him he was going to cut him off without a penny. Jack had accepted that and expected nothing. Now, he thought Father had relented and left him a legacy.

He asked: 'How much?'

'The same as me and Oscar. One third of the residue. There's a small legacy for each grandchild too.'

It took Jack's breath away. He drove the family back to Cemetery Cottages and said nothing. None of them had heard what Leo had said, not even Kate. He wanted to tell her first. It altered everything.

As soon as they got back home, Vicky said: 'I'm going out,' and ran upstairs to change.

Lena took Billy by the hand and said: 'We'll leave you in peace for a bit.' She probably thought Jack was grieving for his father.

Jack put his slippers on and watched Kate make up the fire. When she put a cup of tea in his hand and sat down, he told her about the will. Her face was a kaleidoscope of changing expressions. It was a long time before she asked: 'What will you do with all this money?'

He shook his head. 'I don't know. I've never had much use for it, have I?'

Kate was smiling. 'I wouldn't put it quite like that. You spend much more than I do. You'll be as rich as your brothers.'

'I doubt it – they've had high earnings over the years – but still, we'll be rich.'

'Do you want a better house? Something bigger?'

Jack didn't like change. 'I'm happy here. Do you?'

'I'd like a really nice house, yes, who wouldn't? But it would mean moving, leaving Mam . . . I don't want to do that, not at her age.'

'If we got a big enough place, she could come too.'

'There's Billy to think of, and she won't want to give up her own home.'

'Then we'll stay here for the time being. We should modernise the place, put electricity in and a proper hot-water system. Would you like that?'

Kate laughed. 'I'm used to the oil lamps, but Vicky's always on about us getting electricity.'

'That's because I tell her off for running the batteries down on the wireless. We needed both wet and dry again this week. I suppose we

242

should get it. It would make things easier for you.'

'Jack, I hardly do any housework. Mam does it, and I don't suppose she'd thank you for the latest gadgets.'

'Then we won't. There's charm in oil lamps and candles.'

'Everyone says they're flattering to the older woman.'

'Kate, I do just wonder about the shop. You have to work so hard there. I push more on your shoulders than I should. You look tired sometimes. We won't need the income now, and I wonder whether it's worth keeping . . .'

'No, Jack, don't sell it. Vicky loves the shop. We could show her exactly what to do when she leaves school. Well, she knows already, and business is burgeoning, what with the Box Brownie and the faster roll film. Everybody who wants a camera can afford one now.'

'We'd better put it to her.'

'I've done that several times already. She knows we want her to run the shop.'

'Either way, I'm going to get help in the shop now. We could get out and about more if we had reliable staff. I'm going to use this money to make our life easier, more comfortable, better. You're working too hard, have done for years.'

It was late that night, when they were waiting for Vicky to come in, that Jack said wryly: 'We don't really need money to make our lives easier. All it would take is for Vicky to act like a reasonable being.'

Kate thought Vicky was anything but reasonable. She was spending more and more time with Howard Jenkins and less at home. They had countless rows about the time she came home at night. Kate laid down rules that Vicky constantly broke. It took Kate a little time to work out that Howard was working shifts, and that for one week in three he was free during the evenings. Then Vicky came home very late, night after night, and nothing she and Jack said could alter that.

They debated whether they should tell her about her grandfather's will. Kate was afraid that if she knew she'd have her own money, it would make her even wilder.

'What's the point of secrecy?' Jack asked mildly.

'She tells us nothing of what she's doing.'

'The money will alter her life too. Anyway, you've made no secret of it to your mother. Do you want Vicky to hear about it from her?'

It wasn't until Howard went on night duties that Vicky sat down with them for any length of time and they were able to tell her.

She went off into shrieks of joy. 'We'll be rich. Good-ho. Isn't that

243

great news? When will we get the money?'

'You won't get yours until you're twenty-one,' Jack told her.

She pulled a face at that. Vicky could be sweet-natured and happy one minute, and peevish and disgruntled the next. Worse, she had terrible sulks that poisoned the atmosphere and could last for days.

'You'll still have to earn your living. Have you decided what you want to do?' Kate was rewarded with a blank stare.

'There's the shop.' She was watching her daughter closely. 'We'd like to know how you feel about taking it over when you leave school. We'd show you . . .'

'No,' Vicky spat out. 'No, I don't want to do that.'

'But it's a good business, you'd earn a comfortable living. And you love photography, you already know so much . . .'

Vicky turned on her, full of resentment. 'Mum, I don't want to spend the rest of my life doing that.'

'What *do* you want, Vicky?' Jack was always long on patience with her. 'You're doing well at school; you could train as a teacher.'

She shook her head slowly.

'Or a nurse?' She pulled another face. 'Perhaps you'd prefer to work in an office of some sort?'

'I don't know. I haven't thought about it.'

'Perhaps you better had,' Kate said with exasperation. 'Do think hard about taking over the shop. I'm sure it would suit you.'

'No, Mum, I want to do my own thing. Not take over something of yours.'

The next morning, reluctantly, Kate agreed to advertise for a manager to run the shop. 'I'm not convinced Vicky won't want it when the time comes. She's just a mixed-up child. I don't understand her; at her age I felt grown up, I knew what I wanted.'

'She feels grown up too,' Jack lamented. 'But she's still relying on us for everything. Perhaps that's the problem.'

When they went home that evening, they found Vicky had not yet come home from school. Lena had dinner ready for them set out in her house.

'We might as well start,' Jack said, but at that moment Billy sighted Vicky running up the cart track. She was radiant when she burst into the house. She tore off her coat and hung it behind the door.

Kate was swallowing back the words *You're late* when Vicky said: 'Sorry, Gran, I'm late again.

'Well, you're here now. I've dished up yours too.'

'Get it from the oven,' Kate said, cutting into her lamb chops, 'and come and sit down.'

Vicky was beaming round the table. 'I've made up my mind what I want to do,' she announced. 'Howard has asked me to marry him. That's it. I want to leave school and get married.'

Kate was stunned. 'You can't do that! You've only known him a few months. I don't think he's the right person for you, you'll change your mind.'

'I won't. I've promised to marry him, and Howard's promised himself to me.'

Jack said shortly: 'You're too young, both of you.'

'He's twenty-one.'

'But you're still only fifteen.'

'You asked me what I wanted to do and I'm telling you. We'll wait a bit.'

'Good, I'm glad to hear that.'

'Not too long. Lots of girls get married at sixteen.'

'You won't be one of them,' Jack said firmly.

Kate felt desperate. 'He can't afford to support a wife.'

'He can then. He'll get a marriage allowance and a rent allowance.'

'You don't want to tie yourself to him,' Lena said severely. 'Social upstarts, that's what those Jenkinses are. You're a Courtney and something of an heiress. I suppose you told him you'd be coming into money?'

'Yes, we'll buy our own house then.'

'It's your money he's after,' Lena exploded. 'He didn't ask you to marry him before you told him about that, did he?'

'Rubbish, Gran.'

'Is that how it was?' Vicky wouldn't say. 'I bet it was. You could marry a nice fellow.'

'I want to marry Howard. We're engaged. We'll stay true to each other. He's bought me a ring.' She held her left hand out to show them. 'It's an amethyst.'

'Nothing but a cheap trinket,' Lena snorted with disgust.

'I like it. It's pretty. And I don't need anybody's permission to wear it.'

'You do to get married,' Jack growled.

'We'll wait till I'm twenty-one.'

'You'll have to, Vicky.'

'Truly, Dad, I won't change my mind.'

'Neither will I on this.'

The look in Vicky's blue eyes made Kate think she believed he would. She'd always been able to persuade Jack to do what she wanted.

Kate didn't sleep well. She was afraid they really had something to worry about now. At breakfast, Vicky started again.

'I do want to leave school.'

'Don't be silly, you enjoy it. You got a good School Certificate last summer. You decided to go on to do your Higher, and then perhaps university.'

'That was before I met Howard. School's for children. I've had enough.'

Jack thought schooling should go on well into adult life, but Kate could understand. She'd left school at thirteen.

'You'd like to leave and come to work with me in the shop?'

'No, Mother. Spare me that again.'

'But you're really interested in photography. You're good at it. Exciting things are happening in the trade. All these new filters and lenses. You know so much about it already.'

'I know enough not to want to spend my life doing it.'

'What then? You can't sit about here all day.' Kate was beginning to think she wanted a life of idleness. Had she inherited that from Jack? No, Vicky had always had such energy.

'If you want to be a teacher, you'll have to stay . . .'

'I don't. I'll get a job. In an office or something.'

She nagged so much that at Christmas they agreed she could leave, on condition she attended a commercial college and learned to type.

Jack said wearily, 'We've given in and let her leave school. She's very strong-willed. She'll be at me until we let her get married.'

'We'll just keep saying no. We can't let her get married at sixteen.'

They found a manager for the shop, and Kate had freedom such as she'd never known. She started to do more about the house. Vicky was rarely there; she was spending as much time as she could with Howard. The months were passing and she hadn't changed her mind. She never stopped asking them for permission to marry.

'Perhaps we ought to ask Howard here,' Jack worried. 'Get to know him better. Perhaps we've misjudged him.'

'What about his parents, should we ask them too? And his grandmother? She's here next door but one, but we don't speak to her.'

'We all get set in our ways, Kate.'

'It's been like this since I was a child. The Jenkinses and Frys on one

246

side of the fence, and the McGlorys and Catchpoles on the other.'

Mam was against it. 'Invite him here? That would be encouraging them.'

Kate asked Vicky: 'Have you ever been invited to a meal at Howard's home?'

'Of course.' Her blue eyes flashed defiance. 'Several times. His family's not dead against me. Not in the way you're against him.'

'That settles it,' Kate decided. 'We'll ask them all round here to a meal one night.'

She settled the date by arranging it through Vicky. It had to be a night Howard wasn't on duty. Then she knocked on his grandmother's door and invited her too.

Flossie Jenkins stood with her mouth open and clearly didn't know what to say. She neither accepted nor refused the invitation. Kate asked her again, making it clear she was inviting all the family.

She said: 'Thank you. I have my dinner at midday,' which left Kate still unsure. Vicky confirmed a few days later that they'd all come.

Kate made a special effort to put a good dinner on the table the night they were coming.

'I don't know what you're doing all this for,' Lena said. 'Knocking yourself out for the Jenkinses. Anyway, it's my job to cook the main meal of the day.'

'You can make the pudding,' Kate told her.

'All right, I'll make Queen of Puddings. Though it's a waste of time for the likes of them.'

As it happened, Lena didn't feel well that day, and took to her bed before they came. Kate was cross. She thought her mother was using it as an excuse to avoid sitting down to eat with the Jenkins family. Billy came with a tray to collect food for himself and Lena when it was being dished up.

The Jenkinses turned up in their best clothes but seemed to have little to talk about but Howard. Mother and grandmother sang his praises.

'Such a good son.'

'Doing well in his career.'

'Very bright, he'll get on well.'

'His father was made up to sergeant before he retired, weren't you, John?'

'He's a good catch. Vicky's doing well for herself.'

Kate saw Jack's eyes go up at that. Howard seemed ill at ease, but he didn't dispute any of it. Vicky held his hand for a lot of the time. Kate

247

studied him and wondered what her daughter saw in him.

There was a heaviness about him. His hooded dark eyes gazed out Buddha-like, making him seem somnolent. He said little. Kate thought he was shy with them. Beside him, Vicky flashed like quicksilver and turned to him with adoring eyes.

Jack did his best to be a good host, but Kate felt they were both struggling to keep the conversation going. Nobody's opinion of Howard was changed as a result. But two or three weeks later, the Courtneys were invited for Sunday tea in the flat over the shop. Lena and Billy were not.

'Not our sort, I'm afraid,' Jack said.

Lena turned on him. 'Didn't I tell you that?'

The years were passing and Lena was beginning to feel old. This morning she felt beleaguered with aches and pains, and she was always stiff when she first got out of bed. She struggled across the landing.

'Come on, Billy. Time to get up.' He was the only one needing a morning call now.

'Aw right, Mam.' His head lifted an inch from the pillow, and his almond eyes peered at her over his sheet. As he grew older he was looking more like Mitch.

It always took Billy twice as long as anybody else to get dressed, but he'd been doing it without help for years. He was a grown man now but he never would leave her, and she thanked God for that.

Back in her own bedroom she pulled back the faded chenille curtains to let the light in, and put on her corsets, adjusting them under her flannel nightgown.

It weighted heavily on her mind that Duncan and Freddie had emigrated to Canada. It was such a long way away. Of course, they were having a better life there. They wrote that they'd both found good jobs. And there was still Harry: he was looking for a shore job; he wanted to marry a Birkenhead girl and settle down. Out of all the boys she'd had, there'd be only Harry and Billy left.

When she said anything like that to them, they chorused back: 'There'll always be Kate.'

With her dress on, she called to Billy again.

'I'm up, Mam. Nearly ready.'

Lena was combing her hair when she heard him go heavily downstairs and start raking out the grate. It was his way of helping and she let him do it, though he gave no thought to the dust he raised and it took him twice as long as it should to get a fire going.

She didn't worry about Kate these days. She had a wealthy husband now Jack had received his inheritance. Benedict Rotherfield should have left some of his money to Kate. She was sure he'd have wanted to, and it was only right, but she couldn't blame him for not altering his will. He'd had other things on his mind.

Jack had always been generous. It pleased her to think Kate would never want for anything in the future. Jack had bought her a fur coat and treated himself to a new and smarter car.

They were both looking older too. While Kate's strong features showed no sign of age and there was no grey in her hair, it had faded. It was now more sandy than flame-coloured.

Billy had the fire going at last and the kettle was beginning to sing. It always seemed a long wait for the first cup of tea.

'We'll have our porridge now, shall we?'

'Porridge now.' Billy smiled.

Lena still made porridge at night and left it in the hay box, though Vicky was always telling her that was a very old-fashioned way of doing things.

She sipped at her tea as soon as Billy put it in front of her. It tasted smoky. It often did, because the fire smoked when it was first lit. Even so, she looked forward to it every morning.

Vicky was their biggest problem now. She was giving Kate and Jack a hard time. She never stopped asking for permission to marry Howard. She'd done it again last night over dinner.

Demanded rather than asked, and she'd grown angry with Kate because shed asked her to be home by ten o'clock. None of her boys had been as much trouble as Vicky, and there was more reason to worry about a girl. She just didn't realise what a responsibility she was to Kate.

Lena had lost her temper with her last night.

'That lad you've got isn't worth tuppence. He's dragging you down.'

She was sure Howard was spoiling Vicky's chances all round. 'What d'you want to work in an office for, when you could run a thriving business? You'd earn more from the shop, and you'd have a lot more satisfaction and, yes, pleasure from it. You don't understand what you're turning down.' It didn't make sense to Lena any more than it did to Jack and Kate.

'I do, Gran. I've applied for a job in Mayfield's estate agency. It's what I want. I'm standing on my own feet. I don't want to be beholden to Dad. I want to get married, have a life of my own.'

'You're too young. You'll get hurt. We're trying to save you from yourself.'

Jack said: 'About this estate agency job, will you just be a typist, or is there the possibility of promotion?'

'How do I know? I haven't got the job yet. Anyway, it's only till I get married,' Vicky explained. 'What's the point of training for a career that I'll only have to give up?'

Kate gave Vicky a piece of her mind from time to time. Jack didn't do it, he was far too soft with her, and somebody had to.

'We've spoiled you, given you too much of your own way, my girl. You don't know which way your bread's buttered. Here we are trying to do our best for you and you kick us all in the teeth.'

Jack was overindulgent with Vicky; he did most of the spoiling. Kate said it was because he hadn't had an easy childhood. It had made him over sensitive to the growing pains of others. But it hadn't made him sensitive to Billy; he'd turned his back on him.

Kate went on at Vicky: 'Come to your senses, for heaven's sake, before it's too late.'

Without another word, Vicky slammed out to the bathroom to get ready to go out. The rest of them sat on silently at the table, feeling thoroughly shaken up. Vicky had to come back through the living room to go upstairs to her room. She shot up without saying a word. On the way out, with her best coat on and powder on her nose, she paused beside Lena and wailed:

'Tell them, Gran, what you're always telling me. Tell them love is important.'

Then she turned on her parents ferociously. 'I'll never change my mind about Howard. I told you I wouldn't. He bowls me over. All you're doing, Dad, is making us waste our lives. We want to be married but we can't be. What's the point of doing that to us?'

Billy got up and put his arms round her. 'Poor Vicky,' he said, but for once she pushed him off.

'You don't understand about love,' She went on. 'Howard means everything to me. I don't want to lose what I've got.'

'I'm sorry if that's how you feel,' Jack said stiffly. He looked as though he couldn't take much more. He was getting too old to handle wilful teenagers. Lena could see he was upset; she was too. Vicky was making her feel partly responsible; after all, she had gone on about love to them all.

'Love is everything, Vicky, but you have to have the right person.'

Jack said: 'If you get that wrong, as I did, you make yourself very unhappy.'

'I'm unhappy now,' Vicky wailed as she headed for the front door, and that was only too obviously true.

As the slam reverberated through the house, Billy gasped: 'Poor, poor Vicky.'

Lena tried to cheer everybody up. 'We all need somebody to love, but it's not always the first person we think it's going to be.'

'Absolutely not,' Jack agreed.

'I've lost a whole lot of people I loved dearly, but I still have Billy.' She smiled at him. 'He means everything to me.'

'And I have my mam,' Billy snuggled closer to her and beamed round the table at the others.

'I've found what I want with Kate. I count myself very lucky to have her. I'd do anything,' Jack said, 'to keep her here with me.'

'So would I with me mam,' Billy said. 'Anything at all to keep her here with me.'

'I'm not going anywhere.' Lena ruffled his hair. 'We'll stay together for always, you and me, Billy.'

As Jack got ready for bed, he could think of nothing but the fracas they'd had with Vicky over dinner. It was ruining the peace he'd always felt in his home.

'Are we doing the right thing?' he asked Kate, who was brushing her hair. 'I want to protect her. Girls have to be looked after.'

Kate had fewer doubts about what they did and was always stronger. 'She knows we do it because we love her. That we want her to be safe and happy.'

'We've hung our hopes on her, Kate. We want her to run the shop, to do our bidding. Isn't that what my father wanted of me?'

'We want her to be happy.'

'That's what every parent wants.'

'She's so aggressive towards us,' Kate exploded. 'Wilful and utterly selfish.'

'She can be loving and sweet too, especially towards her grandmother.'

'Do you think she really loves Howard Jenkins?'

'She's obsessed, totally obsessed. I didn't think it would last this long.'

He got into bed feeling depressed. He wasn't handling Vicky as he should, and he felt he was failing as a father.

He put his arm round Kate. The warmth of her body brought comfort, as it always did, but Kate was asleep in minutes, leaving him to worry more. It was not only Vicky; he felt equally bothered about Billy.

Jack knew he had a hang-up about Billy. He didn't know why, but it was there and he couldn't get over it. He wasn't at ease in his company, which was silly.

They ate dinner together almost every night, and ignored each other at the table. Vicky's sulks could poison the atmosphere. Jack felt his attitude to Billy didn't poison things, but just as surely, it tainted.

The first time they'd met, Billy had thrown his arms round him and planted a damp kiss on his lips. Jack had been disconcerted and leapt back from him.

He didn't know why he had, except that at school anything like that had been strongly discouraged and spoken of as unnatural and wrong. When he'd tried to explain this to Kate, she'd laughed at him.

'There's nothing like that about Billy. He kisses the girls with the same joy.'

Jack wasn't used to being kissed by the male sex; in fact, he wasn't used to being kissed at all. His family had shown each other very little affection. He'd been brought up by a nanny and taken downstairs to see his mother at tea time and told to kiss her on her cheek. Occasionally Mother had pecked his cheek in return. Mother had had regard for him, he didn't doubt that, but she'd never shown it. His father was more likely to shake his hand than kiss him. They'd been stiff and formal with each other.

The McGlorys, on the other hand, showered hugs and kisses on each other; it was one of the things he'd so liked about Kate. She was always ready to throw her arms round him. Lena too hugged him from time to time. Billy was even freer with his affection, and Jack knew it shouldn't surprise him, not when he'd been brought up by Lena and Kate. The fact was, he and Billy had started off on the wrong foot and he'd never been able to put it right.

Billy had grown into a handsome man, tall and broad and strong. He had light-brown hair with a touch of gold in it, and big almond-shaped brown eyes with long lashes. They were innocent, gentle eyes; a child's eyes in an adult face. He was very obliging; he wanted to please everybody.

In fact, he radiated affection and love to family, friends and strangers alike, but above all, he was devoted to his mother.

Jack felt he couldn't unbend, that he was failing with Billy just as he'd failed with Leo and Oscar. He didn't understand Billy and he couldn't make Billy understand him.

'Treat him like a child, Jack,' Kate told him often enough, but he couldn't. 'Just relax with him. Time will solve it, you'll get used to him,' but Jack never had. Kate didn't understand it, because everybody else loved Billy.

Jack felt he had plenty of patience with children; he just couldn't reach the right level with Billy. It upset Kate and it upset Lena too, the last people in the world he wanted to hurt.

He lacked the confidence to meet Billy halfway. Just as he'd lacked confidence with his own brothers.

Chapter Twenty-One

1933–1934

Vicky didn't know why she'd applied for a job with Mayfields's estate agency. Howard had thought it a good idea, mainly because their office was in Upton Avenue, within walking distance of both her home and his. He said he could meet her at lunch time when he was on late shift.

When she was called for an interview, she found the building had once been a cottage and was now surrounded by small shops. There were three other applicants, waiting on hard chairs cramped together in the lobby. As she waited her turn, Vicky was assailed by doubts. She was afraid this job wouldn't suit her. She wondered, not for the first time, if she was making a bad mistake. Perhaps she would be better off working in Mum's shop. She did enjoy photography.

She'd have liked to tell Mum so, but it would mean admitting she'd been wrong, and Mum and Dad right. These days she never quite knew where she was with them. She did love them, but when they went on at her it could all flare up into a row in an instant. Dad would assume she'd give in about getting married too, and she certainly wasn't going to do that.

She was called into a large square office with a highly polished wooden floor, and was offered a seat. Four sets of eyes were assessing her minutely. She was introduced to Mr John Mayfield, his two sons Robert and Andrew, and his daughter Sylvia.

'We have five small offices like this scattered across the Wirral,' Sylvia explained. 'I'm currently running this one, but I'm getting married soon and I'll be going to live in London. We're looking for someone to take my place.'

They were a good-looking family and seemed more cohesive than her own. Vicky didn't want to be part of this set-up, though they were pleasant enough to her, and the father was almost paternal in his manner.

Sylvia looked vaguely familiar. Vicky racked her brains trying to remember where she'd seen her before. At school? She thought she remembered her being head girl when she'd first started there. She asked her, and she was right; it brought a smile to each of the faces.

The father asked her about the Courtney shipping line. Even now, years after it had finished trading, everybody remembered it. She told them how the war had reduced the fleet, and they were all sympathetic. They didn't ask about the photography shop; that was small fry by comparison.

They told her something of their business and seemed proud it was a family venture. Vicky decided she didn't want the job. She'd apply for another she'd seen in central Liverpool. She'd be able to go shopping in her lunch hour every day there.

As she was being shown out, Andrew told her they'd let her know about the job by post. He seemed very friendly, rather nice really; it almost made her change her mind.

When she got home. Dad grilled her about what had happened. She told him she didn't think she'd got the job. It was just typical that the letter arrived next morning offering it to her.

Dad and Mum were too loud in their congratulations. She was offered a starting salary of two guineas a week and the promise of a rise within six months if she could run the office by herself.

'Wonderful,' Howard said. 'Now we'll both be able to save for our wedding.'

Vicky felt racked with doubts. She felt she'd worked herself into a corner and there was no way out. In the end she turned up at the office the following Monday morning, gritting her teeth, feeling that she'd have to see it through for a week or two. Sylvia was going to work with her for eight weeks.

'Of course, for us it isn't like work at all. It's been great fun working for Dad. I shall miss it, I know.'

Vicky felt at a loss. She didn't know where anything was kept or what needed to be done.

Sylvia was supportive. 'You'll soon pick it up, don't worry.'

As she walked home after the first day, Vicky wanted to cry. She didn't know why. At times she seemed to be fighting herself. One half of her wanted one thing, the other half wanted something quite different.

She'd been so certain that she didn't want the photography shop, but she hadn't enjoyed the effort needed to get her Pitman's shorthand up to speed, and she'd wondered many times why she'd made such a fuss about leaving school to do it.

Over dinner, the family fired questions at her.

'How did you get on?'

'What are the Mayfields like?'

'Is there much shorthand and typing to be done?'

'Do you think you'll like the job?'

Vicky burst out: 'I think I'll hate it. I'm sure I will.'

'You'll get used to it,' Gran said. 'It can't be all that bad.'

'It's horrible, Gran,' she'd insisted. 'I'm going to have to look for something else.'

Gran smiled. 'You might find you like it when you've been there more than five minutes.'

Vicky ate slowly. She wasn't hungry. She knew they loved her, Dad, Mum and Gran. She didn't doubt that, even in her worst rat mood. Yet she had to fight them and she didn't know why.

'If you'd rather work in our shop, the offer's still open,' Mum said. 'Just make up your mind.'

But she couldn't give them the satisfaction of saying they'd been right, that she'd made a mistake. She'd made her choice and sheer mulishness made her stick to it.

She decided after a few weeks that it wasn't so bad after all. Sylvia explained everything and took to going out for a few hours each day, leaving her to get on with the work. Vicky shared her desk and felt she got to know her quite well in that time. She felt her confidence growing.

She found that Mr Mayfield and his son, Andy, did all the visits to properties and drew up the lists, but they entrusted her to show details of properties on offer and explain all about them to clients who came in wanting to buy or rent.

She also filled up rent books and took charge of the money from the tenants who came in to pay.

Vicky knew Andrew liked her. His eyes had a way of looking into hers and holding her gaze. He'd noticed her amethyst ring the first week she'd worked there. He'd drawn himself up, frowning.

'Are you engaged?'

She'd twisted her ring rather shyly. 'Yes.'

'Lucky fellow. When's it to be?'

'Not allowed until I'm twenty-one.'

His smile had been one-sided. 'All the most attractive girls get snapped up quickly. A slowcoach like me doesn't get a chance.'

There had been no more than that. But he was always friendly and she'd seen his grey eyes look at her amethyst more than once.

In time, Vicky learned to cope on her own at work. She felt she'd settled down and could manage. The Mayfields praised her. Every week, Vicky took in the rent and the rent books not only for her mother and grandmother, but also for Ada Catchpole, because Mayfield's acted as agent to the owner of Flaybrick Cottages.

'It's time they were brought up to date,' Vicky told Andrew; she felt strongly about it. 'No electricity in this day and age. I go to bed with a candle every night, and Gran heats her flat irons in the fire when she wants to press Dad's suits. You tell Mr Donaldson next time you see him that we want electricity. They've got it in the cemetery chapels; it wouldn't cost much to bring it up to us.'

She told Andrew that all the tenants wanted it as much as she did, which wasn't strictly true. Six months later, Mr Mayfield himself told her he'd spoken to the owner and that he'd think about putting it in. She was pleased to relay the news to Mum and Gran, who spread it from cottage to cottage. It was the main subject of conversation there for months.

But what Vicky really wanted was to marry Howard. He was always talking about it, letting her know he wanted it as much as she did.

'I do wish we could go ahead with it. It's what I want, it's what we both want.' He urged her to keep pressing her parents to give their permission.

'We could be independent on what we both earn, in a place of our own. We'll be well heeled when you come into your money. There's no reason for this waiting.'

Howard had a way of letting his hooded eyes search into hers, promising love. There were times when she felt nobody existed but him.

So Vicky kept nagging at her father. She felt he was the weaker link and would give in before Mum. It became a battle that sooner or later she thought she could win. She kept the pressure on, never letting more than a day pass without going on about it. Dinner time was best, when they were all together round the table. She always felt more determined when she'd had a better day at work and was going out to meet Howard.

'I want to get married.' She looked round and caught her grandmother's eye.

'You're like a bad record – stuck in a groove.'

'It's what we want. We can support ourselves. Mayfield's will want me to carry on working. I feel I'm missing out on so much fun, and for what? You keep me here like a child, you won't let me grow up. It isn't fair.'

She felt a joyous surge when Dad dropped his head in his hands. She knew he was about to give in.

'I can't fight her any more, Kate. She hasn't changed her mind in four years. Perhaps it's time to let her do what she wants.'

Vicky fizzed with triumph. She'd won at last. 'I can marry Howard?'

She felt a twinge of conscience when she saw Dad's face showing a mixture of confusion and defeat.

'Why do you keep fighting me?' he moaned. 'I want you to be happy. We all do. I want to give you the best of everything and all you do is kick out at me. Why at me?

'I've tried to protect you. Perhaps it wasn't the right way to go about it, but it's the only way I know. I made a disastrous marriage, Vicky. I don't want the same thing to happen to you.'

'It won't. I'm nineteen, old enough to make my own decision.'

'I was twenty-four.'

'But I love Howard.' Vicky felt victorious. She'd made Dad give in. She'd finally got what she wanted.

Vicky felt her heart flip and toss every time she thought of marrying Howard. Tonight, everything she asked of life was suddenly possible. She'd arranged to meet him outside the Odeon cinema in town.

These days Howard couldn't bring himself to visit Cemetery Cottages, not even to pick her up. He said he didn't like coming face to face with her family; he was afraid they'd go for his jugular. It was nonsense, of course, but they didn't like him and didn't always hide it. He made excuses too: it was out of his way, it was more convenient if she would meet him outside the cinema, or come to their shop.

She saw him waiting for her as soon as she jumped off the tram. 'Success,' she sang out. 'Success, I've done it. Dad's given in, we can get married.'

'Really?' Howard smiled slowly, then took her arm and led her towards the pay desk.

Vicky dragged her feet. 'I don't want to go to the pictures, not after this. I couldn't sit still. There's so much to talk about, to decide.'

Howard seemed slow to grasp what this change meant. 'It's the Marx Brothers, *Duck Soup*. You said you wanted to see it.'

'I did, but not now! I'm so excited.'

'You mean we can go ahead straight away? You've got permission?'

'Yes, I told you. Aren't you excited too?'

'Yes, of course, but what do you want to do now?'

'I'm just fizzing. We have to talk.'

'Let's walk then, come on.' They sat on a bench in Hamilton Square, but Vicky couldn't keep still. She walked him down to Woodside, and when she saw passengers streaming off the ferry, decided she wanted to sail across to Liverpool.

'I knew your father would come round.' Howard was sounding pleased now. 'All we had to do was to stick to our guns and keep saying it was what we wanted. When are we going to do it?'

'This spring? Say in two or three months? Just long enough to arrange everything.'

'That should give us time to find somewhere to live. A place of our own.'

'I can do that at work, won't take any time at all.'

'Rooms to start with, I think.'

'We can do better than just rooms, and what about our honeymoon? Where shall we go?'

'Rhyl?'

'I rather fancy Torquay.' Vicky knew she was going to have the time of her life.

Over the next few weeks, Howard seemed even more keen to tie the knot than she was herself, though he insisted on Rhyl for the honeymoon.

'What's the point in travelling all the way to Torquay? A waste of time.'

Vicky asked Andrew's advice about finding a pleasant place to rent.

'I thought you weren't getting married until you were twenty-one?'

Vicky bubbled over with joy. 'Dad's given in. I talked him into it. I'll want to go on working here afterwards. Is that all right?'

'We'd be sorry to lose you. You know that.'

Vicky felt everything was coming right for her. Now she'd got used to her job, she was enjoying it. The Mayfields made her feel almost part of the family.

Andrew had seen all the properties on their books and knew which were freshly painted and ready to move into. He picked out three he thought might suit her, and took her to see them.

One in particular bowled her over. It was a tiny cottage tucked away in a delightful backwater behind Claughton Firs. She took the particulars to show Howard that night, and as it was already empty, Andrew had said: 'Take the key, then you can show him round.'

'I know he'll love it.'

But she found that he too had heard of a property. A friend of his was moving to a bigger place.

'It's a flat. All mod cons, very comfortable. Just the place for us.'

It took an effort to get him to even look at her cottage, and then he didn't like it.

'Reminds me of Cemetery Cottages, except it's smaller. In fact, it's poky, and the bathroom's downstairs. Look, Vicky, I can't stand up straight in the bedrooms and the stairs are steep and narrow. Then there's a garden; I won't have time to look after that.'

'I could.'

'What, with a full-time job and all the housework? Come and see this flat. Much more practical.'

Vicky did. It was over a row of shops near Birkenhead Park station.

'You can do all your shopping here, and the trains and buses are handy. You can still walk to work. Couldn't be in a better position.'

'It's very busy here, sort of bustling . . .' A train thundered into the nearby station. Vicky had only ever lived in a semi-rural place.

'The park is just across the road. Acres of it, what more could you want?'

Vicky had to admit that the rooms were bigger and the bathroom more modern.

'All the same, I prefer the cottage. It speaks to me . . .'

'The flat gets all the sun. And the rent's lower.' It seemed Howard wasn't going to fall in with her wishes. 'I feel strongly that we should have the flat. It's only for a year or two, until you come into your inheritance. I'll let you choose the house we buy.'

That irked her. 'I buy,' she said. 'It will be paid for with my money.'

'Yes, as I said, you can choose it.'

On the grounds of practicality, she let herself be talked into the flat. She didn't miss his self-satisfied smirk.

He began to ask about her inheritance. He wanted to know every detail.

'Eight thousand pounds plus the interest it's earned since your grandfather died! That's a fortune. It'll make all the difference to us, not having a mortgage round our necks. After we've bought a house, there'll be lots left over. We'll be able to have everything we want.'

It began to get her down. '*I'll* be able to have everything *I* want,' she corrected. It seemed Howard attached more importance to her inheritance than he did to her feelings.

'Of course I mean you. But marriage means sharing. Your money will make a difference to me. You'll let me have my name on the house deeds? I'll feel less of a man living in your house.'

'Of course, if that's what you want.' But she began to see Howard in a different light.

260

He certainly wasn't as quick-witted as his family seemed to believe. She thought him rather slow and staid in his ways. The hooded eyes had promised love, but very little was forthcoming. If she kissed him with too much passion, he'd say: 'We won't anticipate our marriage. I want to respect you, Vicky.'

In fact, it occurred to her that Howard could be quite mean with the kisses he bestowed on her. She began to think he loved himself more than he did her.

They went to Liverpool one Saturday afternoon. Howard wanted her to help him choose his wedding suit. They were walking past Bunnies department store when he pulled her to a stop in front of a window full of ladies' fashions.

'I like that costume. Just the thing for you, Vicky.' He was eyeing a red outfit. 'Suit you down to the ground.'

She liked it. It had the fashionable longer fluid skirt and tight jacket. It was smart. 'For my going-away outfit?'

'To be married in.'

That made her flinch. She thought they'd agreed on a white wedding with all the trimmings. Vicky had tried on several traditional bridal gowns, though she hadn't found one she really wanted. Mum was taking her on another search for it next weekend.

Now, when she heard Howard say: 'Not a white wedding, Vicky, such an expense, buying clothes you'll only wear once,' she felt let down, resentful.

'It would be a waste, wouldn't it? Go in and try on that red outfit.'

She did so. It didn't fit properly and she'd taken a dislike to it by then, though Howard still sang its praises.

His handsome dark eyes beamed down at her, but they no longer moved her as they had. She was finding out that he was selfish and he was mean. They had their first serious quarrel and ended up buying nothing. They went to the first house at the Empire, and though the show was funny, Vicky couldn't laugh.

What really bothered her was that she didn't seem to know her own mind. When Howard took her to a furniture shop to choose some pieces for their flat, she felt she was being rushed into matrimony and didn't like it.

It made her feel confused. As though she didn't know what love was. After years of haggling with Dad to be allowed to marry, now it seemed she didn't want to. The freedom she'd expected to have was nonexistent. Howard had begun to lay down the law to her, and she didn't think he was any more caring about what she wanted than her family had been.

261

She felt closer to Dad, and at the same time she was pulling apart from Howard. Almost as though fighting with Dad was more important than the outcome. She wasn't ready to admit it yet, but she was afraid Mum and Dad had been right all along, and so had Gran.

Vicky felt caught in a web she'd spun herself, and now she was being swept into matrimony. She wanted to stop the bandwagon and make good her escape, but she had to think carefully about what she was doing. She mustn't make another mistake.

She felt very uneasy. She'd been going along with all the arrangements that were being made. Stopping them now seemed like trying to stop an express train. For the last week, the problem had been going round in her head, and she hadn't had a good night's sleep in all that time. She was making mistakes at work and was short-tempered with Billy and Gran.

Last night, she'd finally made up her mind. Everything had gone sour. She didn't want to marry Howard Jenkins. She couldn't go through with it and the sooner she told him, the better.

Vicky stepped out briskly. They'd arranged to go to the pictures again, and Howard expected her to call for him at his home above the grocery shop in Corporation Road.

The sun had not yet gone down; it was a blustery May evening and gust of wind caught the skirt of her blue dress. It was longer than she'd been in the habit of wearing, in the new fashionable, flowing style. She even had to hold on to her new straw hat.

She felt jumpy now their shop was in sight. She mustn't let herself put it off any longer. She'd feel better once she'd got it over.

It had closed for the night and the green blind had been drawn on the glass in the door. Vicky could see herself reflected in it, and again more clearly in the mirror advertising Crawford's Meadow Cream biscuits on the wall beside it. She reached up and pressed the bell that rang in the flat above.

Her blue eyes stared nervously back at her. Her fair curls not covered by her hat were fluttering in the breeze. She'd had her hair cut and set into deep waves the last time she'd been to the hairdresser. Howard had been rude about that; he'd said it looked better left long, and the sooner it grew again the better.

She wished somebody would come to the door. She rang the bell again, and went on assessing her own reflection. She knew that in looks she took after her father. She had the same fair hair, and skin which seemed to have a faint suntan even in winter. She was tall and slender and had the Courtney way of holding her head high. Vicky could see that her cheeks were pinker than usual.

She heard steps coming to the door and the bolts thudding back. She shivered. The awful moment was almost on her.

'Hello, dear, come in.' It was Howard's mother, Miriam, obese but smart in a flowered dress. She treated Vicky very differently now from the way she had when she was a child.

'I'm so glad you've come. I've made your wedding cake today. All three tiers. They've turned out beautifully.' Her face shone with pride. 'Come and see them before Mabel takes them away.'

Vicky followed her reluctantly. She wanted this wedding put off, but she had to tell Howard first. That was only fair; she mustn't blurt anything out now to his mother. In the kitchen, the three cakes were spread out to cool, one small, one medium and one large. Vicky stared at them, not knowing what to say.

'They smell delicious,' she managed at last. 'The whole place does.'

'Mabel ices cakes professionally. She's awfully good at it. I told you I'd asked her to do it? It'll be a cake to be proud of.'

Vicky cringed. 'I'm sure it'll be beautiful.'

'Do you want a sugar figurine on top? A bride and groom?' Mrs Jenkins leaned forward eagerly. 'Or a little silver vase with flowers?'

Vicky swallowed. 'I'll leave that to you and your friend.'

'Flowers then, I think. Can't go wrong with flowers, and Mabel has a little silver vase.'

'Lovely.'

'Howard's bought his wedding suit.' Mrs Jenkins smiled and squeezed her arm. 'I went with him to choose it. Grey pinstripe. You must get him to show it to you.'

Vicky felt desperate. 'Is he in?'

'Yes, dear, but he's only just come. He's getting ready.'

His mother took her into their living room.

'Have a seat, Vicky. Not long to wait now, only four more weeks – are you getting excited?'

Vicky gulped. 'Yes.' What else could she say? She wished Howard would hurry up. 'Will he be long?'

She couldn't stand much more of this, making polite conversation with his mother. What was she going to say when she found out?

'He had to work overtime, dear. He's had a very busy day. The launch at Cammell Laird's – he's been on crowd control. He told you about that?'

Vicky closed her eyes. She'd forgotten the launch. Her mind had been on her own problems, but this morning she'd seen details on the placards outside the newsagent's.

Howard was coming at last. She heard his bedroom door slam and his heavy step on the landing. He'd just had his twenty-fifth birthday, but acted as though he was much older.

'Hello, Vicky.' He was still wearing his uniform. She didn't like going out with him while he was wearing that. It was ridiculous when he was supposed to be off duty.

He smiled, but kept most of the room between them, making no attempt to kiss her. She knew he wouldn't in front of his mother. That was one of the things she didn't like about him. He said he loved her, but he didn't show it. He had a very high opinion of himself. He thought he was a lot cleverer and more important than most. Certainly cleverer and more important than she was.

'I've had a terrible day. I'm whacked. Too tired to sit through a film tonight. I don't think there's anything good on anyway.'

'That's all right.' The last thing Vicky wanted was to go to the pictures with him.

Howard's voice had a slight whine. 'I think an early night for me. I'd just as soon stay in.'

Vicky was alarmed. Now she'd made up her mind to break with him, she wanted to get it over with. She couldn't do it here, with his mother listening to every word.

'Just come out for half an hour. A walk.'

He sighed.

She added: 'There's something I want to tell you.'

'All right.' He sounded reluctant and was slow to put his shoes on. Vicky felt in an emotional whirl.

'A breath of air will do you good,' his mother encouraged him. 'You'll feel better for it.'

'I've had fresh air all day,' he retorted.

As soon as they were out in the street, he folded Vicky's arm through his and asked: 'Where do you want to go? I really haven't much energy.'

'It doesn't matter.' Now she was alone with him, she was struggling to begin.

'Taylor's Wood then?'

'All right.' That left her tight-lipped. Taylor's Wood was right behind Cemetery Cottages. Yet Howard wouldn't come to collect her. The arrangement always had to be that she would call for him. She took a deep breath and told herself that after tonight it wouldn't matter.

Anyway, by the time she'd said what she had to, she'd be near home. It gave her the impetus to begin. She started firmly; she'd rehearsed the opening sentence.

'Howard, I don't think we should go ahead with the wedding.'

'What?' He came to an abrupt halt and swung her round to face him. 'You want to postpone it?'

'No, call it off.'

He looked incredulous. 'Don't be silly, it's all arranged. The church and the reception. I'm paying rent on the flat. You said you liked it.'

'I'm sorry.'

'Sorry! You can't mean it.'

'I do.'

'Do you know how much time and energy I've put into this? Quite apart from the money.'

'I know you're upset. I am too, but it's better to break now. I don't think I can go through with it.'

He smiled, patted her hand in a patronising manner. 'It's just pre-wedding nerves. Lots of girls get them. Not uncommon, I believe. You'll be all right once the knot is tied.'

'No, I've been trying to tell you for a long time.' She didn't want to hurt him, and she knew calling it off at this late stage would. 'I think you're wrong for me.'

'In what way wrong?'

Vicky couldn't exactly say. 'It's a lot of things.' The list was growing. He'd rubbed her up the wrong way too often.

His brow furrowed indignantly. 'You know I love you. You said you loved me.'

'I thought I did. I've changed my mind. I don't any more. I want to call it off.' She knew it sounded miserable, cruel even.

'You've been leading me on.'

'Leading myself on too. I'm sorry.'

She could see anger in his handsome eyes. 'You can't back out now. You'll make me look a fool. At work too; I've applied for marriage allowance and rent allowance.'

'Sorry...'

'Don't keep saying that. Can't we say it's postponed? Illness at home – your grandmother. Something like that.'

'I want to end it. A clean break. I don't want to get married, we wouldn't get on.'

'But I don't understand. You've been going on about your bottom drawer and bridesmaids and things. I thought you wanted it.'

She had wanted it. Once, her opinion of Howard had been as high as his own. She'd thought she loved him.

'I've told you, I've changed my mind.'

'You've found somebody else? That fancy fellow, son of the man you work for?'

Vicky felt her heart turn over. She hadn't got round to admitting that to herself. But yes, she did like Andrew, and she couldn't help but see a lot of him. She eased the ring off her finger.

'You can't break off an engagement just like that.'

'I already have. I was only fifteen, Howard, it all seemed romantic. I was too young to realise . . . I'm sorry, I don't want to upset you.'

'But you are . . .'

'I'm going home, there's nothing else to say. And you wanted an early night.'

'Vicky! No . . .'

'Here.' She held the ring out on the palm of her hand.

'I don't want it back.'

'Take it,' she demanded, and when he made no move, she undid the button on the breast pocket of his jacket and slipped it in.

He caught at her wrist, twisting it until it hurt. 'You don't know what you're doing.' His face and neck flushed with anger. 'I won't let you.'

Vicky snatched her arm back. She'd been scared by his temper before. She didn't think he'd be an easy man to live with.

'What's wrong with me?' he demanded. 'What's made you change your mind?'

Vicky felt tears start at her eyes. 'Let's say I've grown up. I don't want to marry you. Goodbye.'

She meant she'd grown out of him. She couldn't tell him he had too big an opinion of himself and of his family. She'd been flattered to start with, thought he was wonderful, until she got to know him better.

He'd always been cruelly rude about Billy. He'd said he was feeble-minded, dead from the neck up, in his second childhood. Vicky had heard all Howard's nasty ways of describing Billy, and resented them. It should have put her off him much sooner.

Only last month, he'd said, pulling a face of woe: 'I hope you won't have babies like Billy.'

'Why should I?'

'It's in your blood, in your family, so of course you might. My mother says so. It's a risk I'll just have to take.'

That had really upset her. At least by breaking it off, she was saving him from that worry.

266

Chapter Twenty-Two

Vicky left Howard standing on the pavement at the end of Corporation Road. She wanted to put as much distance as possible between them. She was sweating with relief. She'd done it, she'd freed herself of him. As she got closer to home, she slowed down.

She still had to tell her family, and she wanted to get that over too. She was afraid they wouldn't understand; afraid nobody would understand. Sometimes she didn't understand herself. She'd held out for this marriage for four long years, and within weeks of Dad agreeing to it, she wanted to break it off.

Breaking off an engagement was a big thing and much frowned upon, especially at this late stage, when the church was booked and a flat rented.

But it was what they'd pleaded with her to do. Mum would be scathing and tell her she'd come to her senses in the nick of time, but she'd be glad too. She'd tell Dad he'd been right all along, though he'd probably say it himself.

Vicky let herself in through the back door of her home. Nobody ever locked their doors in Cemetery Cottages; there was no need.

'Mum?' She knew immediately that the house was empty, but her mother wouldn't be far. Most likely next door at Gran's house.

Her face felt on fire. She went to the stone sink, turned on the only tap and splashed cold water on her face until she felt better. Then went up to her bedroom and took off her hat. At her dressing table, she combed out her thick fair curls. Her eyes looked overbright and her cheeks deep dusky red. She'd go next door and finish what she'd started. She wanted everyone to know she was no longer tied to Howard Jenkins.

She found them all there. Dad, Mum and Gran were sitting round an empty grate on this warm evening. Billy was balancing on the arm of Gran's chair. Gran saw her first.

'You're back early,'

'I thought you were going to the pictures?'

'Has something happened?' It was Mum who'd noticed her burning cheeks.

'I've broken it off,' Vicky announced. 'I've told Howard I'm not going to marry him.'

There was a moment of stunned silence, before Gran exclaimed: 'What? You mean you've had a row? You've quarrelled?'

'No, well, yes. But it was because I said I wanted to finish with him.'

Dad was all smiles. 'You've come to your senses at last?'

They were all on their feet then, trying to hug her at once.

'What's changed your mind?'

'Thank goodness. I knew it was a mistake. We all did.'

Gran giggled. 'You've left it a bit late – with the honeymoon booked and everything.'

'The church too, and the reception.'

'I've bought myself a new hat for it!' Gran said. 'And I've bought Billy a new suit.'

Vicky laughed. 'Billy's never had a suit before that hasn't been handed down.' He was broader than his brothers and their things were always tight on him. 'You were always saying you were going to buy him a suit that fitted properly.'

'Well . . .'

'And a nice new hat for yourself, you can't complain about that?'

'It's what you need, Mam,' Kate assured her.

'What are the Jenkinses going to say?' Gran was off on another tack. 'This will put Flossie Jenkins' nose out of joint, jilting him like this at the last minute. It's going to be: "What's this I hear? Our Howard not good enough for the likes of you?" '

Vicky said: 'Howard's got a big head. He runs everybody down, you, me, everyone. I couldn't stand that for the rest of my life.'

Her mother kissed her. 'You've done the right thing. Don't let anybody tell you otherwise. Anyway, we never did like him.'

Her father smiled. 'What a bundle of contradictions you are, Vicky.'

'I've got it straight this time.'

'I'm sure you have, love.'

'We're all sure.'

After a cup of tea, they were about to go home when Gran caught sight of Flossie Jenkins in her front garden, dead-heading her roses.

She shot out to her. 'Have you heard?' Vicky could hear her goading her old enemy. 'The wedding's off. Our Vicky's come to her senses at last.'

'Never!'

'It's true.'

'The flighty bitch!' Flossie retorted. 'What's the matter with her? She doesn't know her own mind for five minutes. Well, she'll be sorry, that's all I can say. Very sorry. Our Howard is well out of it.'

Mum took Vicky by the hand, and they went out the back way, giggling.

The next morning, Vicky was late getting up and had to hurry. The blood was coursing through her veins by the time she reached her office. The accountant who had rooms upstairs had already opened up the front door. As she took out her keys to unlock Mayfield's office, the clock on the wall started to strike nine.

She unlocked the smaller of the two desks and removed the rexine cover from the typewriter. It gave Vicky a good feeling that she'd been trusted to run the office virtually single-handed since she was seventeen.

Andy came in on Wednesdays and Saturdays to bank the rent money she'd collected. She counted the cash and checked her figures in the register, making sure they balanced. Then she retyped the list of properties that were on offer for sale. There were two new ones to put on, and five that had been crossed off because they'd been sold.

She was taping the new list in the window so it could be read from the street when she saw Andrew Mayfield coming towards the office. He was striding out in his grey tweed jacket and grey flannel slacks. He was tall and slim, and the wind was fluttering his fair hair.

He saw her and raised his hand in greeting. Vicky waved back, then went to put the kettle on. He always had a cup of tea with her when he came to the office. He came breezing in.

'Hello, Vicky. I've just been to see Mr Donaldson, the owner of Flaybrick Cottages. You're going to get electricity. He says he's arranged for the work to go ahead.'

'Great. I'm pleased. Dad will be too. He was thinking of wiring up our house himself.'

'Really?'

'Yes, but thinking about things is as far as Dad ever gets. Somebody else has to provide the push.' Vicky was delighted that she'd managed to do this.

'It'll be done some time next month.'

'I told Gran it was on the cards. She's worried now about how much it will cost. So's old Ada Catchpole.'

'Not much more than the paraffin and candles do now. I see you've just retyped the list; I've another property to go on it. I should have got here sooner.'

He opened his briefcase on her desk, took out some papers and handed them to her. Vicky put out her left hand to take them. With a sudden movement that made her jump, his hand shot out to catch hers. He turned it over.

'You aren't wearing your ring.'

She pulled her hand away. 'I've given it back. I've broken it off. My engagement.'

His smile broadened into a grin. 'Good.'

She nodded, embarrassed; she didn't want Andrew to think she was flighty.

'I won't ask why,' he said. 'What about coming out with me? If I'm not pushing myself where I'm not wanted?'

Vicky was so surprised, it made her pull a face.

'I mean, with an attractive girl like you, I have to get in quickly. While you've got no other boyfriend.'

She liked him, of course she did, but . . . 'I'm not ready for any more of that, not yet.'

'Any more of what?'

'Being rushed to the altar. Tying myself down. Deciding how I'm going to spend the rest of my life.'

His grey eyes twinkled. 'Then how about a bit of fun?'

'That sounds all right.'

'And possibly the odd kiss; does that put you off?'

Vicky giggled. 'That sounds all right too.'

'We'll take the rest very slowly, I promise.'

'Perhaps not at all. I want my freedom.'

'You were too young to get engaged, that's your trouble. We'll leave all that stuff until later.'

'See how things work out?'

He smiled slowly. 'I think they'll work out all right. What about coming to the Argyll with me tonight? There's a full show, live turns first, then the screen comes down and they show a film. It's Greta Garbo.'

'Sounds fine.' She smiled slowly. 'More than fine: great.'

Lena made the custard pudding and slid it into the oven to bake. It was Billy's favourite; he was always asking for custard pudding. She felt tired, and her legs were as heavy as lead. She'd have to have a rest. She flopped heavily on to her basket chair. Her bunions were playing up too. It was only then she noticed her fire needed making up.

270

She heard the back door open and sank back. 'Where've you been, Billy?'

'To the dead park.'

'You haven't got more flowers?' He bought an impressive sheaf of arum lilies from behind his back.

'For you, Mam.'

'No, Billy. It's wrong to take other people's flowers.'

'Kenny give me them for you.'

'For me, why?'

'Said you were sick.'

'But they're from a grave.'

'No, from outside the chapel. Lots and lots of them today. I helped Kenny load van to go down to hospital. You like them?'

Lena sighed. The fresh scent of the lilies was filling the room. Arum lilies were more funereal than any other flower, and she'd taken against having them in the house.

'Not that sort, sunshine. Your dad would like them on his grave.'

There was a black-edged card nestling amongst them. Lena read it. *In loving memory of darling Josephine.*

'Kenny say cut off cards.' She watched Billy cut through the ribbon and throw it on the fire. 'He say flowers to hospital, wreaths to stay in dead park.'

'Yes, love.'

Her boys had always taken flowers. Stolen flowers, according to Jack. He was against having any of them in his house. There was no way she could stop Billy doing it; he didn't understand. She hoped God would forgive them.

'Come with me, Mam, to take flowers'

'Make up the fire first. I'm tired, Billy, I want a cup of tea.'

'Right.'

Billy knew exactly how to bank up the fire. Hadn't she shown him countless times? He did it with infinite care and attention. He knew how to make a good cup of tea too. Lena closed her eyes to rest, knowing the tea would be put in her hand when it was ready.

'I'm a good boy,' Billy said.

'A very good boy. Fill the coal bucket up for me too.'

Lena thanked God for giving Billy to her. She couldn't manage without him now she was getting old. All her other boys, they'd grown up and left her. Duncan and Freddie were in Canada now. She couldn't say they'd forgotten her, because they wrote regularly, but she'd never see them again, it was too far away.

Duncan was married with a little boy of his own. He wrote that they'd found a better life there. She didn't begrudge them anything. They had a right to do the best they could for themselves. It was Joe and Charlie she wept for, and, most of all, Tommy.

Harry was still living in Birkenhead, and paid over five shillings of his wages to her every week. He came to visit her, mostly on Sunday afternoons. Brought his little boy to see her too, but he didn't care how she managed during the rest of the week. When she'd said that to him, he'd told her Kate would be glad to do anything she needed.

'And you've got our Billy.'

Billy was everything to her now. He was broader and stronger than any of them, and handsome too, with big innocent eyes and lashes that curled up. Billy had never grown up. Everybody thought of him as Peter Pan. Everybody loved him. She had all the love and care she needed from him, and nothing, not even war, could take him from her.

'Come on, Mam. Let's go to the dead park.'

'Let's have our dinner first. There's stew, and custard pudding to follow.'

'Dinner first. Custard pudding.'

'Set the table for me, Billy.'

When they'd eaten and cleared away, Billy smiled his sweet, gentle smile. 'Dead park now, Mam?'

Lena sighed again. She had backache, but Billy never gave up once he had an idea in his head, and she wanted to get the lilies out of the house.

'Come on then, get my coat for me.'

Billy always held her coat out, helped her into it. Brought her hat down from upstairs.

They set out. She could lean on Billy's arm. It was a help to get along. He held the lilies with both his hands, like a bridal bouquet, against his stomach.

When she had a good day, she sometimes took Billy to the live park, where he loved to see the ducks on the pond, but they didn't go very often these days. It was a long walk, and her feet were worse if she walked far.

Billy could come here by himself while she rested on her bed after dinner. He was always in and out. The grave-diggers knew him and sometimes let him help them dig. He frequently swept the paths and helped trim the grass verges. Everybody knew him and talked to him. The dead park was part of his life.

'Hello, Billy.'

'How are you, Billy?'

They called themselves groundsmen now, not grave-diggers, and there were fewer of them than there used to be. They were sitting on the bank in the sun, eating the sandwiches they'd brought for their lunch. Billy seemed to know all of them by name: George and Alfred and Wilf and Kenny. They doffed their hats to her.

When she'd first came to live here all those years ago, people used to ask her if she found it depressing living so close to the cemetery, with gravestones always in view from the windows. Lena had never found it so; she liked the cemetery.

She used to come almost every day when baby Liza died. She'd really missed her, been upset by her death. Upset by Mitch's death too. It was a peaceful place, and comforting to know that when it was all over she'd end up in this grave with them.

It was one of the best-kept graves here. There was no headstone – she couldn't afford that – but years ago her boys had built a kerb of marble pieces round it and the handsome marble vase was always filled with fresh flowers.

She watched Billy take away the wilted flowers they'd put there last week. Then make another trip to bring fresh water. The cemetery brought a feeling of peace, of time standing still. She remembered poor Liza, and regretted that her sons killed in the war were not here where she could remember them too.

Lena walked slowly up the formal cemetery path, hanging on to Billy's arm. She knew she was getting slower. They went out through the great ornamental gates of the back entrance behind the chapels of rest. All they had to do then was to cross the road and climb the cart track.

A few weeks later, Lena was leaning on her front gate with Kitty Watts, while Ada Catchpole recounted the latest news of her daughter, Betty. They all saw the contractor's van as it came bumping up the cart track. A line of freshly turned earth along the edge of the track showed where the trench had been dug to take the main electricity cable. the van drew to a halt outside number one Cemetery Cottages, causing Ada Catchpole to run home.

'Here it comes then,' Kitty said. 'Won't be long now before we're wired up for the 'lectric.'

'Good thing.' Billy stopped sweeping the front path. Lena knew Billy was repeating what he'd heard Jack say the night before. Not all her neighbours thought having the electric would be a good thing.

Most of the tenants came out in time to see the contractor get out of his van and eye the row of cottages. He had a young lad in blue overalls with him, who ceremoniously handed him a large notebook and a tape measure. The man nodded to them as he marched up the path to Ada's front door.

Lena approved of the celluloid collar and cuffs he wore fastened to his shirt with studs; they'd save on washing. He took a pencil from the top pocket of a black jacket going green with age and announced: 'I've come to measure up.'

Lena heard Mrs Catchpole say: 'I hope you aren't going to make a mess.' She was house-proud. 'It's not long since I had new wallpaper in my bedroom. Lovely pink roses all over it.'

'We won't make more mess than we have to. My men are very tidy.'

Lena knew that needn't bother her. Her walls were all distempered white. Billy had helped Freddie do them last time, and would do them over if she explained what was needed and bought the stuff. Perhaps she should have it green downstairs? But no, white again would be best. Easier for Billy. He'd never get an even line round the ceiling if she chose a colour for the walls. She had to be practical.

Old Mrs Fry at number five was frightened. She accosted the man at Lena's gate.

'I don't want any of them new electrics in my house. How do they know it's safe?'

'It's safe, missis. Quite safe. The owner wants all these cottages wired up, so we'll have to do yours. Don't you worry, once you get used to it, you won't know how you lived without it.'

'But I don't know where the light comes from, I won't know how to work it.'

'Archie, lad – bring us a switch.' The boy went to the van and brought an ornate round wall switch to show them.

'You'll be having one of these in every room. Best-quality brass. You just press this little thing down when you want the light on, and up again when you want it off. Couldn't be easier.'

'Let me. Let me.' Billy held his hand out for it, and the lad gave it to him.

'No matches needed, that's what I don't understand,' Mrs Fry worried.

'I can do it.' Billy beamed with triumph and clicked the switch back and forth. 'I can do 'lectric, but there's no light.'

'There will be when we've wired it in.' Archie grinned.

'Come and do my house,' Billy invited. 'I want it.'

'Course I will. We start in a fortnight.'

Archie patted him on the back. Billy gathered him up in a great bear hug in return, Lena couldn't help but see the look of glazed surprise on the lad's face.

'Our Billy's all right,' she hastened to tell him. 'Wouldn't hurt a fly.'

'Squeezed the breath out of me body, he did.' The lad laughed.

'I like you.' Billy beamed at him.

Billy could talk of nothing else for the whole fortnight, and was watching for the van when it came. He pulled Lena outside to see it. The contractor had brought the electrician, a middle-aged man called Eric, who wore a bowler hat and blue overalls.

'Hello, Billy.'

Archie jumped down from the back and started to unload tools, boxes of fittings and great reels of electrical wire. His eyes were watering and his nose looked red and sore. He took out a torn handkerchief and blew hard.

'Give us a hand with this stuff, will yer, Billy? I don't feel up to scratch today.'

Lena knew nothing would please Billy more. He helped carry everything into Ada's house and didn't want to leave. Ada had her mats up and was covering her furniture.

Eric and Archie started gouging old plaster off the walls to make chasings for the wire. They were making a terrible dust that spread everywhere. Billy wiped it carefully off skirting boards and picture rails, then swept it up from the floors with dustpan and brush. That pleased both Archie, whose job it was, and Ada, who was used to having Billy about her house.

'Come and have a cup of tea with me,' Lena invited.

'And leave these men in my house? No! Goodness knows what they'll get up to if I turn my back.'

Lena went home alone. She wasn't looking forward to having that mess in her place. At mid-morning, Billy brought Archie to the door.

He said: 'Can I have some hot water, missis? To make tea.'

'Course you can, come in.'

'Me do it.' Billy carefully filled the kettle from the boiler beside the grate, and lowered it on to the fire to bring back to the boil.

'Our Billy can learn to do anything,' Lena told Archie. Archie brought out his handkerchief again and had another blow.

'You've got a terrible cold.'

'Yes.' He mopped his streaming eyes. 'Awful.' Billy brought out the tea pot and caddy.

'No.' Archie stopped him. 'Just hot water. I've got it all here in the billycan.'

Lena watched Billy peer at the sticky ball of condensed milk and tea leaves at the bottom.

'Not tea.'

'Yes it is. It's all ready. We each bring a billycan . . .'

'Billycan tea!' He laughed.

'We don't like that sort here, do we?' Lena smiled. 'Make a pot for us too, Sunshine.'

When they switched the light on for the first time in number one, Billy clapped his hands and laughed.

'It's magic! I like it. Good stuff.'

The other residents from the cottages rushed in to see it, and admired the beautiful brass rose in the centre of each ceiling. It had the same ornate pattern as the switch on the wall.

'How bright the light is,' Ada Catchpole marvelled. 'Much better than the lamp.'

'Like daylight,' Kitty Watts agreed.

'I want to know about 'lectric. You show me, Archie. I learn it. It's magic.'

'It's science really.' Archie held up some off-cuts of the wire they were using.

'Look, if I take away this brown silky covering, you can see two wires inside, one red and one black. The red is the positive one and the black is the negative. Then if I peel back the red paper and the lead covering, you can see the copper wire inside. The current travels along that.'

Eric the electrician beamed round at them all. 'You see it making light, but it will do lots of other things. Heat things and move things.'

Billy said: 'I help you. I work for 'lectric too.'

Eric shook his head. 'You got to be careful with electricity. It can give you a shock, Billy.'

'What's that?'

'The current will go through you, give you a real jerk. Make you jump.'

'Get me going? Wake me up?'

Eric laughed. 'More than that. Give you a real whammy.'

'I've heard they do that in hospitals,' Ada said. 'To make people better.'

'Bring them back to life?' Billy wanted to know.

'I don't know as I'd go that far,' Eric said.

Billy listened while Archie tried to explain how the wires could be joined together.

'It's magic,' he chortled. ' 'Lectric does everything.'

Archie gave up. 'All right, it's magic.'

No more oil lamps or candles, Lena thought. She always cleaned the lamp glass herself, because once Billy had pushed his hand inside one and broken it. It would be one job fewer she had to do.

After that, they started wiring Kate's cottage. Billy caught Archie's cold, but continued to follow them from house to house as they worked. The cold went through the tenants of the Cemetery Cottages with the speed of a plague.

By the time the workmen arrived at her front door, Lena knew she had it too. Her head ached and her nose streamed, and she didn't feel at all well. With the men working in her house, hammering away and shouting to each other, there was no peace to be had. With all the dust, it seemed to settle on her chest. She was heartily glad when at last they finished and moved on to Flossie Jenkins next door.

She couldn't let Billy follow Archie there, though he wanted to. He wouldn't be welcome in Flossie's place. She asked Kate to bring her a couple of tins of white distemper to keep Billy busy. By then Lena had a nasty cough too, but she got him to paint over the new plaster and freshen the place up a bit, which meant she still didn't have peace to nurse her cold.

Late in the afternoon, Andrew Mayfield called in to Vicky's office at the estate agency.

'How are you all liking the electric light?'

'Love it. Especially our Billy, but he's missing the workmen now they've gone.'

'Had ambitions to be an electrician himself?'

'Well, electrician's mate. He's flashing the lights on and off all day. I hope he isn't going to break something.'

'The switches are built to stand that sort of thing, and he'll soon get tired of doing it.'

'I hope so. He's got a thing about electricity. Thinks it has magical properties.'

Vicky bought some lemons for Gran on the way home from work. She hadn't got over her bad cold, and now it had gone down to her chest. She'd had a sore throat for the last few days. Vicky thought some lemonade would help soothe it.

Gran hadn't got out of her bed yesterday, but Billy was looking after her very well. He made her all the tea she wanted, but he couldn't think of anything different.

When Vicky got home, her mother was busy juggling pans on the oil cooker.

'I wish these potatoes would boil. We were very late getting back.'

Vicky knew they'd been to Manchester to see some new darkroom equipment. They were thinking of bringing the shop darkroom up to date.

'You're not going out tonight, Vicky?'

'No, it doesn't matter what time we eat.'

Vicky chopped up the lemons and made the lemonade, then went to the living room door. Her father was trying to light the fire. He wasn't very good at it.

She asked: 'How's Gran been today?'

'Haven't seen her yet. We gave Billy a call, he says she's much the same.'

'See if she'll have some cod and parsley sauce,' her mother told her, 'and bring Billy down to eat with us.'

Vicky picked up the jug of lemonade and went into Gran's house. There was no fire in the living room grate. That shocked her. Not only did the room seem chill, but Billy needed the fire to make tea and fill hot-water bottles.

She called: 'Hello, Gran?' There was no answer, so she made for the stairs.

Billy was sitting close to the bed, holding both of Gran's hands in his. Gran's face was flushed and her eyes were closed.

'Gran?' Her eyes flickered open for a moment. Vicky put a hand on her forehead; it was burning hot. She gasped: 'How long has she been like this, Billy?'

'She's sick. Got bad cold.'

Vicky's heart seemed to stop, then went bouncing out of control.

'More than a bad cold. You've let the fire go out. You can't make tea for her without a fire.'

'Doesn't want tea any more.' He indicated the cup of cold tea beside her on the table.

Vicky lifted Gran's head and gave her a few sips of hot lemonade. She was afraid Gran would need more than that to make her better.

'She needs the doctor.'

She scuttled downstairs and back to her mother. 'Gran's worse.'

'Did she say she could manage a bit of fish?'

Vicky couldn't believe Mum was so concerned about dinner.

'No! She's *much* worse.'

'In what way? Is it the sore throat that's bothering her?'

'It's more than that now. Her cough sounds terrible.'

'Ada said she'd give her and Billy something at lunch time. Did she eat it?'

'I don't know. Go and see her, Mum. She needs the doctor. I think we should get him here.'

Dad said: 'You know what she's like. She won't have him.'

'Just go and see her. She's all hot.'

'Everything's ready here.' Kate put the fish slice in Vicky's hand. 'Start dishing up or it'll spoil.'

Vicky didn't think she could eat anything. Mum didn't realise . . . She hadn't got the food on the plates when she heard Mum running back. She looked desperately worried now.

'She's really poorly, Jack. Running a temperature. We'll have to get the doctor to her.'

'Tomorrow morning? I'll go down and ask him to call in on his rounds.'

'Now, Jack, please. Tonight. As soon as possible.'

Chapter Twenty-Three

Kate watched silently as Jack put on his coat and went out. Then she hurried back to her mother. What had she been thinking of? She'd been out all day, enjoying herself with Jack. They'd been home for half an hour and neither of them had been near her in that time.

Poor Mam! Kate looked down at her mother's lined face. Her eyes were closed, she was struggling to breathe and there was a rattle in her chest.

'A drink?'

Mam gave no sign that she'd heard. Kate lifted her head and gave her a few sips of Vicky's lemonade. Her eyelids fluttered, but she hardly had the strength to swallow.

Billy was wringing his hands. 'Make her better. Mam doesn't like being sick.'

That brought a lump to her throat. 'We'll do our very best. Go and find Vicky. She's got dinner for you.'

'Don't want dinner. Not hungry.'

'You must eat, Billy, or you'll get sick too. Go on, go to my house.'

Kate felt cold shivers going down her back. She'd never seen Mam as bad as this. She sank down on the chair Billy had left and felt for her mother's hand.

'How are you, Mam?'

Her chest bubbled and wheezed; her eyes remained shut.

'Mam? Mam?' Lena opened her eyes at last. 'How are you?'

'Poorly.' Kate had to put her ear closer to catch the whisper. 'Chest hurts when I breathe.'

Mam had moved with ponderous slowness for some time. She'd leaned on Billy and waved away help from everybody else. Kate tried to think for how long. She wished she'd been more like Vicky. In and out and doing things for her. Instead she'd let Mam wait on her and Jack. She no longer cleaned their house but she still cooked meals for them. She'd let her do far too much and carry on doing it far too long.

Eventually she heard Jack's voice downstairs. He was bringing the doctor up. Middle-aged and balding, he listened to what she had to say about Mam's illness, and took his stethoscope from his bag. He looked serious when he listened to Mam's chest.

'Pneumonia.'

The very word brought numbing dread. The doctor was saying more: '. . . failing health, not a fit woman.'

Mam was to have poultices on her left lung and aspirin to bring down her temperature and help with the pain.

Kate bit her lip. She had aspirins, she could have given her those days ago. She could have made her feel better, if only she'd thought . . .

She had to concentrate then on what the doctor was telling her about making the poultice. A tin was put in her hands. She was to reheat the poultice every four hours.

'I have to warn you,' the doctor looked very solemn, 'your mother's been ill for some time. The crisis is not far away. We may not be able to save her.'

Kate froze in agony. Why had she not noticed her mother's failing health? She'd been home much more since they'd had help in the shop. She should have done more for her. Spent more time with her, given her more sympathy.

'You've done more than most daughters would,' Jack comforted. 'She was taking aspirins, I saw her. Don't reproach yourself. You've done your best.'

'Had you better go for our Harry?' she choked. 'He'll want to know . . .'

'I'll fetch him in the car.' Jack kissed her cheek.

Billy and Vicky came back. Kate sent her home to get an old sheet to make the poultice, and told her how to heat it up. She didn't want to leave her mother now. It was Billy who sat Lena up so that they could bandage the strong-smelling pad to her back.

'Feels nice,' she sighed softly. 'Comforting.'

Lena dozed off then, and the three of them kept vigil round her bed. When Harry joined them and whispered his questions, Mam woke up and another fit of coughing shook her. Billy sat her up again to make it easier for her.

'Thank you, Sunshine.'

Her brown eyes, shining with affection, went round them all, but they came to rest on Billy.

Mam had slept for an hour. Kate tried to send some of her family to bed.

'Go on, Jack, you'll be able to take over later. And you, Vicky. You must, or we'll all be washed out by morning.'

Kate tried to persuade Billy into his own bedroom, which was next to Mam's. He was playing with the pieces of electrical wire that Archie had given him. Kate was in and out until he'd put on his striped flannel pyjamas.

He said: 'She loves me, does me Mam.'

'Of course she does, Billy.'

'And I love her.'

'He loves everybody.' Harry's voice came from the next room.

'Yes, I do then, but I love me mam best.'

Time seemed to stand still for Kate. Harry was dozing in his chair. She could hear Billy tossing and turning in his bed, and eventually he came padding back.

'Is me mam better?'

Mam seemed to come to. 'Hello, Sunshine.'

'Help me sit her up, Billy. We'll give her another drink.' The lemonade was cold now. They plumped up her pillows, pulled her sheets straight.

That woke Harry up too. 'How is she?'

'Kate?' Mam's voice was fading. 'Look after our Billy for me. Take care of him when I'm gone.'

Kate glanced at Billy. She could feel love in the atmosphere now. Mam had always seemed to radiate it to her family, and Billy was her best-loved son. Mam's hand snaked across the sheets to catch at hers. Kate knew she'd been loved too.

'Of course I will, Mam.'

'Promise now.'

'I promise.'

'Thanks, love. Best daughter anyone could . . . have. Always knew that.'

'Mam?' Harry took her other hand. 'Hold on now. You can fight this.'

Kate heard him whisper, 'She's not all that old, is she, Kate?'

She watched her mother lie back against her pillows. She looked more relaxed than any of them.

Harry choked: 'Had I better fetch Jack?'

'Please.' She needed him now. He'd want to do what he could. 'And wake Vicky. She wanted me to if there was any change.'

Kate feared what she knew must be near. Billy was stroking her hand.

'Poor Mam, you'll be better soon.'

Kate heard the back door shut and voices down below. All three were coming back.

Vicky came running lightly up the stairs, bringing a rush of cold night air with her. She bent over to kiss her grandmother.

'Kate, is that you?' The old voice wavered.

'It was Vicky, Mam.'

'Tell her . . .'

Vicky leaned over her. 'Tell me what, Gran?'

'Glad you came to your senses – about that pompous ass. You can do better – than a Jenkins.'

Vicky giggled. 'You're feeling better!'

'Yes . . .' Gran gave a soft sigh and lay back. They all saw the change that came over her.

'She's gone,' Jack said.

None of them moved a muscle. The shocked silence stretched on and on. Kate couldn't get her breath. It was Vicky's sob that broke the spell.

Kate tried to get to her feet, but her knees felt too weak to support her. Her mother's love was here all round them like a wall. None of them could take their eyes from her face. She looked at peace; the lines of age seemed to have faded. She had a half-smile on her lips and she looked twenty years younger.

'What's happened?' Billy wanted to know. 'Is she all right?' He seemed confused.

Vicky took him by the hand. 'Come and have some cocoa, Billy.'

'I need something stronger than that,' Jack choked. 'Come and have a whisky, Harry?'

'Is me Mam asleep? I want her to come too.'

'No, Billy, I'm afraid she's gone.'

'Gone? Where to?'

Kate eyed the body of her mother and felt desperate. 'She's dead. Gone to heaven.'

'She's here.' He pointed to the mound under the sheet.

'No, she's gone to heaven.'

'When will she be back?'

'She won't, Billy.'

'She wouldn't leave me! She promised she'd never leave me.' Billy began to cry noisily.

Kate fetched his coat and made him put it on over his pyjamas so that he wouldn't catch cold. 'Come on, we're all going to our house.'

They sat round the table in the living room. Kate pulled Billy down on the chair beside her, while Vicky made cocoa.

'I don't want to leave Mam by herself,' Billy moaned. Kate felt bewildered too. It had happened so quickly.

By the time Vicky brought the cocoa to the table, Billy had gone.

Harry sipped the whisky Jack poured for him. 'Poor sod. He'll be like a lost soul without her.'

Jack slumped onto a chair. 'What are we doing to do with him? We can't leave him sitting up there with Lena for the next three or four days.'

Kate had to ask: 'Will you take him home with you Harry?'

He said too quickly: 'Mam wanted you to look after him. I heard her ask you to do that.'

Jack said wearily. 'She's always asked a lot of Kate.'

Kate swept her fringe back from her face. 'Look after him Harry, please. Just for a few days until the funeral's over. To get him out of the way. He doesn't really understand and it'll upset him more when he sees us clearing out all Mam's things. He can't live there by himself, can he?'

Jack looked shocked. 'Where's he going to live then?'

'He'll have to come here to us. He couldn't manage by himself. Lucky we've got a spare bedroom.'

'Kate! We'll be looking after him for the rest of our lives. Feeding him, washing and ironing for him.'

'It won't be you that's doing it,' Kate snapped. She was sorry then, she'd never spoken to Jack with such an edge to her voice.

'Come on love.' She felt his arms go round her. 'You go up to bed. I'll run Harry home. This has all been too much for you.'

'But what about Billy? We can't leave him sitting by Mam's bed.'

'All right,' Harry sounded exhausted. 'I'll take him home with me for a few days.'

Vicky stirred. 'I'll get a bag. Pack a few things for him.'

'I'll fetch Billy.' Jack climbed the stairs in Lena's house with Vicky behind him.

Billy was busy over Lena's bed. He had his pieces of electrical wire spread across her and was twisting them in his hands. 'Got to get Archie here. He'll know what to do.'

Come on lad. You're going home with Harry for a day or two.' Jack wanted all this finished so he could go back to bed.

'Not now.'

In the adjoining room, Vicky was tossing Billy's clothes in a bag.

284

She called: 'Come and get your shoes and socks on Billy. He can go in his pyjamas, can't he Dad?'

Jack tidied the wires from Lena's bed, throwing them back in Billy's room. It wouldn't do for Kate to find them spread over her mother like this. Then he led Billy out of the house.

Kate woke to find Vicky by her bed, holding a tray with two cups of tea on it. She looked red-eyed and melancholy.

'Oh Mum, isn't it awful? I can't get it out of my mind that Gran's gone for ever.'

For Kate, the feeling of loss was suddenly overwhelming. Vicky's arms went round her in a hug.

On the other side of the bed, Jack pulled himself up on his pillows. 'You're all dressed up. Are you going to work?'

'I've got to open the office, Dad. I don't want to let them down.'

'You can let them know, once you're there.'

'Yes, but by then I might as well stay. Less to remind me. Unless you want me to help here, Mum?'

'No, love.'

Jack said: 'I should have had a phone put in here. Would have been useful last night too.'

'You keep saying you're going to,' Vicky sighed.

'I will now.'

When they heard the door slam behind her, Kate said: 'Fancy our Vicky thinking of other people. She's grown up.'

Jack reached for his tea. 'Thank goodness. Not before time.'

As soon as Vicky reached the office, she telephoned Andrew Mayfield and told him that her grandmother had died.

'I'm so sorry. What a shock.' He sounded shocked himself. 'You must be feeling terrible. I'll come down right away.'

He let himself in twenty minutes later, and strode straight over and took her in his arms.

'You said she wasn't well. I'd no idea it was this serious.'

'None of us had.' Vicky put her head down on his shoulder and had a little weep. His Harris tweed jacket felt rough against her cheek.

It was only when she heard a customer coming in that she pulled out of his arms and headed towards the cloakroom.

She splashed cold water on her eyes and tried to pull herself together. Her reflection in the mirror confirmed the worst. She powdered her nose, added a little lipstick, but it didn't make her look her usual self.

She heard the customer go and knew Andy was alone again.

She made up her mind to be businesslike. Not let him hold her again. It was the only way she'd be able to stay in control today.

She took Gran's rent book from her handbag and slid it on to his desk.

'She's a week in hand. Mum said to tell you that she'll have the house cleared in that time.'

'Vicky, love, would you like to go home? I can put somebody else in for a day or two. This is a miserable time for you.'

She shook her head. 'It's even more miserable at home. Mum's very upset, she was close to . . . I'll be all right now. I'd like time off for the funeral, though.'

'Of course. Let me know when, and I'll cover for you.'

'What about putting her place on the list of houses for rent?'

'There's no hurry for that. Next week's soon enough. Bring the keys in when you're ready and I'll go and look it over first.' Vicky nodded. It was what she'd expected him to say.

'I don't like leaving you here like this.'

'Probably better if you do. I'll have to get on with the job then.'

He said awkwardly: 'Don't worry about all these lists and things that need typing.'

'No.'

'I don't suppose you'll want to come out with me? We arranged Friday night.'

Vicky felt choked. 'Perhaps I'd better stay home with Mum and Dad for a bit.'

'I think you're very brave.' His brown eyes looked into hers with such sympathy that she felt the tears start to her eyes again. 'I do love you, Vicky. You're sure you'll be all right?'

When Vicky got home from work, Harry was with her mother. She said: 'The funeral's fixed for next Monday.'

Vicky looked at her uncle. 'How's Billy?'

'Terrible. He keeps saying he wants to come back to his mam. He's hard to look after. Giving Ellen a bad time.'

'In what way?'

'He went out and couldn't find his way back. She had to go looking for him. The kids found him near the bus terminus and brought him home.'

Kate asked: 'Was he trying to get the bus back here?'

'Yes, but he had no money for his fare anyway.'

Harry said: 'Mam brought him to see us once. Only once on the bus. Just as well, or he'd know his way back.'

Kate sighed. 'Jack took us all several times in the car, didn't he?'

On Saturday afternoon, Kate asked Vicky to help her bundle up Billy's clothes and belongings.

'I want to move all his things into our spare room. The sooner he's back here, the better.'

'You should have got Uncle Harry to give us a hand with his bed.'

'Kitty Watts is asking two young lads who work in the cemetery to come up. They'll carry the heavy stuff over. There's a nice chest of drawers in Mam's bedroom; we'll move that in for him. Apart from a chair, there won't be room for much else.'

They'd stripped his bed and folded up the blankets in readiness. Kate watched her daughter stowing Billy's belongings in a cardboard carton.

'All this rubbish he's collected,' she fumed. Vicky put in two big lumps of marble from the cemetery, some pretty tail feathers from a magpie and lots of cut-off pieces of electrical wire.

'We'll throw it all out.'

'Not the wire, Mum.' Vicky's young face frowned up at her. 'It means a lot to him. Why shouldn't he keep these things? It's enough that he's lost Gran.'

Kate felt like kicking herself. It made her stop and think how much worse this was for Billy. Why couldn't she look at things as Vicky did?

On Sunday morning, Vicky was washing cabbage at the kitchen sink, helping her prepare the dinner. Suddenly she called: 'Mum, here's our Billy!'

'Where?'

'He's just passed. He's going to Gran's house.'

Kate shot out after him. 'Billy, how did you get here?'

'By myself. Harry wouldn't come.'

Vicky was close behind her. 'Did you come on the bus?'

'Yes.'

'Did you have money for your fare?'

He shook his head. 'Kind lady paid for me.'

Billy let himself into the living room. 'Mam?'

The undertakers had been to put Gran in her coffin. Harry had wanted her brought down because the stairs were steep and narrow.

'Mam's down here now? Why isn't she in her own bed?'

The coffin had been left open in the living room, standing on the trestles provided by the undertaker. Vicky peeped inside. Gran was wearing her best nightdress of cotton lawn; high at the neck and long in the sleeve, it was all soft frills and flounces. She'd kept it in her drawer for years, ready to put on if the doctor had to be called or she had to go to hospital. She didn't want strangers to see her in her well-worn winceyette nighties.

They'd forgotten all about it when they'd called in the doctor, and Gran had been past caring by then. Billy stood staring down at her.

'Make her wake up, Vicky.'

'I can't.' Kate heard her daughter's voice tremble.

'Archie could.'

Jack came to see what was happening. 'No, Billy. Nobody can.'

Kate said, 'Jack, you'll have to go down to tell Harry. He'll be looking all over for Billy. He didn't think he could get this far by himself. Bring his clothes back with you. His room's ready, he might as well stay now. If you go right away, you'll just have time to get there and back before dinner.'

Kate left Billy where he was, staring down at his mother. He was crying.

On the day Gran was to be buried, Vicky left the office before lunch. When she got home, she could feel the tension building up. She'd been dreading the funeral. It was the first she'd been to. The first for Billy too. His face screwed with concern.

'What's going to happen? They're going to do something to Mam, aren't they?'

'Put her in the grave with Liza and your dad.'

'In the dead park?' His eyes were round with apprehension.

'Yes.'

'They mustn't do that. Get Archie. He'll make Mam better.'

Vicky shook her head. 'Archie can't do anything.'

Her father said: 'Come on, Billy. Don't get upset. This is to say goodbye to your mam. You want to do that, don't you?'

Vicky said: 'You come with me. We'll hold hands.'

Her mother sighed. 'Poor Billy, what will he do without Mam?'

The cortège went direct from the house, the coffin carried on the shoulders of six strong men. Billy, Harry and her father were among them.

Billy was wearing the grey suit Gran had bought him for Vicky's wedding to Howard Jenkins. Her mother had asked her to sew a black band round the arm to show mourning, and Dad had loaned him a black tie.

'Mam's never had so many flowers.' Billy squeezed her hand. 'Grave-diggers gave some. Said she was a friend.'

Vicky heard Flossie Jenkins whisper to Gladys Fry: 'Bet they came off somebody else's grave.'

All the tenants of Cemetery Cottages had turned out for Gran's funeral.

Kate was glad they had a manager to run the shop. She hadn't been able to think of the business these last few days. Images of Mam filled her mind all day. She tried to think of the love Mam had had for them all, rather than the loss she was feeling.

She found emptying Mam's house a big job. Jack tried to help, of course. He arranged for the pieces of furniture nobody in the family wanted to go to a saleroom.

Kate felt all the decisions were left for her to make, and it was a big job clearing out all the useless odds and ends that her mother had kept over the years. Jack wouldn't let her scrub the house out; he hired a woman to do it. With Vicky working at Mayfield's, Kate didn't want it said that Mam's house wasn't spotless when they gave up the tenancy. She found it physically hard work, but it was even harder on the emotions.

She was glad to have the job finished, but she'd only been able to find one front-door key when she came to give them to Vicky to take in.

'There should be two to the front door,' Vicky said. 'And one to the back.'

Nobody used keys in Cemetery Cottages. Their doors stood open all day.

'It hasn't been thrown out.' Kate frowned. 'I've been keeping an eye out for it.'

'Don't worry, I'll have another cut. After all these years, Mayfield's aren't going to bother about a key.'

'Over forty years,' she said. 'I was brought up in this cottage.'

It had buzzed with life during those early years. Now it was empty and sounded hollow when she spoke.

'It all looks fresh and clean.' Vicky looked round.

'It's been newly distempered. Well, touched up where it needed doing. Mam had Billy brush it over after the electric light was put in.'

She turned the key in the door for the last time and gave it to Vicky to take to the office.

* * *

289

It was three days after Gran's funeral, and Vicky couldn't get it out of her mind. The particulars of her cottage had just been added to the list displayed in the window, and within a few hours a middle-aged couple came in asking about it.

With a shaky hand, Vicky pushed the details across her desk to them. She told herself they looked the sort Mum and Dad could get on with; the woman was pretty and smartly dressed. She couldn't help but think of such things when the house was next door to them. The woman read aloud to her husband.

' "Old-world two-bedroomed cottage. Parlour, living room and kitchen. Downstairs bathroom/wash house. Electric light. Good-sized garden. Rent: eight shillings and sixpence a week." '

Vicky didn't think that description did it justice. Andy should have mentioned how quiet and countrified it was.

The man was opening a map of the town. He said: 'There's a big cemetery up that way, isn't there? Is it close?'

'Fairly close.' She indicated with her pencil. 'About here.'

'Eight and six a week is a lot if it's next door to the cemetery.'

'Not exactly next door.' Vicky was going off them, but continued to try. 'It's very peaceful there. A lot of people like to be away from the traffic.' That's what old Mr Mayfield would have told them.

Gran had paid only six shillings and sixpence a week, but she'd been there a long time and she'd expected the rent to go up now the electric light was in.

'It's very clean, recently decorated, ready for you to move in.'

Vicky decided not to say she lived next door. They'd find out soon enough if they took it. They were still looking through the list. They also seemed attracted to a house in Upton Avenue for the same rent.

'We'd like to see them both.' The woman smiled at her.

'Yes, but I'm afraid we don't just hand over the keys.'

Mayfield's used to at one time, until the day a prospective client hadn't liked a property and couldn't be bothered bringing the key back. He'd left it in the door and tinkers had moved in. They'd done a lot of damage and never paid a penny in rent. It had caused awful trouble with the owner.

'I can make an appointment for Mr Mayfield to show you round both of them.'

At that moment, she heard Andy whistling as he came up the front steps.

He said: 'Would you like to take them, Vicky? It's only an hour or so off closing time and I've got plenty of writing-up to do here. You can bring the keys back in the morning.'

The couple seemed pleased with that. Vicky took them to the house in Upton Avenue first. It was bigger than Gran's but in a busy road. They didn't seem impressed with it. She headed for home, walking them up past the cemetery.

'It's an enormous place.' The hill was steep and the woman stopped to get her breath back. They eyed the gravestones over the low wall. 'I'm not sure I want to live close to this.'

That rubbed Vicky up the wrong way. The cart track was muddy because they'd had a lot of rain recently. The woman was a town-dweller, and her shoes were not suited to unmade roads like this. She was being left behind. Vicky paused to give her time to catch up. She mustn't do anything to put them off, it wouldn't be fair to the Mayfields.

'Both are nice houses. I think you'd be happy in either.' It was the sort of thing she'd heard Andy say in the office.

She only half listened to what the man was saying. Something about coming up from London. He'd got a job in the Town Hall.

He said: 'It's a bit out of the way and a steep pull up for the wife.'

Vicky thought the neat row of cottages looked attractive. 'It's a pleasant situation.'

The garden looked a bit of a mess. Gran had done nothing much with it for years. Their own garden wasn't up to much either. Flossie Jenkins had complained to Dad about his weeds, and he was talking of hiring a man to tidy it up. Mr Mayfield said untidy gardens could put people off.

She turned the key in the lock and ushered the woman inside Gran's house. It was all so achingly familiar, she couldn't imagine anybody living here but Gran. The woman thought the stone sink old-fashioned. Vicky unlocked the back door and showed them the bathroom and wash house. Neither liked that arrangement. The man started pulling out the dampers in the living room range.

'These stairs are steep.' The woman was puffing by the time they'd reached the bedrooms. Vicky thought her overweight. She was leading them down again when she heard Gladys Fry's voice at the front door.

'Coo-ee, are these our new neighbours?'

'Not sure yet,' Vicky said coldly. Gladys was a nosy parker.

'Not sure yet,' echoed the woman. 'It seems a bit cramped for us.'

'We've got to live somewhere,' the man reminded her.

Gladys would have kept them talking in Gran's living room. Vicky moved them as politely as she could out to the front garden and locked up again.

'Come to the office in the morning,' she told them, 'if you do decide on one or the other. Or we can show you other properties on our books.'

She didn't think they'd take it. She didn't want them to. She didn't want anybody living in Gran's house. It wouldn't seem right. Particularly if they were going to make a friend of Gladys Fry. They stood talking to her for another twenty minutes despite the chill wind.

All in all, Vicky felt it had been a difficult day. The evening was no better. Gran's death was affecting them all. Billy set a place for his mam at the table, and both he and Mum burst into tears when she had to point it out. Dad seemed as miserable as the rest of them.

Chapter Twenty-Four

The next morning, Kate woke to hear Billy sobbing in his bedroom and Vicky's voice trying to soothe him.

'What are we going to do today?' Jack wanted to know. 'We can't continue to sit around here moping. Let's go out, do something different. Life has to go on.'

Kate frowned. 'I was thinking of going to the shop, but . . . Billy's very upset. I don't know what to do for the best for him.'

'If you want to go to the shop, you go. I'll look after Billy.'

She knew Jack was trying to help. Usually he did his best to avoid being left with Billy.

She said: 'One of us ought to go in to make sure the manager is coping.'

It wasn't just that. She wanted to get away from the house for a bit; there was too much to remind her of Mam here.

'I'll run you down and then go and see about getting the phone put in,' Jack told her. 'If we had a phone here, it would be easier to keep in touch.'

Billy was pleased to get in the car – he always enjoyed outings – but in the shop Kate had to find little jobs for him to do.

'Dust these shelves for me, Billy.'

It seemed only minutes before he was back. She praised him; he'd dusted well and was eager to do more.

'Stack these boxes and tidy up the storeroom.'

Another few minutes and he was back. 'Done that, Kate. Done it nicely. Can we go out?'

'Where do you want to go?'

'Find Archie.'

'He'll be working, Billy.'

He nodded: 'Doing 'lectrics somewhere.'

'He won't want you to help now. He'll be working in someone else's house.'

'Want Archie to help me. Do magic for Mam.'

Kate shivered. Jack had been reading his newspaper in the back room. Now he said: 'What about making us all a nice cup of tea, Billy?'

'Will you take him out?' Kate asked him when Billy had gone to the kitchen. She couldn't put her mind to anything else while Billy was here, and his grief was more than she could bear. 'I want to bring the account books up to date, see to things here.'

'Don't work too hard, love.'

'I find the shop routine soothing, after . . .' Kate felt emotionally raw herself. She knew what Billy was going through, and she was full of pity for him.

'Don't bother coming back for me. I'll come home on the tram when I'm ready.'

When the afternoon turned wet and windy, she was sorry she'd said that. By the time she was walking up the cart track to Cemetery Cottages, it was getting dark. She let herself into her house. The living room was cosy, and Jack had a good fire going. He folded his newspaper and got up to help her off with her coat. He kissed her cheek.

'You're cooking something?' Jack never cooked. 'It smells wonderful.'

'Made a big effort today.' He smiled wryly. 'I've got a chicken roasting in the oven. Ada told me what to do with it. She even made some stuffing to go in it.'

Kate collapsed in the armchair.

'You've done too much,' Jack told her. 'I knew you would. You look tired.'

'Lovely to come home and find you've got things ready.'

He'd even set the table. The knives and forks were gleaming on the white tablecloth. Jack had remembered they were only four of them now.

Four! Kate pulled herself upright in the chair. 'Where's Billy?'

'Oh!' Jack's smile of satisfaction faded. 'I don't know. I'd forgotten about him.'

'Isn't he here? When did you last see him?'

'Not for some time.'

Kate was aghast. 'What do you mean, not for some time? You've been here all day, haven't you?'

Jack pushed his hair back from his forehead. 'I took him with me to see about getting the telephone in. They'll come on Friday and . . .'

'Never mind the phone, what about Billy?'

'We did some shopping, then went to a pub for a drink before lunch. We came home and had ham and pickles – you know, left over from the . . . I haven't seen him since.'

There was a ball of worry in her throat. 'He's not upstairs in his bedroom?'

'I'd have heard him if he was,' but Jack ran upstairs to see.

'You should have kept an eye on him. You know how upset he is.'

'He won't come to any harm.' Jack was trying to reassure her. 'He knows his way home, and everybody knows him round here.'

Kate pushed her arms into her coat again. 'I'll see if he's at Ada's.'

'I'm sorry,' Jack said.

She knew he was panicking and blaming himself. The last thing she wanted was to upset Jack too. She said mildly: 'He could be in any of these cottages. Safe and sound in front of the fire.'

She tried the most likely houses first, but nobody had seen Billy during the afternoon. She even knocked on Flossie Jenkins' door, though she didn't think she'd let Billy in. Flossie was out.

Kate went home, feeling on edge. 'He's not here.'

Jack was attending to the dinner. 'I've been thinking – he'll be in the cemetery. You know how fond he is of the place, and Lena's there now. That's where he'll be. At her grave. I'll go and get him. You sit down and rest.'

He poured her a glass of sherry and put it in her hand. She watched him putting his mackintosh on.

'I'm sorry, Kate.'

'Surely Billy won't have been out there all afternoon?'

'He'll be soaked if he has.'

She hovered at the window, watching Jack disappear into the darkness as he headed for the cart track.

Jack felt ruffled. He was cross with Billy for wandering off without saying where he was going. He had no thought for anyone else. It was worrying Kate and would spoil the evening. He'd worked hard getting this meal ready for when Kate and Vicky came home. He'd intended it as a comfort offering.

It was a miserable evening, still raining hard and nearly dark. He'd brought his umbrella, but the rain was gusting against his legs. He hated turning out in it like this, but he couldn't let Kate go when she'd been out all day.

As he was crossing the road to the cemetery gates, he saw a glistening umbrella bobbing towards him. Was this Vicky coming home from work? It was the right time. He waited until she was nearer before he called: 'Vicky?'

The angle of the umbrella changed. 'Hello, Dad. What are you doing out here?'

'You haven't seen Billy? He's gone missing.'

'Oh, no!'

'I'm looking for him. He's probably in the cemetery.'

'In this weather?'

'I had to come and look, to set your mother's mind at rest.'

'I'll come with you. Poor Billy.'

Jack couldn't stop himself complaining. 'He might have said where he was going.'

Once inside the cemetery, the high trees and thick holly hedges bordering the paths made it much darker.

'It's creepy in here at night,' Vicky said, looking over her shoulder.

'Not really.' He wanted to stop her thinking like that.

It was a fair distance through to the newer part of the cemetery. There were fewer overhanging trees and bushes, and it was possible to see a little more. It was easy to pick out Gran's grave, where the mass of flowers showed up white in the darkness.

'He's not here.' Jack felt another needling of anxiety.

Vicky tightened her grip on his arm. 'He's been here, though. Look at the flowers.' She drew him closer to the grave.

'I walked through here this morning on the way to work.' Vicky's voice was tight. It made him realise how much she was missing Lena too.

'All the flowers and wreaths were laid out over her grave. They were still in their fancy paper. Now they're in water.

Jack had taken Kate to buy the wreath of white Christmas roses. She'd written out the card, putting Billy's name on too. But Billy had wanted his own gift of flowers for his mother. Jack had humoured him, allowing him to choose a bunch of big pompom chrysanthemums. Now they were in the marble vase that had been here since Mitch had died.

Another vase at the foot of the grave held the russet chrysanths that had been Vicky's offering, and there were several jam jars on each side, holding other flowers.

'Gran taught him to put flowers in water.' There were tears in Vicky's voice now.

Jack called out impatiently: 'Billy? Are you here?' The only sound was the splatter of rain on their umbrellas, and the sigh of the wind.

'Let's go, Dad. It's scary at night. He isn't here.'

'Billy wouldn't stay out in this. Isn't he friendly with one of the cemetery lads?'

'Most of them.'

'The one called Wilf – doesn't he live at the lodge over there?'

Vicky was nodding.

'Let's ask, he could be there. Or they might have seen Billy and know where he's gone.'

'Good idea,' Vicky said. It was Wilf who came to the door. He had a crust of bread oozing with syrup in his hand.

'I haven't seen Billy today. Been working down the other end. Hang on, I'll ask my dad if he's seen him.'

Wilf returned a few moments later to say they'd none of them been working in the new part of the cemetery and they'd seen nothing of Billy.

Jack sighed. 'Come on, let's go home.' Walking back through the older part of the cemetery, he said: 'There are so many paths and so many different levels. What with the high hedges and trees, Billy could be anywhere here and we'd never see him.'

'There's no reason for him to hide.'

'He might not even see us.'

'If he's not near Gran's grave, I don't think he's here at all.'

Jack knew from the eager look on Kate's face that she'd expected Billy to be in the cemetery. 'I thought I heard you talking. I was so sure.'

'He was talking to me,' Vicky said. 'I met Dad and went with him to look. Billy can't be far, Mum, but he's not in the cemetery.'

Ada put her head round the kitchen door. 'Jack, you can't be trusted to do anything once you get your head in the newspaper. I've put the sprouts on and the custard pudding in to bake.'

'I forgot,' he said. Damn it, he'd hoped to show that he wasn't helpless about the house, and he was keen for this to be a nice meal. He didn't want Kate to know Ada had done most of the preparation.

'The chicken's ready now.'

'Thank you, Ada. What would I do without your help?'

'It's nothing. Lena and me – we cooked together quite a lot. The bunch of dried sage we used in the stuffing, it came from her house, didn't it? I remember seeing it on that hook. I can't believe she's gone. It was all so quick.'

'We none of us can,' Kate sighed.

'Billy will be all right, love. He knows his way home.'

'I can't understand why he isn't here for his dinner.'

Jack was hungry. 'Are you ready to eat?'

'Just going to change my stockings,' Vicky said, running upstairs to her room. 'They're wet.'

'I'll be going so you can get on,' Ada said. 'It's all ready to dish up.'

'She's very kind.' Jack picked up the glass of sherry he'd poured for Kate and sipped at it. She hadn't touched it.

Vicky came down again. 'It's Ada's way of showing sympathy. She was Gran's friend.'

'She kept talking about her.' Kate was blinking hard. 'Telling me little anecdotes about her from the past.'

'Shall I dish up?' Vicky was setting about it. 'I said I'd meet Andy in town, and I don't have much time.'

Jack set about carving. 'I'll run you in, if you're late.'

'Thanks, Dad. There's good picture on at the Ritz, and Andy thought it would take my mind off things. But I don't feel like going – not now Billy's gone missing.'

'You can't leave him standing outside the Ritz,' he tried to joke.

Jack could feel the tension tightening over dinner. Kate didn't seem interested in food. The chicken was overcooked because they were eating later than usual. The empty place set for Billy was a stark reminder of his absence, and so was the custard pudding. He always wanted second helpings when they had that.

'Where can he be?' Kate worried. 'He'll be hungry by now.'

'Perhaps his empty stomach will bring him home,' Jack said, then wished he hadn't. He knew it made him sound unsympathetic.

Even Vicky was pushing the food round her plate. She said: 'I do hope nothing's happened to him.'

Jack didn't like leaving Kate alone while he took Vicky into Birkenhead.

'Come with us,' he said. 'A little run in the car . . .'

'I have to stay. Billy might come back, it wouldn't do for him to find nobody here.'

'Shall I ask Ada to keep you company?'

'No, I'll wash up.'

'There's no need . . .'

'Yes there is. Anyway, it'll give me something to do.'

'Come on, Dad,' Vicky was urging. 'Andy will be there by now.'

Jack drove briskly. It wouldn't take him more than half an hour to drive both ways. The rain was still hurtling down and the gutters were running with water. It meant there was less traffic and fewer people about than usual, which was a good thing.

He was driving past the cemetery on his way home when he saw a familiar figure toiling up the hill. It was Flossie Jenkins. Lena had seen her as an enemy to be avoided, but she was an old woman and it was a terrible night to be out.

He stopped the car. 'Can I offer you a lift, Mrs Jenkins? You're nearly home, but it's uphill all the way from here and the cart track will be very muddy in this.'

'Very grateful, Mr Courtney. You're a real gent.'

She was slow getting her bulk into the passenger seat. Rain was blowing inside his new car and water was dripping from her mackintosh all over the carpet.

'It's an awful night,' she said.

Jack turned the car into the cart track. It rocked over the rough ground as it climbed; not good for any car.

'Billy's gone missing.' He felt weary now. 'We've been looking for him for hours. I don't suppose you've seen him this afternoon?'

'Yes, just before I went out. I've been round to our John's this afternoon. Miriam asked me for my tea.'

'Really? You saw him? What time would that have been?'

'Half one, two-ish.'

Jack straightened up in his seat. This was the only sighting of Billy so far. 'Where was he?'

'Next door.'

'What d'you mean? Outside Lena's house?'

'He went inside.'

Jack felt a rush of disappointment. She was making a mistake, she must be. Billy wouldn't be able to get inside. He parked his car at the end of the row of cottages and said stoically:

'He can't have been inside. It's all locked up. The keys are with Mayfield's.'

'I hope you're not calling me a liar.' Her sudden aggression repulsed him. He could understand why Lena had never liked her.

'I saw him going in with my own eyes.' She was indignant. 'He's got a key. Heard him too. Walking about inside. Going upstairs. It sounds hollow now everything's been taken out.'

Jack took a deep breath, remembering now that Kate had found only one front-door key. Billy must have had the other. Hadn't she asked him?

'You're sure it was today?'

'Of course I'm sure. I wouldn't say if I wasn't.'

Jack went to the front door of Lena's house and tried it. It was locked. He called through the letter-box: 'Are you there, Billy? Come and open the door for me.' There was silence.

He turned to Flossie Jenkins. 'Come in and tell Kate what you've told me. She's worried stiff about him.'

'Billy can't be in there,' he said to Kate when Flossie had gone to her own house. But nothing would stop Kate going out in the rain with a torch to see for herself. First round the back and then round the front, she shone it at every window. They were all closed, and both doors were locked, just as she'd left it.

She asked: 'Do you think he's hiding in there? Refusing to come out?'

'No, Billy would have answered, would have come to the door. Why should he hide from you?'

'I'm sure I asked him about the key. He hid that from me.'

'He thinks of it as his own home. He didn't want to move in with us.'

'He couldn't be asleep in there?'

'There's nothing for him to sleep on, Kate. You cleared everything out.'

'I'd like to get inside, to satisfy myself.'

'Ah, well, Vicky's gone out. Perhaps when she comes back . . . if Billy isn't home by then.'

'I knew something must have happened.' Andy was serious. 'You've never been late before.'

'I've never known our Billy go missing like this.' Vicky was seated beside him in the back of the stalls. She'd been very edgy since Gran had died. She needed life to get back to normal as far as it could. Mum needed that too; they couldn't cope with more trouble right now. Billy's disappearance was cutting the ground from under all their feet.

She hung on to Andy's hand. 'If Billy's lost, he'll be terribly upset. He won't be able to think straight.'

They'd missed the beginning of the supporting film because she was late. She couldn't follow the story. There was a Mickey Mouse cartoon showing now, and though she normally enjoyed them, she wasn't in the mood for Mickey Mouse now.

'I wish there was something I could do.'

'Try to think where he might have gone,' Andy advised.

'We have, and we've looked in those places. Billy hardly went anywhere without Gran.'

The Pathé news started. 'Where did she take him?'

'He won't be in the park now.'

'He could be safe and sound at home by now, for all you know.'

The lights came up. It was the interval.

'Vicky, you're thrashing about in that seat. You can't sit still. I think I should take you home.'

'But you wanted to see Johnny Weissmuller.'

'Let's go.' Andy stood up. 'You can't keep your mind on a film, not with Billy gone. I'll take you home.'

'But you . . .'

'I can't concentrate either when you're like this.'

The rain seemed to have eased off as they waited for the bus. It was almost empty when it came. As she squelched up the cart track, hanging on to Andy's arm, Vicky could see the new electric light streaming out of every cottage except Gran's.

As soon as she saw her mother's face, she knew that Billy wasn't back, but Mum was full of the news that Billy had been seen going into Gran's house early in the afternoon.

'I don't think he's there now,' Dad added. 'He'd have come here for his dinner; that's what he always did, after all.'

'If I could just see inside . . .'

'Flossie Jenkins could be mistaken.' Dad was beginning to look harassed too. 'She's an old woman, she might might have got the day wrong. She might have seen him going in a few days ago while you were clearing the place.'

'The keys are in the office,' Andy told her. 'We could walk down and get them. It's not as though it's far.'

'Dad could run you down.'

'He won't want to leave you by yourself, Mum. It's stopped raining, and it'll make me feel as though I'm doing something useful.'

Jack made a pot of tea. Anything to fill the time. He didn't think it would get them any further if they did see inside Lena's house. He felt the evening was turning into a nightmare.

He'd thought Billy would come home of his own accord once the pangs of hunger began to bite, but it was past his bedtime now and he wasn't so sure.

Kate was on her feet the moment Vicky put her head inside the door to say: 'We've got the key, Mum.'

Jack followed more slowly. They were going round switching on the electric light in every room.

301

'He's definitely been in,' Kate was saying. 'Those muddy footprints by the door, they're his. I made sure the place was clean after the funeral.'

'I was here yesterday.' Vicky was shaking her head. 'Showing people round. We don't know they're Billy's.'

Jack had never known the place feel this cold. There was nothing here at all. He went upstairs; Flossie Jenkins had said she'd heard Billy on the stairs. Lena's bedroom looked desolate without furniture. He flicked the switch in Billy's bedroom, but no light came. He took a look inside; in the half-light, it took him a moment to make out what he was looking at.

It made him draw his breath in sharply. 'What d'you make of this?'

They were all crowding in. Vicky was behind him, her eyes round with apprehension. 'Those are his pieces of wire. What's he joined them on there for?'

'Here's the light bulb; he's cut it off!'

'With these scissors.'

Two pieces of Billy's wire hung down from the ceiling rose, reaching to the floor.

'He's lucky he didn't electrocute himself,' Andy breathed.

Jack watched Kate lean against the wall for support. 'Billy's gone to look for Archie. I know it. He's been saying he wants to find him. He'll have got himself lost.'

Jack said slowly: 'We don't know where this Archie lives. Billy won't either. He wouldn't know where to start. I can't see him doing that.'

'I don't know.' Vicky's face was screwing up with concern. 'These wires . . . Whatever he's up to, it must be connected with them. Ugh.'

'Must be connected with Archie.' Kate's face was white. Jack knew she was frightened.

He had a cold feeling in his own stomach. The wires seen dimly in the half-light looked ominous. They hammered home Billy's plight.

'Let's get out of here,' he said. 'We've got to do something, now.'

Kate's concern for Billy had been growing all evening; now it was gnawing at him. Back home, he built the fire up and Vicky put on the kettle for more tea. They sat round the table.

'I know how to find Archie.' Vicky shot back from the kitchen. 'He worked for the firm that put the electric light in here.'

'Hambles,' Andy said. 'Electrical contractors – from Rock Ferry, I think. We arranged it.'

'I typed the letters. We can find him through them.'

'It's the middle of the night,' Jack pointed out. 'They won't be in the office until morning.'

'Report him missing to the police,' Kate said. 'He's been gone long enough. It's the only way.'

Jack ran Vicky and Andy down to Mayfield's office to telephone. That seemed to be the quickest way to get in touch, and Kate felt there was some urgency now.

'They've promised to send an officer round straight away,' Vicky told her mother as soon as they were home again. She'd brewed a fresh pot of tea and they sat drinking it, listening for the sound of a police car coming up the track.

'They're taking their time,' Kate said after almost an hour.

'Not exactly straight away.' Andrew looked at his watch.

The loud rat-tat on the letter-box took them by surprise. Vicky jumped up first to open the door. Howard Jenkins was standing on the step, chest thrown out, looking very important. His bike was propped against the gate. She felt her stomach lurch; she wished it had been anybody but him.

'Come in.' She stood back. He stepped inside, blinking a little in the strong light, then staring round their living room with all the authority of the law. She'd spoken to him only once since the day she'd broken off their engagement. He'd asked her to reconsider it and she'd refused. Now she felt the heat run up her cheeks.

She brought another chair to the table and he sat down with them, taking out a notepad. He placed his helmet on the table in front of him and fixed his gaze on Andy.

'You know everybody,' Vicky said awkwardly.

He was formal. 'You want to report a missing person?'

Mum said: 'Billy, you know our Billy. He's not been seen since lunch.'

'His full name, please.'

'William Claud McGlory. Known as Billy.'

'His age?' He wrote slowly.

'Address?' He knew the address, for heaven's sake. Vicky felt a surge of impatience; this wasn't going to find him.

'And when did you last see him?'

'Lunch time, we told you,' she said.

Dad explained fully, though Vicky could see his irritation building up too. Then they had to take Howard next door to see the wires they'd found hanging from the ceiling rose.

'What is the significance of these?'

For Billy's sake, they were all doing their best to explain things to him.

'We think he's gone to look for this lad Archie,' Mum said. Andy explained who he was.

'I don't agree about that.' Even Dad was looking worried now. 'Billy wouldn't know where to start looking. You remember, Vicky, how difficult it was to teach him to go round the chemist's shops?'

She said: 'He was scared then.'

'You know what Billy's like. He has to be on familiar ground. I don't think he'd willingly go somewhere he hadn't been before.'

He was looking Howard in the eyes. 'I think you ought to search the cemetery systematically first. It's the most likely place.'

Howard sighed heavily. 'That'll have to wait for daylight.' He snapped his pad shut. 'And first thing in the morning, we'll be in touch with Hambles. We'll do all we can.'

Vicky saw him out.

Mum looked close to tears. 'I don't know how much good that's done. He doesn't seem in any hurry to start looking.'

'I think you should all go to bed.' Andy stood up. 'The night's half over anyway. There's nothing else we can do until tomorrow. I'll open the office in the morning, Vicky, you'll need to sleep this off.'

'I'll run you home,' her father offered.

'It's all right.'

'It's pouring with rain again, and after two. Vicky will never forgive me if I don't. You two go to bed, you look worn out.'

Chapter Twenty-Five

As Jack dropped Andy outside his house, he thought what a nice lad he was.

He was exhausted now, and couldn't wait to get into bed, but he knew as he drove back up the cart track that Kate was not asleep. The light was beaming out of their bedroom window. When he crept up the stairs, he found her wide-eyed and anxious.

'I can't stop thinking of Billy, out there somewhere. You'd have thought Howard Jenkins would have had a look round now instead of waiting till morning.'

'It's a dark night and the rain's coming down in torrents again. Almost impossible to see anything, love.'

'Vicky took the torch round Kitty Watts' outbuildings before she turned in. And all the old pig sties too. He must be somewhere.'

Kate seemed to be folding up before his eyes. He'd never known her be like this; she was usually the strong one in the family. Losing her mother suddenly had really upset her, and she wasn't able to cope with Billy's disappearance on top. She was relying on Vicky and him to handle this. Particularly him. Jack was afraid he was failing again. He was falling short of what Kate expected of him and he'd let Billy down by not taking better care of him.

'You don't think Billy's gone to look for this Archie?' Her green eyes sparkled with worry. 'You think he's more likely to be in the cemetery?'

'Yes.' He sat on the end of the bed and began to untie his shoelaces. He knew what Kate wanted and he knew she wouldn't ask outright for it. 'You want me to take another look? Round the cemetery?'

'There's so many places there. I'll come with you.' She was throwing the blanket back. 'I can't settle to sleep.'

'No, Kate. You stay in bed, I'll go.'

He tied his shoelaces up again and gave her a hug. He didn't think he'd be able to see much until it got light. He'd offered more to calm her than for any other reason.

'I do love you, Jack,' she whispered. 'You're always so kind.'

He let himself out into the night again and shivered. It was pitch dark. He paused by his car, undecided whether to drive it down the cart track, but that was only a couple of hundred yards and he wouldn't be able to take it inside the cemetery.

He decided it wasn't worth the trouble and stumbled down the cart track with the rain drumming on his umbrella. The wind had got up and the rain was horizontal at times. He kept a torch in his pocket for negotiating the path on nights like this. The pale beam showed the rough ground streaming with water, and his shoes, which had been highly polished this morning, were daubed with mud. When he looked up for a second, he stepped in a puddle and felt the cold water ooze down into his sock.

He knew the great wrought-iron gates at the back of the cemetery would be locked, but the little side gate was always open. It gave a loud creak as he went through. The huge mass of the chapels of rest loomed up in front of him, giving some shelter from the driving rain. He stopped. He ought to look inside. On a night like this, Billy would surely seek shelter. But here, so close to home?

If Vicky could look in the old pig sties, he had to look here. Silly to walk past and not do so. The first door was huge and needed all his weight against it before it would open. Inside it was pitch black and airless. He shone his torch round.

'Billy, are you here?' His voice sounded puny under the vaulted roof. He couldn't get out again quickly enough, but he had to look in the other chapel.

Opening the heavy door made a lot of noise. It scraped on the stone floor. He walked twenty yards down the aisle and called again, but there was no answer. He retreated, half afraid to lose his bearings. Then he put out his torch and listened carefully. He didn't think there was anybody here.

It was a relief to be outside again in spite of the rain. He felt bolder out here, between the high hedges of holly and cypress. Without the slim pencil of light shining on the wet tarmac in front of his feet, he wouldn't have been able to see a thing.

He kept calling: 'Billy? Are you there? Billy, can you hear me?' The only sounds were the wind and the patter of rain.

He was feeling as jittery as Vicky had earlier. It was eerie here amongst the gravestones. He rounded a corner, and a marble statue loomed white through the rain, an angel with a broken wing. He'd never felt so much alone.

Jack hunched his shoulders. His legs ached now as he pushed on to the part of the cemetery where Lena was buried. He'd thought this a peaceful place in daylight. Now he couldn't imagine anyone being here from choice. Certainly not Billy.

He tramped on. It was a huge place and more open down in this part. He thought he heard a different sound. He stopped to listen, and it came again.

Was it someone digging? It sounded like the scrape of metal going into earth. He turned off his torch and peered into the dark. He thought his eyes more used to it now, but he couldn't see anything. Surely they wouldn't be digging graves at night? And in weather such as this?

He felt disorientated; he'd lost his bearings. Which grave was Lena's? The geography of the place seemed to have changed. The sound came again, and he thought he saw a figure.

'Billy? Is that you?' Jack tripped over the grass verge and only just avoided a fall. This was Lena's grave, but the flowers had all been moved away from it. There was a new mound of earth . . . He felt his heart lurch.

'Billy?'

'Yes, Jack, it's me.'

Surely not! Cold shivers were sliding down Jack's spine as the first glimmer of understanding sank in. Billy was standing on his mother's grave and had dug some way into it.

Jack was shocked. 'What are you doing?'

'I want me mam.'

Jack shone his torch on the scene, his mind whirling with disbelief. Bile burned in his throat.

'No, Billy, no. You mustn't.'

He stepped forward to take the spade from him, and his feet sank into loose soil. The spade was sticky with more of it.

'Yes, want to take her home. Help me. It's hard to dig.'

He shone his torch over Billy. 'What a mess you're in!'

Billy wasn't wearing a coat. His jersey was so soaked it dripped muddy water, and his trousers were clinging to his legs. Rain was streaming down his face. He seemed to be coated with mud; it was in his hair, everywhere.

'Don't like Mam being here. Want her at home with me.'

'She can't come back. Not now.'

'I want to mend her. Get her right. Have her back like she was.'

'Your mam was ill and she died, Billy,' he said as gently as he could. 'It isn't possible.'

'Might be if I try. You wouldn't try. If you'd done it, then . . .'

'We did our best. The doctor . . .'

'You wouldn't try the 'lectric.' It was a heartfelt wail.

Jack swallowed hard. He had stopped Billy attaching his pieces of wire to Lena on the night she died. Oh my God! He'd thought nothing of it, he'd thrown the pieces of wire on Billy's bed. Then Kate had packed Billy off to Harry's place.

'Archie said it would magic her back. Eric too, bring her round. I got everything ready.'

Jack's head swam, his stomach heaved, but his love went out to Billy, his pity and his sympathy. He put an arm round his shoulders, tried to offer comfort.

'Honestly, Billy, I'd do anything to bring your mam back. We all want her back. If she was here, she'd want to be with you,' he told him gently. 'But she's dead, and nobody can bring her back.'

'The 'lectric . . .'

'The 'lectric can't do miracles.'

'It does magic. Why not that?'

'It can't, not what you want,' Jack said. 'There aren't answers to everything.'

He should have tried to explain to Billy, even let him do what he wanted. It would have settled his mind. He wouldn't have had to do it this way.

Jack saw it as partly his own fault. He should have handled things better. He could understand Billy's loss. There'd been a time in his life when he thought he'd lost everything. He remembered how devastated he'd felt.

He dug the spade into the soil. He had to get all this moved back to fill in that gaping hole, but it was heavy, and he was dog tired. It was beyond him. Should he ask Wilf to do it in the morning?

No! Billy looked on the ground staff as his friends. Better if they didn't know what he'd been doing. It could alter how they felt about him.

'Billy, help me get this soil back. Let's make your mam's grave nice again.'

After a moment's hesitation, Billy started to scoop the earth back with a flat stone. He pushed it down with his feet while Jack used the spade. All the time the rain came down in torrents, turning it to mud. Jack was relieved when at last they had it back and were able to arrange the wreaths and the flowers on top. It didn't look quite as it had, there was mud all over the surrounding turf.

'Let's go home and go to bed,' he said. 'Kate has been worried stiff about you.'

When they reached Cemetery Cottages, Billy was heading for the gate of number three. Jack had to catch him by the hand.

'Billy, you live with us now. Me, and your sister Kate, and Vicky. We're going to look after you from now on.'

Almost as soon as the front door closed behind them, Kate was downstairs, pulling her dressing gown round her.

'Thank goodness you've come to no harm,' she choked. 'Out to the wash house with you. Let's get those wet clothes off.'

Vicky was only an instant behind her, her blonde curls bouncing about her shoulders.

'I thought I heard Billy with you. Thank goodness!' She almost threw her arms round him in a welcoming hug. 'Ugh, you're all wet and horrible. What have you been doing?'

'I wanted me mam . . .'

'What's he been doing, Dad?' Jack was trying to undo the laces on Billy's shoes. They were embedded in mud.

'He wanted your gran back so badly he was trying to bring her home.'

'Dig her up, you mean?' Vicky's face screwed up.

'He thought if he could fix the wires Archie gave him to the power, and then to your gran, it would bring her back to life.'

Jack saw a tear roll down Kate's cheek. When he thought of what Billy had done, he felt moved to tears too.

He said gently: 'It shows how much he loved her and wanted her back. Your mother inspired love in everybody. Billy loved her so much he tried to bring her back to life when she died.'

He could see tears of compassion in Vicky's eyes, and said: 'It won't be easy to fill Lena's place. We'll all miss her.'

'I loved me mam.' Billy smiled tremulously round at them all.

Vicky frowned. 'People will say it was a terrible thing Billy did.'

'Only because they don't understand.' Jack felt he understood him better now. Billy no longer seemed such a responsibility, and he thought he could help Kate look after him. He hoped that between them they'd be able to give him the love and support that Lena had.

'I'm so glad you found him, Dad.' Vicky's eyes were full of admiration for him.

Kate said: 'You did better than the police.'

'Better than Howard Jenkins, anyway.' Vicky smiled.

Jack was so tired, he could no longer think straight. He ached all over.

Vicky asked: 'Some hot broth, Dad? I'm going to heat some for Billy.'

'I'd go to bed if I were you,' Kate advised. 'You've been on the go all night.'

'I'm shattered,' he admitted. 'But we have to let the police know. That Billy's been found, I mean. We can't let them launch a big search at dawn.'

The night had seemed never-ending, and so had the effort he'd had to put into it. Jack was covered in mud himself. He had a quick wash, changed his shoes and socks, and took his new mackintosh from his wardrobe. Then he went out again to his car. If only he'd had the phone put in earlier, it would have saved him a lot of driving round tonight.

At the police station, he told the officer on the desk that Billy was safe at home, then went straight back to his car. Now, at last, everything was straightened out and he could go to bed. When he pulled up outside Cemetery Cottages he rested for a moment and almost nodded off in the car. He felt that it took the last of his strength to drag himself indoors.

The living room was warm, the fire blazed up the chimney. Billy was at the table in his striped winceyette pyjamas, clean and dry now except for his damp hair. He was spooning up broth hungrily.

Jack decided he needed sleep more than food and went straight upstairs and started to undress. It seemed years since he'd been able to stretch out in bed. He thought he heard a car, and was putting on his pyjamas when he heard the hammering on the front door. He paused to listen, and knew Constable Jenkins had returned. This time it had taken him no time at all to get here.

Jack grunted with irritation. He slid his feet into his slippers, reached for his dressing gown and went slowly downstairs again.

Howard Jenkins' helmet was on the table once more. Kate and Vicky were sitting one each side of Billy. Kate had her arm round his shoulders.

Constable Jenkins was unscrewing his fountain pen. 'What have you been up to, Billy? Tell me that.' His voice was ponderous, full of his own importance. Billy said nothing; he was holding on to Kate.

'You've caused a great deal of trouble to everyone, you know that?'

Billy wiped at his eyes with the back of his hand.

'Listen to me, Billy. You went missing at lunch time yesterday. Stop that crying. I want to know where you've been.'

'The dead park. I wanted me mam.'

'She died recently, didn't she?' Jenkins' gaze swung to Jack. His hostile eyes could make him feel uncomfortable; what must they be doing to Billy?

'Buried only last Monday. He's very upset. As you know, she looked after him.'

'Being upset is no reason to disappear. In future, you've got to let people know where you're going, Billy. You've worried your family and you've wasted police time. D'you understand that? Wasted valuable police time.'

Jack felt his fists curl up. He ached to use them, though he'd never fought in his life. He was seeing Jenkins in action, and he didn't like his manner.

'Now then, why did you keep a key to the house next door?'

'My house.' Billy's almond eyes stared back with childlike defiance.

'Not any more.'

'It'll take him time to realise that,' Jack put in.

He was angry with Howard Jenkins. He blamed him for a lot of things, turning Vicky into a problem teenager for one.

'Why did you attach those wires to the electric light?'

'Just a game,' Jack murmured.

'I don't know about that. What about this friend of yours called Archie; did you go to see him?'

Jack could see Billy cowering against Kate. Howard Jenkins was going the wrong way about getting information from him.

He himself had never known how to treat Billy. He'd got off on the wrong foot when they'd first met and he'd never been able to right that. Now he was filled with compassion for him. He knew what it was like to be bullied, to feel helpless.

Jenkins said: 'Look, Billy, stop whining and pull yourself together. I want to know how you spent all those hours you were missing.'

Jack thought the less he knew about it the better. He stood up, scooped Jenkins' helmet off the table and handed it to him.

'It's no good bullying Billy. As far as we're concerned, it's enough that he's been found unharmed. You wanted to put off searching for him until daylight, so surely this questioning can wait? It's now gone five in the morning and we all want to go to bed.' He escorted him to the door. Closed it firmly behind him.

'Bless you,' Kate murmured when he came back.

Jack leaned against the mantelpiece and stared into the dancing flames. Every bone in his body ached with fatigue, but tonight had taught him a good deal, and he no longer felt a failure.

All his life he'd felt inferior because others were able to come up with the answers and he had not. Leo and Oscar had been held up as examples he must emulate if he was to succeed in life.

311

They'd been quicker with their answers and right in matters of judgement when he'd been wrong. They'd oozed confidence in their own ability, while he'd lacked it. He hadn't realised that their confidence was based on their own feelings and not on fact.

Howard Jenkins had that aura of confidence. He'd given the impression he was a quick-witted man of action. Everybody believed he was. They were taking his opinion of himself as the truth.

Jack rarely offered his own opinions; Oscar had ridiculed him too often. Now he smiled to himself. Tonight he'd told Constable Jenkins he ought to search the cemetery thoroughly before he did anything else, and he'd been right. And while Jenkins had wanted to leave everything until daylight came, he'd got on with things and found Billy.

Vicky stirred. 'That showed Howard Jenkins up in his true light.'

'I'm so glad, Vicky, that you aren't married to him. You would have been his wife by now if you'd gone ahead. He's a bully.'

'Horrible.' Billy shook his head. 'Horrible.'

Kate's voice shook. 'I think I'd like us to move away from here now. Perhaps the cemetery is too near.'

Jack couldn't have agreed more. Billy had always gone down there, and they wouldn't be able to stop him. How could they be sure he wouldn't try to dig up his mother's grave again?

Kate went on: 'I want us to be somewhere where Billy can forget. Perhaps we could look for the bigger house we talked of getting, Jack? Not too far away, but . . .'

'A good idea,' he agreed. 'We'll do that.'

Vicky yawned. 'It would be awful seeing new people in Gran's place; better if we moved. Exciting really, a new house. I'll help you look for something special. This one is a bit small for four.'

'For how long will we be four?' Jack raised his eyebrows. 'You'll be wanting to marry this new boyfriend before we're settled in.'

She smiled sleepily. 'I've told you, I'm in no hurry to tie myself down. Andy's fun. He's trying hard to sweep me off my feet and he might even manage it, but I'm not going to be rushed.'

'You take all the time in the world,' Kate told her. 'Come on, Billy, let's all go up to bed.

Despite his utter exhaustion, Jack felt everything would be all right. Tonight, he was seeing profound truths for the first time.

He'd made the mistake of thinking Billy was different, but he was like everybody else. He had his weaknesses and his strengths. There was one thing he did better than anybody else, though. He felt love deeply, and was not afraid to show it.

312